I0681996

RUSTY KNOB

ERICA CHILSON

· RUSTY KNOB · BOOK ONE ·

RUSTY KNOB

Copyright ©2015 Erica Chilson

All rights reserved. No part of this publication may be reproduced, distributed, or transmitted in any form or by any means, including photocopying, recording, or other electronic or mechanical methods, without the prior written permission of the publisher, except in the case of brief quotations embodied in critical reviews and certain other noncommercial uses permitted by copyright law. For permission requests, write to the publisher, addressed "Attention: Permissions Coordinator," at the address below.

Wicked Reads
PO Box 29
Nelson, PA 16940

www.ericachilson.com/wicked-reads

Printed in the United States of America

First Printing, August 2015

ISBN-13: **978-0692505274**
ISBN-10: **069250527X**

Dedication

To my faithful readers, who have stuck by me through the ups and downs, the yanking books from sale, the rewrites, and had the patience to wait until I felt the books were ready. This book is for you, born out of the inspiration during a very trying time in my career. I wouldn't be the writer I am today without you. *Cheers*

The townsfolk of Rusty Knob, West Virginia, see the Gillettes as ignorant wastes of space– worthless drunk sponges. As the youngest, Wynn may be a Gillette, but he doesn't act, nor think like one. At only seventeen, he studies hard, plays basketball harder, and works the hardest.

Wynn is numb to his core, no longer feeling the hits that keep knocking him down to the ground. He's unable to see the bright future laid out before him. Royce Kennedy, a distant relative, tries all he can do to save the youngest generation of Gillettes from the dark shroud of bitter ignorance infecting them via their neglectful upbringing.

Wynn's studying is to the backdrop of drunken chaos, his relationship with friends and family are tainted by a narrow world view, and his life is filled with more questions than answers. His every dollar earned is bled dry come payday, only to have his parents piss it down the toilet or blow caustic smoke to billow in the air.

A warped sense of loyalty forces Wynn to be his family's enabler, and he's paying the ultimate price. With the support system of Royce, the mentor of the school district's LGBTQ online community, and Wynn's friends, they try to prove to Wynn he deserves anything he needs, whether he earns it or not. Growing up in an ignorant wasteland, he never learned love, friendship, and respect are unconditional, can never be purchased, and should never be abused.

Wynn Gillette is at a crossroads. One thing's for sure, he cannot continue on this destructive path. Wynn has to end the only life he's ever known, breaking the bitter legacy passed down from one generation to the next. One way or the other. Permanently.

Good Lord, how am I supposed to survive this?

I'm a pervert.

Being a skinny gay kid in an intolerant wasteland is one thing… being a pervert is another.

My buddy Warren's voice follows me down the drive as I walk to Gillette Holler, combined with the repetitive sound of an axe chopping through rounds of wood. "Kid, just another hour or two ought to do it." A shiver works its way down my spine when I realize who's wielding the axe. "Kade's coming by, so I'ma go fix us up something to drink. Be back in a jiffy!"

"Kay, War!" Overenthusiastic and ever-helpful, I have to close my eyes to the sound of a grown man's voice spilling out of a young boy's throat.

It's ninety degrees in the shade today, and my body reacts to the sight I've been longing to see. I wipe sweat off my brow with the sleeve of my thermal, but I'm not drenched because of the layers upon layers of clothing I'm wearing to hide my rack of bones and scars. I'm sweating because I feel guilty for being keyed-up by a kid who's almost twelve.

I'm a pervert.

A gay pervert.

But I'm not a pervert because I'm gay. No matter what my granddaddy thinks, that is. I'm a pervert because I'm closing in on seventeen and I'm drooling over a child.

I concentrate on walking without tripping over my size fifteens. I've been known to trip over air because of my height. I'm closing in on six and a half feet and barely weigh a buck-fifty.

The first time social services was called in on my granddaddy was because I walked headfirst into a wall. The second time was because I fell down a flight of stairs and broke my arm.

I tripped, I said.

They didn't believe me, they said.

So I lied and agreed with them, I said.

So my granddaddy lost me six months ago because the state thought he was physically abusing me. I get to live in a huge house in town with my new foster dad and brother, and I have a college fund to any school I want to attend. I also have no privacy, especially inside my head because of my three therapists.

You should have seen the look on Dr. Hearst's face when I told him I was a pervert. I laughed for twenty minutes because of it, and left with an increase in my dosage of Lexapro.

Royce Kennedy is my new foster dad, and I would have picked him if I was given a choice. Bren is my new baby brother, and I like him for the most part. Except when I wake in the middle of the night to the little asshole checking to see if I'm still breathing, and when he steals all the sharp knives and cuts my steak and butters my bread for me.

Social Services should feel bad for not believing me in the first place, and I should feel a bit guilty for lying about Granddaddy beating me.

But I don't.

My granddaddy was abusing me by messing with my head—twisting me up by calling me a little faggot, a cock-sucking queer. He said I was too ugly, too skinny, too dumb to make anything of myself. He said I'd end up on the streets, selling my man-pussy by becoming a pimp's bitch– the very street I'd be on when he kicked me out if I ever touched another boy.

Six months back, my social worker came by on a surprise home visit. She found me in a pool of my cooling lifeblood because I missed my dad. Missed him with every fiber of my being, and I didn't want to live anymore, especially with the foulmouthed asshole who was tearing me down every waking moment of my life.

My dad left me nine months ago because a log kicked back wrong when he was felling a tree. The heavy weight crushed his chest and all the organs held within. If the kindest man on earth, the man who was every stereotype of a lumberjack, couldn't survive this world, how was a skinny, dumb, gay kid supposed to survive without him?

I died.

I died, and when I was resurrected, the life I had been living no longer existed and I was placed in a new world with hopes and dreams and a future.

No one else knew I was gay– hell, I didn't even know. I didn't feel the stir until this super-sweet, ever-helpful, always-in-my-face kid broke me. Wynn was only wearing a smile and a pair of cut-off shorts, and I was fucked. Yeah, I'm blaming the victim. Back off! I try to never look at the kid, and I sure as shit will never touch him.

Now when I look in the mirror, I see a pervert staring back at me from the face of a guy who looks like he walked away from a concentration camp, with his frizzy shorn hair and pockmarked skin that seems to think he moisturizes with lard every night.

I'm gross, and Wynn is precious– innocent, kind, and something worth protecting. The fact that he causes blood to pool in my groin makes me physically sick. The first time I woke up to a wet dream about Wynn, I puked. The second time, I felt like an asshole. The third time, I whacked off to the memory.

I've since lost count, my dreams are vivid, and I no longer feel sick about it, either.

I kick a rock, refusing to look at my surroundings. I pop my thumbs through the holes in my shirtsleeve cuffs, making sure my scars are hidden. I walk up the rough pathway to the Gillette's shack, on the verge of losing the breakfast Royce made me and Bren. Sure, I'm nervous over seeing Wynn, but that's not why I'm ready to retch.

Corbin Gillette does his damnedest to force his family to live like rats. Even my asshole of a grandfather made sure I had food in my belly, a roof over my head, and a safe, warm place to rest my head. He may have made me feel like shit, but he didn't outright neglect me on purpose.

When I was younger, Warren and I would try to fix shit around here, to clean the house and mow the lawn, and to help Cora and Willa out with the chores. But I got sick of seeing bruises bloom on my buddy's face for making an effort.

"Ya think yer shit don't stink, boy? Ya think what ta good Lord provides ain't good 'nuff fer ya?"

Warren and I stopped trying, but little Wynn hasn't got the memo yet. I pretend I don't see the sheen in Warren's eyes when all of Wynn's hard work is for naught. Corbin will go on a rampage, destroying furniture and whipping his dick out to piss on freshly scrubbed floors.

"Hello, Mr. Gillette," I say politely as I move to pass the bastard. He's sitting in a broken lawn chair, with weeds growing up near his ears, drowning his troubles in beer while watching his youngest chopping the wood he should be splitting.

Corbin Gillette hasn't worked a single second in his entire life, unless you call drunken destruction work.

"Kade," Corbin says with a sneer. The gleam in his eye suggests he's remembering all the times he beat me, and he's savoring it since he'll never get the chance again.

The man knows– the man knows I have impure thoughts about his boy, and he's beaten me a few times because of it. But Royce Kennedy has more power than Corbin's fictitious God. The bastard hasn't laid another hand on Warren, Wynn, or me since the last time a few months ago when he was kicking my ribs in for staring at Wynn's ass. At least, I think that's why I was being beaten, but it could be the guilt of being a pervert talking. With Corbin, he never really needs an excuse of any kind to take his frustrations out on your hide.

"Are you going to die soon?" flows without thought. I've been obsessed with death since my dad died, since I tried to kill myself. "Why does a bastard like you get to live, while the good ones die?"

"We all go home to the Lord eventually, son." Corbin's voice is soft for a change.

I roll my eyes so far back inside my head, I fear they will never come back down again. I snort at the irony of Corbin believing in an invisible man floating amongst the clouds, reaching down to move human-shaped game pieces. When He gets bored, He flicks a piece from His game of global domination.

I think God needs some competition. Maybe then someone would actually punish the assholes and reward the innocents like Wynn.

I don't believe in an Almighty Power. Royce forces me to go to church every Sunday, and not once in six months of sermons has Corbin Gillette graced us with his presence. But I've heard him a billion times spouting out about God to serve the purpose of infecting his sons with his ignorance.

The fizzy snap of a beer can tab popping draws my attention. Corbin raises an eyebrow at me, always knowing what's playing out inside my head. He points at his youngest son, smirking. In a nasty, snide voice, he rumbles, "Enjoying the view?" Then he swills more than half a beer, eyes never leaving mine.

My eyes tug to the side, unable to resist the power of Corbin's words, then I quickly snap my eyes shut. Not that I can erase what I just saw– no, never that.

Imprinted in my brain is the split-second slice of time of the arc of Wynn's muscular back as he swung an axe over his head. He's still wearing those wet dream cut-off shorts from last summer, even though he's went through two or three growth spurts since. No shoes. No shirt. All messy curls and big, blue eyes, with a tiny blond trail of fuzz leading down his torso, and hard, round ass cheeks flexing beneath denim. Young, sun-kissed skin glistens with the potent, hormone-laced intoxicant of his sweat. I'm just thankful I'm not within sniffing distance, or I'd make a complete pervert out of myself.

The kid isn't even twelve yet, and he's a full-sized man. If it wasn't for the suffering of blood loss as it travels rapidly to my dick, I'd be jealous. I know Warren is jealous of his baby brother.

Wynn is tall for his age, proving he's going to be almost as tall as me when he's full-grown. Except he'll never look sickly because he's skin and bones like I am. His perfect, striated muscles are a curiosity to me, since no matter how much I eat and weight train, I can't grow an inch.

I wince as a montage of naughty acts play out in my mind, the very acts that make me a pervert.

Furious, I lash out at Corbin. "I hope you do the world a favor and rot in this chair," I grit out, knowing he'd kill me if I raised a hand to him. "Worthless waste of life."

"Wait a few years," Corbin drawls out, sounding disgustingly proud of himself. "And I'll be selling Wynn ta da highest bidder. He sure is growing up ta be a fine lookin' lad. My son can be a workhorse or a studhorse, buyer's choice. Better get ta earning some serious dough, faggot, 'cuz Wynn's top dollar."

The back of my hand flies up to stop my breakfast from escaping, amusing Corbin. "I got enough cash to last two years with Willa. I didn't expect to make a dime on the boys, thinking they could bring in money from working. But Wynn's special– special in the way Willa ain't. I suspect I'll be able to live the rest of my life in comfort once I sell Wynn off."

A firm hand wrapping around the back of my neck stops me before I can murder Corbin Gillette in his own yard. I'm tossed closer to Wynn, tripping over my own two feet.

"Get in the house, old man," Warren warns. "C'mon, now. Quit talkin' that bullshit, especially 'round comp'ny."

Corbin struggles to his feet, body ruined from the drink. Warren supports his father as the man runs off at the mouth. "It ain't bullshit. You know it ain't."

"Yeah… yeah… yeah…" Warren releases a strained laugh. "I know you think it's happening, old man. But you keep forgetting how I keep saying I'll kill you first. I'll burn Gillette Holler to the ground with you and Momma in it if you try to hurt Wynn the way you harmed Willa."

"I already got a buyer sniffing 'round for him. I figure if I keep holding out, getting some more work out of Wynn before I give him up, I can increase the price."

Heart beating out of my chest, my eyes seek out the boy who is completely oblivious to what's going down. Wynn is splitting wood like a natural born lumberjack with a wide grin on his face. "Is this true?" I shriek.

"Forget about it," Warren mutters flippantly, rolling his eyes, as he tries to maneuver his dad across their dumpster of a lawn. "This 'buyer' doesn't want anything from Wynn except his happiness. He doesn't want his ass any more than he wants yours. So relax. I hope it's the truth for Wynn's sake, believe it or not."

Bewildered and flabbergasted, "Royce?" spills from my lips.

"Yeah, Dad was upset because Royce wasn't going to pay for a legal adult when it came to me. Royce said if I wanted to leave, he'd take me in, but I better bring Wynn with me. So let's hope Dad's not blowing smoke up our asses, 'cuz whatever else he has planned might not be in Wynn's best interests."

I stare after Warren as he helps his asshole, bastard of a father into the shack, all the while feeling guilty that social services failed to recognize the truth while they left a kid who is being abused in every way possible with his abuser. The state has taken Wynn away a few times, and they always give him back. With me, granddaddy had two interviews and lost me permanently, and all he ever did was call me a faggot.

"Where'd everybody go?" I finally notice the soothing sound of chopping wood ceased when Wynn's voice hit my ears. I ignore the way he makes me feel as a new set of emotions come over me.

Wynn looks at me funny, tiny lips twisting up at the corners like my expression is confusing him. He narrows his eyes as I fight the urge to pull him into my arms, heft him over my shoulder, and run… run and never fucking come back to this shithole.

I take a few steps forward to do just that, but then I realize Wynn would probably struggle, and he's a lot stronger than I am. "Do you need some help? I'm not too proud to admit I can't swing an axe 'cuz my dad didn't get a chance to teach me, but I can stack wood with the best of 'em."

"Thank you," Wynn says brightly, like I just gave him a present that's been on his wish list and he never expected to get it. "Warren was gonna help, but…" He parts his calloused hands– hands that look older than mine already. "I don't mind stacking too. Warren always puts the wood willy-nilly, and then the stack tumbles over. Daddy says to just leave it where it lies, but I like how it looks orderly in a nice stack."

"Me too," I whisper, getting a bit choked up. I never want to see the innocent light die out in Wynn's eyes. It's too precious. "Chaos gives me a headache."

"Yes!" Wynn squeals, sounding like his age for once. "It's like my eyes just go from one thing to the next, making me feel nutty. I like to see stuff where it goes."

"I'm sorry you have to live here, then," I mutter underneath my breath. "Let's get a move on. I do believe Warren took off with the excuse of getting us a drink."

"Oh, that's right." Wynn runs his hands through his mop of curls, and I ignore the strike of longing that bursts in my chest. Something changed in me. I still think the kid is gorgeous, delicious, but I'd rather keep him safe. I want to protect him, cherish him. I never want to take from Wynn something he's not willing to give.

The label of pervert slips from my soul, replacing it are ones that would make my dad proud: Protector. Mentor. Friend.

I reach down for a piece of wood, and then start on creating a solid foundation for a stack. By the fourth piece, I decide I'm going to start using protein powder and lifting weights with Royce. By the tenth piece, I'm sweating buckets, which thankfully cancels out the intoxicating scent of Wynn's hormone-laced skin. By the fifteenth piece, I'm hoping gloves materialize from the sky. By the twentieth piece, I'm getting poked in the shoulder.

"Silly, it's hot out," Wynn reminds me, like I don't freaking feel the Sun melting me into a puddle of worthlessness. He gives a hard tug on my shirt. "I don't wear much 'cuz it's hot outside. If Momma wouldn't bitch, I'd just wear my skivvies to keep my nuts cool. So take your shirts off and put these on." A pair of leather gloves hits me upside the head.

"Um…" I stand here like an idiot with my mouth gaping open, gloves forgotten at my feet.

"You're funny," Wynn thinks I'm playing with him. *God, he's so innocent. I want to eat him alive.* "You must be hot and tired, not thinking straight… Here, let me help you."

Frozen in place, my mind goes on vacation when Wynn's fingers start tugging at my shirts, pulling them up at the waist. My skin flushes bright red when my hip bones show over the top of my jeans, and then I get more embarrassed when Wynn's eyes take in my hollow stomach and boney chest.

Wynn makes a panicked sound in the back of his throat– a cross between a gasp and the baying of a wounded animal. "What'd I do? I didn't even move? How'd I hurt you? Oh, God! What's wrong?" I ramble more and more insane questions as Wynn stands still, blue eyes bulging from his skull like a terrified rabbit.

From one blink to the next, those innocent eyes fill with tears, then Wynn's tearing across the yard. "Warren! Warren! Help! Something's wrong with me!!!" The boy's shrieks of terror will fill my nightmares for years to come. "Help me! I'm dying! I need the hospital. Fix it! W-A-R-R-E-N!" Wynn screams a death knell. "My dick broke!"

My legs crumple beneath me. My ass lands on a piece of wood, but the bruise doesn't even register in with my brain. I bust out laughing hysterically. I shake my head back and forth, feeling no shame for the negative thoughts that scroll on repeat.

"Serves you right, you little shit. You broke me… only fair I return the favor." I fall backward, resting my head on a log. I stare up to the sky, marveling over the ridiculousness of the situation. "Holy fuck!"

A dark cloud passes overhead, blocking out the Sun. "Holy fuck is right, asshole." Warren kicks my thigh. His face is twisted in anger. His eyes are damp with unshed tears. But his lips are curved with wry amusement. "I just had to explain to my baby brother that his cock wasn't broken, and then I had to show him how to take care of business. Pretty sure he's more confused than ever."

Putting up my hands to ward off the oncoming violence, "I didn't touch him," I promise. "Honest."

"I know. I was walking out here from the house when Wynn lost his shit." Warren kicks my thigh again. "Are you gay? I always thought you were."

Every muscle in my body clenches. "Yeah."

Voice tight with silent rage, "Your dick likes my brother?"

"Yeah, but I ain't doing anything about it." I go with honesty for once. "I'm ignoring it. I just started feeling protective over the little shit, and the peckerwood goes and gets hard because of me. Fucked. Up."

"Is Wynn gay?" Warren asks so quietly I have to lean upright to hear him.

"Yeah, but Wynn doesn't understand." I warn, "So don't pressure him, don't tell anybody, and don't tell him."

"Has he always been?"

Now it's my turn to get angry. "I didn't turn your baby brother gay, asshole!" I jump to my feet, ready to destroy a twelve-year friendship. "I didn't even know I was gay until the little cock tease started wearing hot pants around me. And I'm not gonna tell Wynn he's gay until he figures it out on his own. We're born this way, not made! So deal and back the fuck off!"

Warren takes two steps back, face twisted up with shock. He shakes his head back and forth a few times to clear his thoughts, and I worry the stocky bastard is going to murder me with his bare hands. And then he starts laughing.

"You should have seen his face!" Warren howls with laughter. "Wynn was crying, terrified with his dick pointing at the ceiling. God, I remember my first wood. My dick became my best friend. And here my brother is, looking like his dick betrayed him." Warren clutches his side, trying to abate his laughter, and then his eyes change to rage. "Touch him, and I'll cut your nuts off. Go near Wynn's ass, even if he asks for it, and I'll gut you."

Sighing, I roll my eyes. I tug my shirt back into place, not allowing Warren to see my bony stomach. Then I ignore his bullshit by bending down to continue stacking Wynn's woodpile. The boy deserves to have a day off to celebrate the terror of his first erection.

Warren begins pacing around me as I work, confused that I didn't play into his bullshit, but he doesn't help. By the time I get three rows stacked, he's getting agitated. "I promise not to touch him–"

"Thank you," Warren cuts me off.

"I promise not to touch Wynn until he's an adult. If he comes to me, I'm not going to be able to say no. You gotta understand what I mean. I see the way you look at Wynn's little girlfriend." I go in for the kill. "She even bled yet?"

Warren falls to the ground like I swept his legs out from beneath him. "God," he drawls. "Those little shits are so delicious. Makes me feel like a pervert. All I can think about is corrupting Penny..." He lies on the ground with his eyes shut, but then one blue peeper squints up at me. "Yeah, she started bleeding a couple years ago. I thought we should wait, but I doubt I can make it. She's teasing the fuck out of me."

"You're sick," I snarl, getting pissed. "Just because I looked, never meant I planned on touching."

"Penny's a year older than Wynn, for your information… and like you'll wait for Wynn to turn eighteen." Warren rolls his eyes at me. "Like you plan on waiting for him."

My lips twist into an evil smirk. "You owe me a puppy if I'm still a virgin at twenty-one."

"God, I'd rather be ridden hard and buy my own dog." Warren cackles.

"Make it a pug. I always wanted a dog," I murmur. "You owe me your blessing if I wait until Wynn comes to me… and a thousand bucks if I last until he's a legal adult."

"Deal." Warren reaches forward to shake my hand. "Wynn's my brother, that's why I'm going along with this. But I'm not in on this deal when it comes to Penny. I'll be lucky to last another month with her rubbing her ass all over me."

"Pervert," I mutter with a smirk.

Warren says with a wink, "Takes one to know one."

"Takes what to know what?" Wynn pops out of nowhere, looking like a perky puppy. His hair is damp from a shower. He's now wearing a pair of sweatpants because the bat in his pants still hasn't gone soft, and I doubt it would fit in his cut-offs.

"You must really, really want that pug," Warren reminds me smugly. I turn away with a wince and a groan.

Wynn's excited voice reaches out to me. "You're getting a puppy?"

"For both your sakes, you better hope he doesn't," Warren mutters underneath his breath.

•LATE SPRING•
Present Day

"Winnie the Pooh!" Penny's strained voice flows to me amongst the chaos. Every door in the school is emptying students into the hallway. Kids' voices from seventh to twelfth grade meld into an anxious stew of angst. Shoving and taunting, the two sides of Rusty Knob High are obvious: Hillbillies versus Townies.

We live in a constant state of violence, ignorance, resentment, oppression, intolerance, and hatred. We do it to ourselves by not letting go of the past and by thinking too little of ourselves. The townies don't think themselves better, at least not all of them.

My eyes flick around wildly, looking exactly five feet in the air for one of my best friends. But that's not what has me in protector-mode. Penny is my brother's girlfriend, and he'll murder me in my sleep if I let anything happen to her during school hours.

My heart picks up double-time when I don't spot her. Last week, one of my townie buddies made an offhand comment to Penny. She told my brother, Warren, to get a rise out of him. Our fathers' bad blood lives on in their sons, and their sons' sons. The resentment is thick, and the violence is real. Penny was playing a game for attention, and it almost cost Bren his life.

Warren had no problem showing up in Bren's bedroom to issue a warning. I hate violence, and I bridge the gap between the townies and the hillbillies. If I hadn't been there to stop my brother, I have no idea what would have happened.

"Down here!" Penny releases a giggle when I spot her on the floor, trying to grab at a scattering of papers. The girl is immature, no different than the rest of our kin, and she doesn't know any better. But on a daily basis, I want to smack the shit out of Penny to teach her a lesson, and then I want to give her a big hug.

I slide to my knees, shouting over the din of a hundred excited idiots. "That's not your term paper, is it?" Not that it matters none, seeing as how Penny will never graduate, even if she is as sharp as a tack and has the potential to make a difference in this world. Penny wasn't raised to do anything but create another generation of children who mind their elders and do as they were told, even when it's wrong.

I don't think like my kin, so they think me arrogant. I befriend anyone worth knowing– doesn't matter if they are a little one or a papaw. I don't drink. I don't fight. I don't screw. I study hard, play basketball harder, and work the hardest. My daddy says I think my shit don't stink. But I live in the Hollers, so the townies can't accept me as one of their own, either. I'm in the middle, with neither side knowing what to do with me. Since I'm smart, athletic, big, pretty, and a pacifist, they don't know whether they want to respect me and listen to me, or shun me because I'm different.

I swat at a pair of Chucks before they leave a footprint on the title page of Penny's term paper. With a rough yank, I manage to get a handful of pages from beneath a filthy pair of Timberlands.

"My term paper? Ya think?" Giving attitude, Penny sits on her heels, blowing out a deep breath. Her ginger bangs billow, revealing her big, brown puppy dog eyes. Then her bangs fall back into place, hiding her eyes from my view. "Some dumb fuck shoved me when the bell rang, and… WHOOPS!" She flings her tiny hands in the air while pulling a face.

"Figures," I mumble as I get on my hands and knees, hunting for the rest of Penny's term paper. I lost faith in our fellow man around the age of two when I was able to think for myself.

I punch some tool in the thigh when he won't budge. "What the fuck, man–" Bren's insult is cut short when he notices who punched him. "Sorry, man. How about I help ya, Wynn?"

"Yeah, why don't ya?" I go back to rescuing Penny, laughing underneath my breath when Bren drops to the ground next to me, all the while grunting and pushing people out of the way.

I like Bren Kennedy, even if I was told not to because he rejected his roots in the hollers by living in town. He's one of the good ones I befriended, even if he acts like an ass most of the time. In a way, we're related by marriage. My sister married into the Kennedy family, with my niece and nephew being Bren's cousins. Everyone from the hollers are kin some way or another. Plus, Bren's dad is my weekend boss. Royce would kick my behind if I wasn't nice to his son.

"Wynn said to pick up the papers!" Bren shouts into the crowd, clapping his large paws above his head. "So you better fucking pick up the papers! Hop to it!"

I pause to tell Bren thanks, and I even mean it. Students scatter like cockroaches in the light. Some run to the exits like the fires of

Hell are licking at their heels, while others drop to the ground to help out. My faith in humanity returns when every single member of our basketball team– all townies –gets down on their hands and knees to help the hillbilly princess, while our own leave us to fend for ourselves. Bren starts checking out page numbers and begins methodically putting the papers in order.

There are a few sayings in West Virginia that still hold true.

There is no I in team.

Blood is thicker than water.

If you can't make them love you, make them fear you instead.

I am a member of their team, and Penny is going to be my blood, so she is helped because of me. Everybody loves Wynn Gillette, whether they want to or not. It's impossible to bully the kid who will help you out after you spit in his face, especially when he grew to be six foot two. They're not all my biggest fans, and some can be belligerent about it, but they do as they're told.

"How many pages, Penn?" Bren is concentrating really hard on putting the pages to rights as our buddies shove more paper at him. The same boy who called Penny a *rotten twat licker* last week is now being helpful. Waking up to my brother standing over his sleeping form has made Bren leery around Penny.

Breathlessly grabbing for three months of hard work, Penny releases an ironic laugh. "Thanks, Bren." Her eyes flick in my direction, asking for backup. "Just so ya know, I've never licked a twat in my life. If you think pussy can rot, you've been dealing with the wrong type of pussy."

Bren's eyeing me now, but I sit with patience, happy Penny has every single page of her term paper in working order. "Aahhhaaahhhaa… I like you, Penn!" Bren uses my shoulder to push himself to his feet. But as he rises, he whispers in my ear, voice quivering with fear. "Wynn, you make sure you tell Warren I was nice to his girl. I don't want no more visits in the middle of the night."

"We're even," I state with a nod. "All's forgiven."

I don't release a laugh until after Bren and our boys flee the bitchy hillbilly princess. My brother, Warren, visited Bren in the middle of the night with a shotgun to his forehead. If I hadn't been the angel resting on the devil's shoulder that night, the trigger might have been pulled over something ridiculous. Which is why I want out of this godforsaken town.

Since that night, Bren's been the sweetest feller, because I know he pissed his bed from fright. I also know a few more of Bren's secrets, and he has an inkling I know them, too. I get more respect by keeping my trap shut than from the fear I will spill it.

Everybody loves Wynn Gillette because he's the angel on Warren Gillette's shoulder. *If you can't make them love you, make them fear you instead.* The residents of Rusty Knob are fearful I won't meet a girl before I graduate. They're praying a girl will make me stay in town and keep my blood in order.

They couldn't be more wrong.

"All set, Penny?" I eye her over, making sure she's put to rights without a scratch on her. Penny releases a relieved laugh while hugging her paper to her chest. I lean forward and give her a quick kiss to the forehead.

The bitch glares burn the back of my neck, drawing a red flush up my cheeks. I turn to witness three furious girls whispering in hushed tones. I roll my eyes, drawing Penny to her feet, knowing I just put a different sort of target on her back.

I love Penny, attitude and drama included. Doing right by her makes me feel warm inside. What kind of man would I be if I walked by when someone was in need? I have the ability to help, and it makes me feel good when I do. The girls of Rusty Knob don't understand that I care for Penny because she's a human being, not because I'm itching to get into her underpants.

"Jesus, they'd drop to their knees and suck your dick right in the hallway if you asked." Penny shouts at them as we pass by. "Desperate, much? Did it hurt when you fell off the whore tree and banged every guy on the way down?"

"Do you fuck both brothers at the same time, you nasty cunt?" I just raise a brow at Jessica, and whatever else was on the tip of her tongue dries up right quick. I know her secret, too. The pretty blonde is a closeted lesbian who uses Bren's dick for survival in this intolerant wasteland.

"You're a pervert, Jess." Penny flushes bright red. "Thanks for the visual. Because, goddamn, if that was possible, I'd be a fool not to take 'em up on it."

"Eww," I grunt, shuddering at the thought of touching either my brother or Penny. "Stop entertaining that thought," I warn Penny when I notice her eyeing me like a prize.

For some odd reason, Penny's eye-fuckage bothers Jessica. "Don't do Wynn wrong like that, Penn. That's just gross. I see your wheels spinning."

Penny's firing off before I can recover, lunging toward the four girls blocking our exit. "Shut your mouth before I fill it with Franny's girl cock!" I snort, knowing Penny has no bite whatsoever. But then again, she has the Gillette boys watching her back, so she can talk as much shit as she wants. And talk shit, she does.

"You need to buy your brother's bitch a muzzle," Jesse scoffs, and then she turns away to stomp toward her car, with her mute entourage following.

"It makes me feel filthy." I shudder in revulsion. "Like the way to my popularity is through my dick. They don't see me as a person, and now you're eyeballing the fly of my jeans."

"I'm your best friend, do I have to ask again?" Brown eyes rove over me from head to toe, looking for the taint of homosexuality. Penny reaches up, barely able to brush my temple with a fingertip. "You a girl in there?"

I narrow my eyes and refuse to acknowledge such horseshit.

"Every other guy except for Franny would unzip and yank his dick out. You ain't like Franny, are ya, Wynn?"

"Are you shitting me?" I shake my head in disgust, hating how even Penny is infected with the ignorance of Rusty Knob. "Francis is gay. He's not transgender."

"What's a transgender? Ain't those buggers who dress in lady's clothing, are they? 'Cuz Franny dresses like a boy. Nah, that's a tranny. What's transgender?"

I don't answer Penny. Instead, I erase her fears. "Francis is just a boy who likes other boys. It's as simple as that."

"Are you a fag, or whatever that word was?"

"Neither," I repeat for the billionth time. "Do I look like a girl, even on the inside?" I run my hands across my broad chest. "Have I ever turned my head to check out a dude?"

"Nope," Penny pops the P. "But your head ain't turned to look at no girls neither."

"C'mon, Warren's a-waiting." I tug my tiny, ignorant buddy behind me, refusing to acknowledge the fact that for a few years now I've wondered if I was asexual.

If it wasn't for Facebook, I might have taken a sawed-off below the chin by now. I came across a LGBTQ group for the Kentwood

Area School District on accident when one of my classmates was trolling. Their bigoted slurs were infecting my news feed. I made a dummy profile and joined the group, where I easily found Bren, who was too stupid to use a different profile– same for Francis. At least Jessica and my real best friend tried to use pseudonyms.

The stipulations of the group were that you had to be a student of one of the three schools in our district, be between fourteen and eighteen, and abide by Mentor KM's rules. They all soothed me with facts, assuring me I'm not asexual since I do fantasize about other people while jerking off. Their comforting words confused me more, because the imaginary friends I use to get off are always faceless and genderless.

So what the fuck am I?

"You know you can talk to me about anything, Wynn," Penny breathes lightly, showing her sweet and caring side. Her spunky attitude amuses me. The reckless way she manipulates my brother terrifies me. But the soft side of Penny melts my heart.

I tug Penny against my side, wrapping my arm around her shoulders. Like the good brother I am, I escort Warren's girl directly to him after school every day. I miss the first twenty minutes of practice because I have to meet him in the parking lot. But with all things, everybody is real accommodating for a Gillette.

Penny and I have been friends since kindergarten, with Warren six years older than us. The day Penny followed me home after school in sixth grade, was the day my brother lost his fucking mind. Penny grew tits and bled, and Warren turned into a brainless, horned-up dog.

Thinking back, a twelve-year-old girl should have never been on a seventeen-year-old guy's radar. I'm that age now, and I only see them as little girls with pigtails who are trying too hard to look like sluts. Which is exactly why there are so many derogatory West Virginia jokes. There wasn't an idiot in Rusty Knob who would interfere when Warren set his sights on Penny, because we all knew they were destined to get hitched and pop out a bunch of brats.

"How's my girl?" Warren tugs Penny from beneath my arm, glaring at me like he's thinking about tearing my balls off for touching her. He wraps a possessive arm around her waist and kisses the top of her head. "Everybody treating you right?"

Warren's question is more of a warning. A warning he's even issued to me. I've had my ass beat a handful of times because the possessive fuck thought I was lusting after Penny. We made a deal: I'll protect Penny like my sister, knowing someday she will be, as long as he doesn't treat her the way our father treats our mother, or the way our sister's husband treated her. Warren can beat me if I encroach on his territory, but I'll kill him if he ever hits Penny.

My brother is intense. He doesn't share. He's violent, and his threats are promises. But he is faithful, loyal, and a good human being who will treat Penny right.

We share the same personality traits. I dampen down my anger, and he buries his compassion. The only thing that brings out his compassion is me, and the only thing that will bring out my anger is him. Which is why Rusty Knob is terrified I might leave town someday.

"Wynn's my hero," Penny sings, hugging her term paper to her breasts, causing my brother to issue me a warning glare. The brat starts giggling, loving it when Warren turns into a caveman.

"She's just yanking your chain." I thump my brother in the shoulder. "You know how she tests the piss out of you, making sure you're still interested."

"Mmm-hmm," Warren grunts, eyes narrowing to slits as he scans my body– a body that is taller, stronger, and firmer than his own. A body that doesn't stir for Penny... or anybody.

"Jesus, I'm through with you assholes for the day." I turn on my heel and stomp away. "Go use someone else to make each other jealous. I'm your brother for God's sake," I shout at Penny over my shoulder. Sick the fuck of being toyed with, I turn vengeful by dropping a secret I promised to keep. "Grow up before that kid in your gut pops out!"

"Baby?" croaking out my brother's tight throat is the last thing I hear as I jog back to the school to hit the locker room.

THE TEST

Eyes closed, I zone out while I dress in a pair of jeans and my Circle K work shirt. I block out the noise as the rest of the team razzes each other, snapping towels and tossing insults. I'm envious of them, how they don't have any responsibilities and get to be free.

The townies go home to quaint little houses, where they do their homework while their mommas cook supper and their daddies give advice. They have no idea what the reality is down in the Hollers. Which is why the hillbillies resent them, and the townies look at us as *other*.

I hate how I get no relief. I spend my days at school watching after Penny while trying to get an education. Then I deal with my brother's bullshit. Followed by being run to death on the basketball court. On the days we don't have a game, I work until midnight at the Circle K. Only to go home to a shack filled with a violent alcoholic and his zombiefied women.

I actually look forward to the weekends, where my sister's kids, Hayley and Hayden, have their visitation with Bren and his dad, Royce. The Gillettes were against having the twins around their Kennedy kin unless I was there to take care of them. So all weekend, I work odd jobs for Royce, while my niece and nephew get to spend quality time with their uncle and cousin. The more I work, the less I have to be home.

It's obvious Royce and Bren hate to see us go every Sunday night, but I have to get the kids back to their momma and I have to get back to mine. What's hardest is leaving a warm, loving, family-filled home to enter Gillette Holler– otherwise known as the seventh circle of Hell.

I want the fuck out of Rusty Knob, like yesterday.

I was hoping for an academic scholarship if the basketball scouts didn't like what they saw on the court. It was just my luck that they did. I received a scholarship to a state school. One that just so happened to be in Rusty Knob's backyard, so student housing was not included. I'll be going to school for free, but still living in that rat-hole hell our family calls a home.

"We're gonna be late for work again." Jackson Duncan, my actual best friend, nudges me with his shoulder, causing me to snap out of my self-pity. I nudge him back, finding my center just by touching him.

I lean forward on the bench, and begin lacing up my sneakers. "They'll deal," I murmur to myself, eyes cutting across to the idiots who populate our town— the same idiots who will become our future workforce. I know my job is secure, no matter how late I might be once in a while. They won't bitch when their other choices are budding wife-beating alcoholics since anyone with a brain in their head leaves for college and never comes back.

Rusty Knob is filled with racist assholes who hate each other as much as everyone else. We might divide ourselves as Townies versus Hillbillies, but the townies are still hillbillies who don't live in the Hollers. The mentality still weaves its way through all of us, just stronger in the isolated folk.

No matter where you live or where you came from, the most potent slur is fag. The only openly gay person in town is currently being taunted in this very locker room.

"Franny, bend over and show us your purdy asshole." Bren yanks Francis by the arm, but I don't bother intervening because the kid is giggling while he gets tickled senseless. Jack flinches next to me on the bench, but I know he won't jump in to save Francis either.

There are two kinds of people in this world. Those who will kick a defenseless puppy, and those who will pick it up and protect it. Francis is so small and helpless that even the bigots of this town protect him. I'm positive there are other gays in Rusty Knob, but if they look like everyday Joes, they will get lynched in fear their affliction will spread among the population. When a manly man sucks dick and loves it, the homophobes spill out the woodwork.

A couple years back, two towns over, a gay man was dragged behind a car and left on the side of the road for dead. The men who did it to him went free because everyone's lips glued shut when the law came 'round. Word has it, his own family nearly beat him into the grave.

The reason why Francis is giggling while Bren spanks his ass and tells him to go wash the dirty towels, is because no one expects Francis to find another man who is gay enough to touch him. First man to touch Rusty Knob's Franny is a dead man, with Francis surely to follow.

Bren and Francis are protecting themselves with the *bully and the fag* routine. After a bullied chubby girl shouted, "Yeah, I'm fat!

So what?" Bren figured out that if Francis started acting gayer than gay, no one could come up with a good comeback. Francis embraced the slur of fag.

Why do I know all this? My dad thinks I'm gay. My brother thinks I'm gay. Penny keeps asking if I'm a girl inside my head after reading an article about transsexuals in Cosmo. I'm the only man Francis is secure enough to ogle, only because he knows I will never kick his ass. All because I don't go insane, drag a girl to the floor, shove my dick inside her, shoot my seed in there until she's growing my kid in her gut and married to me before I graduate.

I want more out of life. I'm seventeen years old and I want to get a degree and make some kind of difference, even if it's only in a few lives. I want to matter more than the person who goes to work, does a shitty job, then comes home to scream at my kids, smack my wife around, and drink a thirty pack of liquid sandwich while my family goes without. I want to mean more than being the person my family resents behind my back as I put a leaky roof over their heads and rotten food in their guts. I deserve more, and those future kids do too.

The higher you go in Kentwood's educational system, the less Holler-dwelling girls there are per grade. By the time girls hit sophomore year, they start getting picked off by the senior boys, and married and pregnant by the time June rolls around. Only to be used, abused, and tossed away with their kids before they reach eighteen.

Penny is our only hillbilly girl in the eleventh grade, with not a single one in the senior class. All the rest of the girls are on the college track, or dating boys who will go away and come back with a fancy degree and take good care of their women and any kids they have. The social divide becomes wider the older you get.

It's expected of me to marry and have kids right after I graduate. Since I'm nearing the end of my junior year, and the dwindling supply of hillbilly girls hasn't caught my eye, I must be gay. That's the only answer that is possible in the narrowest of narrow minds. I'm gay because I don't want to impregnate a child-woman, get a dead-end job I'll hate, where my wife and kids will run back home to where they came from when I start beating them in an alcohol haze.

Thoroughly disgusted, "C'mon," I mutter to Jack, yanking on his shirt sleeve. He's the only person I speak my thoughts, because even Penny has been indoctrinated into this way of life and will never understand. Jack lives in town, but he understands how badly I want to break the cycle.

Jack has his own secrets he doesn't think I know, because he uses a piss-poor excuse of a pseudonym in our LGBTQ group on Facebook. I've figured out who everyone is from our school in the group, and why they frequent it. Jack sees too much of himself in Francis, and fears what will happen if the truth is ever revealed.

Sad, blue eyes call to me for help, looking as if he's going to be sick. I tug Jack up next to me, wrapping my arm around his shoulders, feeling centered and content with him by my side. He shudders, and then sighs deeply.

Walking together unsteadily, Jack grumbles out the side of his mouth, "Get me the fuck out of here. Watching what Francis and Bren have to do to hide out in plain sight is going to make me puke."

As if Jack called him, Francis materializes in our path. He flashes me a pitiful look, and then in slow motion his hand is reaching out. I sigh heavily, rolling my eyes, as Francis cups my crotch in his tiny, girl-like palm.

"You done?" I direct to the kid molesting me, already suffering through this experiment a few times before– at least this time I'm not in the communal showers. "We good?" His grip flexes, pulsing a bit, and then he removes it. "Don't even think about it," I warn the sadistic twinkle in his eye as I pull Jack behind me. "You start that shit, and you'll regret it."

"Leave Jack alone," Bren calls to his Franny. "We know Jessica sucked his dick last fall. Did Wynn get hard?"

Skipping back to his partner in crime's side, Frances laughs the entire way. "Nah, not even a twitch, boss. It's a pity, 'cuz Wynn's hung like a horse." Bren slaps Francis upside the head, not appreciating the reminder that his Franny craves cock.

"You just mind your own business," Bren warns Francis as I drag Jack from the locker room.

"What do you think they'd do if you got hard?" Jack gasps when we breach the outside of the building, spilling out into the student parking lot.

"There wasn't a snowballs' chance in hell I was going to get hard," I remind my buddy. We've spoken at length about how nobody turns me on. He understands that I'm not like normal folks who just know what they want.

I remember the first time I got wood, I thought I was dying. In a blind panic, I ran to Warren to show him. He laughed, dragged my ass into the bathroom, turned on the shower, told me to get in, and then grabbed my hand and squeezed Momma's conditioner into it. I stood in the hot shower, crying so hard I was hyperventilating, not knowing what was happening. Warren made a vague gesture with his hand, and then left the room. Like an idiot, it took me two weeks of standing in the shower with conditioner in my palm, every single time I sported wood, before I figured out what I was supposed to do.

My dick confuses me.

"If I would have gotten hard, I would have dropped dead on the spot," I mutter when I snap out of my thoughts.

"I mean…" Jack stops talking abruptly, and then veers around my pickup to get into the passenger side. When we both get into the cab and get situated, he continues. "I mean, forget about who was receiving the fag test. Most of us have been targeted. I mean, what would happen if someone actually got hard when Francis cupped them?"

I smother a laugh as I pull out of the parking lot. "Truthfully, I think if Bren were to cup the dudes, he'd probably yank a few out of the closet. But Francis… he's… there is something the opposite of sexual about him, and I don't mean because he's gay. He's childlike. Innocent. To be protected. So I doubt he's gotten anyone hard in his life."

"You're right… I was just…" Jack takes up stuttering all the sudden. "I… I worry, because I get hard for no goddamned reason. Like if something tastes good, or if I feel sleepy, or warm and cozy, or if a stiff wind blows."

My head hitches backward as a peal of laughter spills from my lips. "Ain't that the goddamned truth." I snort a few times. "I think Francis is the anti-erection. I go soft just thinking about him. Fuck, my dick would stay hard thinking about Penny, and you know I ain't feeling her. If I was hard and anybody touched me, I'd stay hard. It's not a fag test. It's a guy with a dick test. It just is."

"Yeah, when Jesse blew me, I wasn't thinking about her. I was just hard. I didn't even get off. She told everyone I did to save pride." Jack shifts around uncomfortably. "So, say someone failed the fag test, what would they do?"

"The basketball team?" I mull that over while I park in my reserved employee parking spot at the Circle K. In other words, I park next to the dumpsters. I can't tell Jack what I really think, how Bren isn't looking to out gay kids, but to find himself a trustworthy '*friend*'. Bren's behavior is all an illusion. "All talk. No bite. They're just looking for another victim to pester."

"Okay." No longer looking green around the gills, Jack hops down from my truck. He flips the lid on the dumpster to contain the smell so it doesn't permeate my interior.

"But…" I snarl when I see some lazy fucker left the trash next to the bin instead of inside it. I flick the lid back open, toss the trash bags into the dumpster, and then shut the lid again. "Our fathers… our uncles… our grandfathers… It's not their sons you should be worried about."

"Fourteen months and I'm out of here," Jack threatens as he charges into the Circle K, ready to tackle the shit job we were given.

Leaning over the counter, getting into my face, "I can't believe you told Warren I was pregnant," Penny chastises me. Her brows pinch together in the middle, like she's trying her damnedest to get those fake tears to spring from her eyes but failing miserably.

I know who Penny truly is. Flawed. Jealous. A manipulator. I can only tolerate her because I love her like a sister. I can't go around punching everyone who annoys me, because my hand would be broken and all of Rusty Knob would be hospitalized. So, instead, I just accept it and move on.

My last nerve snaps, and I pray Warren won't execute me in my sleep. "This sucky, boring ass job that I hate so goddamned much, is going to put food in your kid's gut." I point at Penny's rounded tummy. "Here you are, worried about a term paper that means jackshit since come June you'll be married and living in Gillette Holler. You won't even make it out of junior year, I suspect."

"Winnie the Po—"

"No, you're gonna listen, and listen good," I warn, getting into Penny's face like she was mine. "Since I turned twelve, I've been supporting my family of lowlifes, my brother included. I already put food in the mouths of my niece and nephew, my momma and sister, and your worthless baby-maker. I'm not gonna be around forever. I hoped the news that Warren was gonna be a daddy would light a fire under his ass to get a goddamned job and quit acting like our worthless daddy. I'm gonna live my own life, and I ain't gonna be fathering your kids until the day I die."

Penny mimics a fish, eyes bulging and mouth gaping open. "I… I… I thought we were friends? I thought you loved me like a sister."

"I do." I lean backward, wanting to end our conversation. "I graduate in a little over a year, lest you forget since you won't be joining me. I want more for you than the life I'm living. But y'all are cut off after that, 'cuz I'm gonna get my own life. It's about time y'all fend for yourselves."

"I'm pregnant," Penny sputters, aghast.

"You ain't dead," I say flatly, hating how Penny is forcing me to speak like her. When passions arise, my roots show. "You got enough energy to spread your thighs for Warren still, and he's got enough life in him to make children. You assholes can get jobs and support your kids. You need to do that instead of lying around on your asses in filth, while your kids raise themselves, waiting for me to put food in the fridge. Just like my daddy and momma and my sister."

Penny stomps across the floor toward the exit, nearly taking out a display of potato chips. "I ain't like that!"

I just roll my eyes. "I love you, Penny. I always will. But you were raised like that, same as Warren was, same as I was. But instead of hating it, you saw it as normal. You could break the cycle if you realized there was a better way of living. You're a smart girl, but you got knocked up on purpose because your momma told you it was time to get out of her house and into mine. My house is hell, and it makes me sick to think you'll be living there."

"I ain't like that!" Penny shouts again. She jerks the front door open with force, proving being pregnant isn't a disability. "I ain't!"

"Prove it!" I shout at the closing door. I narrow my eyes as Penny stomps across the parking lot toward Warren's idling, piece of shit car.

I know I'm going to regret our fight around two in the morning when I wake to a sawed-off to the forehead. Maybe Warren will pull the trigger this time and put me out of my misery.

It's Friday, which means it's payday. Which means I'm going to want to shoot myself within minutes of getting home anyway.

Carrying a crate of milk to the cooler, "Only fourteen months," Jack tries to cheer me up, but it only makes me feel worse.

Fourteen more months of working a dead-end job where I don't get a penny of my wages. Fourteen more months of my family sinking their teeth into me. Fourteen more months before I go to college yet still remain in Rusty Knob, West Virginia.

"I'll miss ya, bro," I say to Jack on his next pass through with another crate to stock the cooler. "I hope you find what you're looking for wherever you end up."

"I will." He flashes me a cheeky grin that transforms until it looks painful. "You can always come with me."

I shake my head sadly. "Nah. I'm a Gillette. Loyal. Blood comes first."

Words projecting like sharp weapons, "You're a Gillette. Shouldn't they put you first at some point? You weren't born to funnel money into their chaos."

Words stinging me, I blow out a deep breath, and decide now is the perfect time to close out the register. I jump when a hand thumps down a Gatorade on the counter.

"Anything else?" I ask, not bothering to look up while I press a few keys on the cash register. My cheeks flush bright red, knowing the customer had to have heard my fight with Penny and everything I said to Jack. I'm a quiet guy, so I'm a bit freaked.

"No," comes a cold voice. I shiver, eyes flicking up to meet the most violent stare I've ever encountered. I'm a big dude, the next to the biggest dude in all of Rusty Knob, with this guy being the biggest.

"It'll be $2.49, Kade," I mutter, getting tongue-tied because Kaden Marx is murdering me with his feral stare. I want to mutter, *"What'd I ever do to you?"* like a pussy. I mean, I'm a nice guy. I've spent my life making sure nothing violent happens, and Kade is glaring at me like I kicked his puppy and then pissed in its wounds.

A heavy palm slaps a ten on the counter, and then lifts the Gatorade. "Keep the change."

Confused, I mutter, "Thank yo–"

"Don't buy booze with it," Kade cuts me off. "I don't want your dad pissing my money down the toilet, or your mother breathing it into her lungs, or your sister shooting it into her veins, or your brother snorting it up his nose. If you don't use it on yourself, then feed those dirty assholes who call you uncle."

The Gillette in me erupts. "Aren't you those dirty assholes' teacher?"

"Yeah," Kade grunts. He reaches over, grabs a bar of Ivory from the shelf, and then slaps another ten on the counter. "Keep the change. Keep the soap. Buy some detergent with what's left. When Hayley and Hayden walk into my classroom come Monday, they better not burn my nose hairs off with the tang of drugs, booze, and shit and piss on their skin and clothing."

"What the?" I stammer, at a complete and total loss as Kaden stalks out the front door. "What'd I ever do to you?" slips out, even though he can't hear me.

"I'm sorry?" Jack's upward inflection makes the apology sound like a question.

"What the fuck was that about?" I stare down at the bar of soap and the two tens, paying Jack no mind.

"I'm gonna go finish up in the back. I'll walk home tonight since you've yet to close out the register. I'll see ya Monday at school."

"Yeah, bye." I continue to stare at the money and soap, confusion and hurt warring in my emotions. "What the?" Snapping out of it, I remember it's payday. I begin closing out the cash register while Jack locks up the front, and then disappears into the back of the store.

Cash register closed out, the front locked up nice and tight, I tear open the envelope containing my pay. "Motherfucking payday," I snarl. "I hate you!"

I close my eyes, hoping against hope that I got my full pay this week. "Christ," I whimper. Thirty-seven hours, and I only got paid for five. Not even enough to pay for a tank of gas. "Daddy, if I had the balls, I'd shoot you dead."

I press the itemized invoice on the counter, detailing the charges my father had amassed this week while I was at school. Daddy sneaks in here when I can't stop him, and charges thirty packs of beer for himself and cartons of cigarettes for my momma to his seventeen-year-old son's tab.

My boss doesn't stop him because they are buddies. I started working here when I was twelve, under the table because it was illegal, because someone had to pay my daddy's tab when he was too goddamned worthless to do it himself. I work so my father can drink, which puts him in a foul mood, so it's my fault he knocks my mother around, and then he pisses my hard-earned money down the toilet.

Yeah, I could quit. I've been there and done that. My father beat the fuck out of me because he was sober, and I spent three nights in the hospital. I had to go back to work to pay my medical bills. Daddy threatened this would be an endless cycle unless I just went to work like a good son– a son who wasn't in physical pain. Either I pay for Daddy's beer, or I pay for more medical bills. My choice.

PULL THE TRIGGER

As my truck rumbles over the ruts in the hard-packed dirt path, my eyeballs jiggle in my head and my nuts get pounded into the bench seat. Slowly simmering, my anger gets the best of me with every jarring movement.

Sometimes I envy Warren for his ability to pick a target at random and release all of his pent-up fury. But mostly, I envy him because he can get lost inside Penny and forget the world.

I refuse to hit back because the thought of anyone hurting as badly as I do makes me choke on misery. No matter how low of a lowlife they may be, no one deserves this existence. When I accidentally insult someone, it never leaves my thoughts until another fuck-up buries it.

Gut churning, my tires hitting junk in the yard signals I've arrived home.

I glare out the windshield with bitter hatred at the trash heap known as Gillette Holler, understanding why Daddy drinks like a fish, Momma smokes cigarettes by the carton, Warren snorts powder up his nose, and Willa has a needle plunging into her shrinking veins.

To forget.

To commit slow suicide.

To be a coward.

I don't drink. I don't smoke. I don't do drugs. I won't fight. I can't fuck. All I can do is smile and keep on a-giving.

A crooked shack greets me with light glowing from the cracks between the rotten boards acting as siding. The majority of Rusty Knob's homes have painted siding, double-pane windows, insulation, sheetrock, and solid framing, with a waterproof roof over their heads. They also have a hardworking daddy and a good momma, with a couple of smart kids I go to school with. For the rest of us who were born to shit parents, there are portions of our home where animals can crawl in to lay down next to us while we sleep in our beds. Where I have to go outside, pluck a piece of junk from the yard, and then nail it over the hole while the rest of the family gets a broom after the coon curled up on one of our cots.

It's not a home. It's a motherfucking dumpster.

My eyes rove across the yard. My path is lit by the huge bonfire blazing in the center of the trash heap. The grass is so high it brushes my nuts when I walk to the front door. Somewhere buried deep within the mass of green are the prehistoric remains of seven push mowers and the chassis of a John Deere lawn tractor. My worthless family is so lazy, they will step over a mower with weeds choking it to death, instead of starting the bitch and clearing the land.

Who am I kidding? They won't mow the lawn because then we'd see the junk littering like a wave of misery across our land.

The bonfire leaps a few feet, its flames licking at a plastic chair– Daddy's favorite. A sick smile twists my lips as I watch it melt and then collapse into itself as fuel for the fire that spreads. I calculate how far it would have to grow for the flames to sweep to the shack.

As fast as it started, it's a pity the fire extinguishes when it meets a solid metal barrier– Daddy's recycling pile. His cash accumulating interest, he likes to say when he's drunk. When isn't he drunk? He's a dreamer. Always waiting for the price of metal to rise, and then he's going to make the motherlode. I've watched the price of metal go up and down in my seventeen years, and that pile has neither moved nor grown, but it's rusted to the point that it's worthless just like Daddy.

Daddy loved to sit in that green plastic chair he stole from the sanctimonious bitch down the Holler, where he'd stare at the fire and toss his spent soldiers into the recycle pile at his back. Irony, the fire ate his chair and his beer can barrier saved him from certain death.

"Cora, ya fat hag! Get me a beer!" Daddy's voice bellows from the smashed out front window. Momma isn't fat but she is a hag, and she's never not gotten that piece of shit his motherfucking beer.

Momma's only job in life is to sit in her rocking chair, guarding Daddy's beer while smoking like a chimney. She won't work. She hardly cooks. She sure as shit doesn't clean, because you can't polish a turd, she likes to say. She says her children are grown, so she's done raising 'em. She shouts at her grandkids while filling the house with the scent of cigarettes while leaving a pile of ash at her feet... and then she passes Daddy a beer from the never-ending supply I bought.

From my seat in my truck, because my muscles refuse to move me to the house yet, I watch my father's hand rear back, whipping my mother's face to the side.

Momma's offense?

Momma didn't get Daddy a beer quick enough from the thirty pack resting right by his side. She had to get up and cross the room so he wouldn't have to exercise his elbow by reaching for his own warm skunk piss.

I don't react after witnessing the act of violence since I was born. I stopped flinching a decade ago, learning how if I tried to step in, Momma got beat worse and I broke a few necessary bones.

I don't even feel bad when Daddy hits Momma anymore, because I wanna hit my momma too. I want to hit her for ever spreading her legs for that worthless asshole. I hate her for creating Warren, Willa, and me. I want to kill her for letting Daddy growl at us kids, strike us, and destroy anything we've ever tried to build. I hate her for pushing Willa out of the house when she was only fifteen because it was time to rear her own children, knowing Willa would either be abused or find herself back home with kids suckling at her teats.

Momma didn't want better for her only daughter. She wanted Willa to experience the same suffering she had. Because in this world I live in, if you want to rise up and find a better life than the one your parents provide, their ignorant pride gets bent. You get pounded in the face because your momma and daddy see it as a grave insult, as if you think what they gave you wasn't good enough– they see it as if you're judging them.

"Ya think yer better than me, don't cha, boy?" A meaty fist explodes against my face, dropping my ass to the floor. *"Guess what? You ain't shit, son. You ain't never gonna be shit 'cuz yer a Gillette. Ya best come ta terms with that ta-day."*

Every time I look at my sister– who Penny reminds me of time and time again with her quick wit and squashed potential – I blame my momma for ruining Willa. Willa is a shell, just like our momma. She won't do shit. She won't lift a finger to raise her children. She won't even cook the food I bring home to warm their bellies. She hasn't been right since her husband was locked up for beating her so badly that she was in the hospital for eight weeks. Momma blames Willa because Donny Kennedy was sent away for seven-to-twelve years for attempted murder, saying she brought it upon herself. My sister should have just laid back, spread her legs, and taken the hits by her husband's friend that night like he ever so politely asked.

Willa was nineteen years old.

Daddy put Momma in the hospital for saying it was Willa's fault, not that that will erase the words once they were spoken. When Daddy finds the gumption to defend his daughter, you know it was fucked up.

I can't do it anymore.

I just can't.

My family is a disease.

I don't understand sitting around bitching about your shitty lot in life, complaining about how horrific your parents are, and then acting worse than they do. That's what Warren and Willa do. They sit around and get high, saying how bad our parents treat them. How we went to bed more often with empty bellies than filled ones. Instead of getting a job and righting the wrongs, they sit there, snorting and shooting up the money that Hayden and Hayley need to survive, and they do it in front of the filthy, hungry kids.

"*Ya hungry, boy?*" Daddy lifts his beer to his vicious lips, and when he pulls away he's smiling– taunting me as he drinks his liquid sandwich while my empty belly growls. "*Ya better git used to it until ya can feed yerself.*"

The victims became the worst victimizers.

I don't drink because it destroyed our lives, same as drugs and smokes. We didn't have food in our bellies or clean clothes on our backs, but my parents had the funds to pollute our air with their smoke and piss beer down the toilet.

It's like an infection weaving its way through my family, already sinking its teeth into Willa and Warren, and it won't be long before Hayley and Hayden and Penny's unborn babe are infected too.

There's something about me that makes me immune.

I might not have ever gotten hard looking at somebody, but that doesn't mean I can't get it up to use it. After watching the rest of our kind spit out kids they won't raise, and watching my sister's soul die because of sex she didn't want to have, my dick is staying in my pants. I will not create children my family will destroy.

I won't hit another soul unless it's for protection after sitting vigil at countless bedsides.

My life is an expansive landscape of misery, where I work my ass off with no payoff. There is no warmth to be found. No soft, safe place to rest my head. There's no pleasure or connection. I'm just a walking organ donor for when my parents and siblings' bodies finally fail. I'm destined to watch them slowly kill themselves on my dime, and I'm powerless to stop it. I can't walk away because blood comes first for a Gillette.

I can't stop the cycle, but I can stop my misery of growing older while allowing them to kill me slowly as I watch them die.

Knowing years from now the scenery will never change, my eyes drink in the panoramic view of Gillette Holler. I stare at my father exercising his elbow by raising the beer can to his lips every minute and a half. To the side of Daddy is Momma, her arm getting the same workout with her smokes. I can almost hear the rasp of the lighter as she inhales to make the cherry grow bright. Somewhere in the filthy depths of our shack, six-year-old Hayley and Hayden sleep, with Warren and Willa roaming around these hills yonder.

I reach behind me to the gun rack crossing the back window of my truck cab. After years of practice, I find my shotgun resting in my palms. Eyes never leaving my daddy and momma, I press the nose of the barrel beneath my chin and pull the trigger.

Click.
Click.
Click.

No matter how many times I pull the trigger, my mind can't wrap itself around the fact that nothing happens. Snarling, I toss the shotgun into the passenger side of the truck, and then I pound the ever-loving fuck out of my steering wheel.

Screaming so loud my ears ring and my voice breaks, pure violence erupts from my throat. "MOTHERFUCKER! GODDAMNED MOTHERFUCKING THIEVES. YOU STOLE MY AMMO! YOU STOLE MY MOTHERFUCKING AMMO!"

Vision shot to shit because I'm sure I blew a few blood vessels, I gasp uncontrollably while my mind spins over how low those worthless cocksuckers I call family are willing to go. So much for blood coming first. I really am just a tool they use.

"You through yet?" Warren draws my attention to where he's resting his forearms against my open window. I blink a few times to clear my vision. What is revealed is my brother's wide mouth twisted up in a bright smile with tear tracks staining his cheeks.

My brother releases an amazed laugh through the pain. "'Bout time. I knew it would be a payday that would finally break ya."

"What?" I roughly rasp out, voice gone from screaming.

"You're a brave asshole, I'll give ya that much. Ya see…" Warren adjusts himself in my window until he's comfortable. "When a man is as calm and good as you are, and he ain't got nobody besides his own hand to drain his sac, and he refuses to release his primal nature with his fists, he's bound to break sooner rather than later. It was only a matter of time."

Eyes held wide in horror, "Our life is a living nightmare," I breathe.

"Sure is," Warren drawls out. "And I ain't like Daddy, neither." Reaching over, a dirty fingertip taps my temple. "I can see those thoughts spinning in your head. See, every night before payday, I take the ammo out of your gun and the spares from the glove box. Then I sit out here while you sit in your truck stewing over how life drew you the short straw. I'd wait for you to do what you finally did tonight. Next morning, I always put your ammo where I found it."

Bewildered yet awed, I try to mutter, "Why?"

"'Cuz I only got one brother." Warren leans forward and kisses my forehead. "And I love him like no other." He tugs my heartstrings, and then pisses me off. "I respect him because he has principles, and he'll take care of us because we're incapable."

"You're *not* incapable," I mutter begrudgingly.

"I didn't mean me. *Us*, as in the Gillettes of Gillette Holler. Kennedy or not, I meant Hayley and Hayden, because they have Gillette blood flowing through their veins. I meant my baby when it's born. I meant Penny and Willa. Not me. Not Momma and Daddy. Those assholes made this goddamned bed, and they can lie in the filth they created. So, see, I ain't letting you go. I ain't letting you end your life. I'm making sure you get the education you deserve."

"I don't want to be here anymore," I seethe, heart beating out of control from the ferocity and truth in my words. My eyes light on my shotgun sitting next to me. It's calling to me to end it all. "When I pulled the trigger, I meant it. How could you take that away from me and force me to suffer?"

Eyes as clear as a summer sky hold me captive. "Ain't no take-backsies when it comes to death. There's a lot of people wishing they weren't dying, and you have no right to go before your time." Warren chucks me on the chin. "You ain't no coward, Wynn, and I ain't gonna let you act like one. If I gotta stick this shit out and see it through, you're gonna too."

"What? You called me brave, but now I'm a coward?" My voice cracks as I stare down at my worthless excuse for a shotgun. It's of no use to me without its ammunition. What am I supposed to do, bash my skull in with the stock? I don't have the nuts to do that, which is why Warren's calling me a coward right now. My finger itches to prove him wrong.

"Brave and coward are just different sides of the same coin of suicide. Don't think I ain't been where you are. Don't think I ain't been through this with Willa every fucking day for the past three years. Every. Single. Goddamned. Day."

"Willa?" Years of suffering and burdens and hard truths cause tears to sting my eyes so fiercely I have to bite my lip to contain them. The pain causes me to forget all about my own bullshit. I forget about my aborted attempt at blowing my chin out through the top of my skull. I finally remember I'm Wynn Gillette, and my blood comes first.

"While Momma and Daddy are lost to their addictions, and you're at school taking care of business and my Penny, I'm here medicating our sister. I'd rather have a zombie, knowing we can get help cleaning her up after you've made some good change at whatever high-class job you get coming out of college. It's just my way of making sure Willa is still alive when the twins graduate, get married, and make her a mamaw. In the meantime, I know a standup guy like you will take care of the little ones as if they were his own."

"War–"

"Listen," Warren cuts me off by cramming his dirty palm over my lips. "They ain't got no daddy. If that asshole shows his face in Rusty Knob, even the middle class douches will shoot him on sight. I ain't in a position to raise my own kids, let alone someone else's, while I try to keep my siblings alive and my parents off their asses."

I wrench my head to the side, forcing Warren's hand to slip free from my mouth. I scrunch my face in distaste when the sickly sharp scent of drugs wafts up my nostrils. "What am I supposed to do?"

Leaning in my window, "Get the fuck out of here, that's what," Warren snarls. "Get. Out. Of. Gillette. Holler. Forget where you came from and be who you are. Don't leave Rusty Knob, but never come up this dirt road until you know you'll never take a sawed-off to the chin again. I mean it."

"I don't think I can do that," denial is thick in my voice.

"You will. You're gonna call up that weekend boss of yours. Royce is gonna give you a place to lay your head 'cuz he's Hayley and Hayden's uncle too. You and the twins deserve a nicer place than this shithole. A real home befitting a man of your goodness and intelligence. And every cent you earn will go in your pocket for your future."

Words flow numbly from my tongue on autopilot. "Everyone needs me."

"Shut the fuck up, Wynn." A rough slap connects with my cheek, and I don't even blink from the contact. This is how it is with Warren and me. We love each other, and we have funny ways of showing it. If my brother is worried, he hits me out of reflex. If he's angry, he gives me the cold shoulder after a thorough beating. But through it all, I know he loves me no matter what.

"It's true!" My voice pitches up high in a whine. "They do need me. They can't survive on their own."

"Arrogant asshole! Don't judge me in your head, and then cut off my balls when I try to be the head of the family. You're the baby, goddamnit!" Warren's palm smashes down on the hood of my truck, startling me. "Act like it for once. You need to get out of here. You need more."

I mumble rapidly, "I don't think I can do it."

"You're one brave motherfucking badass killer," flows from my brother's tongue without a hint of sarcasm. "You just pulled the trigger on yourself. Not once but three times. You can do anything. I need this from you. I need to get my own shit together, while keeping Willa in one piece, and I need you to take care of Penny and the twins for me while I do it. We good?"

I mutter a lame promise. "I'm not sure how, but I'll try."

"Good." Warren pats the hood of my truck again– this time he does it with a grin on his face. "Get a goddamned blowjob while you're at it. I don't care if it's from some townie skank or a dude's piehole, but I want you to get off with another human being. You ain't a machine, Wynn. Men only need a few things in life, and when they don't get 'em, they either turn up dead or an addict. Food. Sleep. Sex. Work. Play. Love. Family."

"It's time to break the cycle," I breathe out on autopilot.

Warren reaches into my window, curving his arm down to pull the handle to open my door. With a big grin, he tugs me out of the truck. "Time to break the cycle. The next generation of Gillettes will not be drunks. They will be a smarty pants like their Uncle Wynn."

"I'm not that smart. I'm so fucked in the head that I'm not the best example." Sputtering, my tone is laced with awe and horror, "I just tried to kill myself for shit's sake."

My brother ignores me while he pulls me across our yard of weeds and debris. I nearly upend a few times before we get to the front door. A push mower almost puts me on my ass, but it's a tar bucket that twists my ankle.

"Watch where you're going, bro!" Warren drags me to my feet when my sneaker gets caught on an old chainsaw chain. "Heads up, Momma was yelling about Hayden having a faggot haircut all afternoon, then she broke out the shears."

"What?" I gasp, subconsciously fingering my hair. "Faggot?"

"I know." Warren tries to placate me, thinking it's me who's offended, when I'm thinking about Jack and Francis. "I know. Momma and Daddy don't know no better, but that's no excuse."

"Hayden and I have the same haircut– so do you." I shudder, thinking of being held down as a kid as my momma sat on my chest and hacked off my curls. "It's a bit long, but we can't help the curls. They gave 'em to us!"

Warren smirks, but it's a mix of anger and sadness with no happiness to be found. "Remember how Momma's so fucking ignorant that no matter how many times we try to tell her the twins aren't identical 'cuz they are a boy and a girl, she don't get it? Well, Momma mistook Hayley for Hayden today, and butchered all of her pretty curls."

I hiss, "Jesus Christ," with a wince.

Warren rounds on me quick as shit, yanking my t-shirt in his fist. He pulls me down until we're eye to eye. "Get them the fuck out of here, ya hear me? Tonight! And don't come back!"

My brother's eyes are bloodshot from tears, not drugs. But it's the terror flashing over his face that breaks me. "What about you? Come with us…" I'm not too proud to beg.

"I got shit to do, brother," Warren says lightly, taking a step back from me. His fist unclenches, and then he smooths my shirt until he pats the wrinkles out. "Instead of enabling Momma and Daddy while trying to provide for the kids, you take all that money and carve out a comfy life for yourself. I'll be following you shortly. I've got to get me a job, now that I hear I'm gonna be a daddy, and I've got to find a safe place for Willa."

I reach forward, gripping the doorknob, not wanting to enter Hell. "What about Penny?"

"You're Penny's brother, and you're gonna keep her in line, make sure she educates herself proper and gets a job. You hear me? I'll be with her around the time the babe is born." Warren twists the knob, and then shoves me into the house. "Daddy and Momma can rot in hell," flows to my ears as Warren runs across the lawn like a coward, managing to miss all the trash that kept tripping me up.

A scowl pulls my lips as I watch my brother sink into his dilapidated car with a passed out Willa in the passenger seat. The backseat is stuffed to the roof with garbage bags– no doubt everything of any value they have to their name. Peeling out, rocks spit in all directions from beneath the tires.

I stand, feeling more than lost, as my brother and sister flee into the night. When the cloud of dust settles, I step inside our shack for what I hope is the last time.

DIDJA EAT YET?

Daddy's pale blue, bloodshot eyes are the first thing I see, not the dilapidated surroundings. The main room only has a recliner and a rocking chair to one side, with a small table surrounded by mismatched chairs. The plywood kitchen has empty cupboards, a forty-year-old fridge, and a wood stove used to cook and heat the shack. We have a single bathroom that has Daddy saying we are spoiled rotten assholes because he had to use an outhouse his entire life. There are three bedrooms haphazardly attached to the main room: Momma and Daddy's, mine and the twins', and Willa's. Warren sleeps in the main room on a cot shoved up against the front wall.

Compared to how Daddy was raised, he thinks we are ungrateful shits because this is a palace. *"Gillettes don't need no better,"* he says on a daily basis. *"Who the fuck do you think you are, The President of The United States?"*

The smell is the first thing that assaults me besides Daddy's crazy glare. It's a combination of cigarette and wood smoke that dries out your nose until it bleeds, the dank, sweet scent of stale beer, the rot of garbage juice, and the tang of piss because Daddy can't hold his bladder no more.

I've learned to never look away from Daddy's gaze or turn my back until we've established contact. His tall body may be emaciated, but when he blows a gasket, he could take down a charging bear.

Daddy's not drunk enough to make sense yet.

"Where's yer worfless brover off ta dis time a night?" He glares at me as if I'm the sole reason our lives are a living nightmare. Only wearing a pair of shit-stained, grungy white undershorts, Daddy's ass is fused to his recliner, which is the source of the nose-wrinkling ammonia stench.

"War had shit ta do." My words easily slip into Daddy's diction. If I try to speak a coherent sentence, I get the piss pounded out of me for insulting him.

Daddy lost interest in me the second I didn't have anything interesting to say. The man ought to have a bulging forearm from all the twelve ounce curls he does. Elbow bending, a can is pressed to his lips again.

Everything about beer leaves me feeling bitter hatred. Like a hillbilly version of Pavlov's Dog, the popping sound of a can opening fills me with dread, waiting for a biting tongue or a flashing fist. The fuzzy zing to the nose of a fresh beer makes my stomach roil, especially combined with the satisfied moan Daddy gives when it hits the back of his tongue. The sickly sweet scent of beer cans lying around in the sun smells like broken promises and abandoned dreams.

If you were hit in the face with a hammer every single day, would you be able to look at a hammer without feeling pain? Would you flinch? Or would you remove every hammer from your environment to protect yourself? Only problem, the hammer isn't hitting you in the face; it's the fist wielding it. Even without a hammer, the asshole would find a way to torture you.

I've never understood, how after everything, Warren is able to touch the vile poison without reliving every horrific detail of our lives that has been at the hands of an alcoholic. I wish I could blame my daddy's mistress for all of our troubles, but it's not the beer's fault Daddy is a worthless waste of space.

Even if we removed the beer, we'd still be stuck with Daddy.

Self-preservation. Acting on instinct, I sweep in fast, grabbing a can of warm skunk piss from the thirty pack resting at Daddy's feet. He bares his yellowed teeth in a snarl, like I'm the one stealing the beer I bought in the first place. I remove the bent can from his fist, and place a fresh soldier in his grip. "Thank ya kindly, son," Daddy says with a nod.

Peace offering accepted, I'm able to turn my back now that I'm no longer in danger. "Didja eat yet, Momma?" I don't bother asking the alcoholic in the room. He sees no need for food since it dilutes the effects of his beer. But the truth of it is, is that even a small morsel passing Daddy's lips tears his guts up something fierce. He's on a liquid diet that is slowly murdering him. His body is cannibalizing itself, organs eating themselves from the inside out, leaving an empty husk of bitterness for us to handle.

"I had a dab of deer meat and brown gravy on toast," Momma replies, tapping the edge of her smokes on the side of the rickety end table to drop her next cig out the hole in the soft pack. She brings the pack to her mouth, grips a filter with her lips, and then pulls the pack away while keeping her prize in her mouth. The red lighter that is a permanent fixture in her right hand rises.

My eyes flick away as Momma lights up, unable to watch but I can't turn off my hearing. The rasp of a lighter does bad things to me, same as popping the tab on a beer can. I clench all my muscles to keep the visceral reaction from quaking my entire body.

Momma's barely forty but looks nearing seventy compared to Rusty Knob's townsfolk. Withered skin wrinkled around her eyes, a mouth puckered from taking drag after drag off her smokes, and a yellow tint to her skin and hair from the toxins in her bloodstream. Judging by Willa, Momma must have been a beautiful woman before she allowed Daddy to ruin her– before she ruined herself. We all got Daddy's clear blue eyes and Momma's sandy curls. It turns my stomach to see such a waste of life– to look at my parents.

"Hayley and Hayden?" I glance in the sink to make sure I see three dirty plates that ordinarily I'd be scrubbing before I settled in for the night. I breathe a sigh of relief that Momma fed her grandchildren at some point today.

Punching his boney thigh, "War better git his own damn house!" Daddy starts in on his nightly drunken rant. "I ain't gonna feed none of his goddamned brats. Someone should have drowned Willa's. Hayden's gonna be a murderer, just like his daddy… and Hayley's gonna be a bad wife, just like her momma. I ain't got no more money to take care of you multiplying ingrates."

"Yeah, I hear ya," I mutter, hiding the disgust in my voice. I channel the patience of a saint.

I hope you fucking drown in your beer, you goddamned bastard!

Feed us? The deer meat in Momma's belly was one I poached last week when the kids were starve-gutted. I could have gone to jail if I was caught. Once the carcass was dragged onto our land, I was safe. No one, especially the authorities, will cross a boundary line. Daddy and Warren will shoot trespassers on sight, even if they have a warrant.

"Payday, ain't it?" Daddy grunts out, turning his palm over, asking for what little cash I might have left. Wiggling his fingers like a hungry fish, he catches the involuntary flash of loathing that crosses my face. "I'ma start chargin' yer ingrate ass rent, boy. Yer livin' up 'ere in the lap a luxury, got food in yer belly 'n a roof over yer head, 'n ya give me that goddamned look?"

I slowly walk backward toward the twins, keeping Daddy in my line of sight. Next to me, Momma's disinterested. "I made five hours this week. Just enough to put gas in the tank to make my way to the Holler. I have nothing more to give ya."

Daddy's getting agitated, but not nearly as agitated as I am. "Maybe ya better git yer ass back to work, son. Ya need ta pay yer own way if ya plan on stayin' in dis house. While yer at it, tell Mr. I 'ave more money than God, Royce Kennedy, he's late on his child support."

"*Child support?*" My voice twists with anger. "Royce isn't their daddy." I close my eyes, mind spinning out of control. "*Pay my way?*" I pay all of the bills. I'm the person who fills the fridge with food for the twins since Daddy uses the food stamps and sells the food for cash. Daddy drinks his disability and Willa shoots up her welfare. Momma's smoking whatever money Warren gives her.

Vein in my head throbbing, fists clenched at my side, I almost killed myself earlier tonight just so I wouldn't have to walk away and leave them behind. "I'm done," I announce, my words slipping back into proper English. "You're right. I shouldn't be living here anymore. It's time I'm on my own way."

Leaning forward, Daddy places his beer on the floor by his side, which means he means business. "Using those fancy words like the world God give ya ain't good 'nuff. You think yer shit don't stink like the rest a us?"

I'm frozen in fear, worried I'll have to defend myself for the first time in my life, knowing I would put my daddy in the hospital. "I'm a grown man now," is my only reply.

"That ain't it," Daddy snarls, face transforming into that of a monster. His paper-thin skin stretches over bladelike cheekbones as his lips form cutting words. "If it weren't fer yer blue eyes, I'd think yer momma was running on me with a townie 'round the time you were made. Nothin' I ever did was good 'nuff fer ya. Always turning up yer nose at the food I put on the table. Always out in the yard trying to mow the lawn, trying to fix shit and clean the house. Couldn't leave good 'nuff alone, as the way God intended. If I wanted a winder fixed, I'd have fixed it."

My rope snaps. "I'm not going to apologize for mending a window when it was snowing inside the house, when I knew you'd never get around to fixing it. You have no idea how ridiculous you sound, do you? You have no idea how goddamned ignorant you are.

My wanting a different life doesn't have a cocksucking thing to do with you."

"Don't disrespect yer daddy like that," Momma speaks up because Daddy is speechless. Her words soothe him some, but they weren't said out of respect. It was my mother's defense mechanism. If Daddy unhinges, everyone in this house will become his target.

I don't know if my conscience will survive leaving my momma behind, but I know I won't live long if I don't leave. Warren's right. Momma did this to herself. But I can't blame her as she didn't know any different. But then again, neither does Daddy. Why is it I know better, then? Explain that.

"You don't need to worry about feeding anyone but yourselves. You'll have nobody bleeding you dry, and every cent you earn can be spent on you and Momma." *They earn no money* is what will plague me for the rest of my days. But maybe they will use the money the government gives them in the way it was intended.

Hell freezes over. Santa Claus fits down nonexistent chimneys and passes out gifts to the Gillettes for the first time in our lives. The Easter Bunny shits out chocolate eggs and leaves them in a basket like a happy yet demented version of a litter box. Daddy stops drinking and Momma stops smoking, and I finally get some feeling in my dick.

Yeah, ain't none of that happening. "Good luck," I mutter as I back up toward my bedroom door.

"Is it Christmas?" Daddy turns sarcastic, thinking I'm joking.

"I'm serious." I turn my back on my parents, knowing none of Daddy's triggers have been tripped. "Warren and Willa left for parts unknown. I'm going to go in my room and remove Hayden and Hayley from this house, and you're not going to stop me. Got it?"

"Don't ever come back, ya ungrateful ingrates!" Daddy shouts at my back as I enter my bedroom. It takes everything in me not to shout back that ungrateful and ingrate means the same thing.

I shut the door behind me, securing the tattered blanket over the opening to keep the stink and sound from infecting our private space. Nothing short of a shotgun could stop Daddy's bellows right now.

For seventeen years, there has been an imaginary boundary line between my safe haven and the rest of Gillette Holler. Once I passed the threshold, nothing could harm me. It was a bullshit lie I made up in my mind, but it was how I survived the night to meet the next morning.

It makes me sick to see that the twins have adopted my survival strategy. They are precious, and shouldn't have to use this room and me as their lifeline against an abusive, Crypt Keeper-looking drunk and his abused and even more abusive hag of a wife and their zombiefied mother.

Gillette Holler is for the dead– those dead inside and out.

Once, a long, long time ago… Warren, Willa, and I were innocent children. We were pink-skinned, bright-eyed, and curious yet unafraid. That was snuffed out by our parents and the situations they created. I already see how the first six years of Hayden and Hayley's lives are infecting them, and it stops tonight.

Willa, not quite herself since she was torn from us when she was a child-bride, had the good sense to pass her kids off to me when she returned to Gillette Holler. I'm big and strong enough to protect them, but smart enough to use my words instead of violence to do the job. I was thirteen when the twins became my responsibility, vowing they would have the childhood I never received.

I've worked hard to fix our hundred square feet of privacy. My olive drab cot is from the Army and Navy store. It's draped with the patchwork blanket Penny and I made in Home Economics back in eighth grade. The bare-bulb ceramic lamp, which I found tossed in a townie's yard with a **FREE** sign on it, is resting on the small table I nabbed from the side yard. I sanded the table down and put a whitewash on it, same as with the dresser I bartered from one of Warren's buddies. The dresser is filled with tiny clothes I bought for the twins at secondhand shops, with the bottom drawer filled with little kid books, while the top holds my school books and basketball trophies. The walls are covered in the colored pages of activity books and cute drawings from the time since the twins could hold a crayon. There's a scattering of stuffed animals and toys I got at the Salvation Army to take the sting of violent words and the stench of broken dreams from wafting in from the rest of the shack.

Our room isn't anything to look at, but I'm proud of it. It's clean because I've taught the kids to pick up after themselves– something they pretend not to know, instinctively knowing Daddy would see them as budding ingrates who think their shit don't stink because they don't want to wallow in their own filth like swine.

Our floor is covered with the recycled carpet Bren's dad gave me when he replaced the carpeting in his rental house. Royce Kennedy is going to be our savior once again.

From the Holler, Royce's daddy and wife passed away in a tragic car fire when something electrical went on the fritz. Ford issued a recall to save countless lives, leaving a little boy without a momma– Bren. Royce took the insurance money and the insanely huge settlement and put it back into Rusty Knob. He created jobs to employ laborers who want to work. Every time a family leaves the area, Royce buys their home, and then houses those who will respect his property and give back to the community.

The townies love Royce Kennedy, and the rest of Rusty Knob loathes him, calling him a traitor for bettering himself. My boss is always saying he sees something in me, something he sees in himself. He's tried to get me to quit the Circle K, even knowing why I worked there, wanting me to come work for him fulltime while still going to school and playing basketball. Every Sunday he begs me not to take the kids away from him, saying he'd give us all a better life if only I'd let him.

I always tell Royce blood is thicker than water, and he always counters with how the twins are the only blood Bren and he has left.

I hadn't realized I had that backward. If you care for someone, then you should want them to better themselves. Staying stagnate, or worse, lowering yourself to another's level, is not loyalty. Loyalty is rising above it all, and taking those who can't help themselves with you.

"Uncle Wynn?" Hayden's sleep-slurred voice fills the room. His tiny paws rub at his closed eyelids. "Is Papaw going to hit you again?"

"Nah, little feller." I kneel down beside the rickety toddler bed that Hayden and Hayley are squeezed into. I bought the bed at a yard sale a few years back, but they've both since grown out of it. I work all week to pay for Daddy's beer, and all weekend to pay for whatever bills I can swing. When the kids get out of this bed, it will be the last time they touch it.

My fingers flutter through my nephew's wild curls, and he smiles through his sleepiness. I reach over to nuzzle at my niece's hair, finding uneven, chopped off curls. But when moving the strands reveals something much viler, I nearly careen into the living room and beat my parents to death.

Whatever happened while I was at work tonight is why Warren and Willa got out of Dodge and Daddy was so passive when I insulted him to his face.

I bite back the need to clench my fists. My voice is light, but the words squeeze between gritted teeth. "What happened to Sissy's cheek?" I run a light fingertip along the blooming bruise, not wanting to wake the little girl just yet.

"Papaw and Mamaw were fighting over how Sissy didn't have faggot hair because she's a girl. I don't know what faggot hair is, but Sissy's hair ain't no different than the girls in our class."

"There is no such thing as faggot hair, Hayden. I never want you to use that word again, unless you're repeating something someone said. If another kid uses it, tell them it's not nice."

"I promise," he vows with determination.

"Good. What happened next?"

"Mamaw thought Sissy was me, and she don't take no backtalk. I kept screaming for Mamaw to look at me– to see me –so was Papaw. Momma and Uncle Warren walked in during the tussle, and Sissy fell on the floor into a pile of her hair."

I can't look away from Hayley's bruised cheek and shorn off hair. "What did your momma do?"

"She got real furious, and started hitting Mamaw in the back. She got backhanded real good by Papaw. Uncle Warren dragged her out of the house after he told us to go to bed. Sissy and I stood by the door a-listening, and we overheard him telling Mamaw and Papaw that they better agree to anything you said, or else he's gonna burn Gillette Holler to the ground."

"Well, that explains so much," I mutter to myself. "I need to make a phone call, and while I do, I need you to sit here real quiet-like. Okay?"

"Kay," Hayden whispers, laying his head down next to his sister's, and then he pretends to go to sleep.

I move my cot to the side, drop to my knees, peel the carpet back, and then pry a wedged floorboard up. Beneath that is my secret cubbyhole. I pocket all the cash I have hiding, and then I palm my cellphone. I flip the lid open with my thumb, and then I turn it on. Royce had bought me a burner phone, making me promise to show the kids how to find it and use it.

I've never had a reason to use it until tonight.

I press the green button after I scroll through the contacts, only finding a single phone number listed. I stare at my six-year-old niece and nephew as they pretend to sleep as the call goes through.

"Wynn?" Royce's voice comes muffled, followed by a cuss. "It's two in the morning. Did something happen?"

"Shit! Sorry," I rasp out, feeling like a heel because I woke him. "I know you don't get much sleep as it is. I didn't think before I called."

"Forget it." The sound of rustling fabric reverberates through the phone. "Whatcha need, Wynn?"

"That job offer still on the table, the one with a place to rest my head?"

"Always. I take it something major happened to change your mind, eh?"

"You could say it's been an interesting night– almost my last one."

"Who? Tell me who tried to hurt you!" Voice stiff with fury, "Wynn, I mean it. Tell me!"

I spit out the truth before I can stop myself. "Me. I couldn't take it anymore. Warren stealing my ammo changed my outlook on life. Seeing Hayley's hair shorn off by my momma was a wakeup call. But the bruise on Hayley's tiny cheek from an elbow jab is what made me say the hell with them. I know you'll want us at your house, but I'm not comfortable with that."

"Christ," Royce hisses. "I have a few places open right now, but I have a few conditions."

"I know. I have to quit the Circle K, keep up my grade-point-average so I don't lose my scholarship, continue to go to off-season practice so I'm fit for the university team, work for you the rest of the time, graduate, and I'm not to support any able-bodied males over the age of eighteen."

Royce's stance is that even though I act like a man and he treats me like one, I'm still a kid. I can help anyone younger than me, but I'm never to help a man who can help himself. My boss is in his late thirties, and he refuses to help any of the men in town older than him unless they are open to change. Royce says you shouldn't try to teach an ignorant, old dog new tricks when you could take the effort to make a real difference to someone who not only needs it but wants it.

"Damn straight, Skippy," Royce says with a chuckle. "I love how you pay attention. Wish my kid wasn't deaf."

"You're Bren's daddy; he ain't gonna listen to you. No way. No how. I'll admit, he's a pain in the ass, but he's just confused."

A rough throat clearing vibrates my ears, letting me know Royce knows what I'm hinting at even though not a soul has ever whispered the truth. "I need to decide where to put you. How many are leaving Gillette Holler?

"Three are leaving Gillette, but we're picking one up in Franklin Holler on our way to town. It's just me and the twins, and Penny 'cuz her momma is pressuring her to move out. She's carrying Warren's kid now– her momma's ploy to get her hitched and out of her hair."

"Goddamned, ignorant assholes!" Royce sputters a few more choice cuss words before calming down. "What the hell happened to Warren? Why isn't he taking care of his own mess? And you are *not* leaving Willa behind with those deadbeats you call parents." Royce's voice quivers with rage. "I mean it, Wynn. The only reason I haven't stepped in before now is because I knew you were keeping an eye on Willa and her kids."

Royce feels responsible for my sister because it was his brother who married and brutalized Willa, and Royce was the one to stop it. The man he tore off my sister, the man who was inside her, never made it to trial. He was found dead a few days later from an apparent hunting accident. If Willa's ex-husband ever gets out of the pen, he'll have an accident too.

After everything settled down, Royce offered me a job, paying me outrageously as long as I paid the bills and put food in his kin's belly. In a way, he was using me while helping me. He wanted to make sure his money got to its intended target without being wasted on my parents.

"Warren is on a Willa mission. They peeled out of Gillette Holler about an hour ago for destinations unknown. I'm sure we'll be hearing from them sooner rather than later. Warren said he was doing what he was doing to keep Willa alive."

Royce is quiet for so long that I have to ask, "You still there, boss?"

"Yeah…" His breath shudders out. "When Willa was in the hospital, I asked her to move in with me. Bren was only thirteen and he needed a momma, and the twins were toddlers who needed a daddy. I told Willa I'd take care of her– protect her –and I wasn't looking for anything else in return. Even then she was just a child, not much older than my own son is now. I just wanted to keep her and my niece and nephew safe." Another deep shuddering breath. "I failed."

"You didn't fail, Royce. You didn't." I slump to my cot, suddenly exhausted. "Warren told me I was cutting his balls off because I wasn't letting him do his job as the head of our family. Willa is her big brother's responsibility now."

Sounding incredulous, "And you have faith in Warren?"

"Shit, yeah!" I pause, not sure if I should tell Royce the truth. But then I realize if anyone deserves the truth, it's him. "I pulled the trigger tonight. I pulled it, and I was confused to why it didn't go off– confused as to why I didn't die. So I pulled it again and again. Warren's been protecting me from myself all this time, and I didn't even know it. Have no fear, Royce. Willa is safe."

"Wynn… if you pull that shit again, I'll shoot you myself," Royce threatens, causing me to bark a sharp laugh.

I'm smiling even though I shouldn't be under the circumstances. "I'm suddenly cured– Warren Gillette, the ammo thief, inoculated me against insane, suicidal attempts. Pulling the trigger must be what sex feels like."

Royce's snicker warms my skin. "I don't know what kind of sex you're having, kid. That's hella explosive, blowing your brains out… Get out of the holler. Anyone who can use inoculated in a sentence doesn't belong there. Pack your shit, pack the kids' shit, and then go get Penny. I'll meet you out front of my place in a few hours– say seven? I should be able to drag Bren's ass outta bed by then."

"Will do, boss." Out of nowhere, I start to get choked up. "Thanks. I… I wouldn't be here without Warren, but I also wouldn't be getting out of here without you. Thank you."

"No one deserves the life you've been living. But if anyone deserves better, it's you. Get to trucking, Wynn. We got a lot of ground to cover this weekend, because y'all will be in class come Monday morning."

"Yes, sir," I say into an already disconnected phone.

"Are we moving to Uncle Royce's?" Hayden asks, no longer pretending to sleep.

"Not with him, no. But he's gonna find us a real place to live." I stand up, having no clue where to begin. "You close your eyes and pretend to sleep, okay? Keep your sissy nice and warm– comfort her."

I stare down at the kids lying in a bed that's way too small, and my heart swells. No one will raise a violent hand to them ever again if I can help it. They won't have to live under the constant strain of addiction, never knowing if they will get a smile, a scream, or a punch to the gut when they walk in the front door. This life won't warp them until they think what is wrong is right.

Even if I fail, I'll only fail at the small things. Knowing my parents failed at the big things and I'm still a good human being, means even if I mess up time and again, the kids are going to be just fine.

I shove my cellphone into my front pocket, pushing the wad of cash deeper, closer to my body and farther away from my daddy's clutches.

I was honestly going to kill myself tonight, ready to call it quits. Heart pounding, chest rising as I breathe rapidly, I use the high to conquer my cowardice.

When you live in a hovel, there is no need to use the front door. "Don't be scared. I'm only making us an escape hatch like in Marvel comics. Cover your heads with your blankie."

Covering my face with my forearm, I draw in a deep breath, and kick out with my exhale. The noise of splintering, dry-rotted wood is deafening, noxious dust billows around us, but the kids don't even blink.

"I'm glad you trust me so much," I mutter to myself more so than to them. Laughing, I gape at how fragile this shack truly is. One well-placed kick tore out an entire section of exterior wall, proving my suspicions that there were no studs from one room to the next. The only thing holding this rat-trap together is headers and footers. I can easily back the pickup truck up to this hole and shove our shit in the back.

"I'm getting the truck. I'll be right back. If Papaw or Mamaw comes in here," I glance at the heavy lock I latched on our door, "remind them how Uncle Warren said he'd burn Gillette Holler to the ground, and tell them Uncle Wynn says there isn't a fool in all of Rusty Knob who would take them in."

DON'T MIND YOUR ELDERS

The sun is just breaching the horizon as I drive down the rough, rutted path from Gillette Holler toward the town of Rusty Knob. After several hours of packing our things into the back of my pickup truck, where I had the kids scavenging the lawn for furnishings I could refurbish– if it's in the yard dumpster, it's fair game– we're finally greeting a new dawn.

I pull up front of a real house– one of those houses with siding, functioning windows, and roof that doesn't leak. There isn't junk piled up in the yard, except for the part cars lining the back field. The grass is cut with regularity, and there is a swing set and a sandbox among the blooming flowers. Even their driveway is graveled, and the dirt road has been oiled to keep the dust down.

Franklin Holler.

I don't know what Penny's momma was thinking, trying to hitch her daughter to a Gillette. Daddy is scum compared to this normalcy. Penny's daddy is the town mechanic. He's got a shop in the center of Rusty Knob, but he keeps his part cars up here yonder in the holler because of town ordinances.

The infection runs deep is all I can figure. Penny's momma was married young, so she thinks that's the way of life. The Franklins have lots of mouths to feed, but they have a proper momma and daddy raising them.

I don't get it. I'm sure Penny would call it love when I'd call it stupidity. I wouldn't go hitching my star to Warren, least not until he grows up some. Penny didn't need a man until she got knocked up. Before then, she could have got herself an education and a profession. She would have carved out a real life for herself.

I don't have anything against becoming a momma. I just don't believe in becoming a momma when you still need your own. Today's a new dawn for all of us. Kids be damned, Penny is gonna live up to her potential.

"I'll be back in a few minutes." I lean over to ruffle both their mops. They flash me an identical set of grins, which is why they always confused Momma. Pale, chubby cheeks pinked, they're excited after running around the yard looking for treasures. Now they're raring to go on their next adventure with Uncle Wynn.

I pull the keys out of the ignition just to be safe. Hayden and Hayley are Gillettes, after all. "Read up on my homework," I tease them, reaching over to flop The History of The United States Government textbook into their laps– they can look at the pictures of monuments they might get to see now that they left Gillette Holler.

I get three steps up the front walk when the door swings open in welcome. Mrs. Franklin is waiting on me. No doubt she knows why I'm here, seeing as I have a tarp-draped pickup truck filled with furniture.

Mrs. Franklin is a mamaw-looking woman: rotund, somewhere in her forties, with gray hair pulled up on top of her head. She leaves the holler to go farther than Rusty Knob. She's one hundred times smarter than my own momma but still ignorant when it comes to the way of the world. She also bakes the world's best apple pie. So no matter whatever nastiness she's about to spew, I can't be angry with her.

"Warren said he wasn't gonna marry my Penny," reaches my ears before I get to the front door. "Your worthless brother is gonna abandon his children. You here to marry my Penny in his stead?"

Instead of feeling warm and cozy over the prospect of having a family, my guts wrench so tightly I almost puke on the spot. My nuts tug up so close to my body, they try to turn themselves into lady parts.

When I cuddle Hayden and Hayley, I get the tingles. That warm, pleasant sensation I can only assume is love. I feel it sometimes when Warren and I get to talking about important things, and he'll chuck me on the shoulder and laugh. I feel it around Penny sometimes when she's being a dipshit, and I always kiss her forehead while I'm basking in the glow. I get that same warmness when I lean into Jack for support, and when I chat with Royce. I crave that sensation after feeling cold down to my marrow since the day I was born.

But the thought of marrying Penny and bringing my own kids into this world, leaves me with frostbite.

"No, Mrs. Franklin. I'm not here to ask for Penny's hand in marriage." I feel like cow shit when the hopeful expression on her face warps into anger. "Now, listen. I'm not saying I'm not going to take care of your Penny, ma'am. I'm here to do just that. But, see here, I think of Penny as my sister, and I can't do my brother such harm as to steal his girl. I'm here to take care of Penny until Warren can… and he will," I promise, knowing I'll make him.

"You're gonna force my baby to live in sin? I don't think so. Penny ain't no whore, especially not to a Gillette."

"Ain't nobody ever gonna touch Penny that way besides Warren. If they tried, I'd be violent for the first time in my life, believe me. We're gonna live right in Rusty Knob, somewhere nice. We're both going to graduate. The baby ain't gonna stop Penny from getting an education. She's gonna work somewhere, and she's gonna help me take care of the twins." I point at the pair of faces smushed up against the driver side window– nosy brats. "When Warren's done doing what he needs to be doing, he's gonna come back here and do this right proper with Penny, and she's gonna be a grown woman when he returns."

"Why couldn't Penny have fallen for you, Wynn?" Mrs. Franklin asks the same question I've asked myself many a time.

"Love don't work that way," is the only answer I can give. The truth is terrifying. I know the misery and love of family, and that's what I feel for Penny. But I've never felt the emotions that are necessary between a husband and wife.

Mrs. Franklin steps to the side, revealing a tiny, young girl with huge, brown eyes and tear-splattered cheeks. Penny's hand is subconsciously cupping her belly, right over Warren's baby. I can see the war raging inside my friend. She wants to go. But she's so terrified of the unknowns, she'd rather stay where she knows what to expect.

"Will you do this with me?" I ask, knowing she'll get that we're both feeling the same way.

Gillette Holler is calling to me like a lost coonhound puppy– howling and howling a somber song of loss. Its pull is mighty strong, but the wounds are throbbing and so raw that I know better than to give into the call.

Penny shakes her head, causing her coppery ponytail to bob up and down, making her look twelve instead of like a momma.

Penny's name isn't Penelope. She was named after the cent piece because of the color of her hair. Fingertips brush tears off her freckled cheeks as she starts toward me.

"What do you need from the house?" I hitch my thumb over my shoulder, showing there is room for Penny's stuff in the bed of my truck.

"Git in the truck with the children," Mrs. Franklin orders Penny. "Everything in this house belongs to your father and me. I'll decide what you're taking from here, and Wynn can carry it."

Harsh.

Leaning forward, I grip Penny's arm when she loses her step. Fresh tears splatter her cheeks but she doesn't look back. I curl her into my side, escorting her to the passenger side of my truck. Now the warm sensation returns, like I'm doing good and feeling good because of it.

The kids press themselves to the windshield, following us as we move around the front of the truck. When I pop the door open, they almost fall out. "Nosy brats," I grumble with affection, causing Penny to crack a smile. "Shove over. Make some room for Aunt Penny. She's gonna read you the second Mrs. de Winter's passage about Manderley. It's about time Penny caught up in English class."

"Seriously?" Penny begins bitching immediately.

"Seriously," I order with a not-so gentle shove into the truck. "Hayden loves it when I read my assignments to him. He falls into the story. Hayley just likes dozing to the sound of my voice. They both loved the description of Manderley, wanting to visit."

"I don't know if I wanna live with you," Penny grumbles, hating how I'm gonna force her to reach her potential instead of sit around and rot. Her lips curve up into a grin when she sees my scowl— forever baiting me.

"Last night, I dreamt I went to Manderley again," I prompt as I hand Penny my worn-out copy of Rebecca.

Penny teases me. "You're such a girl." She chuckles softly with the kids while she shifts them around until one is beneath each of her arms.

"Not that horseshit again," I warn, sick to death of Penny calling me transgender simply because I don't have my cock in one hand and a beer can in the other.

Reciting from memory in a pleasing lilt, Penny surprises me. "The road to Manderley lay ahead. There was no moon. The sky above our heads was inky black. But the sky on the horizon was not dark at all. It was shot with crimson, like a splash of blood. And the ashes blew toward us with the salt wind from the sea."

"YAY!" The kids whoop and holler, clapping and acting silly, the deep words having no impact on their tiny minds.

Feeling warm and cozy, I press Penny's forehead to my chest, and then I lean down to kiss the top of her head. "You've been doing your homework, after all," I tease as I pull away.

I tell Penny I'm going to go deal with her momma by quoting, "It wouldn't make for sanity, would it, living with the devil?"

Penny's next words follow me up the walk, giving me new insight into why our English teacher tries so hard to get us to read the required curriculum. "I believe there is a theory that men and women emerge finer and stronger after suffering, and that to advance in this, or any world, we must endure ordeal by fire."

Just how Royce said a boy who knows how to use inoculated in a sentence shouldn't live in a Holler, a girl who can recite Daphne du Maurier shouldn't live in one, either.

"Listen up, Mrs. Franklin," I speak with direct frankness to the woman staring at me like I've grown a third head. "Penny's stuff belongs to her, whether it's in your home or mine. Point me in the proper direction to retrieve it."

"This is the way it's done," Penny's momma says sheepishly as she turns to walk inside the house.

I skirt around the woman, cutting her off. What I say next isn't for Penny, but for her younger sisters and all of her nieces to come. "Don't think it didn't scar me for life, seeing my sister sob and shriek as my daddy passed her off to a man twenty years her senior, knowing what was gonna happen to her when he got her home. This is why I'm taking Penny right now, knowing she will be warm and safe and loved."

A wash of tears rushes over Mrs. Franklin's eyes, but she's too strong and bullheaded to let them fall. "I lived through it, and it's only fair my daughter does, too. At least she loves Warren."

My face twists up with frustration. "See, that's what I don't get. You mothers do it to your own daughters. No one else is. Mr. Franklin would have kept Penny here until she finished college if you'd let him. Seems to me, if it hurt you so bad when it happened to you, you wouldn't want to inflict such suffering on your own daughters. Just 'cuz it's been done, doesn't mean it's right. Just my take on things."

"Mind your elders," is Mrs. Franklin's lame comeback.

"Maybe if you'd challenged your elders to think outside of their tiny world, they'd learn something." I charge down the hallway, knowing which room Penny shares with her sisters. I look at little

Molly for direction, and she points out which drawers belong to her big sister.

I yank the drawers from the dresser, dumping their contents on Penny's bed. "Maybe the elders don't know what the fuck they are doing, and when we listen to them, we end up doing the wrong goddamned thing. Seeing on how you consider a young girl old enough to become her child's elder. That's just a thought from someone who thinks for himself."

Molly, taking the initiative while her mother is stunned stupid, begins gathering Penny's things and stacking them nicely on the second patchwork blanket we made in Home Economics.

"There is a big difference in following an ignorant person blindly to your own destruction and minding your elders. Don't stunt your daughters to the point they can't think for themselves, and then force them to birth children when they are still children themselves. Then force the same bullshit lies on them that your grandmothers made up because they didn't know any better. It's not a legacy. It's enslaved ignorance."

"Wynn Gillette," Mrs. Franklin says in warning, and Molly begins tearing shit off the walls and tossing it onto the blanket. Out of nowhere, Hannah comes out of the depths of their shared closet with a huge armful of clothing still on their hangers, and then she makes a mad dash to the front door. Kids start spilling from the woodwork, gathering Penny's things because she deserves them.

This generation is going to change West Virginia. Just seeing how much the Franklin kids stick together melts my frostbitten heart. It's even defrosting Mrs. Franklin a teensy bit but pissing her off more.

I lean forward, gathering up Penny's blanket like a tarp. "I'm going. I'm going. I'm going." I chant to the angry momma at my back. Whether a townie or a hillbilly from the Hollers, nobody likes being judged, especially by a seventeen-year-old boy stealing their daughter.

———————

The last of Penny's things are secured in the back of my pickup. All of her family is scattered about the front yard, looking sad and worried. All but Penny's momma, because she never followed us outside. The twins' faces are glued to the side window again, while

Penny hides beneath the hood of her sweatshirt, not able to say her goodbyes.

"Is your daddy already at work?" I ask Jeb, Penny's younger brother by two years.

"Yeah," Jeb whispers while running his hands over his freckled cheeks to remove what he considers cowardice.

I grip Jeb's shoulder and squeeze, but my words are directed at Penny's four sisters as well as little Jeb. "I cried when my sister was taken, too. I was ten and Warren was sixteen, and neither one of us could stop it. Believe me, we tried. But Daddy had taken all the guns from the house knowing how we'd react. That night, we huddled up in bed together, crying. It's okay to be sad, but you need to understand this isn't the same thing."

Jeb doesn't say anything, but his head flicks up. I can almost see the tears evaporating in his eyes. Molly and Hannah walk right up to me, while Deanna and Sarah inch a bit closer. Penny is the oldest, and they're terrified whatever happens to her will happen to them when the time comes.

"See, Penny's already a sister to me. I'm just taking her with me, is all. She's still gonna go to school. She's still gonna walk down to the shop and visit with you and your daddy. You're still gonna see her at school, and you can visit our home whenever ya want." I chuck the kid underneath the chin. "Bring your sisters with ya, but leave your momma to home until she starts thinking for herself."

I walk away to a chorus of byes and a bunch of hand waving. I ignore Penny's hiccupped sobs as I pull away. I'm thankful she keeps her head buried in her hoodie, because the twins are smushed up against the rear window, seeing exactly what I'm seeing in the rearview mirror.

Molly, Hannah, Deanna, and Sarah run after the truck, yelling goodbye and waving like crazy mad, with their new leader paving the way. I can tell Jeb is going to do a better job at keeping those girls safe than Penny ever could.

"Is that Bren?" Penny's eyes widen when she takes in the boy she sicced Warren on leaning against the porch railing of a huge two story house on the outskirts of Rusty Knob. "What's going on, Wynn? I thought we were meeting up with your boss."

At the sound of their cousin's name, the kids start squealing something fierce. Hayley's in love with the big idiot, latching onto him in a way she's only with me, which makes Warren jealous. "Bren! Are we playing with Bren today?"

"Penn, ya better open that door right quick, or the kids are gonna maul ya." The door pops open before Penny can even move, with the brats tearing across the yard. They tackle Bren and fell him to the ground. His peal of laughter is sweet to my ears but disturbing to Penny.

"Appearances ain't always what they seem, Penny," I say as I swing out of the truck. "Sometimes ya gotta look a little deeper. Bren's a good guy at home and on the basketball court, but he's a bit of a dick at school."

"Why?" Penny asks, catching up with me. "I don't get it," she mumbles, confused as she stares down at Bren tickling his tiny cousins. "Look how he treats Franny."

I don't go into it. I was angrier than a feral cat when Bren started hanging around Francis, until I realized he was protecting the gay kid in the only way he knew how. It was someone making fun of Rusty Knob's Franny that led me to finding the LGBTQ group on Facebook in the first place.

I liked how it was a community for our school district to deal with the ignorance. When I got on there, I thought I was open-minded, but I only realized how narrow I truly was. The moderator is a man in his twenties who educates us by posting videos and articles, saying West Virginia is stuck in the 1990s. Everyone is welcome. It's not just gay, bi, and questioning kids in the group. A few of their straight friends hang out in there to show their support.

I was smart enough to make a new Facebook profile: Rusty West. Because Rusty Knob is not exactly friendly to those who are different. I didn't want to end up getting beat because I don't know what I am. No one would guess Jack is known as Virginia Duncan, or Jessica is Kentwood's Cutie. Bren and Francis only turned their profiles to private, thinking no one else in the group was from Rusty Knob. Francis is always voicing his opinion, and so is Bren.

"Just treat Bren like an asshole at school, and be friendly with him the rest of the time. That's what I do."

We stand at Bren's feet, watching him look carefree. Penny asks, "Why not just be buddies, then?" and that draws Bren's attention to us.

Penny doesn't get it, so I educate her. "It's safer this way. Trust me. Don't ask any more questions." I reach down to yank Bren to his feet. "They turn into happy puppies when your name is said. Gonna have to buy 'em a kennel."

Smiling brightly, "I think we better call the groomers, then." Bren ruffles Hayley's hair, letting the shorn off curls slip through his fingertips. "That is a righteous haircut, my little badass. But I think you're due for a trim. I'm gonna go run in the house and call around to see if we can get you into the hairdresser."

Bren untangles from the kids, laughing when they try to reattach themselves. He nudges me with his shoulder, gaining my attention, and then whispers in my ear. "Don't think I missed that bruise on Hayley's cheek. If you hadn't left your daddy and momma, I would have shot every last one of you Gillettes until the state was forced to give me my kin."

"Bren!" Penny coils up for attack. I reach over to stop her with a Warren-patent-pending-maneuver, wrapping my hand over the lower part of her face to silence her. She struggles and tries to bite me.

"Not today," I caution Penny not to bite the hands that feeds. "Bren has every right to feel as he does. I don't blame him. It's just him and his daddy left, and these kids are part of 'em."

"Any women and children in my yard better git their asses in this house for breakfast!" Royce shouts as he steps onto the porch. "Sorry, Wynn. You're a grown man today," my boss says with a huge grin as he tosses me a lunch sack.

Before I catch my breakfast, the kids are shrieking, "Uncle Royce! Uncle Royce!" and crawling up the steps to the front porch to attack the short, burly man.

"What the hell is wrong with Willa?" Penny whispers in my ear while Royce herds the children into the house. "Why didn't she drop these kids off here years ago?"

"Ignorance," I grunt bluntly. "Willa was a year older than you when she was beaten and raped. She went back to the only life she knew how to live. Loyalty, most certainly. Fear, most definitely. Thought she didn't deserve the best house in all of Rusty Knob, probably."

Penny twists up her freckled face, confused as all get out. "How do you figure that?"

I just narrow my eyes and shake my head as I walk back to my truck, feeling Penny's eyes burning into my backside. I whisper to myself when I settle into my seat. "Because that's how I would feel. That's how I've always felt when Royce offered me a different sort of life. It's how I felt when I was awarded a scholarship. Like I was being disloyal for leaving them all behind. That's how I know."

Large hands pound the hood of my truck at the same time, "Dumbass," hits my ears. I jump, and then a blush creeps over my skin like I was caught in the act of doing something bad. Bren climbs into the passenger side, wearing a shit-eating grin.

Bren's a younger, skinnier version of his dad, with thick brown hair and warm eyes lacking happy, laugh lines. Not too tall, but not too short. Someday Bren will fill out to be rugged like Royce. Just like I know Hayden will, especially with how stocky Warren ended up being. I'm just tall and athletic, whereas they're built to be workhorses.

Right now, though, Bren is intimidated by me, and I find it funny, knowing how he'll be able to knock my ass to the ground when he finally fills out. He always gets antsy when trapped in a truck cab with me. But, today, Bren's balls seem to have dropped.

"You need to rethink the definition of loyalty, Wynn. They ain't worth it. Not because they don't have any money, or because they are undereducated. It's because they are nasty human beings who would rather hurt than help."

I drop my breakfast into my lap, and then close my eyes. "That's my momma and daddy you're talking about," I snarl my warning. My hands grip the steering wheel to contain my violence, until my knuckles turn white.

I don't know where Bren's courage is coming from. "My papaw was illiterate, but he was a kind, hardworking man who put his family first. The house was small, but it was warm and clean, and all bellies were filled."

"You don't know what it's like," I mutter while tears sting my eyes. "Going to bed starve-gutted until you feel hollow inside. Not being able to get warm, no matter how close to the fire you stand…"

"Yeah, we got more money now than we can spend. We didn't earn it at first, and we'd return it if it meant we could get Papaw and Momma back. We'd gladly take to living in Kennedy Holler to this house, just to have the dead resurrected. But that wasn't my point." Bren reaches over to grip my shoulder, and then he gives me a good shake with his large paw. "We still work because we need a reason to live. We ain't got no family, and Daddy ain't got no woman. But we're good people."

"The best," I breathe the God's honest truth.

"Your momma and daddy ain't," Bren twists out. "They're the type who would lay down and die instead of moving two feet to the left to safety. *Can you believe that truck hit me in the center to the road? How dare they? Gimme money! My leg's broke, better tap the beer!*" Bren taunts in a comical voice, but he's being serious. "They ain't even loyal to themselves, so why should you be to them?"

"You sound so much like Royce right now, it ain't even funny. Do I need to check to see if your dad's hand is playing ventriloquist with your behind?" I release a humorless laugh. "Can I have Bren, Kentwood's douchebag bully back?"

"Nah, I only perform that act Monday through Friday, eight a.m. to three p.m., and before and after basketball games. The rest of the time I gotta be me." Bren picks up my lunch bag. "Eat your breakfast. We gotta lotta work to do today, and Dad's gonna need our help later this evening."

I reach into the brown sack, knowing I'll find an English muffin sandwich filled with scrambled eggs and a sausage patty, just like every Saturday morning. Sunday mornings are biscuits covered in sausage gravy, and we eat at the table as a family before church. Suppers are always takeout being eaten while we play board games on the living room floor.

Royce doesn't make me do much work. He basically gives me busy work so I don't feel guilty he takes two days a week to make up for the other five shitty days the twins and I lived through.

"Thanks," I grumble around a large bite of sandwich, knowing Bren cooks on Saturdays and Royce on Sundays.

"So… Dad's crew just got done remodeling the old Sutton place over on Holland Road. He thought that would be perfect. It's small, but it has three bedrooms. The school is just a street over if you cut through its backyard, and then the neighbor's yard too. It won't take much for Penny to take the kids to the park on weekends. You'll have a few of the team as your neighbors with Jack at the end of the street. Nice and safe."

"Bren–"

He stops my protests by pressing my sandwich closer to my lips. "Nope, I was told to make you listen. Dad's been planning this for the past four years, knowing Willa would never give in, so he'd have to help the kids through you. He's been waiting for you to be grown enough to see you had a real future. He had the same plan for Warren, but your brother couldn't be swayed, no matter what. You ain't the only kid Dad helps out, but you're one of the only ones he considers family."

"Jesus." I scrunch up the bag, hoping Bren will look at my hands instead of the tears on my cheeks. A man has to have some pride.

"Dad doesn't like spending the money he made because Papaw and Momma died. He calls it blood money. Everybody is so goddamned prideful, saying they won't take a handout, but their actions are so worthless it disgusts him. We've been doing all we can. Dad started scholarships, having the teachers tell him which kids are deserving. He's fostered a kid who lost his dad. He created a few businesses to employ the townsfolks so they don't think it's charity. Everybody has to have a reason to live besides drowning in misery and addiction, and he's giving them one. We can't take that money to the grave, and we ain't gonna spend it on bullshit, neither."

I just stare out the windshield of the ancient truck Royce hooked me up with when I was fifteen so I could drive the twins to him for the weekends. Before me is Rusty Knob, a place everyone in the hollers hates out of pure jealousy. It's another world than the one I grew up in. It's quaint with its tree-lined, paved streets, nice houses, mommas and daddies who raise smart kids, and their happy dogs trotting at their sides as they walk down sidewalks.

Most of us in the hollers, we live like trash because our parents keep telling us that's all we're worth because that's how they see themselves. No, that's not true. That's just how my parents see us.

At Rusty Knob Elementary and Junior/Senior High School, there is a clear divide between the townies and the hillbillies because of an ignorant sense of loyalty. The kids don't play together, because those from the hollers won't allow it. If you intermix, you get your ass beat for being a traitor. If you join the sports teams or try to get an education, then you're being hoity thinking your shit don't stink like the townies. If you work in town, you must think you're better than your kin. The hillbillies would rather starve than swallow their pride and leave the hollers to work in town.

I have two close friends: Penny and Jack. One is from the hollers and one is from town. My friends don't speak to each other because they've watched me get beat since kindergarten.

Folks in the hollers are all against the townies, but we don't like each other either. We're divided again by our kin, while the townies are lumped together into a big, powerful group of people who have money and influence, and the education to wield both. It's our own ignorance that segregates us from the townsfolk who want us to join them.

We're Rusty Knob.

Bren hands me a hanky when I didn't realize I was still crying. "Mop up your eyes. We need to get a move on. I called the team. They're helping us unload the truck and set your shit where it goes. Then we're going over the storage unit to find what else you're missing. Dad's addicted to those estate auctions, then he donates it all to the Salvation Army."

"Um… yeah." I scrub at my eyes and blow my nose. "Sorry. Don't know what's up with me this morning. If Penny saw me like this, she'd start in on her horseshit again."

I navigate the few blocks to the house Bren described, getting choked up all over again when I see ten guys scattered in the front yard– every single one of them a townie.

Bren hits the dashboard with a flat palm. "Welcome home!"

"No more. We have what we need. Let's get out of here." I turn to walk out of the large storage unit housing all of Royce's purchases. They've already pushed me into taking a big mattress for Penny, a pair of twin bedframes and mattresses for Hayley and Hayden, a table and chairs, three dressers, a sofa, a few lamps, and tried to force me to take a television.

"C'mon, Wynn. Don't be a jackass!" Bren pounds me on the shoulder. "Give me some backup, Jack. Tell your boy he needs a bed."

"NO!" I push the mattress away. "I've got the cot I bought at the Army and Navy store. Give it to someone who truly needs it. We only need the essentials. No spoiling me or Penny."

"I know better than to say anything," Jack says to stop Bren from going off at the mouth. "The little ones have beds, and you hooked Penny up with a full-sized for when Warren wanders home. Let the man keep some pride when it comes to the shit he uses."

"Look!" Bren charges around me, and then comes back with the railing to a crib. "We should take this now. Penny will need it in about seven months."

"No," I say forcefully. "Everything bought for Penny's baby will be by Warren, Penny, or me. Nobody else. Just as Royce can give the twins what they need to survive, but nothing more. I took the dresser and the mattress for Penny, but that's it. Nothing for me. Only shit the kids will be using will go into that house unless I buy it or build it myself."

"Fucking hillbilly pride," Bren grunts out, angry that I won't just accept all of his charity. He stomps from the storage unit, and the sound of my passenger door slamming follows thereafter.

"You really should take that TV, though," Jack starts in again, using a smooth man voice that is at odds with his little kid body. He tries to wrap his arm around my shoulders, but he's too short. He settles with just leaning against me in solidarity. "For the kids. Kids like TV. Cartoons and shit… Then you and Penny could watch the news. Ya know, keep abreast of the goings on in the world."

My best friend is manipulating me into giving in, but I can't allow it. "They can play outside, do their chores, do their homework, read and color. We don't need a TV."

"Lost cause," Jack sighs out as he steps away from me. He says loudly for everyone's benefit, "I tried!"

"Computer?" Duane, our tall Small Forward, pops out from behind a large hutch like a demented, big-toothed Howdy Doody. He thrusts a laptop at me. "It doesn't look very old. It's like my mom's."

"No," grits out between my teeth even though my hands are itching to clutch it to my chest and never let it go. "We can use the computer lab at school and the library. Plus, Royce always lets me use his desktop in the office."

"You sure?" Duane comes closer, noticing the lust in my eyes. "I could hook ya up with my internet password. For a few bucks, I could put an extender in your house. I'm just two houses down, neighbor. You could borrow some internet for homework."

"I... I... I... shouldn't." I close my eyes to block out the sight of my greatest temptation. "I can't. Thanks for the offer."

"I'd die without Wi-Fi," Francis calls out from the depths of the storage unit, where he's hunting for his own treasures. He's created a pile out front, saying he's going to barter a price with Royce, when we all know Royce will just give it to him. "Netflix. We all share our usernames and passwords. Binge-watching and binge-eating is a townie tradition. A life without Facebook. Tragic."

Jack and I snort, both of us addicted to Facebook. Then his narrowed eyes cut to mine, asking me a silent question. He believes I never use Facebook because Wynn Gillette's profile is inactive. I just smile to throw him off center.

Realizing I'm on Facebook all weekend at Royce's, "Take the goddamned laptop, Wynn," Jack demands, when he's never raised his voice to me before. *Busted!* "If you must, pay Royce for it in installments at the price he paid in the auction. But you're not leaving here without it. Ya never know when you might need WebMD."

"I... I... I..." I start stuttering again, fingertips curling into my palms against the urge to pull the laptop from Duane.

Jack grabs it out of a smirking Duane's hands, then he speaks the coaxing words of the devil. "You know you want it. Just take it!

What about when you start college? You wanna be the only kid without internet access?"

With outstretched arms, I reach for the laptop just as Adam did with the apple. My fingertips curl around the edges possessively, and then pull it until it's mine. I press it tightly to my chest, feeling an undesirable sensation burst in my chest.

"Sweet!" Duane high-fives Francis. "I'll hook up the signal extender this afternoon. Pretty sure we got one lying around somewhere."

"I've got the Netflix info!" Francis turns giddy. He wraps the laptop charger around my neck, and then pinches my ass. I allow it patiently, knowing the poor kid is starved for attention. "It's like teaching a baby how to walk and talk! What should we force on Wynn first? Game of Thrones?"

"Shameless," Jack says with a straight face, and then busts out laughing.

"Ass," I mouth to my buddy, knowing all about that show.

"Irony, my name is Frank Gallagher, the Urban Hillbilly," Duane sings.

"That is too fucking funny." Francis gooses Jack, causing my buddy to blush. '*Franny*' only has the balls to pester Jack and me because we are too nice to embarrass him. "Wynn better stay away from Shameless until he's used to regular living. God, his hillbilly mind is gonna explode."

"It's like they're from another country," Duane teases, and it makes me bark a laugh.

"Try another planet," I add in, meaning it. "You're used to me, and I'm straddling the line between two worlds. Penny's the same way, with her daddy having a business right in town. A real hillbilly like my daddy…"

"I've had my ass beat by enough of them," Duane mutters. His eyes cut to Francis, as if he's thinking what we're all thinking. Francis has a target on his back, and he better stay out of the hollers. "Violent. Feral. Shotguns. That's all I'm saying."

"Just stay in town and walk the other way in school," is my only advice. "There is no reasoning with the old timers. They are set in their ways, and telling them different will get your head shot clean off."

"Such a way with words," Francis bats his long eyelashes at me, giving me a hungry look I can recognize but I've never felt.

Nothing against gays, but my balls just shriveled up. I might not know what I want, but it ain't Franny. Don't get me wrong, he's adorable, and he's got a natural sexiness the girls try to copy, but he freaks me out. Francis is the buddy who molests me on occasion to get a rise out me.

In a daze, I walk out of the storage unit with my new laptop clasped to my chest and its charger wrapped around my neck like an electronic scarf. I hug it, never wanting to let it go. It's one of the things I've always wanted, something most take for granted, but didn't think I could ever have.

Royce has shoved down my throat how to manage money for the past few years. He taught me the value of a dollar by writing down everything I earn, how much I spend on necessities, and what I should have had left over to buy the things I earned. He says everyone should do that to see what they waste. Like spending more on beer and cigarettes in a week than the monthly mortgage of a nice house in town. According to Royce, Daddy and Momma spent hundreds of thousands of dollars during my lifetime on smoke that pollutes the air and piss filling a toilet, with nothing but deteriorating bodies to show for it. All money neither earned, either pilfered from the state or stolen directly from Warren, Willa's, and my pocket.

I never wanted to believe Royce, even with the evidence of nearly four hundred a week of my Circle K earnings paying for their vices. It's a new dawn, and I can finally see clearly.

"A laptop instead of a mattress? Nice…" Bren drawls out when I get into the truck cab. "Welcome to the year 2002."

Eyebrows scrunched with confusion, I turn over the ignition. "It's 2015, remember?"

"Exactly," he deadpans

My fist flies out to mock-punch Bren in the shoulder. "Fucker!"

Bren snickers while rubbing his arm. "I've got one word for ya, brother. YouPorn."

From the corner of my eye, I can see Penny looking at me while smothering her giggle with the back of her hand. "What?" I ask again for the tenth time in the past few minutes.

We're sitting on our porch steps. Penny's keeping an eye on the children in the front yard, and I'm doing some of Royce's busywork. I look down at the invoice again, making sure the number is correct, and then I input it into the Excel file.

"It's been almost two days, and you've yet to let go of your new baby. You even take your laptop into the shitter with you. I bet you spooned it last night." A girly giggle slips past her lips. "It's so fucking cute, I just can't stand it."

"Shut up," I snap, but then I crack a smile. "I'm trying to work here, remember? I've got to log in enough hours to offset our rent." She rolls her eyes, knowing full and well it's just a bunch of bullshit Royce is tossing my way to take away any guilt I feel over living off him.

"I have some good news," Penny announces, but then she's running down the porch steps before she can share the wealth. "Hayley! No! You don't hit the townie kids. They bruise too easily. What'd I tell ya?"

Hayden is unfazed. He hands the poor kid who was just hit upside the head the purple sidewalk chalk Hayley didn't want to share. The little boy, Tomlin, smiles brightly and draws the last arc of his rainbow.

"No hitting townies, Aunt Penny," Hayley parrots back in her girly, sing-song voice. It's my turn to smother my laughter. "I sorry. I forgot that they bruise easier than the rest of us."

Eyes bugging out from my skull, *They do not,* I mouth to Penny. "It's just ignorant bullshit passed down the generations so our parents don't have to come out of the hollers to bail us out of the principal's office."

"It's true! They bruise easier," Penny argues, and I worry about her level of intelligence.

"Oh, really?" I set my laptop down for the first time since I took it from the storage unit yesterday morning. "Explain high school, then. We're all bloodied and bruised in that war."

Penny's brown eyes widen impossibly large, pleading with me to go along with her, then I realize what she's up to. The kids have to go to school with townies, live in town, and they can't act like hillbillies. I get it, but I don't like lying to them. I won't promote their ignorance, even if Penny is trying to not be embarrassed by their behavior.

"Hayley. Hayden. Both of you c'mere a second. Please." I widen my legs on the steps, making room for them to stand in front of me. They come to me easy enough, always listening to me. "Don't hit anyone. Never. Hit. Not because they might bruise easier, but because it's mean and nasty. Understood?"

"Yes, Uncle Wynn," Hayden agrees solemnly, and then he walks back over to Tomlin– his friend from school who's now his next-door neighbor. The kid sits back down, and continues to add to their sidewalk landscape.

"Hayley, as long as you're not using it, you have to share. You can only use one color at a time, same as they can. So just wait your turn, and they will have to wait theirs. Next time you hit someone, I'm gonna hafta take your chalk away and force you to watch your friends and brother use it."

"Fine," Hayley bites out, glaring at me like she's a grown woman and I'm the disappointing brat, then she stomps back to the sidewalk. I breathe a sigh of relief that she behaves, no matter how begrudgingly.

In the holler, we don't share. If we want something, we beat the crap out of whoever has it and then take it. Once we have something, we fight to keep it.

"The girl's gonna be the troublemaker," I say to Penny when she retakes her seat next to me on the porch step. "Acts just like Warren. It's her new badass hairdo giving her that attitude. Only six-year-old girl I've ever seen with a curly fauxhawk."

"Hayley's a cute, naughty shit, for sure." Penny laughs, remembering all the attitude she's had to deal with in the past few days from my niece.

"No more Hillbilly-isms. Just talk straight to the kids and tell them the truth. If Hayley keeps hitting, start taking her toys away and make her clean something. She needs to learn acting like a little asshole doesn't make her tough."

Penny releases a nervous laugh, and then nudges my shoulder. "I think maybe my surprise should be yours."

"Huh?" I freeze midway as I grab for my laptop.

Voice filled with pride, "I got a job," Penny announces. "It's what I wanted to tell ya before Hayley turned into Rocky... I'ma start calling her Rocky from now on."

I groan when I notice I still have a thick stack of invoices to input. "What's the job?"

"Childcare." Penny glares in my direction when I snort. "I guess I can't be telling the townie kids hillbilly fables, like how they bruise easier."

"Guess not," I say with a straight face, but then my lips quirk up at the corners. "How'd you come upon this?"

"After church this morning..." Penny groans, and this time I do laugh. The girl had never been to church in her life. "I waited with the other mommas while Bible School was letting out, then we all went to the park together to watch the kids play. I was chatting with a lady who runs the daycare." She turns to me, huge brown eyes bugging out of her skull. "Can you believe those weirdos have other people watch their children while they work? The little fuckers are like ten and still being watched."

I bite back a snicker. "Inconceivable that they wouldn't want their kids running around like heathens, getting into trouble and hurting themselves. I mean, at fourteen, they better move out and start a family of their own."

"Stop making fun of me," Penny warns, sounding genuinely upset.

"Sorry, sister." I rub her back to take the sting of truth out of my words. "So, you'll be watching these kids who are old enough to look after themselves?"

"Newborns to fourteen, with the older kids having extended study hours in the church. I'm to start after school until six o'clock when the last of the parents show up. They're okay with the twins coming with me as long as they don't start any trouble. I guess most of their classmates will be with 'em. I'm to fetch all the kids from the elementary school and walk 'em to the church, give 'em a snack, and then run 'em ragged on the playground."

"Sounds perfect, actually." I squeeze Penny to my side and drop a kiss to the top of her head. "I'm proud of you."

"Maybe if I... if I do a good job, they'll let me place the baby while I'm at school so I can graduate." Penny's eyes cut to me, a childlike hope filling them. She knows she messed up by trying to snag Warren by getting knocked up on purpose, but instead of regretting it, she's trying to learn from it and move on. "Ya know, maybe how those mothers do it when they go to work?"

After witnessing the generosity of the townsfolk firsthand, I don't doubt for a second that the ladies would allow Penny to do just that. If she fits in, they'd probably let her work there fulltime after she graduated. We all see their help as charitable arrogance, like they gain a point in their favor for turning one of our own against us. When in reality, they just get that same warm feeling I get when I help my family. That feeling I call love.

I drop another kiss to Penny's head and squeeze her again before I let go. I drag my laptop onto my lap, and then pick up the invoices.

"Well…" Penny sighs loudly as she stands up. "I guess I better walk all those kids back to their houses. Get me some practice on walking kids like they're dogs." I chuckle at how flat her words sound. "Still can't wrap my mind around the townies leashing their dogs and walking them down the street. They're dogs. Let them be dogs. Next thing ya know, they'll be leashing their kids."

I bust out laughing as Penny rounds up the neighborhood kids.

"You wanna hit the dishes while I pack the lunches?" I reach up to pull the peanut butter jar from the cupboard, still amazed I'm in a house that has siding and a roof, let alone actual, functioning cupboards.

"I'll do it in the morning," Penny skirts the task, trying to weasel out on working, just like she did with fixing supper.

Sure, all I did was boil a box of pasta and dump a jar of sauce on it, but I was trying to work at the same time. Which is why I said no TV in this house. Even the twins tackled the sweeping, with Hayley manning the broom and Hayden the dustpan. Meanwhile, Penny was out on the sidewalk gabbing with the neighbor lady.

"No, Penny. Tonight," I order. I bite my tongue against any further comments. I start assembling four sack lunches with PB&Js, bananas, and juice boxes, so all we have to do is grab them out of the fridge in the morning.

"Ya know, Wynn," Penny starts in, sounding like my momma when I'd point out her shortcomings. "I'm gonna be working. I ain't yer slave. We're roommates. You ain't my daddy or my husband, so you don't get to tell me what to do."

I think, "*You sound so mature right now.*" But I say instead, "I understand that. I do. But I worked all day yesterday creating a home for us. Then I stayed up all last night because I wanted Royce to know how appreciative I was. Then I continued working after church, where I had to stop to make dinner. I haven't slept since Thursday night and we're hours from it being Monday."

"I said I'll do it in the morning," Penny stresses over her shoulder as she stalks out of the room.

"I ain't fighting with ya, Penny," I raise my voice so it will follow after her. "But we both know how this will play out. How do I know? I've lived this way my whole life. Your momma took care of you, and I ain't your momma or daddy. Come morning, there will be breakfast dishes piled up on dried-on supper plates, and no one will do 'em. Then come supper time tomorrow, another batch of dishes will pile on that 'cuz you went to school all day and then work. Then what?"

Hackles rising, Penny points at me from her position in the living room. "I ain't the maid, Wynn."

"Neither am I," I volley back. "Whoever cooks the food, doesn't do the dishes. To ask me to do both isn't fair, especially when we both know you won't be doing the yardwork either."

"Morning." Unrelenting, Penny stomps out of the room grumbling, "I'm going to bed."

Fuck it!

I twist the taps, and then squeeze out some detergent onto the dishes. If Penny wasn't here, I'd have to do this shit all by myself anyway. It isn't fair because she is here, but at least she was mindful of the kids so I could concentrate on working for Royce.

"Penny had no plan on doing these here dishes," I speak to the empty kitchen, not letting the truth of my words bog me down. "I'm alive for one thing– that almost ended for me. I'm standing in a nice house, with nice things, with actual dishes to wash because my belly is filled. I don't have an ornery drunk pissing himself and abusing us, and there's no smoke giving me nosebleeds. I'd say Penny being obstinate is the least of my worries."

"You like talking to yourself?" Jack's amused voice flows from the screen door. "No shock on Penny shirking her duties, though," comes as he steps into the kitchen.

Happy to see an unexpected, friendly face, I turn to look at Jack over my shoulder while I dry my hands on a dishtowel. "Hey, buddy. What are you doing here?"

"I was in the neighborhood–"

"Literally." I laugh because Jack lives at the end of the street. "Unreal. When I came for a visit, it took me fifteen minutes to drive from the holler into town."

"I like it. It's convenient to be able to bug you when I get the hankering." Jack takes a plate from my hand and begins drying. "I was sent by the basketball team as their emissary. I come bearing top-secret security codes for Wi-Fi, Netflix, and Amazon Prime, with a list of shows, movies, and music that are a must. Bren wanted me to say, and I quote, '*one word: YouPorn.*' Not sure what that was about, but I'll be finding out come bedtime."

I snort. "Bren's such a douche that I can't dislike him."

"Ya know, maybe watching some porn isn't such a bad idea." Jack drops a bomb in my kitchen, "Rusty West. It might arouse you."

I freeze, muscles locking up. A plate slips between my fingertips, but Jack's catching it before it hits the bottom of the basin. "Mind you, I'd wondered for a while, not knowing if I should ask. See, this guy is in a Facebook group I'm in. I don't know if he realizes, but the moderator only lets kids from our school district into this group. So finding two guys with the same unique situation in the same area, is a bit of a stretch."

"Is Virginia Duncan standing in this here kitchen?" I act all aghast. "Rusty Knob, West Virginia," I admit, "is a heck of a lot more creative than West Virginia, Jack Duncan. But nowhere near as stupid as Bren Kennedy and Francis Parker."

Jack hip bumps me, pushing me out of the way so he can finish the dishes. "We're creative." He releases a deep, evil snicker. "Bren and Franny are in-your-face obvious. But we can't tell anyone."

"Or it could get bloody. Yeah?"

"Yeah," Jack mutters softly, lost in thought. "I think Bren knows who we are, because he constantly tests you with the fag test, but never me. It terrifies me just the same that I might get tested."

"I don't think Bren is trying to out anyone," I reassure Jack. I haven't had the balls to ask Bren outright, but his reasoning is obvious to me. "I think Bren's trying to find someone he can trust. That BJ you had with Jessica must have confused him. I mean, the guy says he's bi. He has no problem getting girls, but that itch has got to be growing. An itch he ain't gonna let Francis scratch."

"Jesus Christ, yes!" Jack shouts, flinging the dishrag to plop on the kitchen floor. "Shit! I got a bit overexcited there," he mutters as he picks the rag back up. His cheeks are redder than a ripe tomato. "Sorry. Speaking of itches that can't be scratched, as cute as he is, Franny doesn't do it for me. Just not my type."

"No shit, sugar." I bust out laughing, thrilled that I'm finally able to understand my best buddy. "No wonder you always look sick when Bren is mock-flirting with his Franny. You're jealous. You've got a bit of a crush, don't ya?"

"But I can't do anything about it, even if I wanted to." Jack slumps, hip propped up against the countertop as he tugs at a frayed string on my dishcloth. He won't look at me. "God, this conversation is bizarre. Never thought I'd be having it."

I think about that for a split-second, and then shrug. "It's freeing, actually. I feel better now that it's out in the open."

Satisfied that I'm not judging him, Jack continues. "Bren flirts with Virginia Duncan in the group because I'm listed as a bi female. We get away with it and no one bats an eyelash. But truth be told, we're dealing with a gay kid who uses a false identity and a bi guy who could have anyone he wanted as long as they didn't have a dick."

"First, Royce knows what's up, so Bren's daddy ain't stopping him. Second, no matter how he plays, Bren isn't stupid, either." I tug the dishcloth from Jack's grip. "Your last name is Duncan, for cripes' sake. Bren knows you aren't a girl and he knows it's you, and he flirts with you anyway."

"Nobody ever says anything," Jack grumbles. "We all go online and commiserate, and then pretend it never happened while we hang out every day. I don't get it."

"I can't answer for the rest of 'em, but I was waiting for you to spill the truth to me, not wanting to put pressure on you. Not to sound like Mentor KM, but you coming out should be your choice." I dry a plate, and then put it in the cupboard. "You're my best friend, and Bren is like the pesky little brother I never had, so I'll watch your back if you can't wait until you get to college to scratch that persistent itch."

"Thank you, but I'll wait." Jack hesitates, choosing his words wisely. "Can you…"

Fuck it!

"Penny can finish these dishes she promised to do in the morning. If she doesn't, I'm eating her sack lunch myself. That would fix her wagon." I toss the dishrags into the empty basin, leaving the dirty dishes to soak in the other side of the sink. I grab ahold of Jack's sleeve to tug him out the screen door.

I sit on the top step of the front porch, marveling over how different my life was from a few nights ago. It isn't as dark here in town, but there is a peaceful sensation that settles over me, blanketing me in that feeling I call love. Hearing the peepers not getting drowned out by the bellowing of coonhounds is a pleasant surprise. I thought it would be nosier in town with all the people living here, but it's quieter somehow. Sometimes silence is deafening. But then again, Daddy's bitching isn't echoing off the hilltops.

Jack bumps my arm with his shoulder, being that he's almost six inches shorter than me. He does it again, trying to gain my attention while comforting me. "Do you even know what the itch feels like? I don't want to rub it in, but I'm curious."

"Truth be told, yes and no." I sigh, finally putting a voice to something I've always left unsaid. "The empty void is suffocating, and I'd do anything to fill it up. I can't help but wonder if it's worse than how you feel. I mean, I get horny for something I don't understand. I know how to take care of business, but it just isn't very filling. Like living off PB&J when you really want a steak."

"You're good at dealing with going without, for sure. But, do you... do you ever look at someone and want them?" When I don't answer or protest, Jack starts lobbing questions at me left and right. "What's it like when you jerk it? I know you weren't using porn, so what do you visualize?"

"What's it like for you?" I ask instead of answering something I don't know how to explain.

"I kept... I kept looking at girls how everyone else was, but it did nothing for me. I bet you feel like that all the time. I would concentrate on it so hard, it would give me a headache."

"How'd you know?" I finally ask the one question that I'd been too hesitant to ask. "How'd you figure out you were gay?"

My buddy releases the most ironic laugh I've ever heard. "JV basketball changed that for me. I couldn't stop popping chub in the locker room. It didn't take long for me to figure out why. All those naked, sweaty boys. It was a buffet put on just for me every practice. The showers are my greatest pleasure and nightmare combined." Jack shoulder bumps my arm again. "Now I enjoy the view while feeling petrified someone will notice I sprouted wood."

Feeling envious, my curiosity gets the best of me. "Then there's the itch?"

"Then there was the itch that started to tingle and turn into a burning need when I was around Bren. It's like my body picked Bren, knowing we'd both like the scratching."

My voice comes small, unsure. "Did you ever feel that with me?"

"The itch?"

"Yeah." My breath catches, scared our friendship is about to change.

"Nah," Jack rasps after a heavy pause. "Don't get me wrong. You're the best view in school. But I never burned for you."

Bitter disappointment flows through me, and I'm surprised at its source. "Guess that means your body is telling you I'm not gay then, eh?"

"Don't know if that's how it works or not. We both know Franny is gayer than gay. I just want to protect him, not diddle him." Jack gently head butts my arm this time, so I know I'm not going to like what comes next. "Sorry, I can't help ya out, bud. I don't know what you are."

"Me either." I take a deep breath. "I was kinda hoping you could tell me. It's one of the reasons why I tried to…" Feeling closer to Jack more now than ever, I blurt out the truth, being selfish enough to force my best friend to help me shoulder my burdens.

In a rush, "I tried to kill myself Friday night," I spew before I can take the words back. "I couldn't deal with the long stretch of misery without someone to make me feel warm, ya know?" I shudder, my body reacting to the endless cold I suffer with. "Warren and Penny have each other, no matter how tough shit gets. Royce? He's alone, yet he's got Bren to hold onto. You? At least you know what you want. Having a crush, even if you can't act on it, must make you tingle something fierce."

Reaching for me, "Shit, Wynn," Jack cries. Smaller than me, he tries his best to wrap me in his arms, rocking us slightly on the front porch steps. I grip him back just as fiercely, fingers clenching into his shoulders, twisting in the material of his t-shirt. I try to ignore the fact that I'm drenching his shoulder from my leaky eyes, and I pretend I can't hear the sniffling sound emanating from his nose.

If I'm busy, I can ignore what I've done. But in the quiet, it comes rushing forward, causing my heart to beat a rapid tattoo against my ribcage as the panic sets in.

I was a hairsbreadth away from not experiencing this moment–not being here for Jack when he needed me most, and my best friend wouldn't have felt useful because I wouldn't have been here for him to comfort and support. We need each other, and I almost destroyed that. Almost, but only because of Warren. Because I *did* pull the trigger.

I've never felt this level of shame, even with who my parents are and where I come from, and I have no idea how to handle it. All I can do is suffer through the assault as my body violently shakes to release the pressure.

We don't speak for a long while, but it's comforting just the same, calming my anxious reaction to the truth of my actions.

The pleasant warmth buzzes its way through my body, unfreezing me. I know it's not the same thing Jack was describing, but at least I know I won't grow cold as long as I have loyal friends and good family.

Jack pulls away first, having to tug my arms from around him. He leans to the side, far enough away so he can look me dead in the eyes. "Someday, you're gonna meet somebody, and they're gonna rock the world beneath your feet. It'll feel like an earthquake. It will be petrifying yet exhilarating. You'll feel sick– heartsick. But you'd do anything to continue feeling that way, no matter how much it hurts."

"That sounded like that was from firsthand experience," I mutter as I finally release Jack out of our embrace. "You got something to tell me, Jack?"

"I better get going." He rises to his feet, and then hops down the steps before I can stop him. "We've got school in the morning, after all. Gotta get rested up."

"Uh-huh," I grunt, not appreciating his evasion.

Jack goes a few feet down the walk with his back turned to me so I can't see his face. His words flow quiet, but I can hear them well enough. "I may or may not have had a kiss a few months back. A kiss that dropped my ass to the ground. I will not admit that what was once a crush is now something more. But I'll say, seeing the person I might love fuck a swath through Rusty Knob, feels a lot like dying. Especially when said crush loves every minute of it."

My eyes drink in the sight of Jack's slouched shoulders as he walks away from me. I don't know what it must feel like to want someone so much that you'd get jealous. But I think finding out would be worth the pain. Getting that type of kiss, now that would be worth everything.

With a heavy sigh, feeling weary to my bones, I stand up to walk back into the house. I open the screen door and nearly careen into a tiny slip of a girl wearing a floor-length nightgown.

"I don't want to fight with you," Penny murmurs. My heart aches to see tears swimming in her eyes, but it's pounding furiously for another reason entirely. "I'll pull my own weight. I promise."

Hesitantly, I ask, "You didn't hear anything on the porch, now did ya?"

"Not a word," Penny agrees, but she's lying to comfort me. She steps forward to rest her cheek against my chest, silently asking me to kiss the top of her head. I oblige, slipping a hand around her back to hold her for a moment longer.

I pull away with a, "Night, Penny," and then walk through the house toward my bedroom.

Penny's, "Wynn, you better promise to live to be one hundred and ten," will haunt me for the rest of my days, because the gravity of what I tried to do is finally sinking in.

WYNN GILLETTE BOUGHT ME A DRINK

Standing in the hallway of the little school, with Hayden holding my left hand, I try to wrangle Hayley with the other. The mommas walking their kindergarteners and first-graders keep stopping to say how cute I'm being, calling me a good big brother. I don't bother to tell them I'm the uncle, because not many kids become one at the tender age of eleven. Looking at how Hayden and I are behaving, the townsfolk assume we're one of them, compared to the wild young'uns running down the halls without any supervision.

"Now let me fix your dress." I squat down to adjust the hem on Hayley's dress, but she squirms and strikes out at me with her tiny fists of fury.

"I don't wanna wear no dress." Hayley hits the top of my head, but her words are filled with pouting instead of anger. "I want my pants back."

"Double negative, Sissy. You're a girl. Girls wear dresses." Hayden informs his sister, earning her ire. He's an old soul who sounds just like Warren when you get him going. A budding misogynist who begs me to teach him the proper way to speak. I can't seem to wrap my mind around that.

"Hayden." I roll my eyes and shake my head as I reach up to tug Hayley's shorts back into place. We have to keep her tushy covered while on the swing set. "Girls can wear pants all they want. Hayley, the reason you're in a dress is because I had to toss your clothes out. We'll go after school to the Salvation Army and get you some pants. Okay? Will that do? Will you be good now?"

Hayley grunts at me, but I take that as a good sign. "Let's get you kids to Mr. Marx." I rise to my full height, taking a tiny hand in each of my own. A fluttering of laughter fills the hallway, so I glance over my shoulder to see a young momma checking out my ass.

Blushing, I mutter, "No shame, I tell ya," underneath my breath. I should feel flattered, but all I feel is envious that I don't get to experience whatever brought heat to that momma's face.

This is the first time I've done this with the kids. Where we come from, the parents tell us to get on the bus. We ride around the hills for over an hour, picking up our neighbors, then we get dropped off in the parking lot. It's up to chance whether or not the kids get to where they're supposed to go. The teachers do their best to keep everybody in line. It's how I was raised, and it's how Hayden and Hayley spent kindergarten and most of first grade.

But this morning, I saw all the kids in town skipping down the street. Most were with their older siblings, but the little ones were holding their mommas' hands. So I took the initiative to deliver Hayley and Hayden to Mr. Marx personally. Plus, Kaden Marx and I have some unfinished business to attend.

Mr. Marx is wearing a huge smile, not that I give a hoot what else he's wearing– teacher clothes, I guess. But the smile is bright and happy, completely the opposite of the icy, taut scowl he gave me on Friday night.

I snort in amusement when *knee high to a grasshopper* comes to mind. Mr. Marx is so tall, the first graders aren't much taller than his kneecaps. He's standing in the center of a circle of kids running around and around him while giggling and acting silly.

I feel a bit envious of Mr. Marx. The fact that he loves his job radiates from him, glowing pure happiness. But my envy is quickly replaced with that warm sensation, because I'm glad that someone is doing right by these kids and loving every second of it.

The twins yank on my hands, alerting me to the fact that I stopped in the middle of the classroom to watch their teacher play with his students.

"Sorry," I mutter brusquely, shaking out of it. "C'mon," I give a tug to get us all moving again. I grip their hands tightly, not wanting them to scurry off to their friends. I've got to show Mr. Marx how fresh they look and smell.

I step up to the circle, but I don't break into the arc the kids are creating. "Mr. Marx." I clear my throat, waiting impatiently while the twins yank and tug, trying to run off.

"Uncle Wynn," Hayley whines, fed up. "Let go."

My hands start sweating, so I have to grip tighter. The little brat figures this out, tugging harder and harder. "Hayley Willamina Kennedy," I warn, using her full name to get her attention. She freezes beside me, huge blue eyes flicking up to light upon my face.

Mr. Marx's smile transforms into something naughty. His lips curl up at the edges like he finds me amusing. That dang smirk tightens my belly muscles, but it angers me more because he's making fun of me with just a look.

"I can mind these kids better than you can," he's thinking.

"Well, I should hope so. It's your dang job," spills from my mouth.

Shit!

Mr. Marx chuckles while waving his hands about like they're fluttering in the wind. "Go on, now. Go on and play," he sweeps the kids away from him, and they scatter to the four corners of the classroom. "It's a bit like herding cats, or using a funnel to collect water."

My kids just stare up at their teacher like he's their god.

Figures.

I stand frozen beneath Marx's heavily-lidded stare, unsure what I was going to say or do. It's odd, being looked down upon. I don't mean judged– that's an everyday occurrence from everyone. I mean literally looked down upon. I'm six-foot-two, and I'm staring at Mr. Marx's nose instead of his eyes.

"That's some rocking locks, ya got there, Hails." Mr. Marx flutters the top of Hayley's curly fauxhawk. "Setting a trend in the elementary school with your Rockabilly dress and hardcore hairstyle."

Hayley tugs on my hand to get my attention. She whispers like it's a secret, "I want more dresses, Uncle Wynn." The little minx is already crushing in the first grade.

Fuck!

I just bust out into hysterics– a combination of stress and amusement. I let go of the kids' hands, and they finally slip free. Hayley doesn't want to leave her teacher's side, but her brother won't allow it.

"Girls should wear dresses," my nephew is going off again. "But I think you ought to be wearing pants. C'mon over to the reading nook. I want to get a good book before they're all taken."

Trying to contain his laughter, Mr. Marx is biting the corner of his lip, his crooked front tooth leaving a dent. I ought to know, I seem to keep staring transfixed in that general vicinity. With a deep breath, my eyes snap up to meet his, deciding I better do what I came here to do in the first place.

"I have something…" I get a bit tongue-tied because he's not glaring at me for once. Kaden Marx was one of Warren's friends when they were growing up. I saw him constantly when I was a boy. But I haven't been around him much since. When I am, he's usually glaring at me. I'm a bit thrown off by the old Kade making a reappearance. "I have something for you," I try again.

"Oh, yeah?" Mr. Marx relaxes, shoving his hands into the front pockets of his teacher pants. He's telling me he's Kade now, just another kid from the hollers. "The kids look really good, Wynn. I… I'm happy that you got the fuck away from your parents and took the twins with you. I couldn't stand by and allow their futures to be trampled. We all know social services will not breach a boundary line for fear of their lives."

My eyes drop to look at Kaden's shiny teacher shoes. "What you said… what you did… how you made me feel… it had its intended impact. I couldn't keep living that way anymore."

"I'm glad you made the right decision," comes muffled to my ears because my pounding heartbeat is drowning out all other sound.

I wince, knowing I didn't make the right decision at all. "You can thank Warren for that. Trust me when I say my decision was piss-poor."

Kade shifts on his feet while ducking his head to get into my line of sight. But I can't look up at him. "Ignorance is not the absence of intelligence. Rather, it is the absence of knowledge. Just open your eyes wider, is all. You have no reason to be ashamed of your roots, Wynn. Your past will shape you far more than those who grew up here in town. You'll appreciate every meal and every dollar you earn."

"I feel that already." My shoulders curl in on themselves, shrinking me further.

"Your father is scum. I'm sorry to say that, but it's the truth. You need to hear me when I say that isn't how it is in every house in the hollers. They are dirt poor people who don't have an education enough to realize they can have more if they tried to achieve it. That's all. When sons like you and I try for more, their pride gets bent. They are good people who love their families, and they don't know any better because their eyes are shut. You just drew the short straw with the piece of shit abuser you call daddy."

I finally look up into Kaden's earnest, hazel eyes. "Why do you always act like you hate me?"

Kade steps back and straightens up taller. "Because you were blinding yourself on purpose, pretending you couldn't see the truth. It's like what you were saying to Penny at the Circle K on Friday

Night. You weren't meeting your potential. It was on purpose, and it pissed me off."

"Understood," I agree, shaking my head up and down. I cram my hand into the back pocket of my jeans, and pull out what I came here to do. "Here."

Larger, warm hand wrapping around mine, I shiver a bit while the transfer takes place. "Seriously?" Kade's eyebrow hitches and his mouth quirks up in the corners. "How are your math scores?"

"What?" I grumble, bewildered. "I just took it last month. I got a 760 for my SAT math score. Not perfect, but prit'near."

"Well, that explains it." Kade hangs his head as if he's disappointed in me. I can only see the arch of his nose, and the top of his head. I never noticed how he wears his thick curly hair in a bun like a girl, but his slow movements draw it to my attention. "It's those missing forty points that have you giving me my twenty bucks back, plus the bar of Ivory. Seems like I'm coming out ahead on this."

Blushing bright red, I mutter, "Huh?"

Voice quiet yet solemn. "Yeah, I drank the Gatorade for two bucks and some change, and bought this here soap… but now I have my twenty bucks back, already pissed the Gatorade down the toilet, and I'm holding a bar of Ivory. Seems like we aren't even, are we?"

"You shittin' me?"

Kade looks up abruptly, face splitting into a huge grin. "Obviously your math skills leave something to be desired, or else you're a proud sonofabitch who's putting me in my place. Which is it, Wynn? Should I be thanking you for handing me my ass, or should I get you a math tutor?"

I look away quickly, blushing to the roots of my hair. "I'm handling… I mean, *handing* you your ass," I drawl, chuckling a bit underneath my breath.

"I'ma keep this soap on my desk." Kade twists to the side, placing the bar of Ivory by his nameplate. "I like it when students give me gifts. I'll have to find that Gatorade bottle and keep it as a souvenir to remind myself about the time Wynn Gillette bought me a drink."

I have the sudden urge to fan myself like the mommas and mamaws in church during a sermon. I look away, unable to gaze at Kade's grin. I clear my throat. "So, what'd you get on your SATs, Mr. Smarty Pants-Teacher Man?"

"Not as good as you," Kade admits without putting up a fuss. "I haven't known Royce since I was a boy like you have. My eyes weren't as open as yours are. I met him when I was a sophomore, and he turned my life around."

Shocked but not shocked, "Royce paid for your schooling?"

"Yeah, and I'm paying it forward." Kade gestures around his schoolroom. All the kids– townies and hillbillies –are playing together and getting along. "I used to be a bit like Penny, thinking dogs on leashes were ridiculous. It took me a long while to assimilate."

My eyes narrow, causing Kade to huff a laugh. "I was the dog-walking neighbor Penny was referring to. I also stole her fable about townie kids bruising easier." He flashes me a huge grin, keeping one eye trained on the rest of the room while looking at me with the other. "I'm going to employ that trick on my first graders."

Mind spinning, wondering if Royce has been talking behind my back, I ask, "Small world, coincidence, or on purpose?"

"Small world, Wynn," Kade comforts me in a soothing yet deep voice that crawls down my spine as it caresses my name. "I live across the street from you in the blue house with the white trim. I'm the jackass walking his tiny pug a billion times– day and night." Kade leans in and whispers near my ear, causing me to shiver again. "Let Penny in on this secret– dogs chase cars, but sometimes they chase back."

"Are you serious?" I mutter sarcastically.

Nodding like he didn't hear the sarcasm, Kade's ear brushes my cheek. He grimaces, and then says, "Splat," while clapping his hands together in front of my face, breaking our moment. "I love my dog, so I leash him."

"Jesus," I rasp out in a gust, turning abruptly so Kade can't see my flushed face. "I better get going. I already missed homeroom. I'm sure I'm late to first period."

Kade straightens to his full height and takes a few steps back. He clears his throat, and rubs his palms on his teacher pants. "Yeah, guess I better teach these hellions how to read and write. I started in September. It'd be bad to get chastised before I put in a full school year, yeah?"

"Yeah," I drawl, nodding. My feet are fused to the floor. For some reason, I suddenly want to rejoin the first grade. "I'll be seeing ya around, I guess."

"I'll be hearing Penny bitching from across the street, I suspect. The quality of the neighborhood just decreased." Insulted, I step forward, but then Kade's laughter hits my ears. "I'm joking, Wynn. I like it. It reminds me of my momma."

"I'll rile Penny up some more for ya, then," I say in parting.

FLUSHING TRAITORS!

Dazed, I wander from the elementary half of the building into the high school side. I have no watch, and there are no bells between periods in the little school, so I guess first period has already started. My chat with Kade felt like it sped by, yet I know it took quite some time.

"Sorry, Mrs. Kerry," I mumble when I sneak into Field Biology. "I got held up in the little school." I lean against the door, closing it with my back, waiting to be told to either sit or hightail it to the office. I'm not worried, though. All the teachers respect me because I respect them.

Looking up from her desk, "Not a problem, Wynn," Mrs. Kerry chirps happily. She marks me present on the roster with a flourish of her hand. "We're doing a lab today, so join a group."

I push off the door with a, "Thanks." I turn to weave around the lab tables, looking for Jack, and what I spot has me missing a step. "The fuck?" I mutter underneath my breath.

Rusty Knob High is segregated– the students segregate themselves. The townies in the front, the hillbillies in the back, and the middle is where students hide out. There is a lot of jealousy and prejudice. If a townie tried to sit in the back, they'd get their ass kicked, and whoever they were trying to sit with would have a few broken bones for being a traitor. If a hillbilly tried to sit in the front, the townies would look at him cross-eyed but not do anything about it. However, he wouldn't be present in school for a few days afterward because he would be a traitor. The middle is where people like me sit– someone who belongs to both sides –and can access both sets of their friends.

Penny always sat in the back. Jack always sat in the front. I always sat in the middle. At the front-most lab table, Jack and Penny are sitting together like the best of friends, and Francis is joining them.

"What's this about?" I take the seat that I can only assume is meant for me, and a ruckus starts in the back the instant my ass hits the plastic.

"Fucking traitor!"

"Asshole townies are stealing our people!"

"Gillette always thought he was better than us!"

"You can keep Warren," Duane shouts from the table opposite us, "But we've always had Wynn."

Bren makes a spooky face. "They stole me too. It's so much fun here. We have cable."

I go to cover my mouth to keep my laugh contained but end up covering my eyes instead. "You idiots are playing with fire. They will seriously fuck you up."

"We stole one of your girls too!" Duane reaches over to grab Penny's arm. "But then again, you gave her away when you wouldn't let her sit in her usual seat."

"What?" I jump up, flipping around to face my people. "Is this shit true? Is that why Penny's up here?"

"If the bitch wants to live in town, then the bitch ain't allowed to sit back here no more. Them's the rules." Danny Macomb is surrounded by a group of kids who are trying to blend into the background by being quiet, because we are all sick of this shit.

In little school, we were all friends. Then the stories our papaws, daddies, uncles, and brothers passed on to us bred ignorance. We went from friends to feeling pressured into hating one another because our elders said so. But most of this school hates these unwritten rules, and would just like to hang out with the friends we made in kindergarten.

"Rules change," I declare, and then sit down. I ignore the hushed whispers and nasty slurs that are tossed Penny's and my way. "I'm sorry." I reach out to tug Penny under my arm. "I knew this was going to happen. I just wasn't prepared."

Mrs. Kerry just looks up from her desk, waiting everyone out. The teachers know better than to get in the middle. This bullshit dies down rather quickly, but always rekindles off school grounds.

"Well," Penny snuggles into me for a second, and then pulls away. "I always wanted to know what the view looked like from up here." She looks around while wiggling in her seat. "Pretty spiffy. I feel smarter already."

"Oh, shush!" Francis puts his palm in Penny's face. "I don't give two flips about Townie/Hillbilly politics. I just want to know what put that color in Wynn's cheeks. Our boy looks positively flushed."

"Yeah, Wynn." Bren leans over from his lab station. "Why were you late? But better yet, who the hell were you with?"

"No comment." I manage to hold a straight face for all of five second, but then my grin spreads far and wide.

Eyes going wide, "Holy shit!" Jack thumps me on the back. "Holy fucking shit! Who?"

"Don't get too excited," I mutter. But then I bend forward to hide my face in my hands. "It's nothing. It's not what you think."

"Fuck too, it ain't!" Penny tugs at my hand, trying to decipher my expression, so I press my face to the tabletop to cool off.

"What's up?" Duane pipes in. "I don't get what the big deal is."

"Wynn?" Jack whispers in my ear. "Are you okay?"

"Fine!" I squeak out. "Can we please change the subject? Maybe actually do our lab? Some of us have to keep up their grade-point-average or they lose their funding."

"Look at that blush creeping up the back of his neck," Francis purrs salaciously. "Yum!"

"It was YouPorn, wasn't it?" Bren manages to get everyone off my ass by cracking us up. "I knew that would be the cure. Porn cures all wounds."

"That's time, douchebag," Penny grumbles. "Even I know that. Time heals all wounds."

"But porn is quicker," Bren banters back.

I walk home after practice, bogged down with a handful of bags filled with little kid clothes from the thrift shop– pants. I got lots and lots of pants. I also found Penny a really nice mirror to hang on her bedroom wall for a few extra bucks. I want to feel guilty for treating myself by buying an oscillating fan, but my room is hotter than Hades. Properly built and insulated houses retain heat, I've found out the hard way. I was used to the constant breeze blowing through the knotty, rotten wall boards in Gillette Holler.

When I thought I couldn't afford a better way of life, I was looking at the few dollars I managed to save every week. I never took into account that I wouldn't be supporting my parents' habits or well-being. These past few days, I've saved at least fifty bucks on gasoline. I don't have to drive fifteen minutes each way every single day to get to town. I just walk everywhere I need to go. Plus, the lack of wear and tear on my ancient truck means I won't have to buy replacement parts so often. I know Royce is lying about the price of rent, and he's still paying me way too much for so little work, but it feels good. I don't feel like a charity case.

Pride.

I tuck my purchases on the porch, wanting to surprise the kids after they've helped with chores and finished the phony homework assignments I come up with on the fly. I can hear Penny, Hayley, and Hayden chatting inside the house, but they aren't what greets me first. Our porch has some new additions.

Sitting on my porch is a green, metal lawn chair that's older than my daddy. It's covered with a thick floral cushion, with a sticky note attached to its armrest: **Keep your ass comfy while you work, ensuring you'll work longer**.

Next to the chair is a newer metal table with a sticky note stuck in the center of the glass top: **Keep your shit in order and off the floor**.

A wooden crate is hiding beneath the table, out of foot traffic. It's filled with tools, paint brushes, cleaning rags, a wooden block, and a couple of packs of assorted grit sandpaper: **If you don't know what this shit's for, then I don't know what we've been doing these past few years**.

Off to the side is an old-fashioned rocking chair. I already know it's my next project since it's covered with three sticky notes stapled together in a long list: **Sand me. Do I look sanded enough? Yes? Sand me some more. Do I look perfect yet? Your vision sucks, Wynn. Put some elbow grease into it. I want to look like I did when I was first crafted. Now wash me– wash me until I'm slippery under your fingertips. Dry me like you own me, sugar. Sand me again, ya lazy hillbilly. More of that rinse/repeat action. Time to make me shine– you know where to look.**

Chuckling to myself, my eyes land on a can of clear-coat hiding next to the chair. The can lid is covered in half a dozen sticky notes: **I ain't no fool! You think I'm a fool, Wynn? Sand me again, buddy. That wasn't good enough. I said I wanted to look freshly crafted, remember? Rinse/repeat. Take the brush and dip it in the honey. Oh, yeah! (I'm not the Kool-Aid man!) Brush me real slow, make it feel real good. Let me dry. Let me dry even longer. No, sit yer ass back down and wait. I'm not ready yet. Now I am. I wanna be roughed up again. Rough me up, Wynn. Run that block of wood covered in extra-fine-grit sandpaper along all my curves, and then caress me with a rag. Now slick me back up again and wait until I'm dry. I'm ready to leave now. Our date has become very disturbing, and I wanna go home to my daddy. Pick me up. You know I like your big hands under my arms. Carry me across town to my daddy's porch. He wants me facing the road, so we can people-watch together. Ya know, sit there a-rocking, waiting for friendly callers to come a-knocking.**

Royce's perverted humor is genetic. It's where Bren got his douchebaggery. Feeling warm inside, I chuckle for a few minutes as I gaze at the task Royce wants me to perform. Before now, what's turned into a hobby was for survival. I love refinishing furniture and building it from scratch. It's rewarding and useful.

I'm shaking my head, still chuckling, when I turn for the door. I need to start my homework and bicker with Penny over who's going to cook supper tonight. Out of the corner of my eye, I see a little dog walking its owner down the sidewalk, and my body lights on fire.

"Evening," I mutter as I duck in the front door, trying my damnedest to hide my blush.

"Evening," Kaden's voice follows me into the kitchen. "Tell Penny they walk kids on leashes at amusement parks."

That has my face whipping to the side. "No shit?" Kade's rich laughter lingers in place as he continues walking his ankle-high dog down the street.

Face boiling from a flush, I'm relieved to see Penny standing at the stove cooking while the kids sit at the kitchen table with their Crayolas. I try to creep past as quiet as a church mouse so she doesn't see me.

Penny slaps the dishrag against the counter when she catches sight of me, causing my steps to falter. "Jesus Christ! What's gotten into you today? Your face is redder than Saturn."

"Saturn is the planet with the rings," I correct her, hoping to go cool off in the bathroom. "You're thinking of Mars."

"No, I'm pretty sure it's Saturn," she mumbles as she turns back to the stove.

"Yeah, sure." I smother a laugh. "What's for supper?"

"I don't rightly know." Penny's voice is faint as she stares down into the pot she's stirring. "I'm not much of a cook."

I come up behind her, curious now. "Hopefully it's edible," I say as I peek over her shoulder. "Why is it gray? Are there any foods that are naturally gray?"

Penny turns abruptly, glaring at me. "Quit distracting me. What has you so flushed?"

"It is eighty degrees in the shade today, ya know?" I back up slowly until the table bumps my hip. I sit down in Penny's seat, and turn to the kids. "How about we play Uncle Wynn's homework while Aunt Penny stirs the gray *food*?"

I pull my backpack off my shoulder, unzip the top, and start piling my books on the table. Hayden grabs for anything dealing with English class, while Hayley goes straight for my Government textbook. She likes the pictures.

"Wynn Erastus Gillette," Penny pulls out her momma voice. I think all female creatures are born with one. I heard Hayley wielding it on her brother this very morning. "You got that look– that look your brother always gets when–"

I cut Penny off by babbling nervously. "Well, Warren's my brother. Can't be helped that we look alike. Our little man looks like War too. I don't hear you complaining about our looks, especially since your kids are probably gonna take after us."

"You know what I mean." Penny employs the narrowed stare along with her momma voice. "It's the same look that Warren gets on his face before he starts chasing after me because he's hungry."

"Maybe War just wanted some of your gray food. We should freeze some for when he comes home."

Penny growls like a pissed off kitten. "I did hear you and Jack talking on the porch last night. So I'm a bit confused. I wanna know who's riling you up so much that you're getting all moony-eyed."

"What do you think about this Supreme Court Justice?" I ask Hayley as I turn to today's assignment. "He looks pretty old, doesn't he?"

"He looks smart," flows from Hayley's mouth as she runs a fingertip along the lines of the image. "Judges make the rules, right?"

"Nope. The Legislative Branch makes the rules. The Judicial Branch enforces them."

"I thought old people's minds got feeble," Hayden butts in.

"Wisdom, nephew. We call that wisdom. Feeble is when you don't work your mind or body, so it gets weak. Just like arm muscles." I flex my biceps, popping the muscles out. "If I stop working, they will shrink. If you stop using your mind, it does the same thing. Except with disease– that can't be helped none."

"I want to grow up to be wise," Hayden announces as he tugs my textbook closer in front of him. "I like the looks of this man. He does look smart."

"Are girls allowed to make the rules?" Hayley tries to yank the textbook away from her brother, but he's not having it. Hayley hops her chair closer to him, so she can see the book better. "I wanna make the rules. Hayden can enforce 'em. But I wanna be in charge."

The twins and I continue on this path as I do my homework, with Penny in the background slamming pots and pans. "Are men born with the ability to shut their ears to a woman?"

That warm feeling in my heart is radiating with the force of the Sun. I start chuckling. "Yeah, it's our only defense against a woman's momma voice."

"Shush now, and eat your… plate of gray." Penny sets our plates on the table, and then nudges my books to the side. "I'm sure it's tasty."

I swallow thickly as I stare down at the viscous mass glued to my plate. "Do we have any pepper?"

Penny growls, "No," while never taking her eyes off of me.

"Kids, did you know kings and queens employ royal food testers to see if they've been poisoned?" I stick my fork into the funky-textured *food.* "We might be getting a dog... and some pepper." I choke down a bite, holding back a shudder as my taste buds revolt.

Everyone digs in after I swallow.

I down half a glass of water, trying to flush away how it coats my tongue. It's surprisingly tasteless. I'm not sure how Penny accomplished that feat.

"Royce has been in contact with Warren," Penny begins, and I forget all about eating. "I guess he found 'em an hour or so after you called him Friday night. He told me at breakfast on Saturday, but I wasn't to tell you until now. He feared you'd be upset and not settle in well."

"Explain," I say calmly because I'm afraid I will bark out the order instead.

"Willa..." Penny looks at the kids to make sure they don't understand. "Was in bad shape, Wynn. Warren confided in me about it every day. That, and he was always worried about you. Rightfully so. He took off thinking a change of scenery would help, but Royce caught up with 'em and managed to make it back before you showed up at his front door the next morning."

I set my fork down, food long forgotten. "I don't understand."

"Warren took Willa to a..." Penny glances at the kids again, and my heart starts beating into hyper-drive. "To a facility. He used the fact that he was the eldest brother, saying she wasn't able to think for herself. Royce paid for it, of course. Warren's staying in the facility's family housing while Willa gets better– something to do with family sessions with the doctor, and how Willa won't say what's ailing her. It's gonna be a long while before they come back."

"How long?" I still, terrified of the answer.

"Around three months, I suspect. It's what Warren was hoping to do once you got a good job. He didn't want to tax anyone that wasn't family on Willa's account. But Royce is very persuasive, saying the longer we waited, the worse it would get."

"Drugs? Like rehab?" I snort, thinking of my daddy and momma. "I've never drank a drop, puffed a smoke, or taken a hit, knowing I'd be hooked from the get-go."

"Partly drugs." Penny takes a deep breath, then turns to the side to hide her face from me. She pats her eyes dry with a paper towel. "Mostly mental, though."

"Jesus H. Christ!" I hop to my feet. "I'm sorry. I... I... I need to take a walk and think. I'll be back." I kiss a set of brown curls and a copper, and then stride out the door.

"Royce!" I holler the instant my feet touch his front yard. "They're my family. How dare you keep this from me?"

Raising from his crouch at the side yard garden, "Well, hold up now," Royce mutters calmly, hands raised out in front of him. "We'll get this settled, but it has to be civilized. I don't know what you're going on about."

I stand over the man I've come to respect over the past few years with my hands curling into fists and tears threatening to fall. "They're my family, and I'm a grown man. It's none of your concern. It should be me taking care of 'em."

"Now, you listen here, Wynn Gillette, and you listen good." Royce rises to his full height, still inches shorter than me. What he lacks in height, he makes up in bulk. Royce feels huge and commanding, even when I'm looking down at him.

Meaty palms land directly in the center of my chest, push hard, and then I find myself flat on my ass, staring up at Royce. "That's better." Apparently he didn't like looking up at me while we *talk*.

"You're a goddamned kid. Ten years from now, I'll still see you as a kid. You and Bren are only a few weeks apart in age. Do you honestly think I'm going to allow you to deal with adult bullshit while you're still a junior in high school?"

My eyes slip shut as my heart breaks. "You don't think I can do it?"

"Knock that pride horseshit off, Wynn." Royce kneels beside me, still hovering over me. "It has nothing to do with whether or not you can do it. It's that I think you shouldn't have to. Someone should be looking out for you for once. I see you as my son, and I'm going to treat you that way. I want to show you how the world works, teach you to handle it, and then watch you try to deal with it on your own. No matter what, I'm gonna be behind you, waiting to hold you up should you fall."

"You're too good of a person." I glance away, feeling there are people out there that need Royce's help more. "I don't deserve it."

"You might not be my son by blood. But, by George, you sure do act just like me." Royce reaches out to help me sit up. "Warren told me what you did to yourself on Friday night. Which is why someone your age shouldn't have to deal with this shit."

Wincing, I look away from him. "I'm sick about it. Sick down to my marrow."

"Everything is going to be okay as long as you let the adults take care of the heavy lifting. When you're my age, you can take over so I can retire." Royce settles down next to me until we're both sitting cross-legged in the yard.

Deflated and exhausted, "The garden looks good," I mutter lamely.

"Don't change the subject, boy." Royce chastises me, but he's grinning from ear to ear as he looks at his large vegetable garden. "Whether by blood or marriage, you and I are kin. We share Hayley and Hayden, and they need both of us. My son doesn't have a momma or siblings. He's lonely. Bren won't tell you this, but he's always been keen on you as his brother. He's nuts about those kids."

I accuse my boss of manipulating me. "Are you trying to make me emotional?"

"No, I'm explaining why I've done what I've done." Royce breathes deeply, and then looks down at his fingers. He starts playing with a blade of grass, as if he's scared I'll rebuff him somehow.

"What happened to Willa is unforgivable. First off, I shouldn't be telling you this, but you ought to know. Your daddy sold Willa to my brother for a few thousand dollars. Donny wanted a wife; he bought a bride. I tried to stop it, and I'll never forgive myself because of it."

My breathing picks up until I'm panting. I clench my teeth along with my fists. I've never felt this violent surge of pure hatred before. It's like if I don't harm something, my skin will burst like overripe fruit. I feel rotten, inside and out.

"It is what it is, Wynn. Your daddy is an asshole. If he was educated, or rich, sober, or had a good job, he'd still be a goddamned asshole. It's just who he is." Royce grips my shoulder, rhythmically trying to calm me. "Bad thing is, though, poverty, ignorance, and addiction changes an asshole into a despicable creature who in all rights should be put down. Just like my brother and his rapist buddy. It's an epidemic in a way. Bitter negativity feeding on itself like cannibals until no one is safe."

"I hated Daddy so much I tried to kill myself. I hated him because he fucked me up to the point that I didn't think I could leave him and keep the guilt from eating me alive. But I loved the kids more than I feared my conscience."

"That's what Warren was hoping, Wynn. Ya know, leaving was more loyal than staying."

"I get that now. That's why I feel sick about what I almost did."

"A man needs an education, and I don't mean college. He needs to learn a trade, get a job, and provide for a family. I don't mean a nuclear family, either– a family could just be yourself and your friends. It's giving back what you take from this world. It's ingrained in our DNA. We have to have a reason to live. Goals, or whatnot. We have to see those goals realized. If a man sits around doing nothing but being negative, and he doesn't have the brains in his head to figure out how to fix his problems instead of drowning in them, then he's going to be a hate-filled sonofabitch who is toxic to all those he touches."

"Momma?"

"Your momma, too. Wynn, she ain't no good either. There's being abused, and then there is being a victim. She sat around and let you kids be abused, then she auctioned your sister off to the highest bidder. Your momma did that, not your daddy."

"That night will haunt me for the rest of my life– Willa's screams."

"Yeah… Well, I'm sorry you had to see that." Royce's eyes glaze over and his face pales. "I have a nightmare about your sister I revisit myself every time I close my eyes."

"I miss Willa." My lips quirk up at the corners. "I ain't seen the girl she was since I was a little fella. Penny reminds me of who Willa used to be. It's why Warren took a shine to her, I suspect."

"Willa's still a baby, Wynn. She's only twenty-two years old. She's got a lot of living ahead of her, and I'm gonna force her to live it." Royce pauses, looking decidedly uncomfortable. "When she comes back from treatment, she's moving in here."

Shocked, "What?" tumbles past my numb lips.

"So are the kids, *and* so are you," Royce stresses.

"I don't see why I have to move in here," I argue, feeling flustered, betrayed, stifled, and a billion other emotions I can't name. I move to stand up, but Royce reaches over and shoves my ass back to the ground.

"Hayley and Hayden need a constant in their lives. You've been that for the past four of their six years. Willa will need as much support as possible, and she won't stay here without you."

I roll Royce's words around in my mind, deciding whether or not that is true. Willa is very anxious. If you move too fast, she flinches and curls into herself. If anyone needs something familiar, it's my sister. I just never thought I'd be the one who provides her with that comfort.

"After you finish up college, and get the career you want, you can move wherever the heck you want. Until then, you need a real dad just as much as the twins, and I'm gonna be that for you. We could have a real family without assholes, addiction, and negativity."

"Royce–"

"You don't get a vote, son, because you're still a kid." Royce squeezes my shoulder. Hard. "Same as Bren is still a kid. Hell, you're parenting Penny, and she's almost a year older than you."

"Penny needs someone to keep an eye on her. She's a menace," I mutter with affection.

"Which is why you're not living here just yet. You're showing the girl how life should be. When the time comes, Warren and Penny will be staying in the house you're living in now. After I give them the tools to do it, they're gonna carve out a life for themselves. They both gotta have jobs, and goals, and a reason to live, so that their babies will have a bright future with happy parents."

"You're too good," I repeat.

"I ain't, not really." Royce shifts in the grass as if he's uncomfortable. "I might have ulterior motives."

"Oh, yeah?" I challenge Royce to answer me for some reason, even knowing he doesn't want to. "What are they?"

"I'm lonely, too," he admits brusquely, and then clears his throat. "I want my son to have a big family– the family I couldn't give him with his momma –but I want it for me more. I've spent a lot of lonely nights with a lot of blood money. Money is no replacement for the living, breathing person who made my heart beat. I only feel better when I improve the situations of the people of Rusty Knob who deserve so much more."

"I actually understand that." I smile even though I feel as sad as I do happy. "Doing good makes me feel warm. Doing bad makes me feel sick. Doing nothing makes me feel dead inside. The rest of the time, I just feel alone in this world."

"See? You and I are a lot alike, son." Royce wraps his hand around the back of my neck and pulls until my cheek rests on his broad chest. "Now, you're gonna stop stomping down sidewalks, being angry about shit you don't understand. You're going to do your homework, go to school, show Penny how to behave, and keep an eye on our niece and nephew. Then, when you've got a spare minute, you're gonna refinish Willa's rocking chair."

"Christ," I croak, and then I burst out crying. Body quaking with violent sobs, my fingers twist in the fabric covering his chest. Like a dad should, Royce holds me together while I threaten to shatter apart.

I don't know, maybe a part of growing up is dealing with the fact that everything is fleeting. They say home is where the heart is, but they aren't speaking of a physical sense of home. That *home* is the warmth I feel. But to those who live in poverty, home is a physical place, and we know there are never any guarantees you'll keep it.

While I was in Gillette Holler, it felt as if I owned it. It was my daddy's land, his home, his bills, and his mess. Yet I felt a proprietary claim, even though I was just a kid.

Here, in Royce's rental house, I feel out of place, like I didn't earn it. In a way, though, it's no different. Royce is just a better version of the father I always longed to have. Yet I feel guilt over sleeping in these four walls covered with a stable roof while eating food someone else gave me.

My daddy saw me as an obligation– another mouth to feed until I was old enough to feed myself, and feed him while I was at it. To Royce, I'm not an obligation but a gift. He wants to feed and house me to make me strong. He's not doing it so I can take care of him in the future, but so I can take care of myself and those who need me.

My daddy taught me I could be the king of Gillette Holler once he was gone. But he was going to be belligerent and jealous until then, tainting how I'd see my future sons as competition. Royce is teaching me I can be anything I want to be, and he'll want nothing in return but my respect.

One view is a narrow slice of life. The other is so wide, it's humbling.

Knowing this, as I lie on the cot I bought with my own money, listening to the fan I also bought with my own money, while in another man's house, I promise to be patient.

I'm seventeen years old. I *am* still a kid. I'm not allowed to have legal custody of my niece and nephew. They would have been taken away from me sooner rather than later if I hadn't left Gillette Holler with them. Social services won't step foot into the hollers, but they can take the kids from the elementary school with ease. Kaden wasn't trying to insult me last Friday night. He was warning me that they were coming for the kids, and he was disappointed I wasn't doing a dang thing about it.

I know how it goes. I was removed from my parents' care on three occasions. Once because a teacher got into trouble for washing my hair in the drinking fountain on picture day. Mrs. Elroy meant well, but the school board caught wind. In the end, Mrs. Elroy was suspended for a semester, and Warren, Willa, and I were taken from my parents for a few hours, and then delivered back into hell.

Times changes, laws get more stringent, families corrode, and the twins wouldn't have been returned to Gillette Holler.

I know Royce is humoring me with the kids, knowing Warren is his only opposition. We all have the same tie to the twins– uncle. I'm powerless right now. I'm not even old enough to own property, or vote, or get married.

But someday... I will be old enough. Someday, I'll give more than I received. Someday, I'll grow up to be somebody's Royce Kennedy.

With great patience, because today isn't someday, I open *my* laptop. Royce bought it, and he's never going to make me pay for it. He did so to get that warm feeling– his only defense against the bitter cold of loneliness. I now understand this, and I don't want to take that sensation away from him by putting up a fuss. I appreciate the gift, and I'll never take advantage, which is exactly why Royce *chose* me as someone he'd be proud to call family.

With the back of my wrist, I scrub at my eyes, and then I decide to be a kid for the rest of the night. I have food in my belly, a pillow under my head, and everyone I love is snug in their beds. I allow myself to not feel guilt over taking care of me for a change.

I log into Facebook, quickly scrolling through my feed. I don't have many friends on this account since I don't want anyone to know me. But all fifteen members of **Kentwood Area School District: LGBTQ Community Group** befriended me. Bren and Francis are the only ones from Rusty Knob who use their actual names. The rest are smart enough to use aliases.

Most of the posts on my feed are from chatter in the group, with Bren and Francis commenting, liking, and sharing everything from everywhere like it's their job.

Francis Parker: Is corn really blue? Where do blue corn tortilla chips come from? Is there a slutty ear of corn out there somewhere? Does it tease the male ears of corn but doesn't put out so they turn blue? I shall call this blue corn slut... Jessica.

Bren Kennedy shared a video: Children of the Corn Trailer.

Bren Kennedy shared a link: Blue Corn– Wikipedia, the free encyclopedia.

Bren Kennedy shared a link: Jessica: Urban Dictionary.

I keep scrolling and scrolling through mountains and mountains of inane bullshit from those two idiots before I can find anything from the other thirteen members.

Virginia Duncan: I quit my job today. It just wasn't as fun without my ex-coworker. My boss was a total dickwad anyway. I think he robs from the poor and gives to the drunkards. So, who wants to spot me a twenty?

Bren Kennedy commented on Virginia Duncan's post: Free weights or crunches? I'm an excellent spotter. Go steal a case of beer from the Circle K, and we can split it while we workout. Your ex-boss won't mind. He'll just go hire one of your relatives to pay for it. JK. No, I'm not. Sorry. Not sorry.

Francis Parker posted an image on Virginia Duncan's Timeline: Hans and Franz with a photoshopped Bren in the foreground flashing a twenty dollar bill.

Kentwood Cutie: I sucked another dick today. Nope, still a lesbian. Just thought I'd make sure.

Bren Kennedy commented on Kentwood Cutie's post: Did they pass or fail step #2 in the fag test, sugar? I'ma start a new test for you, where I make cuties suck my schlong, and those who fail I'll send your way. We'll call it the dyke test.

Kentwood Cutie commented on her own post: I'll ignore the slur since I'm sure you meant it affectionately. It's about fucking time you paid it forward, ya selfish prick.

Kent Wood: Seriously, why do we bother with these stupid names? It's three small schools? I see you bastards all the time. It's an easy process of elimination when Bren & Franny only interact with Duncan, Cutie, and Rusty– all from Rusty Knob. It doesn't take a genius when Bren is the Ram's Power Forward, Franny is their score keeper, & 'Cutie' is their cheerleader cocksucktress. Which begs the question, is the Q in our group their Point Guard who's never looked twice at anyone? Is Virginia really a dude? I mean, Duncan is on the Center's jersey. What the fuck is in the water over in Rusty Knob's locker room? Hormones? Then you have dipshit Kathy Emerson from my school sticking like glue to me and Wood Kent. That leaves seven of you lying bastards in Hillock Corners. Why can't we just be real? It's a closed group, and we all have something to lose. –Josh Truman, Hornet Point Guard. Furrow Creek High of Furrow Creek. GAY!

Kentwood Area School District: LGBTQ community Group: How are the kids in my neck of the woods this evening? Hit the group P.M. for a chat since Josh decided to out himself and a bunch of others on FB. This is NOT a suggestion–Mentor KM.

Jesus fuck. Josh's status update blasted out to his entire friends' list. Kent Wood or not, it was set to public. Numb, not sure how I'm feeling, I click the group message.

Mentor KM: Josh, if you were in arm's reach, I'd wrap my hands around your skinny neck and twist until your pea-brained head popped off.

Bren Kennedy: Shit! Mentor is piiiiissssssssseeeeeedddddd.

Mentor KM: Yes, I'm pissed, Bren. This is life or death. Coming out is a personal choice that should never be taken lightly, especially in our area.

Kathy Emerson: Assfuck! I've got three years left in the pustule on the horse's ass called Furrow Creek, West Virginia. I bet you feel real liberated tonight when you only have to suffer this shit for a few more weeks before you graduate and move to Rhode Island. The rest of us are left behind to clean up your fucking mess.

Virginia Duncan: I use this name, not because my family could give two shits about whether or not I want to get head from a girl or a guy, but because we live in the most intolerant state in the country. Remember that gay guy in Hillock Corners who was dragged behind a car? He was in his thirties. We have no way to protect ourselves! My parents know I'm gay, and they want me to stay alive.

Bren Kennedy: Reason I'm so 'out' there with the fag test and fucking girls left and right is because half the people will actually believe I'm bi, and the other half will doubt it. It was the best defense. I don't care if word spreads about me because I've already confused the fuck out of them. But my friends… if anything happens to them, I'm chartering a bus to Rhode Island, motherfucker. Don't doubt me. I've got 74,000,000 from the Ford Motor Company, a sawed-off, hillbilly blood, and I won't go to jail. Fuck you very much, Josh!

Francis Parker: I'm not as gay as I look and act because Bren and I devised a plan to keep us both safe. He confuses them, and I become so queer they avoid me like the plague. I'd love to live in a world where that wasn't the case, but we aren't there yet. In less isolated areas, sure. But we don't live there, do we? I'd like to live long enough to actually go to Berkeley. I'm not a flamboyant silly boy. I am a human being, and I'd appreciate some goddamned respect!

Kentwood Cutie: Is the irony lost on anyone else? We came to this group because we felt so alone in our schools surrounded by hate-filled slurs and ignorance. We developed a sense of community that I looked forward to every single night. It got me through the rough times when all I see ahead of me is two more years of high school, and then a life in Rusty Knob. I am the only lesbian in Rusty Knob, at least the only one we've been able to find. Maybe I ought to visit Furrow Creek more often. The irony is that one of our own betrayed us in the name of feeling free, but all that accomplished was to take our freedom of privacy away.

Mentor KM: I vetted each and every single one of you before I allowed you in this group. Phony names or not, I know who you are. I grew up in one of your towns, went to the same school, dealt with the same pressures, and it wasn't that long ago. At one point, I contemplated suicide. I didn't see my life changing. When I got accepted to college, moved away from town, I found a WHOLE WIDE WORLD OF DIFFERENT. Every shape and shade of different, and I finally fit in. I came back home to give you kids, and the kids that follow you, HOPE! Don't shit on my dreams by throwing spiteful temper tantrums.

Bren Kennedy: I knew I liked you, Mentor KM. Well, you know I love you like a brother, but that's beside the point. I think you're a great guy, too.

Mentor KM: Thank you, Bren. I appreciate that.

Bren Kennedy: You're not going to say it back? … …. …

Mentor KM: Clearly I put up with you, so there is that. I love you, too. Now knock it the fuck off and shut up.

Virginia Duncan: Kennedy? You're holding out on us! You KNOW Mentor KM!

Mentor KM: No comment on that… So, let's talk about some positives. 1: the post was removed. 2: It was up for 12 minutes. 3: It was a dummy account, so not that many saw it. 4: the ones who would retaliate most likely weren't on FB at the time, or they don't have access to internet outside of school hours. 5: Josh is in FB timeout for being a prick. 6: Anything good happen today? Seriously, hit me with something inspiring.

Wood Kent: I'm sorry my brother is an asshole. I'm Libby Truman, btw. I'm another Q. Jessica– I mean Kentwood Cutie – Hillock Corners is a bunch of cowards ghosting in here but never putting in their two cents. But 3 of the 7 are lesbians… so it's your lucky day. YAY!

Francis Parker: Now that is awe inspiring, & my odds of getting laid just diminished.

Bren Kennedy: Rusty West got aroused today… so he might not be questioning anymore. Don't know by who, but he was rocking the blush.

Rusty West: WAS NOT!

Bren Kennedy: Fucking creeper. I thought you were sleeping. Dad said you were exhausted. & you SO did. You were still sporting wood with that flush in Field Bio.

Rusty West: Shit, was I?

Francis Parker: Uh, yeah! It looked good on you, too. So, who's the lucky fuck?

Kathy Emerson: Maybe Rusty doesn't belong here anymore.

Kentwood Cutie: Only if it was a girl. Who are we to judge? Even if Rusty is straight, he earned his right to stay in the group.

Virginia Duncan: I know who. He's been popping chub around this person since September. He doesn't even realize it.

Rusty West: Have NOT! NOT! NOT!

Virginia Duncan: Shout caps? Really? Dude, I'm your best friend. When this person came into the Circle K, you popped chub, without fail. Completely oblivious. You've been blessed, and I felt sick for enjoying the view.

Bren Kennedy: Who?

Francis Parker: For the love of all that is… evil. Answer the question!

Mentor KM: Who?

Wood Kent: Shit, even Mentor wants to know. Shit just got real!

Mentor KM: WHO?!?

Rusty West: How do you know if you want someone? If what Duncan says is true, I don't feel it. It's not the same urgency as getting antsy so you jerk off in the shower. I don't get it.

Virginia Duncan: He really has no clue. It's like it doesn't register or something.

Bren Kennedy: I've been keeping an eye on this, and I think it's because he has to feel more for the person. He's too nice. He'd probably feel guilty for wanting someone. This person he doesn't realize he's getting off on, probably should give 'Rusty' permission to want him/her. WHO THE FUCK IS IT, DUNCAN???

Virginia Duncan: What are you gonna give me for the answer?

Bren Kennedy: Whatever you want, sugar.

Mentor KM: The mind is very complex. I took a lot of courses on human sexuality. I think Bren is onto something here. There is chemistry. There is friendship. Lastly, there is love. Sometimes chemistry blooms to friendship, which translates to love. Sometimes friendship can turn to chemistry, and translate to love. Often times, chemistry fades and friends gravitate apart. I've felt chemistry. I have friends. But I will only have sex with someone I love. There are people who need trust and intimacy to let go enough to feel pleasure. I'm one of them. Maybe Rusty is like me, too. Maybe he's so skittish, he can't feel chemistry. I know he has many friends.

Francis Parker: deep… I have friends. I've never felt anything else. Maybe that's what has you confused– fuck it– Wynn, I've never wanted anyone at Rusty Knob. I've never looked at them and just wanted them. I like looking at you and teasing you because you're so pretty and big, and you don't get pissed at me. I know when I get to Berkeley my world will open up, so I've never felt sad about it. I get that you're different because you don't recognize when someone arouses you, so you can't put a label on it. Wynn, you aren't a label.

Mentor KM: Labels make us feel safe. Labels group us together so we don't feel lonely. But you're right. Labels create a divide, like it's them vs us. It's why the minority groups feel so isolated, because they don't hold the seat of power. We need to remove labels unless it's used as a descriptor, and with that goes the fear and power.

Virginia Duncan: Forget labels. Don't stress over whether or not someone makes you hard. This person (and we both know who I'm talking about) do you want to hang out with them? I don't mean how you want to sit around and do nothing with me or Bren. Do you want to keep talking to them? Do you think about them all the time? Do you blush like a fucking lunatic just because you heard their voice? Because, Wynn, if you do, that's your answer.

Bren Kennedy: Wynn, you need to stop stressing. You made me cry, bro. Like seriously fucking cry– blowing snot and everything. What you did Friday night, it made me hate you a little bit. I idolize you, and you go and do something so fucking stupid… My mom died. We didn't want her to die. But her death saved countless lives. Yours would have been for nothing. It made me sick. You made Dad sob. You made him break a door when he punched it. You need to get your shit straight, bro. I'm your friend, your family, and I love you. Your loss would have killed this town. I would have blown you myself if it meant you'd figure your shit out. Jesse has tried many times.

Mentor KM: BREN! Stop ignoring me. ANSWER OUR P.M. NOW!

Rusty West: I feel sick with myself. I didn't mean it.

Virginia Duncan: What if you didn't have Warren? It wouldn't have mattered that you didn't mean it. You'd still be dead, and we'd be planning a funeral right now. Your family would have been broken more than it already is. It would have solved nothing.

Rusty West: I've come to terms with why I did it.

Bren Kennedy: Sorry, bro… don't hate me.

Rusty West: What? Why? What the hell? Someone's knocking on my front door.

Bren Kennedy: News flash! HOLY FUCKING SHITBALLS OF FIRE! Mentor KM lives in Rusty Knob!

Running through my living room, I weave around the furniture. My front door is reverberating with forceful pounds, causing me to hurry and nearly upend over the coffee table. Whoever it is, is hitting the door with the side of their fist, and they're going to wake Penny and the kids.

"What the hell?" I quickly unlock the door, and then twist the knob, realizing too late I probably should have checked to see who was pounding. "What's so urgent? It's after midnight."

"What did you try to do?" Low and cold, I recognize the voice before I take note of the fist gripping my throat. Kaden does to me what Mentor KM promised Josh– wrapping his meaty fist around my throat and squeezing. "You are so fucking stupid. Goddamn you!"

"Shit!" A grunt is forced from my chest when I'm slammed against the outside wall of my house. The back of my head hits siding, and then my feet are being dragged off the ground until Kaden and I are eye to eye. I freeze, scared yet exhilarated, while Kaden glares at me with his nostrils flaring.

I jerk around, arms pushing off his shoulder, while trying to place my feet on the ground. Kaden releases his grip on my throat, only to capture both of my hands. Fingers braceleting my wrists, he presses our hands above my head.

"Why?" flutters across my lips. "Why?"

"Why did you try to kill yourself? I know you're Mentor KM, because nothing is that coincidental."

My question throws Kade off, so he starts babbling. "I'm a teacher– mentor –and it's my initials. It's not that big of a stretch. It's more obvious than all of your classmates' aliases. I have to hold myself apart from the students. If some bigoted father found out his kid was in my group, he'd say I turned his kid into a fag, or that I was trolling for my next fuck. That's how this sick shit always plays out. So I use Mentor KM. But I figure bigots are fucking idiots in the first place."

"Why did you try to kill yourself?" I repeat, hating how disappointed in myself Kade makes me feel. Like I haven't murdered myself in my head repeatedly over the past few days for the stupid bullshit I pulled. Like it didn't cure me from ever doing it again. Like I'd never wish the destructive thoughts that were going through my mind at the time I tried to kill myself on anyone, even my worst enemy.

"You first," Kade snarls, all vestiges of the friendly elementary school teacher vanish.

"You know that movie Sliding Doors? Where if you take one path, this happens? But if you take the other, something else happens?" I'm calm in the face of Kade's rage, finally able to put words to my emotions. "Well, I was unable to see another path before me. I saw an empty expanse of misery, and I wanted to end it once and for all. Somehow, I ended up ending one path and starting one I didn't even know existed. For that, I am eternally grateful."

Kaden's facial expression softens. Instead of smashing me to the wall, he leans into me, using his weight to hold me in place. "We have that in common. I don't need to explain the details to you, but it was the same shit with me. My life was similar. My grandfather was an abusive drunk, but my father was like you. Calm and passive. Good. My life took a horrific turn when my father died and my grandfather took custody of me."

I murmur, "I'm sorry." I want to reach out and comfort Kade, but he's holding my hands above my head, using his body as a fulcrum point. I'm rendered immobile, but a twisted part of me likes it– is comforted by it.

"Bren didn't know the details. He just said you tried to kill yourself. I'm asking for details now. But before you hem and haw, saying you want mine in return, know I tried to kill myself when I was sixteen. I'm no longer a danger to myself. But you pulled this shit four days ago. It might feel like a lifetime to you with all the changes, but it was only a heartbeat for me. Spill."

"I…" My eyes slip shut.

Raw.

Exposed.

Ashamed.

Kade presses deeper into me: Forehead resting on mine. Nose pressing against mine. Mouth a hairsbreadth from connecting with mine. He breathes, "How?" directly into my mouth– hot and moist.

"I was sitting in my truck after you handed me my ass at the Circle K. I just… I'd got yet another empty paycheck. I worked another week to fuel my daddy's addiction. I was the one killing him, no different than if I pointed a gun at his forehead and pulled the trigger."

"You're the first enabler I've ever heard who actually gets it." Kade brushes my forehead with his, moving my hair away from my eyes so he can see me. "I have been so pissed at you since I came home. I just wanted to shake you and scream, '*Knock it the fuck off, Wynn!*' But I knew you weren't ready to listen."

"I get that." I release a self-deprecating laugh. "I was sitting in my truck, staring at the shit world I lived in, looking at my daddy drink himself to death and my momma smoke herself into an early grave. I knew I'd be the one taking care of them at the expense of myself. I was destined to be an active participant in their deaths, no different than an assisted suicide by funding their addictions. I couldn't live that way, and I couldn't see another way of life. My eyes were squeezed shut to the possibilities."

"You can only help those who are willing to help themselves for a reason, Wynn. That help isn't monetary. It's education. You teach someone how to take care of themselves so they can show others in turn. To spend all that time and energy, and most often money, you're taking it away from someone who truly needs help. Some people aren't fixable because they like how miserable they are– they thrive in it. For you to attempt suicide over people who are truly worthless, means you were taking away all the good *you* could have done in this world."

"I know that *now*," I whine, voice breaking. "I get it, okay?"

"It's not okay." Kade's voice is stiff with anger yet filled with compassion. "But it will be eventually."

"You asked me, why did you *attempt* to commit suicide? What you don't understand is, I *did* kill myself. The person I was is dead– the way I saw the world around me. It wasn't a matter of not taking enough drugs or not slicing deep enough. I did the irreparable. I put the barrel underneath my chin, and then I pulled the trigger. When it didn't go off, it was a conscious decision on my part to pull it again. Then I did it a third time just to be sure."

"Wynn. No…" Kaden's hands unlock from around my wrists, where they begin fluttering around my face, like he's envisioning the nightmares I've had whenever my eyes are closed or open.

I would have turned my head into liquid. A shotgun beneath the chin would have blown my brains out of my skull and exploded my face. I've admitted this to no one, but I haven't kept any food down since. The vision pops into my head at random, and it makes me physically sick.

I almost didn't see Saturday's dawn.

"That wasn't an attempt. I did it. I fucking did it three times. I can't use the excuse that Warren removed my ammo, because I didn't know that." The words start pouring out of me, quicker and quicker. "I did it. I feel sick about it. I can't change it. Goddamn it, I wish I could change it. I didn't even kill myself, and I regret. If I had…"

"Shh… it's gonna be okay. I promise." Kaden envelopes me in his arms, rocking me back and forth. For the second time in less than twelve hours, I break down sobbing. I fear I'm going to be doing this with great frequency. I melt into Kade, comforted by that fact that he's bigger than me. Kaden can hold me up and protect me from myself.

"It's like my life sped up to when I'm actually going to die, and it's been playing all the moments from that point to when I tried to kill myself, but only in reverse. It's showing me what I would have missed if Warren hadn't been on Wynn suicide watch."

"What's it showing you?" Kade rasps in my ear. "What would you have missed?"

"Just stupid shit that makes me feel warm inside, yet makes me ache thinking I would have missed it. Like someday Willa will be herself again. Penny and Warren will get hitched, and they're going to have a billion kids and grandkids who will go nuts when I visit. Hayden is going to grow up to tell his wife she can't wear pants, but she's going to wear the pants in the household. Hayley is going to be a lawyer because she's a know-it-all, but underneath her suit she'll be covered in tattoos and piercings. It's going to take Bren forever, but he'll figure out he's already in love. Royce is going to get remarried, and then complain how his kids will be graduating when he's wearing Depends."

Kade's laughter is warm and rich. He curves around me, cupping the nape of my neck in his palm with his fingertips splayed in my hair. "That sounds nice. But what about you? Where are you in all of this?"

"Shit." I whimper, eyelids drooping. An enlivening yet drugging sensation waves over me. I snort in surprise when it finally clicks, but I choose to ignore it. "In these dreamscapes, I'm just an outside observer seeing what I'd miss in my loved ones' futures because they're what's important to me. Obviously I'm not, or I wouldn't have tried to kill myself. But now I realize that if I love them, I'll protect myself because they love me."

"You have no idea," Kaden says as he steps away from me, leaving me feeling bereft. "Look out there," he orders, pointing in the general vicinity of the sidewalk. I gasp in surprise at what comes into focus. "There'd probably be a few kids from Hillock Corners and Furrow Creek on their way here if they knew where you lived."

"Bro…" Bren approaches my porch hesitantly, stopping at the bottom step. "I was worried Mentor KM was going to hurt you because you're a fucking moron."

"So were we," Jessica pipes in, with Francis and Jack as her backup. "When you stopped messaging us, we got worried."

"So we ran out of our houses to investigate," Jack adds, but he's grinning.

"Mystery's solved, yeah?" Francis is wearing a pout. "I'm jealous. I'm going home now." He stomps his way down the sidewalk with his head hanging low.

"What the hell?" I mutter as I watch Francis go.

"Wynn, you're a rockstar. Dayum," Jessica drawls. "You managed to catch Mentor KM."

Sputtering, I make an unintelligible sound of exasperation.

"Oblivious, I tell ya." Jack grabs Jessica's arm. "C'mon, let's go home. We can practice the fag and dyke tests in my bedroom again. Both of us might get off this time."

"Hey!" Bren looks from between me and our friends' retreating backs, torn between talking to me and joining them. "Hey!" He decides sex is more important than friendship and jogs down the sidewalk. He abruptly stops and turns to face us. "Just so ya know, you could pound nails with that thing. That was what they were talking about– your mystery crush revealed. Don't look down, but I think it's contagious. Kade is gonna be hurting soon. Night!"

Confused, all I can do is watch Bren run off. "Assholes, wait up! If you're gonna play, let me join. I'm bi. I can please you both. Jack, I'll give you a blow job instead! You'll like it more. I promise."

"You've never given a blowjob in your life!" Jessica alerts the neighborhood.

"I've had enough of 'em!" Bren shouts. Lights turn on in adjacent houses as he runs down the street. "I can learn! Practice makes perfect. Wait up!"

Of course, I look down, but Kade is twisting out of view. Clearing his throat brusquely, it takes a few tries to get the words out. "Hope Bren doesn't tear a hamstring chasing after them."

"He's probably already in Jack's bedroom, completely naked and stroking his cock. Bren can outrun and out-sex everyone on the team."

"Yes," Kade utters. Then he releases a funny laugh. "Let's remind me how you're only seventeen years old, a high school junior, and I'm now a faculty member. Please remind me of that often. You being my neighbor with no adult supervision, while raising my tiny students, is totally throwing my equilibrium out of whack. Bad Kade. Not an adult."

"What? I don't get it," I murmur, suffering blood loss. "What are you, twenty-two?"

"Twenty-three, actually…" Kade backs up slowly. "And you're off limits." He hops down the steps, and then jogs across the street. When he gets to his porch, he yells, "See ya around the neighborhood!"

Muttering to myself, I lock the front door, and then weave my way through the living room in the dark. "Fucking bizarre. My life is fucking bizarre." By the time I make it to my bedroom, my hand is already jammed down my pants, taking care of business.

"Life has been kind to you, my brother," Penny's voice startles a shriek out of me.

Tearing my hand out of my pants, I whisper-shout, "What the hell?" I yank my t-shirt down to cover my bulge. "Why are you in my bedroom, sitting on my bed?"

"Yeah, I guess I didn't think that through." Penny bites her bottom lip in indecision. "Your dick is bigger than your brother's."

My hands are already cupping my ears before I can shout, "Shut up!"

"It was a compliment. Warren isn't exactly small, ya know?" I bug my eyes out, pleading with Penny to shut the fuck up.

"What do you want?" I bite out between my gritted teeth. "I'm busy."

"I can see that, Dirk Diggler." Penny gets up from the edge of my bed to walk over to my bedroom door. Finally. "Someone was pounding on our front door. I watched them choke you, slam you against the house, and then yell at you. Then I saw you get all moony-eyed again, so I came in here to wait for you. I was going to ask if you were okay. But, as we've both figured out, I didn't think that through. I forgot how that look translates into sex. I can't unsee you jingling your thingy, but I thought I ought to compliment it."

"Good night, Penny," I groan, humiliated beyond belief. I fall to my cot when she exits to the hallway.

Peeking back into my bedroom, Penny gives me a thumbs up. "Only you would pick the unobtainable. Jesus Christ, Wynn. I'm impressed."

"Go away." I cover my eyes with my forearm. "I want to jerk off while I can still remember the feeling of getting hard because I want to fuck someone other than imaginary friends."

"Have fun!" is followed by a bottle of hand lotion hitting my stomach. Blessedly, my door latches before I die of embarrassment.

In less than two seconds, my cock is slicked up with my fingers gliding up and down it. I've never touched myself in bed– always in the shower. My eyes are closed, and I'm fantasizing about taunting lips, a warm laugh, and a strong body... I learn it doesn't take a shotgun beneath the chin to blow my head clean off.

•LATE SUMMER•

"How's this taste?" Penny shoves a spoon at me, hitting my front tooth. I either open my mouth or risk bodily harm. "It's potato salad," she assures me, as if I couldn't tell by the mayonnaise and potatoes I'm swallowing down my throat.

"Hmm…" I drawl. "Maybe a bit more pepper?" Penny's kitten growl has me chuckling. "Just kidding. It's tasty. Warren will love it."

Penny's smile is brilliant, with her freckles disappearing in the wrinkle at the top of her nose. "You promise?"

"Honest." I tug her ponytail. "The salad is really good." I gesture to the dishes lining every surface in the kitchen. "Everything looks delicious. I'm really proud of you."

She hops on her heels, clapping, and then jumps up to kiss my cheek. "It was that cookbook you gave me. It really helped."

"*It was necessary*," I mouth to Jack, but he doesn't see me because he's sneaking a bit of icing off the icebox cake.

Everything Penny used to make was gray, even when it started out another color. For the life of me, I couldn't figure out how that was possible. When Royce had me rummaging through his storage unit, so I could pass out essentials to those in need, I came upon a huge cookbook. If anyone was in need of a cookbook, it was Penny.

Penny turns pensive, voice breaking a little as she speaks. "I'm gonna miss you, Wynn."

"I'm not going anywhere." I sound flippant, as if I don't care. But it's all an act. I'm scared shitless yet excited. But a bit sad, too. "I'm sure you or Warren will come a-hollering, wanting me to fix this or that. You'll still see me in school every day come next week. It's not like I'm moving across the state or something. I'm two streets over, is all."

"It's just not the same." She pulls me in the billionth hug. I've suffered through this for the past week straight. Every time Penny sets her sights on me, I'm getting embraced. I won't lie; I do enjoy it. Her tiny belly is growing and it presses into my hip, like my new niece or nephew is hugging me too.

"Warren will keep you busy." Jack taunts, and Penny shoos him from the kitchen by snapping his ass with a dish towel. Laughing,

"The ol' boy has gone without for three months," flows from the porch and beyond.

I make my escape. "I'm just gonna see if I forgot anything, and then I'll help ya finish setting up for Warren and Willa's welcome home party."

"The house feels so empty now." Penny's words make my heart ache, but her sniffle breaks it.

I wander from room to room in the small house, making sure nothing important was left behind. For the past three months, we've been slowly filling up the spaces with more belongings than I've ever owned in my lifetime. Most of the furnishings were things I found at the flea market, thrift shops, online yard sales, and actual yard sales. I get a lot of pride out of refinishing something, turning it into what it was meant to become.

A refinished piece of furniture is a bit like me. The old Wynn lived in Gillette Holler with his eyes squeezed shut to the truth. The new Wynn will be starting senior year on Monday, will be living in a household filled with people who love him, and has a future to look forward to living. It won't be easy, but nothing a bit of sandpaper and a fresh coat of paint now and again can't fix.

I didn't take much with me when I moved my stuff to Royce's house this morning, because I wanted Penny and Warren to enjoy everything I left behind. My old bedroom still has my cot and dresser, just in case someone needs to crash for the night or longer– my way of paying it forward.

The twins' bedroom is completely bare, but that's a good thing since the baby will need it. Hayley and Hayden wouldn't have been comfortable going from one bed to another, anyway. It wouldn't be fair when my greatest wish for them is stability. Yesterday I got them situated at Royce's. They enjoyed their sleepover with Bren, not realizing it was permanent. At a few weeks into their seven years, Hayley and Hayden are living where they will stay until they either graduate from high school or college.

I find nothing we truly needed was left behind, and that depresses the piss out of me. Fighting my emotions, I make my way outside. The yard is set up with several folding tables and chairs for the party. Even the god-awful decorations Penny and the kids made don't manage to cheer me up. I'm excited to start this new chapter in my new life, but I'm terrified of what condition my siblings will be in when they arrive. The unknowns are scary when the known I was living was so pleasant and warm.

Bren nearly tackles me, arm hooking around my neck. He bends me at the waist so he can reach to give me a nuggie. "How's my new big bro?" I fling my arms out to stop him, but he's behind me.

"That's kinda creepy." Jack cuts in, saving me from being assaulted. "If Wynn is your new brother, and Willa is his sister, then wouldn't that make Royce the grandpa to Hayley and Hayden? That's some twisted, West Virginia shit. Grandpappy uncle daddy?"

Bren drops me to the ground, annoyed with Jack and taking it out on me. "My dad is only thirty-seven. He isn't elderly by no means. He wants to raise 'em as his kids, dumbass."

Jack reaches down to draw me to my feet. He brushes leaves off my back in apology. "What does that make Willa to him then, huh?"

I chuckle as Bren gets all flustered: red-faced with his hands combing through his short, black hair. "Other than Dad's sister-in-law? I don't rightly know. Dad doesn't talk much about it. He tells me what to do, and I pretend to do it."

"Pretend?" I eyeball Bren. "You're such a bad liar."

"Don't make me look like a pussy in front of Jack." Bren whispers out the side of his mouth toward me, but Jack hears him anyway.

"You don't need Wynn to do that for you." Jack's been playing a hard-to-get asshole, and it's amused me to no end because it confuses the piss out of Bren. "It's obvious when I look at you that you're a daddy's boy."

"Duncan!" Bren is flummoxed, arms waving around erratically as he tries to think up something to say.

"No comeback?" Jack releases an evil, taunting laugh. "I thought so. Wynn doesn't need to make you look like a pussy 'cuz you always smell like one, making me want to puke."

"Ah!" I drawl, enlightened. "I get it now."

Jealousy.

"What'd I do wrong, sugar?" Poor Bren's so confused, he's just looking around for an answer, gazing heavenward for some help from above. Then his eyes bulge from his skull and a huge smile slips across his face.

"Oh, Jesus. Fuck. Not him again." Jack breathes out next to me, but not because he wants our newest arrival. He's sick of my fixation because it's hurting me, while Bren thinks it's hilarious.

My eyes drink in what's causing such a commotion. Kade strolls across the street– all six and a half feet of him. All I want to do is climb him like a tree on a warm summer's day, and then hang off one of his *limbs*.

Kaden is headed right in our direction, and my pulse starts going haywire and my palms sweat. "Thank the Lord I wore a jockstrap today." My boys snort at me when I whimper in pain from my dick's circulation getting cut off. "I wasn't sure if he'd show, so I was being prepared."

I lived through seventeen years of never having anyone trip my trigger, and now I wish I'd revert back to that. If Kaden is in my general vicinity, or if I think about him, my dick turns to granite. This summer he was my across-the-street-neighbor and always starring in my thoughts. I can't remember the last time my dick was soft.

"Hello, my groupies." Kade greets us in a voice as warm, smooth, and intense as whiskey. One sip, and I'm already drunk. "When's Warren getting home?"

Bren's talking back and forth with Kade, but I pay them no mind. I use this as an opportunity to check him out. I'd always wondered what Kaden's hair would look like out of his man-bun. This is the first time Kade has gone out in public with his tight, chocolate brown curls flowing to his shoulders. I reach out in awe, unable to stop myself, and an angry hand swats mine away.

"Leave Mentor KM's pretty hair alone," Jack cautions. "We're in public, remember?"

"Shit," I hiss, snatching my hand away. This past summer I've turned into a crushing girl. I'd sit on my porch just to see Kade walking his dog. It was like a simple hello was currency. The man has shut me down at every possible turn. Not to be deterred, I've had the best summer of my life– just me and my hand.

If Kade would let me finger his hair, I'd go whack off with that hand. I've turned into a sick puppy.

Part of the reason I'm so sad to move is that I can't stalk Kaden anymore. But the highlight is that my crush goes to school with me. In perfect West Virginia fashion, my crush just so happens to teach at the school, not study there.

"Jack? I don't call you Virginia Duncan in public. Please don't call me Mentor KM when we aren't in the group. Okay?" Kade flashes us a humoring smile. "No hard feelings. I just want to make that clear. It's for the same reason you just told Wynn not to touch my hair."

"Understood, Mr. Marx," Jack squeaks out, sounding embarrassed.

"Kade," he stresses. "Only tiny humans call me Mr. Marx. I'm not old *yet*."

"Wynn, get ahold of yourself." Bren hits me upside the head because I'm leaning forward and hanging onto every word coming out of Kade's mouth. "You're looking like a fool."

I blush bright red to the roots of my hair. But, otherwise, I'm rendered dumb, deaf, and mute. I rub my sweaty palms on my jeans, and then shove my hands in my pockets. I just look around, unsure what to do next.

"Well, I better go wrangle up the twins," Bren says in parting, but then he stops when he's a few paces away. "Jack, make sure our boy doesn't do or say anything stupid." His order was actually a way to ensure Jack doesn't leave, I hope.

"I'm not *that* bad," I mutter.

"Wynn, you're pretty obvious." Kade flashes me a huge, shit-eating grin when his words hit my ears. "You're still a kid yet. You'll get over it eventually. When I look back at how I must have looked when I was your age, I want to kick myself in the nuts. I'll never forget the time I had a kid get hard for me, and he screamed like he was dying."

"Fuck," shudders out my lips. I fight the urge to hide my face behind my palms. I'm Wynn Gillette– the only member of my family that has his shit together. If Bren is warning me that I look like an idiot and the guy I'm stalking is saying I'll want to kick myself in the nuts in a few years, then I've got to knock it off.

"I'm gonna go now," Jack announces, but his feet don't move. "I only came over to help Penny set up for the party. I'm not family… so… I'm gonna go."

I reach out to grip my buddy's arm. "Stay. Someone needs to keep Bren in line. Family or not, the last time Warren saw Bren was when he threatened Bren with bodily harm. It's best that we have people here to act as a buffer."

"I feel out of place, but okay." Jack sighs, acting put out. If my crush on Kade is obvious, Jack's obsession with Bren is in-your-face. "I'm going to go see if Penny needs any more help. Later."

I peer down the street, acting like I'm not embarrassed. "I'm actually not standing on the sidewalk just to look like a dolt." I blush brighter. "I'm the welcome wagon. Warren ought to be pulling down the street at any moment."

"Wynn?" Kade leans down a bit to whisper in my ear. "It's fine-- how you feel about me. I'm flattered, and it's not as obvious as you think. Only the kids in the group get it. Everyone else is oblivious."

"Are you sure?" My tone hitches higher. Kade puts me at ease, making me feel comfortable to say anything that comes to my mind. "Because I'm so humiliated right now, I want to hide underneath a rock."

All Kade does in response is release an amused chuckle.

"I know…" I look at my feet, having no shame when it comes to saying whatever comes to mind, but being embarrassed about what I feel. "I know I don't know what I want yet. I'm just figuring it out."

"Exactly," Kade says, reaching over to pat my shoulder. My skin jumps at the contact, but otherwise I try not to react. "I don't mean this as an insult, but you're still a kid. You can't understand something you haven't had any experience with. A few years from now, your uncertainty will be a fleeting thought because you'll know yourself better. So don't beat yourself up over anything."

"I look like an idiot," I mutter. "I mean, I'm this manly looking guy but I'm acting like a chick around you. Penny uses this against me every single day."

"Wynn," Kade laughs my name. His hands curl around my shoulders, and then shake me slightly, forcing me to join him in laughing at myself. "There is nothing about your reaction to me that screams *girl*." Dropping his hands, Kade's voice changes, deepening. "It's almost like I can feel the testosterone pouring off of you. Lord knows, I can practically scent it."

My eyes flick up to connect with Kade's, and then widen at what I see staring back at me. A throat clearing has me stumbling back a step like I was caught red-handed.

"Warren's car is approaching," Royce informs me. He wedges himself between Kaden and me, and then folds his arms over his broad chest. He flashes us both a disapproving look that makes up for the silence that surrounds us.

"Nice day, isn't it?" Kade tries to engage Royce in conversation as all three of us stare straight ahead. "Perfect for an outdoor gathering."

Royce looks to the side toward Kade and away from me. "Be the man, got it?" is his warning.

"More obvious than I thought, I guess," is Kade's raspy reply.

Royce steps forward when Warren's car pulls up to the curb. "I'm a dad. I see everything."

I walk forward, mumbling, "It's my fault. I'll try to behave. I just… I just can't help it. My body has a mind of its own."

This time Royce grabs my shoulder. "You feel what you feel, son. Just as Kade owns how he feels. But the grown man better act like one, got it?"

"You're blaming Kade for what I'm doing?" I blurt out, amazed. "What the hell, Royce?"

"*Just drop it*," Kade mouths to me while rolling his eyes. "Royce thinks I'm a pervert."

"*You* think you're a pervert," Royce growls. "I'm just being a dad."

"Dude? What's up with the standoff between the three of you?" Warren asks as he slides from the driver's side. "I feel hostility." He lunges at me, taking the very breath from my lungs, wrapping his arms around my chest so tightly I can't breathe, and then he squeezes tighter. "Baby brother!"

Warm and solid, healthy and happy, Warren feels so good in my arms that emotions assault me in every direction. My nose tingles and my eyes water because Warren smells like home. I hang on for dear life. I'd never spent a day away from my brother in nearly eighteen years.

"Three months felt like an eternity without your bullshit." I laugh through the tears, rocking my brother back and forth while patting his back forcefully. The hollow thud is loud in my ears. "I've missed the hell out of you, you stocky sonofabitch." I muss up Warren's dirty blond curls.

"Me too. Me too. I missed you too." Warren's attention span is short, because now he's hugging me while his eyes flick around wildly, searching. Distracted, he spots Kade again. "Hey, you! It's good to see you." Slipping away from me to greet his buddy, I'm left behind, as always. Having Warren's sole attention was short-lived, just the way it's always been.

My sister is leaning against the car, like she's too petrified to move. Small and fragile, Willa hides behind the fall of her blonde curls as she hangs her head low. She's near Royce, like she's watching him with one eye as if he's going to attack her, but scared to step away because she needs him for protection. This is the Willa I've known since I was fourteen, but I see a bit more life peeking through.

Hesitant, I say, "Hi," in a chipper voice. I don't walk forward and hug my sister, because I have to give her time to decide if that's what she wants. I learned this from experience, after being a little boy and wanting to hug the sister I remember, and she'd lash out, shrieking bloody murder when I'd get near. Awake or asleep, Willa's terrified screams always haunt my mind.

Clear, bright, and sober, blue eyes flick up to connect with mine, and then a small smile tilts the corner of Willa's lips. She reaches a hand out, and mine is in hers in a heartbeat. We don't say anything. We just look at each other, gripping our hands together, not too tight and not too loose. No words need to pass because we both feel the warm pleasure of family zinging through our blood.

Royce pats my shoulder, grinning like a fool, then he softly disconnects our hands. He leans down into Willa's personal space, and I'm surprised she doesn't flinch. He whispers a few words in her ear, and she nods in reply.

The *tap… tap… tap…* of tiny sneakers thudding against the sidewalk hits my ears, to the soundtrack of Penny's excited squeals and giggles, announcing Penny and the twins have finally realized Warren and Willa made it home safe and sound. From the corner of my eye, I watch as Warren grabs Penny out of the air as she launches herself at him. He swings her around, looking like he won the lottery. No doubt, Penny was what was distracting him so.

Hayley and Hayden run around me, trying to get at their momma, but Royce stops them with a firm grip to the back of their necks. He holds them back, giving Willa a moment to center herself.

I can almost feel Kade curling in on himself as he witnesses a mother terrified of her own kids. If it wasn't for the fact it's what I've seen since they were toddlers, I'd be screaming in pain. I reach over, resting my hand on Kade's forearm to settle his nerves. I leave it there for a moment, and then allow my arm to fall back to my side.

Willa looks at Royce, then looks at me. With a deep breath, she mouths, "*I can do this,*" and then she squats down to the height of her kids. Holding her arms out, "Hayden? Hayley? Give yer momma a hug."

Royce doesn't let go of the kids' necks, his large fingertips denting into their skin a bit in silent warning. He walks them a few steps forward, then nudges them into their mother's arms, but he never lets go.

I turn completely around, deciding to stare at the house, because I can't handle looking at my sister struggling to hold her own children, with the kids I've practically raised for the past few years looking to their momma like she's a stranger.

Stressed. Over-emotional. I start to chuckle when I realize we're all facing the opposite direction. Kade's next to me, acting as a silent, brooding wall, with Jack next to him looking uncomfortable. Bren's arm wraps around my shoulders, and I pretend I don't hear him sniffle.

"This ain't gonna be easy," Bren says to me. "At all."

"I know," I reply. "But we can't avoid it like I've always done. We can't force it, but we can't ignore it."

"Dad said to let him deal with it," Bren warns. "You hear me?"

"I'll try," I promise.

"You'll do," Royce orders as he walks past me, holding Willa's hand while she holds Hayden's, and Hayley's is clutched in his other hand. "You'll do," he warns over his shoulder, issuing me the dad stare.

"Yes, sir," I mutter falling in line behind them.

Copper hair a streaking blur as she skips across the yard, Penny shouts with glee, "Welcome home!"

TYING FLIES

Most of my family, all of my new family, and two of our friends, surround a rickety table right in the front yard. I'm in between Bren and Kade, with Jack sitting on Bren's other side. Hayley keeps sitting on my lap, and then sitting on Bren's, and then switching back and forth, as if she's trying to reassure us both that we're still her favorite.

Sitting across from us is Warren with Penny fused to his lap, her arm thrown over his shoulders. Warren keeps whispering in Penny's ear, and her resulting giggle is so sweet it's giving me cavities.

Royce is sitting directly across from me, eyes flicking around like he's ready to pass out ass whoopings.

Hayden is the calmest of us all, instinctively knowing what his momma needs. He's talking low and slow, updating her on everything she missed.

Willa's better than I expected, but still not up to par with being a functioning human being. She's spooked, looking like everything is overloading her senses.

"Boss?" Warren nudges Royce in the side with his elbow. "What hellish job are you forcing me to perform? Do I get a few days off first, or do I start the minute I'm done chewing my food." He sounds disrespectful, belligerent, and slightly antagonistic. But that's Warren's way. The fact that he'll actually work is a huge step in the right direction.

Royce's voice is firm yet understanding. "You've had a twenty-three-year vacation, War, with a three month escape from reality. I'd say you're gonna work when I tell ya to work."

"I get it." Warren puts his hands up in surrender. "I'm just being a dick. I don't want to end up like Daddy, and I don't want my kids ending up like Willa, Wynn, and me."

"What's wrong with me?" I act all offended, and then I crack a smile. "Joking."

"Dr. Kline said you were to stop being evasive," Willa cuts in, shocking us all. Her voice is confident for once. "No more acting like an asshole."

"Sorry, sister," Warren mumbles, looking properly cowed.

Royce eyes Willa the entire time he speaks to everyone at the table. "Warren, you'll be working on the landscaping crew until the snow flies. You and Penny will get home at the same time, so I'm leaving you be every evening. But you've got to find a hobby–doctor's orders."

Penny leans back a bit, giving my brother the stink-eye. "Why would the doctor be giving you orders, Warren?"

Warren ignores Penny, and that twists my guts into knots. "Hey, Kade do y–"

Hand clasped over Warren's mouth and chin, "No, motherfucker," Penny warns. "You answer me. Now."

"Iwasinrehabtoo," Warren grumbles so quickly we can't decipher his words. "I have to become a productive member of society. I have to get a job and keep it. I have to treat everyone with respect, especially myself. Willa and I both have to find sponsors and go to NA. Lastly, I'm to find a hobby to occupy my downtime so I won't look to drugs and alcohol."

"Why wasn't I told?" Penny takes the words out of my mouth, so I sit frozen in my chair, mind spinning out of control. "Why did you lie to me when we spoke on the phone, when we wrote to each other?" Penny's voice breaks with the same betrayal that's washing over me. "Why, Warren?"

"Baby," Warren croons, eyes turning shiny. "I didn't want to worry you." Then my brother turns to me. "You had so much shit you were dealing with. I lied to protect you. So hate me if you must, but I kept my trap shut for your sake."

The tension surrounding us is so thick you could cut it. "I… I… I…" All I can do is stutter, I'm so frustrated and shocked.

"What were you asking me?" Kade breaks into the heavy silence.

"Do you still have your papaw's fly tying equipment and supplies?" Warren tries to sound pleasant, but his eyes are darting around like we're all disappointed in him.

I reach across the table to still my brother's tapping fingertips. "Whatever you gotta do, you do it. You have nothing to be ashamed of, and I'm proud that you got yourself some help. Whatever I feel about that is about me, so don't you worry about it."

My words were directed to Warren, but it's Willa who visibly relaxes. My brother and sister are a little under a year apart in age, and have always been close. Their addiction was shared.

Daddy's last words to me, where he wondered if I was some townie's kid, hit me like a ton of bricks. I've always been different–other. I've never truly been a Gillette, at least not in the sense that I belonged. I don't want Warren and Willa to think I'm judging them just because I didn't turn to vices to deal with my shit. I just want them to be happy and healthy.

Underneath the table, Kaden rests a heavy palm on my knee to reassure me. A jolt runs up my spine, clearing my head and making me gasp in shock.

Royce's eyes are on me before I can close my mouth, giving me the '*I see everything*' dad look.

"Yeah, Warren," Kade begins speaking like his thumb isn't stroking my knee. "I hate that sonofabitch for so many reasons, but I appreciate him teaching me how to tie flies. I picked it back up after I came home from college."

Like an idiot, everything Kaden says is intriguing. "You fish?" I ask, hoping he'll fish with me sometime.

Kade's, "I don't fish," deflates me. "So I've been selling the flies over at McDivitt's Sporting Goods."

"Do you think it'd be okay if we shoot the shit every once and while, and you could teach me to tie flies?"

Feeling like a teenage girl, I rest heavily against the back of my chair, pouting because my brother is stealing his buddy back when I want to be the one spending time with both of them.

"I think that's an excellent idea," Royce says with a grin, and I resent him a bit for it. "I think Kade would be a good influence on you, Warren." Eyes flicking in my direction, he says, "This way he'd get some friends his own age."

"I was thinking of crafting a new fishing pole since we left ours in Gillette Holler." I turn to Kade, "I could make you one, and Warren and I could teach you how to fly fish. It would be a good opportunity to teach the little ones."

"Yeah," Warren says enthusiastically. "After work, I'll check to see if I can get a good deal on some reels. Dr. Kline would definitely approve of this as an appropriate hobby. Tying flies is creative, and then you're left with something useful, and fishing is calm and soothing. Fruit for your labors. Plus, whoever cooked this spread, would make a mean fish fry."

Bren leans into me and whispers into my ear while Warren goes on and on about food and hobbies. "Dad should have known better than to try to cock-block you. You're too smart. He always traps me in my own shit. I've made his skills rusty."

"Don't know what you're talking about," I mutter, managing to pull off looking guilty and innocent at the same time. "You're invited too. I'm just wanting to spend some quality time with my big brother."

"Uh-huh, sure ya are." Jack leans forward so he can talk to me without Bren's head in the way. "I'll be joining ya just to see how this train wreck plays out."

"Mmm… mmm… this is real good grub." Warren wipes his mouth with a paper napkin. "It's quite the spread. I know Wynn didn't make it since it's not covered in pepper."

"Ass." I toss a dinner roll across the table, the trajectory is Warren's face. My brother grabs the roll before it smacks him upside the head, and then takes a big bite out of it. "I'll have you know, I taught Penny everything she knows about cooking."

"It's true," the girl in question pipes up from her seat on Warren's lap. "Wynn got me this huge cookbook with a red gingham tablecloth on the cover. It has yellowed pages, but it's got a lot of great recipes in it."

"It was a long road to edible food," I drawl, causing Hayley and Hayden to giggle. "In three months of grocery shopping, Penny kept forgetting the pepper. Then, when I'd bring it home, it would up and disappear."

"Imagine that," Penny breathes in disbelief.

"I like to fish," Royce announces out of nowhere. "No one goes fishing until Wynn has made poles for everyone at this table, and Warren has fashioned us some flies. No one hits a fishing hole without all of us," he declares.

"Dad's got mad skills," Bren breathes into my ear.

I grin, happier than a pig in shit. Bren thinks I'm trying to get Kade alone so I can molest him. That's not the case. I want to get to know him. It's not sexual, no matter what my dick is shouting. I just want to spend time with the people I care about. Nothing would make me happier than all of us spending time together as a big, happy family.

Warren and Willa are addicts, but so am I. I'm addicted to that warm sensation that surrounds my heart. I never had a stable family, and I'll do anything to feed my addiction.

"Here, baby." Warren spoon-feeds Penny some potato salad. "We've got to keep you from starving our little feller." Rubbing her belly while feeding her with the other, I drown out the rest of the syrupy sweet words flowing out of Warren's mouth directed to Penny and her baby bump.

There is sweet, and then there is overkill. With anyone other than Warren, I'd say they were empty words.

I look across the table at Royce, who's still glaring at Kade because I sat next to him. "I'm glad I'm coming home with you. I would have shot myself again if I had to put up with Warren's baby talk." All conversation ceases, so I throw in a, "too soon?" as a joke.

"Dr. Kline thinks you should see a therapist," Warren says pointedly. "I agree."

Betrayal slams into me out of nowhere. A surge of violent pride grips me. "You had no right!" I shout, fist hitting the side of the table. "No right to talk about my shit with a stranger."

"You need help," Warren says calmly, but then grins. He points at my red face and the vein throbbing in my forehead. "Proof you're a Gillette, after all."

Seething, I draw breath in and out of my lungs to calm myself. I concentrate on Kade's hand gripping my knee, centering myself on his nails digging in. Warren and I are two sides to the same coin. I'm capable of acting like him, and he's capable of acting like me.

"You cured me," I whisper.

"It doesn't work like that," Warren presses. "Dr. Kline gave me the number to a therapist who specializes in kids who are gay. Not to, like, cure it. But for you to understand it, so you won't keep trying to blow your brains out."

"My taking a shotgun barrel to the chin didn't have a dang thing to do with my dick." I shut my eyes as I close in on my breaking point. My fists clench on the table edge. My breathing becomes shallow.

Kade stands abruptly. "I have a loose riser on my back porch." He grips my shoulder and yanks me from my seat. "Wynn's gonna fix it. We'll be back when we're through."

"No!" Warren shouts.

Royce shocks me with a, "Go!"

Head whipping to the side like in the Exorcist, Warren glares at Royce, then looks back at me. "Sitcha ass down, baby brother. I know who you are, even if you won't admit it. I also know Kade real well. I ain't gonna allow you to use '*carpentry*' as a way to forget that you need professional help."

"Carpentry isn't a euphemism for *that*," Kade sputters, insulted. "Neither of us do *that*, especially not together."

"Bullshit!" Warren sneers. "I thought we were friends, and here you are stroking some part of my baby brother's body underneath the table."

"So much for not being an asshole," Kade growls. "I'd hoped you'd grow up in rehab, but I guess not. Wynn's about to go Gillette on your ass, fuckface, and I'm saving him from himself."

"Euphemism for what?" I mutter, confused, as I'm dragged away. I keep looking over my shoulder at my brother, who's being held in his seat by Royce. It cools my need for violence some, but not by much. "I doubt Warren knows what the word even means."

"You're so innocent, it terrifies me. Some asshole could take advantage of you, and I don't mean physically." Kade yanks me across the street by gripping my arm, and then veers us around his house to the backyard. He pushes me down until my ass lands on the porch step I'm supposedly repairing.

"Don't move, take steady breaths, keep your eyes on the gnome in the middle of the yard, and wait while I get us some iced tea." Kade's feet fall heavily as he pounds up the stairs. "I'll be right out."

My mind is spiraling out of control. Every emotion I could possibly feel is hammering me at once. My heart is battering the inside of my ribcage. A violent shaking starts in my fingertips and works its way through my hands, up my arms, and into the rest of my body. A cold sweat beads at my brow. My lungs are collapsing and expanding as I exhale and inhale rapidly.

Doing as I was told, I locate Kade's gnome. A shocked snort manages to erupt through my involuntary rage. Kade's backyard is dinky, with a small dog run for his pug and little else. There's a perfect square of garden pavers, and on the central most edge sits the gnome.

"Who has a zombie gnome?"

"I do," Kade mutters from behind me, and then a glass of tea is lowered in front of my face. "Here."

I reach up, taking his offering, with a lame, "Thanks." I wrap both hands around the glass damp with condensation, but I don't take a sip.

"Zombie gnome's name is Suicidal Tendencies. It's a coping skill I learned from one of my therapists." Kade takes a seat next to me on the step, his hip and shoulder brushing mine. "The gnome is a focus object. When I'm hit with emotions I cannot control, I'm to come out here and focus them on the gnome. Sometimes he's my best friend. Sometimes he's my worst enemy. Suicidal Tendencies can't talk back or leave me– he's very patient, never judges, and always listens to my shit."

Turning toward Kade, "Is Warren right?" My voice dips low, flooded with fear. "Do I need a therapist?"

"No," Kade whispers. "You need someone who will listen. Someone who understands. But that person can't be clinical. You need to connect with them in order to trust them. And that person has to have been in your shoes at one point. You need a constant. But unlike me, yours needs to be flesh and blood."

"What's the difference?"

Kade takes the glass out of my hand, and then sets it on the step beneath us. He rests his arm on my thigh, with the inside facing up. "Shit," I whimper when I take in the puckered scar bisecting his arm up the middle, from his wrist to elbow.

First I trace the line with a fingertip, causing Kade to shiver, then I cover it with both hands, trying to pretend it never happened. It reminds me of when Kade was covering my face, trying to erase the fact that I almost pulverized my entire skull with a shotgun.

"I meant it, too," Kade breathes, and then lifts his right arm to show me it looks the same as the left. "I was resolved. I was through living. It wasn't a spur of the moment decision. I researched how to do it right."

"How did you…" With the shoe on the other foot, I stumble over the words, just now realizing how difficult it is for others to ask this question of me. "How did you survive?"

Kade leans forward, picks up the glass, takes a long sip, and then puts the glass back down. "I nicked the artery in a few spots, but missed it entirely the rest of the way. It took a lot of blood to bring me back to life, which now makes me feel guilty because I took blood away from people who really needed it. Maybe someone died who shouldn't have because they wasted it on me."

"Oh, Christ," I groan, fingertips biting into Kade's forearm. I experience a light bulb moment of my own. "What a pair we make. Now I understand why everyone wants to throttle me when I pull that martyr bullshit. The shoe's on the other foot now, and I want to punch you in the face for saying shit like that."

The corner of Kade's mouth tilts up into a sardonic smirk, and then his crooked front tooth is pressing into his bottom lip. "Make sure you tell Royce I cured you of your self-deprecation. Maybe he'll stop glaring at me when you're around."

"No way, man… no way. That's between you and Royce." I shift uncomfortably, worried Kade doesn't want me to know the details, but I need to know them. "I get how you survived– medically. But… how did you not bleed out? Who was your Warren?"

"Your brother is an asshole, but he's the best asshole ever." Kade chuckles, a wave of emotions rolling over his features, as if he's remembering their good ol' days. "My social worker found me during a surprise home visit. She was making sure I didn't trip again." He does the drink routine again, as if nervous. "She was the same lady I was going to call to remove Hayden, Hayley, and you from your home."

"I guessed right on that, then," I mutter to myself, somehow knowing if I hadn't left my parents, we would have been taken from them instead. Permanently this time. Knowing I did it on my own gives me a sense of power over my life.

"I had a lot of stitches, and even more therapy. I was removed from my grandfather's care, but he had supervised visitation. Since I had no other family, I was placed in a foster home."

"Royce?" I guess, because it has Royce Kennedy's signature written all over it. No doubt, the twins and I would have been given over into his care anyway.

Same destination. Different path.

"Yeah. I was sixteen, almost seventeen." Kade leans back, resting on his elbows. I sneak a glance at him, and follow the direction of his eyes. He's connected to his focus object, talking to Suicidal Tendencies instead of me.

"I get how hard this is for my friends and family now." I lean forward, resting my elbows on my thighs, feeling hopeless– lost – and for once it's not about me. "I can't imagine… I can't imagine the world without you in it." My throat goes tight on me all of the sudden. Whether it's a glare or a grin, I look forward to just being around Kade. Always have. "Jesus, this is hard. Why'd you do it, Kade? Why'd you try to kill yourself?"

Voice taut with painful emotions, "Grief mostly," Kade breathes the words. "I lost my mom when I was real young, and my dad stepped up. I don't think I'm capable of loving anyone as much as I loved him. He was a kind and gentle giant. Soft-spoken and patient. He was my daddy, my momma, and my teacher. Dad was my best friend– my hero. He was my world… and one day he was gone."

Voice changing from soft to harsh, Kade gruffly grits out, "Logging accident at work. He was felling a tree, and the chainsaw kicked back. The tree fell in the wrong direction, and it landed on his chest– pulverizing everything beneath it."

Tragic, there are no words, so I simply rest my hand on Kade's knee like he had for me earlier.

"For hours on end, I would just sit and stare at the door, waiting for Dad to come home. Only thing was, he was never coming home again." With a deep breath, Kade looks up and away, and then his eyes settle on Suicidal Tendencies again. "Still to this day, I'll lay in bed, trying to remember the deep timbre of his voice, remember the way he smelled like sawdust and pine sap, or the way his eyes would crinkle up in the corners when he was smiling."

Kade rests his hand over mine, twining our fingers together, seeking comfort. "Dad reminded me of a big bear. He was taller than I am now, with a wide chest and shoulders. But I was never afraid of him, even when I barely came up to his knee. He wore flannel, jeans, and huge work boots, and sometimes I dress like that to remember him."

"I can't imagine how comforting it would be to look in the mirror and have someone you love staring back at you." I gaze at Kade, instinctively knowing he looks exactly like his father. "I want to punch my reflection sometimes, hating how perfect Gillettes look when we're broken in every way that matters... but this isn't about me. Your hair? Did your dad wear it long?"

Kade's deep laughter stuns me stupid, causing a sensation I've never experienced to slither up my spine. "Dad shaved his head, hating how people would comment on his hair. My grandfather made some shitty homophobic slurs, so I started growing it out when I was seventeen as a way to spit in his face. When I visit him, I make sure to wear it down."

"Rebel," I mutter with a smirk.

Kade squeezes my hand, signaling the happy portion of our conversation has met its end. "When I talk of suicide, I tell everyone it was because my grandfather was a drunk bigot who abused his faggot grandson. But that's not the entire truth. Three months after Dad passed, I woke up so terrified I had pissed the bed. I couldn't remember... I couldn't remember my father." Kade's voice is lifeless yet panicked, as if he's nothing but a ghost of himself.

"I could remember nothing of him. Not even what he looked like. I was so distraught, I didn't realize I could just reach for his photograph. Instead, I took my grandfather's hunting knife to my forearms."

I gaze at the zombie gnome, and its name hits me so hard I recoil backward. "You're not tempted to do it again, are you?"

"Sometimes," Kade admits the truth like it doesn't wound me. He leans back upright again, and rests an elbow on his thigh, keeping our hands connected on his other leg. "I *miss* Dad to the point I feel alone in this world." Kade's voice hitches, forcing him to pause. "But I know he would be furious at me for trying to kill myself."

"He'd blame himself," I mutter, another realization dawning.

"Just like Warren is blaming himself right now. Royce too, ya know?"

"I get it," I gulp out. "Sometimes I want to kill myself because I was so goddamned stupid for trying it the first time. I know it makes no sense, but I have to punish myself somehow."

"There's a reason you're alive. It's best you deal with that fact," Kade orders. "We all have a reason for existence. I'm still here to save others like me. It's why I became a teacher, but I'm waiting for the guidance counselor position to open up. When I applied, all we had was first grade available. I was qualified."

"I wanna grow up to be someone's Royce," I admit. "You want to grow up to remember your daddy."

"The gnome is the part of me who doesn't believe himself worthy. He's a lifeless zombie with suicidal tendencies." Kade squeezes my hand. "The man sitting next to you, realizes he is worthy. That's why you needn't worry that I'll harm myself. I have a bunch of confused West Virginian kids who will always need my help. Every year, more kids will grow up and realize they aren't just like everyone else, and that's okay."

"Warren was wrong," I admit. "I wish I could say I was gay, or straight, or bi, or asexual. Anything. I don't need a therapist to help me embrace it. I'd welcome the truth with open arms."

"You need the label," Kade points out. "Without it, you feel lost. Ya know, I was the same way."

"What?" I gasp out, shocked, and Kade just looks at me while nodding his head up and down.

"I was confused. All of my friends were fucking girls left and right, your brother especially." Kade's grin is huge when I recoil from the turn our conversation has taken. "Warren took to sex like it was an occupation."

"Oh, my God," I groan, tearing my hand away to clasp my ears. "Please, no more. Penny tells me too much. Some things you can't unhear."

Kade just laughs at me, and then reclaims my hand in his. Warm. Strong. Larger than my own but softer. I like his hand wrapped around mine. Something so simple warms me like the hottest of fires.

"I wasn't interested. At all. I *tried* to be interested. I felt empty like you did, I'm sure. I didn't understand what was going on. Then one day, right after I tried to kill myself, I was visiting a friend, and I saw this manly kid running around in just a pair of dinky shorts with his little round, hard ass cheeks hanging out. I had known this boy since he was born– it was nothing new. But that day, it was like being struck by lightning. After it clicked, my dick was finally able to communicate with me."

"I'm not there yet," I mutter, ashamed, and then the truth just spills from my lips. "My dick does as it pleases, and I don't know why it does, or that it's even doing it. Most of the time, I have to look down to see that I'm hard. I must look like a fucking moron, cupping my crotch all the time, checking to see if my dick is still attached."

"Not always, though." Kade releases a snicker, one that could only be classified as naughty and evil. "You get this look on your face when you and your dick are copasetic. Starved."

"NO!" I clasp my ears again, laughing self-deprecatingly. "I can't talk about this subject with you, not when it's about you."

"Oh, so you admit you're receptive to your cock's signals." Kade tips his head back and releases a dark, sinful laugh that has me whimpering with a combination of humiliation and lust. His eyes land on my face, and then he shouts, "There's the look!"

I fold in half, hiding my face against my thighs, while wrapping my arms around my head. I'm so dang hard, my balls are threatening to explode. "Jesus, why am I enjoying this torture so much?"

Kade rests his elbow on my back and leans on me. "Because making fun of yourself releases the stress." He sighs deeply, and then pulls me up so I can't hide my face from his view.

"I'd gotten hard for one little cock tease, so I wasn't quite sure if I was gay or a pervert. I mean, I seriously thought I was a pervert." Kade's face twists up into a grimace. "Thankfully, I never saw this kid again for years after Royce and the little shit's family caught on."

"Wow…" My eyes bug out in shock. "I need the rest of the details on this story. I'll beg."

Kade flashes me an odd look, like I should just know the details. "Whole lotta keep-away has been happening over the past six years… I didn't accept I was gay until college. Late bloomer. But then my dick was pointing out what he liked like a divining rod. I took his hint and slapped a label on myself. Since my dick has never pointed out a girl, the label was the right one."

"Other than you…" I trail off, knowing Kade will get what I can't say.

"Wynn?" Kade tugs my hair so I'll look at him. "My version of schoolyard flirting, I was taunting you in the Circle K for months, and you were oblivious to the fact that you were tenting your pants. I think you need to open the lines of communication. Somewhere your wires got crossed, and you're ignoring the signal."

"Why can't I be normal?" I hate how whiny I sound– pitiful.

"That's the problem, right there." Kade points at me, and then himself. "Normal. Being gay *is* normal… for me. I don't know. Maybe it was all the faggot slurs out of your father's mouth, or how sex got twisted up with violence with what happened to Willa. I don't even know if you're gay, or if it's just that you feel comfortable around me. But you need to tune in to find out."

"Thank you," I breathe like a prayer. "I mean it. Thank you for talking to me. I needed this. I really did."

"I know," Kade breathes back. "It's what I meant about how you needed a flesh and blood human being with experiences and wisdom to share, not a ceramic inanimate object, and not an impassive therapist who doesn't know you and will never *get* you. This is why I'm on this planet, to help people like you– people like us."

"I'll never try to kill myself again." I stand up, unable to sit still while I say this. "I know it was stupid. I know it was wrong. And I meant what I said about Warren curing me."

"I know. It's why I said you don't need a therapist." Kade stands up, grabs my hand, and then starts walking me around the perimeter of his back yard. "But you do need to say it out loud."

I hold it in. Maybe it was five times around the backyard, or fifty, but I finally say what's killing me. "Guilt. Shame. Fear. I wake up in the middle of the night and puke my guts out. I look in the mirror at my face, tracing where I would have liquefied my flesh and bone. It could be a week, or a day, or even a minute, and I find myself doing the same thing. It's a compulsion now. I don't know how to accept what I did, why I did it, that I survived, and be able to swallow the guilt and shame so I can move on."

A firm hand wraps around the back of my neck, drawing me into an embrace. Kade grips me to his chest, whispering soothing words against my hair. I hadn't even realized I was crying, that's how disconnected I am at all times.

"God," I cry, clasping my arms around his middle as tightly as I can, not caring that I'm dampening his shirt with my tears. "I needed this."

Hugging Kade is different. His strong arms are holding me, holding me up and holding me together. I take comfort in how safe he makes me feel. It's not me taking care of Penny, Hayden, or Hayley's needs. It's not me cleaning up Willa and Warren's messes. It's not a mock-punch of affection from Bren and Jack. It's not Royce trying to comfort me without coddling me, when he's so much smaller than I am.

Kaden is strong enough in all ways to support me, and I needed it. Maybe someday, I'll be strong enough to support him back, if he'll let me.

"It'll be okay. I promise... Shh... it's alright. It gets better– easier. Just let it out." Kade brushes my hair off my forehead, and then nuzzles it with his cheek. "When you find the answer on how to release the guilt and move on, I'll need you to tell me. Until then, we'll just help each other cope. Okay?"

"I like you because you're older than me, stronger than me, taller than me, bigger than me, and smarter than me," I mutter in a very serious tone. "So if I figure this out before you, the universe will implode."

"You, little shit," Kade grumbles when I start laughing.

"Little shit?" I point at my chest. "Who, me?" I quickly turn around or risk fainting from blood loss. "Seriously, Kade, you can't blush and look at me like that. My dick might think you're interested, and then we'll have to take up carpentry."

I charge across the yard the instant Kade releases a growl. "Innocent, my ass. I knew you were fucking with me." He hooks his arm around my neck, steering me toward the street.

"I just wanted to hear you say Warren thought we were gonna screw. I was torturing the both of us." We both huff out a laugh when we spot my family. They're all sitting on one side of the table in the yard, all the chairs facing Kaden's house. The look of shock on their faces when we start toward them is priceless.

"If you were a girl, they wouldn't be checking for a hymen. Beware, Royce will ask the status of your pucker, worried about penetration." Kade sounds like he's joking, but there is a thread of truth in his words and a whole helluva lot of hurt. "I don't think I'm a pervert anymore, but they're still looking at me like one. Yet they never bothered when Warren was a grown man putting it to Penny."

"I hate that I understand what you're saying." A bit of my earlier rage leaks back through. "I want to be mad at Warren, but I can't be."

"Same here." Kade releases a laugh. "The Warren who left here three months ago, he wouldn't have suggested a therapist. He would have called you a faggot, shamed you in front of everyone, and then dropped your ass at a religious cult retreat that would *cure* you of your perversions. I'd say he's had some progress."

"That's not even funny." I chuckle a few times. "But it's so freaking true, isn't it?"

"Hillbillies, I tell ya."

SOLD

It takes walking down an entire street before I gather the courage to ask Royce what the deal is. We just left a distraught Penny alone with Warren. Not that she's not thrilled to have Warren home. But for three months it was *us*: Wynn, Penny, Hayley, and Hayden. Now Penny feels like we're leaving her behind with a childish junkie– she picked Warren; she can keep him.

"Were you ever going to tell me Kaden is your foster kid?" I try not to sound like I'm interrogating Royce, or angry with him, but it seeps through anyway.

"Honestly, I didn't think it mattered." Royce just shrugs the best he can while holding Hayden's hand. "I'm not the only one keeping secrets, Wynn. Were you ever going to tell me your *issue* resolved itself by setting its sights on your *adult* foster brother?"

"I don't really think that counts, Dad." Bren snickers, thriving on the drama. "Kade hasn't lived with us in four years. Technically, Wynn hasn't even lived with us yet."

Eyes narrowed, "Why didn't you tell me?" I accuse Bren.

Bren flashes me a naughty grin, so I know he's going to taunt me. "I was going to wait until Christmas morning, and watch your shock when lover boy showed up to open presents."

"Snarky ass," I growl. Willa's sweet laughter hits my ears, and all the stress and pressure melts away. If she thinks my predicament is hilarious, then I'll try to amuse her more often.

Not serious, but wouldn't be surprised, I ask Royce, "Do you have any other sons I should know about?"

"Yeah, two of 'em," Royce answers immediately.

"Who?" My heart clenches with betrayal and hurt. "I don't understand all the secrecy. This was major, and you somehow forgot to tell me this shit?"

"You're such an idiot." Bren hits me upside the head. "You're walking with us, dipshit. Yours truly, you, Hayden, and Hayley are Dad's kids. With Kaden getting an honorable mention of '*like a son.*'"

Eyes squinting, I mumble, "Legally?"

"Yes," Bren says, still sounding amused, but Royce talks over him. "I was awarded guardianship in May, with the legalities finalized in the end of July and two weeks ago."

"How is this any different than with Kade?" I ask Bren, knowing he'd tell me the truth quicker. But, instead of answering, he takes Hayden's hand away from Royce, and then puts his other hand on the small of Willa's back, ushering them up the street so I won't upset them.

"I don't want to upset anyone, but shouldn't this be a big deal?" I ask Royce in a hushed tone, knowing the kids and Willa can still hear me. "Everything I've known my entire life has changed, and no one consulted me." My voice cracks under the strain of stress. "You just hid me away down the street, piling busywork on me so I wouldn't notice."

Royce squeezes my shoulder. "I understand, son. I get how frustrated you must be. But it had to go down this way."

"Then explain it to me!" I demand. "I have a right to know."

Royce sighs heavily, but eventually gives in. "The difference between Kaden and you kids is that you're not my foster kids. I was awarded guardianship of Kaden until he reached the age of majority because his grandfather was unfit to raise him. After that, I had no legal ties, but we continued to have a father/son relationship."

"I don't understand how I'm any different? I mean, I'm seventeen years old already."

"When my brother married a child, it drew me to the Gillettes. I've been keeping an eye on you since you were ten. You know that."

"Yeah, it wasn't obvious at first. But as I got older, I figured out you were taking care of me the best my parents would allow." It's my turn to squeeze Royce's shoulder as I get choked up on emotion. "I appreciate it. But at times it makes me feel like you think I'm incapable of taking care of myself."

I wait for Royce to deny it, but he doesn't. So I get to the heart of the matter. "You're talking around what I'm asking. Why is that?"

"Fine." Royce sighs again, but this time he rakes his fingers through his dark hair. "About a week after you left your parents, I had sole parental rights to you, Wynn. You are my son in every way to me, blood or not. Out of respect for your roots, I didn't go forth to change your birth certificate and your last name."

I can't mask the hurt in my voice. "How?"

"We'll discuss that when we get home, okay?" Royce's voice holds a deep well of sympathy and compassion, and I can't be angry with him when he looks at me that way. "The difference is, according to the state, the four minors walking with me right now are my children, versus how I was only Kaden's guardian for a year and a half. I'll be your father by rights until we die."

"What about Willa?" I gesture at my sister's back, trying to convey how lost I'm feeling.

"I signed over my parental rights before I went into treatment." Willa doesn't turn around, but she does respond for herself, instead of Royce taking over. I'm a bit shocked because she's not the zombie I remember.

Dumbfounded, I blurt out. "Permanently?"

"Yes." Willa releases Hayley's hand, who immediately latches onto Bren. My sister slows up until Royce and I are walking beside her. She turns her head and actually looks me in the eye.

"But you're out now. Are you saying they aren't your kids?"

"For the first time in my life, I did something selfless for my children, Wynn." Willa's voice breaks, so I decide not to say another word on the subject. But she keeps speaking anyway. "I had to give Royce temporary guardianship or else the state was gonna take the twins away, and there was no guarantee I'd ever get 'em back. I was logical for once."

"Hey, it's over now," Royce murmurs gently to Willa, and then he turns to me. "I visited my brother in prison and forced him to sign his parental rights over to me. Then Willa gave me permission to petition for adoption, listing Willa and me as Hayley and Hayden's parents. Willa didn't give up her children. She is their mother in all ways. Forever."

"But… what the hell?" I stammer in shock, feet missing a step until I stumble forward. "Did it go through?"

"Two weeks ago," Royce's voice shudders out. "It took longer than it did with you because of the odd situation. It was a bit messy with how Willa and I are living together and sharing the children, but not married or coupled. It helped that I was their biological uncle. Under the circumstances, they understood how I'd want to care for my sister-in-law and her children."

Royce's house comes into view. Sensing that I'm about to boil over again, Bren immediately snatches the kids up under each arm and ushers them into the house, with Willa following quickly behind.

"Why didn't I know any of this? I didn't know anything!" I shout. Frustrated and hurt and angry, the Gillette violence in me erupts. "It was about me and the twins, and no one told me! What the hell, Royce?"

Speaking in a calm and quiet voice, "They were adult issues and your input wasn't necessary." Royce tries to calm me down, but all he does is piss me off more.

"Royce, do you hear how that sounds?" My body starts to vibrate with how powerless I feel. I wipe the sweat off my forehead with the back of my hand, and refuse to acknowledge how high my voice pitches. "You haven't said it, but I can read between the lines. My parents didn't want me anymore."

"You listen to me, Wynn." Royce grabs my arm and drags me across the yard toward the barn, so we're not making a spectacle of ourselves in front of the neighbors.

"I've been sick with worry, and it changed nothing." Royce opens the barn door, and gestures for me to move forward. I've never been inside it before. Even my curiosity can't overpower my need for answers.

"I wasn't about to spread the misery around. All it would have done was force you to worry over whether or not I was awarded the children. If I hadn't been, the state would have stepped in and taken them from us."

Body shaking, "shit," slips from between my quivering lips.

"No one in their right mind would have given them to your parents, to my imprisoned brother, or your junkie siblings. Blood ties be damned, they are not fit parents. The only choice was me. If that didn't work, you were too young. The kids are adorable and smart and tiny, and they would have been adopted out in a heartbeat!"

A fist crunches against a support beam. I stare in awe as Royce loses his shit. The man has never been anything but calm and supportive, and this new side of him feeds into the chaos spinning around in my head.

"All this was going on while I spent all of my time playing happy home with Penny and the twins, while stalking Kade?" I crumple to the floor, feeling sick to my stomach. "It makes me feel so goddamned worthless, like I was living a lie."

Royce crouches down next to me. He grips my chin, forcing me to look at him. "You. Are. A. Child." His enunciates every single word, breath billowing across my forehead. "That has nothing to do with whether or not you are capable of shouldering the burden, and everything to do with the fact that you shouldn't have to. I am your father, and if I couldn't do this without you, then what a shitty father I make."

"I could have helped you, though," I whisper, averting my eyes away from his. "That's what's hurting the most. I'm not a selfish asshole. I would have done what I could."

"You did, Wynn. You took care of the kids and Penny all summer." Royce settles next to me, sitting on the barn floor. "You kept them happy and healthy. You kept Bren out of my hair. So instead of stressing, I could actually focus on getting everything finalized. It's over now. There is no sense in opening up old wounds."

"You're talking around what I really want to know, Royce." I cock my head to the side, staring at him. "Why is that?"

"Don't ask," Royce breathes, and then turns away from me so I can't see the sheen of tears in his eyes. "I don't know if you'll hate me, if you'll lose respect for me, or if you'll actually understand."

"My parents?" I ask the back of Royce's head, since he won't look at me. His shoulders are sloped, folding in on themselves.

"I told you not to ask," Royce grits out. "They aren't your parents. *I am*. That's all you need to know."

My words lash out forcefully like a fist. "I deserve an answer!"

"I don't think you can handle it yet, son." Royce turns back around, letting me see the agony etched across his face. "Just let it go and trust me. You're too fragile right now."

"That was answer enough. You said it was simpler for me, quicker. Now you're upset and refusing to tell me the truth." I rise to my feet, and then stare down at my *father*. "They gave me away, didn't they? My parents, they signed me away, and the petition of adoption went uncontested, didn't it?"

"Wynn, please." Royce scrambles to his feet. He stares up at me. "I beg of you. Stop."

Vein in my forehead throbbing, fists clenched, I open up my mouth and bellow down at him, "Answer me!"

"They didn't give you away. They didn't want to sign. They refused to take care of you, and they refused to let you go." Royce starts whispering the truth, like he doesn't want me to hear it. "You wouldn't have survived going back. Fuck, Wynn. You tried to blow your brains out. I would have done anything to ensure your continued health and happiness. *Anything.*"

"What happened?" I demand, and Royce answers.

"You're a minor, and they were your parents. Legally you couldn't live on your own. They were going to have me arrested, knowing it would ruin any hope of gaining the twins. They were using you, Hayley, and Hayden as leverage. They were going to force you to go back to them, and it would have killed you." Sympathy flashes across Royce's features, or maybe it is pity. "I gave them what they wanted all along, just like they knew I would."

I accuse, "What did you do?"

Royce waits a heartbeat, closes his eyes, and then destroys me. "They sold you."

SACRIFICE

I lunge to the trash barrel, losing everything I ate today. Body-wracking sobs compress in my chest as bile pours from my throat. I try to grip the edge of the barrel, but my strength is waning. Royce holds me up until the last of the spasms pass, and then he gently tugs me to the floor.

"Shh… Just rest a moment." Listless, I lie on the wood floor, unable to move or think. My eyes track Royce as he steps over to the far wall. He reaches into an ancient refrigerator, hand coming back out gripping a bottled water. He yanks a shop towel off the roll, and then comes right back to me.

Royce sits down next to me, and then maneuvers me around until my head is resting on his thigh. He unscrews the cap on the water, and then hands it to me. He presses the blue shop towel into my other hand.

"When I was a boy," Royce begins in a soothing voice, lulling me a bit. "I always wanted a big, red barn. Just a whim I had… After I met my Annie, I decided I better build one. I worked night and day, trying to save enough money so I could marry her."

Royce pauses to wrap my fingers around the bottle tighter. "Drink," he orders. I take a sip, and he rewards me with more of his story. He never talks about himself. Neither does Bren. It hurts them too much, so no one bothers asking anymore.

"I bought this chunk of land on the outskirts of town, right where we're sitting now. I had big dreams, and I would stop at nothing to gain them. I worked from the time I was fourteen until nineteen, and I still didn't have enough. Annie's daddy said I couldn't marry her until I owned land. So my daddy sold everything he had– everything. Just so I could afford this. Sacrifice."

Royce points at the towel gripped in my fist. "Wipe your face." I do as I am told and earn some more story. "I bought a forty-year-old trailer for a thousand bucks. It sat where the garden is now. Then Annie's daddy allowed me to marry her. My daddy lived with us, because that's what a good son does."

Royce's words are a punch to the gut. I start sobbing again, body quaking with the force. "Shush now. There'll be none of that.

I'm not passing judgment. You need to listen to the rest, and you'll see where I'm headed."

All I can do is shake my head as I swallow my tears. I take another sip of water, and then wash my face off again.

"We were struggling real bad. We all were working constantly but getting nowhere. My daddy, Annie, and me. Then Annie got pregnant with Bren, and I started working harder. We were barely surviving. But the one thing we were was happy. We had each other, and all of us were willing to make sacrifices. I don't know if it was an act of God, but my daddy and Annie made the ultimate sacrifice."

Royce reaches down to take the water bottle back, and then he drains half of it. "You see, us loving each other wasn't because we were perfect. The ability to love someone says more about you as an individual than the person you love."

"My parents don't love me," I rasp, throat burning from the bile I passed. "First they sold Willa, and then me... always to a Kennedy."

"They're incapable, Wynn. It has nothing to do with you, or Willa, or Warren, or Hayley, or Hayden. Because I love you guys more than words could express. The only thing it has to do with is them."

"I want to be surprised that they did this to me, but I'm not." I breathe the rest. "It still hurts, though. I don't ever want to be like them."

"That's my point. I didn't work hard because Annie was amazing. I worked hard because that was the type of man I wanted to be. Annie loved me because that's how she was. My father sacrificed everything for me because he was that type of person, not because I was God's gift of a son."

"I'll try to remember that." I clear my throat. "But it will be hard."

"It's a lesson you have to be taught over and over again. Every time you want to slip back into this bullshit, you have to remind yourself of what you have, not what you lost."

"They lost me." My earlier rage returns. Muttering in a dead voice, "I lost nothing," is a declaration.

"Don't," Royce warns, shaking me a bit. "Don't turn into them because they weren't capable of loving you. Keep your eyes open to what you have."

"I'm trying, but it's so fresh." I try to sit up, but Royce won't let me. "I promise I won't hurt them or myself, but I can't make myself not feel what I'm feeling."

"Let me finish what I'm trying to say, and maybe it will help open your eyes." Royce looks down at me, waiting for me to calm down, and then he begins again. "We had nothing but each other. Every week we were going more and more into debt, with less and less to eat, but we were happy."

"You wanted to know why I tried to kill myself– that's why. That was the life I was living, only there was absolutely no happiness. How did you… how did you find happiness inside all that misery?"

"Silver linings. Faith. Hope. A wide world view. Not wallowing in shit." Royce shrugs. "Take your pick, but it's easier said than done."

"I've been trying, Royce. Really trying. But it just keeps coming and coming… and coming…"

"Appreciate that it can always get worse, so know what you're living through now is not as bad as you think it is," Royce warns. "I was at work and Bren was at school. My dad was taking Annie to the doctor because she was pregnant again."

I just stare up at Royce's face, barely feeling the tears spilling from my eyes to fill my ears. Nothing in my life will ever be as bad as what Royce and Bren had to live through. It's time I got over myself.

Eyelids shuttering his emotions, Royce continues to torture us both. "Right in the middle of the highway, the car burst into flames, turning into a blast furnace. My pregnant wife and father were trapped and burned alive."

A whimper erupts from my throat. I squeeze my eyes shut and press my face against Royce's thigh. This is why Royce and Bren don't talk about it ever. It's hard to hear, but harder for them to voice.

"A faulty ignition switch. They paid the ultimate sacrifice, leaving Bren and me to never have to worry financially again."

"Blood money," I whisper. My mind plays hundreds of times when Bren would shut down because someone said he was lucky to be rich.

"Money can't bring a loved one back from the dead, and it can't buy happiness, but it has the power to change lives." Royce shocks me by smiling down at me. "The first thing I did was build me this big, red barn. I knew that would amuse my daddy as he watched me from heaven. Then I built Bren a big house– the house I planned on building his momma. That garden is in tribute to my own momma."

A sharp laugh escapes me. "Leave it to you to see the silver lining."

"I was in a bad place for a long while. Some days I fall back into that. Tragedy strikes, and God works in mysterious ways. Blah… Blah… Blah… Instead of sleeping, I would lie awake thinking. Why did Annie, our unborn baby, and my daddy have to die? Was it to save countless lives? To give Bren and me the resources to help the lives in this town? Why did Donny buy your sister, and then try to kill her? Was it so when she's able, she can share her story with women who are in similar situations?"

"I think that's the only way to deal with it." I move to sit up, and this time Royce allows it. "I feel like shit for being mad at you, and yelling at you." I look him directly in the eye while I apologize.

"Just because someone else's situation is worse than yours, doesn't mean you aren't feeling what you're feeling." Royce clears the air with the wave of his hand. "Now I'm positive that shit wasn't God's plan. It was simpler than that. All of these events culminated so we were all in a hard place that would bring us together– make us stronger.

"Now that huge house will be filled with family. Willa will have a strong man to take care of her, and I will have a family to make happy. Bren will have those siblings he's always needed. And you will feel wanted and loved for the first time in your life."

I have to turn my head, looking away from the sincerity glowing from Royce's face. I'm not sure if I can handle hearing anymore, but Royce offers me no relief.

"Anna and the babe died. My daddy died. Willa was almost murdered and left wounded, and Donny was imprisoned. We can't ask God why when it's so obvious it was to bring us all together."

"I… I…" Feeling overwhelmed again, I decide to make a joke. "I don't know if that's true or not, but it sounds better than bad shit happens to good people."

"You can be such a wiseass sometimes." Royce laughs at me, but then it dries up quicker than usual. "Wynn, we could stress on the hows and whys of it. We could throw up because of the stress of it. We could allow it to alter who we are, until we take a shotgun blast to the chin or a hunting knife to our forearms… or we could just accept that there was a reason, even if we don't understand it."

Royce stands up, and then reaches a hand down to help me rise. "We move on is what we do."

"Big, red barn, eh?" Curiosity gets the better of me, and I finally take a look around. "Apparently I'm not a dreamer, because I had no whims when I was a kid."

"You're still a kid," Royce reminds me. "You've still got time to dream some shit up." Catching the look on my face, "Except that. Don't be dreaming about that. No being alone with Kaden Marx. I mean it."

I ignore Royce. I've never had a dad who gave two shits, so being told what to do doesn't sit well with me. "This is nice. I like it out here." I wander around the barn, taking note of all the woodworking supplies. "I could live out here. Maybe I'll go get my cot and make myself to home."

"That's why I brought you in here." Royce picks up a rasp, focusing on it instead of me. "My office is where I escape. Bren jogs. Kade ties flies. That's why Willa and Warren's doctor required that they find a suitable escape." He presses the rasp to my chest, and I clutch it in my hands. "No one will come into this barn unless you invite them."

"What?" I mutter to Royce's retreating back.

Royce turns on his heel to face me, and continues to walk backward to the door. "Maybe I was dreaming of a big, red barn because someone else was gonna need it. Ya never know. The Lord works in mysterious ways."

My eyes bug out in surprise, and "Shit," flows from my lips. I place the rasp back on the worktable, noting all the new tools littering the surface. "You didn't have to do this. I don't want to run you from of your own barn."

"I built it and never saw a use for it," Royce admits while wearing an odd grin. "I only need a bit of space for the lawn tractor and garden supplies."

My mind's already imagining the possibilities. "Wow… thanks."

"Hey, Wynn?" Royce calls from the door. "If you care about someone, you have to make sacrifices. You have a bright future ahead of you, and Kade has goals that shouldn't be hampered. I'm not telling you to stay away from him because I'm being an asshole. I'm saying it because you need to hear it."

"Why?" I blurt out. "I can't help how I feel. It's not like Kade feels the same way back. Is it because I might be gay?"

Royce just stares at me for a minute, and then shakes his head back and forth. "I don't care," he sounds mildly insulted. "The adult will always be held accountable. Keep your dick in your pants around Kade, so he can keep his job. That's what I'm saying."

I glare at Royce. "It's not like Kade would ever take me up on it," I sputter out, exasperated. "Seriously?"

Royce tilts his head back and laughs, and then laughs some more. "Keep it in your pants around Kade until you're an adult and no longer a student of Kentwood Area School District. If you have to scratch an itch, do it with someone who has nothing to lose, someone who doesn't mean anything to you."

"Wow… Dad… way to give shitty advice." Bren's voice flows into the barn before he appears. "Advocating casual sex. It's no wonder I'm a slut."

Royce's head hitches to the side, setting his sights on his son. "Were you eavesdropping?"

"Did you suddenly forget who I am?" Bren steps into the barn. "Jeesh. Ya think you'd learn." Bren starts foraging around the worktable, like he knows what he's searching for. "This is nice. It's like someone knew exactly what you needed."

I'm relieved there's no note of jealousy in Bren's voice. I think of Warren and how he doesn't share– he wouldn't even share our shitty father.

"We can share the barn if you want," I mutter, unsure what else to say.

A brilliant grin brightens Bren's face. "Thanks, bro. But I think you need somewhere to get away from me… thanks, though." He drops the tack hammer back to the worktable. "I had to come out here because Willa's manning the stove, and I ain't sure she knows how to cook."

"Christ!" Royce hisses as he peels out of the barn.

Bren chuckles. "That got rid of him, now didn't it?" He leans against the table, still laughing. "Actually, Willa's reading the kids a book. I just wanted Dad to knock his shit off."

Uncomfortable, I start organizing my new tools. "Are you ready for preconditioning training tomorrow?"

Bren rolls his eyes. "Don't change the subject… but yeah, I'm ready. Three months without practice is killing me, and I miss our boys."

"Me too. I haven't touched a basketball in way too long."

"I'm just going to say this, and get it out of the way," Bren warns. "Dad's not just being a dad. There's something about you and Kade that's fragile. You feeling me?"

"I have no clue what you're saying, dumbass." I get defensive. "I. Am. NOT. Fragile. I could kick your ass if I was so inclined. I just don't believe in violence."

"Truer words… truer words," Bren chants just like his father does. He picks up the hatchet. "If Kade is caught in a compromising position with a student–" The hatchet blade severs a piece of rope. "Now you feeling me?"

"Yeah, I'm feeling ya." I take the hatchet away from Bren, and then hook it on the peg board. "No borrowing my tools until you know how to take care of 'em."

BACK OFF!

Proving Penny's thinking wrong that I'm a girl in my head, my first desire isn't to curl up in a ball and cry my eyes out in my bedroom. I just learned my parents saw me as a possession that could be bought and sold, and I fear Royce thought the truth would have me grabbing for the nearest shotgun. But I'm surprised I'm not surprised.

No longer Daddy and Momma. Corbin and Cora Gillette just put me in debt again. I have no idea the price tag I had slapped on my ass, but I'll have to pay Royce back somehow. Not only did Royce take me in, having to feed, clothe, and put a roof over my head, he had to pay to get me first.

Disgusting.

Instead of getting angry, violent, or stewing in misery, I find something else to dwell on. I can't be bought and paid for. While I will show respect and thankfulness, I will not sit down like a beaten dog and do as I was told just because cash exchanged hands.

When I'm told not to do something, it makes the need buzzing in the back of my mind that much stronger. The only thing I wanted to do tonight was the one thing I was warned against. I want to feel my kind of normal after learning my entire life was a lie, and I'm going to do it.

Armed with my canvas tool bag, I sneak away from my new home without being bogged down with guilt and shame.

I've never had anyone tell me what to do, to the point where I wanted to listen. All the bullshit my daddy spewed was during violent, drunken episodes. My parents didn't care what I was up to as long as I gave them what they wanted. I just spent three months acting like a grown man with a family. It rankles a bit to be told to back off.

It's late, but not too late to bother the neighbors. I make my way around Kade's house to the backyard. My eyes light briefly on Suicidal Tendencies as I head to the back porch, wondering how many secrets the chunk of ceramic knows and wishing it could spill a few.

I'm not here to seduce Kade, not like everyone thinks. I just want to say thank you for talking to me today, for making me feel safe and understood. I feel a bit guilty going against Royce's wishes, when I owe him so much. But I just couldn't resist doing something that had no strings attached.

I kneel to the side of the porch, paying mind to the lush hosta. I press on the riser, looking for its faults. I see nothing wrong, so I make my way to the other side of the porch. Immediately I spot the crack running along the riser. I fish around in my bag, looking for the pieces of metal I fashioned earlier. I grab my screwdriver and a few screws, and get to work securing the growing crack.

A light flicks on overhead, the glow lighting my work. "Wynn?" Kade calls out from the porch. "Is that you?"

"I'm almost finished," I call back. "I'll be on my way when I'm done." I affix the last piece of metal, holding it in place while I set the screw. "It's a good thing you brought this up. If the crack grew any wider, the steps might have collapsed on your heavy ass."

"I appreciate it, Wynn," Kade's voice is closer. I look up to see him leaning over the porch railing above me. His hair is loose again, so it takes me a second to notice his worried frown. "But you and I have to get something straight."

My hands fall to my lap– my screwdriver landing on the ground. "Royce got to you, didn't he?" I start putting my tools away, and then I zip my bag up like it pissed me off. "I just wanted a few minutes to do what *I* wanted to do. I wasn't doing anything bad."

"Wynn," Kade breathes like I'm killing him. "We can be friends. I like talking to you so much. But I can't be with you the way you need me to be."

I slip on the shoulder strap, and then rise to my feet. I flick a hateful glare at the zombie gnome as I walk away, because the grotesque thing will hear all the words I hoped Kade would whisper to me.

"Wynn! Stop!" Kade calls out. "Come back here!"

I keep walking, bitching at myself inside my mind with every step I take. *I'm an idiot. Why did I think he'd like me back? I just wanted to be friends. I love Warren and all, but how is he a better friend than I could be? I understood when I was a kid how it was Warren and Kade, and I was the annoying little brother tagging behind. But I'm a man now. Is it because I wanted to touch Kade? Maybe kiss him? I just wanted to show him how much I like him, make him happy. What's wrong with me?*

Lost in my thoughts, my feet hit the sidewalk. I'm jerked backward forcefully by a hand on the back of my t-shirt. I release a high-pitched shriek of surprise as I'm dragged off the sidewalk to the grass.

"You like that I'm stronger than you, remember?" Out of breath, Kade reminds me of the taunt I issued him earlier today. He tows me to the backyard with ease, proving how much stronger than me he truly is. Once we're out of the nosy neighbors' sight, he presses my back to his chest, wrapping his arms around me to immobilize me.

"I'm not trying to… seduce you," I bite out. Struggling, I fling my head from side to side. Kade grunts when my chin connects with his shoulder. "I don't know why, but I just wanted to hang out with you. Is that too much to ask?"

"No," Kade breathes into my ear, voice dark and heady. "That's not the issue." He shifts, and then my tool bag falls to the ground. His thick arms bind me tighter, and I try not to melt into him. "You're still a kid. A very confused kid. The fact that we've talked about some heavy shit isn't helping. It's a recipe for something that can't happen."

"Why not?" I challenge.

"I want you, is that what you want me to say?" Kade shouts the words, and then he lets me go. "Fuck! I want to kick my own ass." With a forceful shove, I land on the ground. Ass-planted, my palms are abraded by the ground. "You turned me into a pervert!"

"What the hell, you nut job? A pervert? You're the one spouting how being gay is our normal." I'm frozen on the ground, confused by the lost yet terrified look in Kade's eyes.

"I'm not a pervert because I'm gay," Kade snarls, voice slurring. "I'm a pervert because of when I started wanting you."

I try to get up, but Kade barks, "Stay down there– keep away from me!"

"Fine!" I shout back, my voice quivers with rejection. I try to get to my feet, but slip on the damp grass. "I'm going!" I scramble to my feet in a rush to leave.

"NO!" Mouth open like he's screaming, with great force, Kade shoves me back to the ground. "You're listening."

Stunned stupid, I glare up at the asshole version of Kade who used to come into the Circle K– the one who would be nasty to me for no reason.

"Shit!" Kade walks in a circle while yanking at his hair. "If I'm not around you, I'm good. If I chat with you in the group, I can keep my professionalism."

Hope bursts inside me. "Are you saying you like me?"

Kade stops moving, freezes, and then thaws. "Ya think?" he mutters sarcastically. "But we have some issues we need to discuss, both require you backing off so I can keep my sanity. No sweet gestures that make me want to pull you into my house and lock your ass in there with me. You have to stay away from me."

Turning belligerent, I mutter, "I don't want to."

"I know!" Kade bellows. "That's the problem."

"I don't really see the problem here." I sit up and fold my legs underneath me. "We seem to be on the same page. I just won't tell Royce I'm spending time with you."

Kade just glares at me.

"What? What'd I say that was so bad?"

"What you said is exactly what I expected you to say, and I'm not making fun of you." Kade drops to the ground to sit next to me. "I'm a grown man– a teacher. I have to be above reproach. But at the same time, there is something niggling at the back of my mind, like what they would accuse me of is the truth."

"Accuse you of what? I'm not in the first grade. I'm months away from being eighteen. I'm not asking to fuck you. I just want to get to know you."

"That makes it worse," Kade sputters. "Look around at this intolerant wasteland, Wynn. I know when you're finally able to slap a label on yourself, you'll be shouting that from the rooftops. But I don't have the courage or the luxury of doing so."

I lean forward, and whisper against Kaden's cheek, "I can keep a secret."

Kade jerks away, eyelids shuttering the hazel of his eyes, and then he groans deep in his throat. "You're so innocent– naïve. It's so intoxicating. You have no idea. Which is why I know what Royce says is the truth."

I demand, "What truth?"

"If I come out of the closet… if I get caught with a student in my school district… if they figured out I'm Mentor KM… I'll lose the job I was born to have. In a few years, I can come out if I'm in a committed relationship with an adult."

"Well, lock that fucking closet and stay in there, nice and safe." I don't say '*with me*' but Kade's glare says he read my mind.

"All it takes is one rumor and my life is over. Even if I don't lose my job, the rumor will infect the town. Old bigotry exists. If I'm outed, they won't want their children in my care, thinking I'll make them gay, or worse, that being gay somehow makes me a child molester– that pervert your daddy, your brother, and Royce have called me for the past six years. Even in the group, I have to be apart from it, only intervening with advice and encouragement. Bigots, and normal folks alike, would see it as an abuse of power, like I'm picking out a victim to fuck by exploiting their need for a place to belong. That's the truth of it."

Jesus, I feel so small, like I have to beg, and I hate it. "How is being my friend the issue?"

"Because–" Kade takes a deep breath, and then pierces me with his angry stare. "You want me, and maybe it's only because I make you feel safe. Maybe it's because I was there when you needed someone. Maybe not. Maybe so. But I'm not willing to find out."

"So that's it." Rejected, my hands fall to my lap, suddenly lifeless. "Just like that? I'll see you at Sunday dinner at Royce's, or when we're opening Christmas presents, or just walking around town. I'm supposed to just wave? Or are you going to ignore me? All because we're attracted to each other and you're afraid."

"You don't get it," Kade bites out. "I'm not a high school kid. I'm not Warren's buddy who used to come over to shoot at beer cans."

I jab my fingertip against his hard chest. "You're still you, Kade."

"I'm not that guy anymore, Wynn." He grips my finger, prying it away from his chest, and then he places my hand back on my lap, a safe distance from him. "I have three degrees and a mortgage. I want to be in a position where I can help the kids in this shithole, not have that stripped away because of a quick lay."

I test the words out on my tongue, "A quick lay?" while narrowing my eyes in a combination of anger and hurt.

Kade knows his words sting, yet he says them anyway. "We are *not* equals yet, and I won't stunt whatever we could build by starting a parent/child relationship with a high-schooler."

Completely floored, and unsure how to deal with it, I ramble, "Jesus Christ. You make me sound like a toddler. You call yourself a pervert but then make me feel like a stalker." The shakes start in my fingertips again, working their way through my hands and up into my arms. My stomach twists in on itself, readying to erupt. I've got to get the hell out of here before I'm sick. I breathe the word that is repeating over and over again in my mind. "Harsh."

"Wynn, I have to be harsh, because you're not hearing me. I think you're an incredible person– smart, witty, addictive. I'd love to be your friend but I can't be. I can't want you. I can't share myself with you. I can't touch you. You're going to have to back off."

The breath in my lungs seizes. My heart feels like it's going to implode. I gaze out at Suicidal Tendencies, needing something to anchor me. "I'll leave you be. I just… I just need a moment to get my feet beneath me."

Fingers twist in my hair and yank my head backward with violent intensity. "You're hearing what you want to hear, Wynn. You're not actually hearing what I'm saying." The fingers tighten, drawing a groan from my throat and another unfavorable reaction in my groin that I don't want to acknowledge.

Angry, hazel eyes glaring down at me, Kade's tone is laced with desperation and fear. "You have to stay away from me for my own sake. If a rumor starts, you'll look like a rockstar for bagging a teacher, enough to where they'll forget the gay connotations. To every adult, you'll be my victim and I will be your predator."

"I get it." I breathe, "Sacrifice."

Kade's fingertips release my hair abruptly, and I slump to the ground. "Wrong." His amused chuckle flows over my skin, prickling me with rejection. I have no idea what he finds so funny, when all I feel is sadness. "Patience is the word I'd use. At seventeen, waiting ten seconds seems like an eternity. I want to be your mentor until I can finally be your friend. Maybe in a few years, we'll be on the same page, and we can be lovers. Stop acting like I'm murdering you and razing your world."

"Don't laugh at me," I snap, trying to get to my feet. With a firm hand, Kade just yanks my ass back down next to him.

"I'm sorry, but you're hilariously a typical teenager." Fists clenched, Kade's laughter makes me want to resort to physical violence. He leans into me and whispers. "I'm not insulting you, Wynn. I used to act exactly like you. I find it endearing… intoxicating. Hotter than Hades." Kade shoves me backward; my elbows dig into the grass. "You have to get your ass away from me before I do something neither one of us will regret."

"Not a problem, asshole!" My palms lash out, landing in the center of Kade's chest. I lunge away from him, and then launch to my feet. My reaction just makes him laugh louder, which twists the blade of rejection even deeper. "Maybe if you'd stop yanking me closer and not letting me leave, I could get out of your sight!"

"Teenagers," Kade says with an evil snicker. "Remember those days? Pure fucking torture."

My head whips around, wondering if Kade is losing his marbles.

"The worst," my brother steps from the shadows. "I've got one across the street that's driving me to drink." Warren reaches for me, but I dart away. "See what I mean? The most illogical creatures known to man. Cute little shits, though. Ain't they?"

"The cutest," Kade murmurs. "Make sure Wynn actually heard what I said. No way could I get that point across to Royce and keep my nuts."

"What the fuck is this?" I demand, balling my fists up at my sides, never feeling more like a Gillette than I do now. "Were you listening this entire time?" My voice breaks with humiliation. "That was private!"

"Teenagers are predictable," Kade says, causing Warren to start laughing again. "Like Royce was going to let you out of his sight for five minutes, Wynn. Don't forget, I've been through this for the past six years. If Royce could, he'd wipe our asses after we take a shit." Noticing that I'm still confused, Kade finally explains. "Warren and I were ordered to wait for you to show up tonight."

Rubbing his ear dramatically, my brother groans. "My ear hurts from getting lectured. It's ringing, cold, and feels numb. Royce is worse than the counselors at rehab."

When Warren reaches for me again, I don't jerk away this time. I expect him to pound me like when I was little, but he just pats my back, trying to comfort me lamely.

"At least Royce didn't threaten your manhood." Kade mounts the back steps I just repaired, and it's like a punch to the nuts. "The man guilt-tripped me so bad I almost started crying."

"Yeah, the man's a heartstring tugger. Hey, say hi to my dog!" Warren chirps happily. "Is Pervert doing well without his daddy? I ain't seen him in three months."

I turn on my brother. "What the fuck? You don't have a dog?"

"Perty– my pug was a gift from Warren on my twenty-first birthday," Kade says through gritted teeth. "And I suggest we drop this thread of conversation, or I might drag your brother into my house and write you a check."

"Good God, do it!" Warren groans. "Not only would you both feel less frustrated, I could finally relax. I already had to buy you a goddamned purebred pug, don't make me ante up a grand when I can't afford it."

"Well, as you heard, you owe me your blessing now, so can you please get Royce off my ass."

"Royce is your dad, not mine," Warren reminds both Kade and me.

Kade flashes me a blinding smile so large his teeth glow. "Make sure Wynn gets it, okay?" and then he disappears into his house. The sound of the deadbolt locking closes off any possibility of us forming a friendship.

My eyes sting, and I refuse to acknowledge why. My mind is spinning maddeningly. Half of me wants to cry, while the other half says I need to man-up because I got what I deserved.

Nothing.

Just because I'm itching for someone, doesn't mean I'm entitled to them wanting me back. I feel like such a foolish asshole right now. I want to crawl in my bed and hide out for days, and I never want to speak to any of these bastards ever again.

"Well, brother…" Warren picks up my tool bag, shrugging it over his shoulder. "In Gillette speak: Kade wants you to sow your oats, grow up some, and then he'll fuck your brains out if you're still interested. That clear enough for ya?"

"Crystal," I mutter darkly.

"But from one Gillette to another, I beg of you to somehow get into his pants before you turn eighteen. The judgmental, self-righteous prude needs to be knocked down to size. Plus, I've got a pregnant woman on my hands, and I ain't got the money to lose."

"What are you going on about? Are you drunk? High?"

"Nah, just stacking the odds in my favor, is all."

"What odds?" I narrow my eyes at my brother, but I know him. He ain't gonna give in. So I drop it. "I didn't come here to fuck Kade. I don't even know if I want that. I only wanted to say thanks for being my friend, and I end up with it being thrown in my face and being dicked with."

Warren follows me as I head for the sidewalk. "It's because you're too nice," He schools me in his warped version of adulthood. "Nice guys always finish last. Ya gotta take what you want, not ask for it." He drops to his knees right on the sidewalk, begging and pleading with me. His hands are clasped like he's praying. "Please, if you love me, you'll *take* it. Soon."

Getting a clue, something snaps in me, so I reply to my brother the only way I can, with hostility. "It's no wonder you're buddies. Y'all are fucking pricks."

Still on his knees, Warren, pointing at my old front porch– his new front porch –where Penny is standing with her arms folded over her chest and a fierce scowl on her face, "That's what she said!"

•MID-AUTUMN•

BACON AND EGGS

"It's almost been two months," Royce reminds me. He grabs a waffle off the stack, and then pours fake butter-flavored syrup all over it. "Are you ever going to talk to me again?"

Bren, Royce, and I prefer real maple syrup, but since Willa and the kids love that sticky stuff… which is one of the reasons I don't talk to Royce anymore. I never get my way.

"I talk to you," I reply shortly. Instead of being conscientious, I hog all of the bacon by picking the platter up and dumping its contents on my plate. Undeterred, Bren just reaches over and grabs a fistful, then he passes bacon out to everybody.

"No, you *answer* me," Royce stresses. "You're proving me right by acting like a kid."

"I *am* a kid, remember?" I mutter sarcastically. "I'm not a grown man who should have any say in his life. I'm supposed to act my age. So I am." I reach for the platter of scrambled eggs, but Willa smacks the back of my hand with a spatula, and then puts a scoopful on my plate. "Kids don't talk to their parents. They don't listen to 'em, either." I reach for the ketchup, and Hayley snatches it and hides it in her lap.

I don't like eggs without ketchup.

There are four kids in this house, and somehow I managed to become the bad apple. I don't even recognize myself anymore. Used. Abused. Shot. Sold. Bought. Adopted. Betrayed. Rejected. Bet. After my maggot parents and Royce, Kade, and Warren made me feel and look like an asshole, I decided to give them what they were asking for by actually acting like an asshole.

My family is learning to work around me. They've had more than a few breakfasts without bacon and eggs, and every conversation I've had with anyone over the age of seventeen has been one-sided. Even my teachers are fed up with me, and I never thought I'd see the day.

Being angry is exhausting, and I feel guilty over making everything about me instead of blending us into a family and making Willa feel safe and comfortable. I've been through a lot, and I felt I earned the right to be a selfish prick. But I've punished us all long enough. I want *me* back, but I fear that Wynn no longer exists. I decide it's high time to speak my mind.

"I'm over you adopting me against my will, because I get it." I speak the words, but they sound hollow. For the first time, I realize I might actually have an issue with Royce adopting me like an unwanted, throwaway puppy. "I'm dealing with all my freedoms being taken away for my own protection. But what's been eating me is how you made me feel like a predator– some kind of stalker."

With the edge of my fork, I slide all the bacon on Bren's plate, and then the eggs on Willa's. I've been eating too much because I end up throwing most of it back up and I'm trying to keep on some weight.

"Wynn." Royce uses his sympathetic voice, but it only makes me feel pitiful.

"It wasn't… I didn't…" I stumble over my words, not wanting the kids to hear the word I need to use. "I'm humiliated. Mortified. I didn't want to play *carpenter* with Kade." My voice breaks from trying to finally release my bottled-up emotions. "I wanted to get to know him. Not know him like I did when I was a kid, but how two grown men know each other, but more than that."

"I know," Royce starts in, but Bren cuts him off. "That wasn't the problem. Kade is older than you. He's frustrated, and it's making him ornery. He was looking at you like *carpentry* was the only thing on his mind. Ya feeling me, here? He wanted to nail you. Hard."

Blushing bright red, I hide my head in my hands and sputter between my splayed fingers. "Not that I would have minded none, but I'm sure your imaginations are running wild."

"The only innocents at this table have Gillette blood flowing through their veins." Bren swats the back of my head so I'll look at him. "My well-honed carpentry skills can spot an easily manipulated *friend*, and I'd put Kade in that category too. He has the knowledge but he's never put it into practical use."

"Bullshit," I blurt out.

"Language!" Willa smacks the back of my hand with the spatula again, causing the twins to giggle. We've all had our asses tanned for cursing.

Wincing, I try to rub the sting away. "That's gonna bruise."

"I agree with Bren's assessment of Kaden," Royce says brusquely. "I suggest we change the subject."

Ignoring his dad, "I know you've been ghosting in the group," Bren accuses me, and he'd be right. It's been almost two months, and I've yet to type a single word in the group, but I'm always there. Lurking... watching.

"I tried to get Kade to tell me the juicy shit when he'd come home on weekends from Penn State, but he'd clam up and get embarrassed. So we've all been working together to get his story for you. But he just keeps calling himself a late bloomer, and leaving it at that."

"I was watching when he brought up the college roommate." I can't help the feeling of violent jealousy that strikes my gut. I grit out in a nasty tone, "Kade's not innocent."

"Subject change," Royce repeats. "Wynn, I don't want you walking Hayley and Hayden to their second grade classroom. Stay out of the little school."

"Are you shitting me?" I raise my hand before Willa can smack it. "Don't even think about hitting me. No one could censor themselves after that horseshit."

Royce grabs my hand, spreading my fingers against the tabletop. He stares pointedly at my sister. "Nah, I think I'll let those go," Willa drawls. "That was a real shit move on your part, Royce."

Recoiling, Royce lets go of my arm. His brown eyes look to be swimming in his head, but his lips are upturned at the corners. Willa's never talked back to him before, and it's having an odd effect on the man.

Hayley turns to Bren. "Well, shit... am I allowed to say shit now?"

"As long as it's not at school, sure." Bren releases an evil snicker. "Why not? What's the big f'n deal?"

"Kade is coming over for Sunday supper, so that is not why I said that." Royce glares at all of us, probably wishing he'd never dreamed of a huge, dysfunctional family. "I want the kids to be more independent. What I meant to say... I want you to deliver them to the little school, and they are to find their own way from there. It's not so you won't see Kade. It's because they are old enough to do it themselves."

"I'm sorry," I mutter, ashamed. "I feel like an ass... Oops." I reach over to grab Willa's spatula, and then I whack myself. "I earned that one."

"I think you earned this." Hayden steals the ketchup– kid sauce –from his sister, and passes it to me.

"I'm sorry I've been so… awful." I blink a few times, forcing my eyes to appear dry.

Bren elbows me in the side. "You need to *blow* off some steam. Trust me when I say it's like taking a happy pill."

"Seriously?" Having the patience of a saint, Royce rolls his eyes. Since Willa's giggling, Bren doesn't get into trouble for conversing about oral sex at the breakfast table. "Y'all have too much time on your hands. Willa's joined Rusty Knob Volunteer Fire Department Auxiliary. So from now on, we're all going to be helping from time to time– get into the community spirit."

Chair almost clattering to the floor, coming to his feet, "We have practice starting next week!" Bren shouts. "Then we have games. I don't have any time to myself as it is. I went from being an only child to…" Bren's hands flutter, pointing at all of us surrounding the table. "To *this!*"

Unfazed by Bren's theatrics, Willa asks, "Don't you always have practice?" But she does look confused. "Am I missing something?"

"That was preconditioning," I explain to my sister. "It's just to keep us in shape. Regular practice is torture. Coach Nichols beats the shit out of us." I yank my hand from the table. "Shit's an approved word now that you've used it. Fair's fair."

"This is nonnegotiable," Royce declares as he pushes away from the table. "I know your schedule better than you do, so you can't pull any shit over on me." He stalks over to the kitchen island, grabbing the kids' sack lunches. "Since it's a Friday, I'll extend the curfew until one a.m. Fair?"

"I'm not complaining!" Bren claps excitedly. "Sign me up for the next chicken barbeque if you're willing to extend curfew every weekend. Craft Fairs? Car Shows? Sign my behind up!"

"You're hopeless." Chuckles flow from my lips as I reach for my backpack. I feel freer than I have in months. "Ready, little ones?" I call as I walk toward the door. "Sorry about breakfast, Willa. I was being a shit."

"No problem," Willa calls back. "Have a good day at school!"

"Wait, Wynn," Royce collars me before I get a few feet out the door. "You need this." He hands me a to-go cup of some kind of gray sludge that is probably one of Penny's recipes. Confused, I just stare at it. "It's a protein shake so you'll get some quick absorbing nutrients."

My heart constricts. Royce knows. Speechless, all I can do is nod my head. But I'm positive he reads what I'm feeling directly from my thoughts.

Down the sidewalk, Hayden's voice flows to my ears. "I'm pretty sure the word shit is gonna get overplayed."

Walking into the gymnasium, I draw up short. "Why is Francis doing cartwheels?"

Franny is short, with a curvy behind and muscular legs. He's got a waist that indents like a girl. The kid's shorts ride up every time he lands on his hands, showing off his jockstrap. This isn't out of the ordinary for him, but it's still not something I see every day.

"If Franny's not careful, he's either gonna get beaten or violated." I shake my head, worried about the guy. Jack shudders next to me, not sure if he's getting turned on or is going to be sick.

"I don't understand Franny." Jack shudders again. "He's so normal when we hang out. But then he goes and ruins it by being sexy."

I raise an eyebrow at my best friend, finding it odd how we're complete opposites. "You find Franny sexy? If I had a type, I'd think it was burly."

Jack snorts. "No shit. You have no idea how you and Kade look side by side. Intimidating and hot as fuck. I'm into someone who can't break me in half. I only weigh a hundred and thirty pounds, and Kade would suffocate me."

Out of nowhere, Bren puts me in a headlock, jumps on my back, and starts shouting, "Giddy up, brother! Giddy up!" I struggle to throw him off, but he's too strong. Light as a feather, though, which is probably why Jack is sniffing around him. "Giddy up!"

"Are you high?" Jack asks for me.

Letting go, I decide to act carefree like Franny. I break into a run. "Fuck it!" I shout as I charge across the gym with Bren on my back, with Franny as my destination.

"Clarification," Jack shouts as he runs after us. "Are you both high?"

"I've got exciting news!" Bren shouts into my ear. "Oh, good! Franny's protecting himself," is his odd explanation for our scorekeeper displaying his assets on the basketball court.

My face scrunches as I come to a dead stop. "The fuck?" I drop Bren on the floor, but he takes it in stride. Jumping to his feet like a demented Jack-in-the-box, I begin to wonder whether or not he really is high.

"I overheard Coach Nichols." Bren rubs his hip and mouths, "*Ouch...* Anyway, you know it's my favorite pastime."

"I thought being a whore was your favorite pastime," Jack grumbles, still feeling a bit bent out of shape. We've bonded the past few months over being spurned by our crushes. "I'm positive you pay for it."

"Wait," I put my hands out, stopping them both. "A whore is the one who gets paid, right? Are you saying Bren's so good he gets paid?"

"Thanks for the compliment, Duncan." Bren puffs out his scrawny chest. "So, anyway, we're getting visitors, so Franny is being *fran*tastic!"

"High," Jack says at the same time I say, "Nucking futs."

Coach's shrill whistle has us all flinching. "Git yer asses on the bleachers! ASAP!"

Like a small horde, all twelve of us run across the court, and then sit our asses on the courtside seats. Coach Nichols can be a scary sonofabitch– he reminds me of what my daddy would be like if he was only thirty and sober. We're all sitting prim and proper, with our hands folded in our laps, when the side doors open.

Leaning into me, "Are we being invaded?" Jack breathes in my ear.

Smirking with arrogance, "I tried to tell you, but you wouldn't listen," Bren whispers back.

"Oh, wow..." My mouth hangs open, catching flies. "Unreal."

In a wave, Furrow Creek's Hornets flow from the boys' locker room, both the JV and Varsity teams. At the same time, Hillock Corners' Tigers escape the girls' locker room. Both sides glare at each other, like they don't know what the hell is going on either. It's almost comical; they turn to us, register they're trespassing, and then take a quick step back.

"Alright! Alright! Alright!" Coach Nichols claps sharply while shouting at us. "Every fucking year our rivalries get in the way of making it past districts."

"Where's Willa's spatula when you need it?" Bren snickers in my ear. "We are still on school grounds, right?"

"You cocksuckers annihilate each other on the court, and then invade territories, until we're so off kilter, we can't play worth a shit. We're done."

"What Coach Nichols is so eloquently trying to say–"

"Well, pardon me," Nichols sings in a haughty tone while pulling a face. "You just go right ahead and cut me off on my own court, and speak for me while you're at it. Hillock Corners is filled with sanctimonious bastards and inbreds!"

"RAMS!" We shout as a unit, just barely edging out Hillock Corners', "TIGERS!"

"Silence!" Coach Danvers screams above the insult slinging. "Jasper, you're instigating the same rivalry we're trying to eradicate."

Coach's name is Jasper?

"You talk like a tool, Crispin." Nichols sneers at the more intelligent man, but then he shuts up.

"Crispin?" Bren snorts. "Are we seriously going to listen to some little dude named Crispin?"

"I'm going to get down to brass tacks," Danvers starts again. "Unless Coach Smithers wants the floor?"

"Why didn't we get that man as our coach?" Jack whispers in my ear.

"Nichols is a brute, but we're better because of it," Bren answers. "Danvers probably allows his team to make all the decisions instead of being their coach. Diplomacy is for losers."

"What's that make Coach Nichols?" Duane leans forward, trying to talk to us a few guys down the bench. "A communist dictator?" We all shrug and nod in agreement.

"Pretend Furrow Creek isn't attending this train wreck," is Coach Smithers' response. "I want no part in this insanity."

"You're only as good as your competition," Danvers begins, and I decide to respect the well-spoken man. "We spend pre-season and post-season practicing with our own teams. We play against other teams a few times a week during the season. But that isn't enough to learn, to grow, not only as a team, but as individual players."

"Danvers?" Duane calls from courtside. "So if our team sucks, we can't get any better, because we're practicing and playing against people who can't play for shit?"

"Winning against last place only makes you runner-up loser," a lanky kid from Hillock Corners shouts. "We're never challenged."

"If it wasn't for basketball camp every year," a short, stocky kid from Furrow Creek breaks in. "I'd only ever practice with my team."

"Excellent." Danvers claps. "We're getting along, and we're understanding. Progress."

"Listen up, ya lazy fuckers!" Nichols shouts. "The practice schedule stays the same, with the exception that Hillock Corners and Furrow Creek will be bussed here every afternoon. You'll have a different coach every day, in a rotation."

"No more rivalries," Smithers finally speaks up. "No more sabotaging each other. During practice, you will be known as the Kentwood Area School District team. But during the season, you will play against each other as usual. You will know each other's strengths, weaknesses, and how your minds work. It will make for a stronger, more challenging game."

"We hope this will lead us to victory." Danvers claps again, and Bren snorts at the ridiculousness.

"Yeah, but only one team can win districts," a boy from Hillock Corners sounds as baffled as we feel. "Only one of us can move forward."

"Then I guess the better team will win, ya dumb fuck," Nichols goes off at the mouth again. "Don't be a pansy ass like your coach. Man up."

"Whichever team progresses shouldn't matter." Danvers turns diplomatic as expected. "You can take pride that your school district is representing us, and that you helped strengthen the team that makes it to the playoffs."

Duane turns to us, "We do anyway. What's the big fucking deal? The Rams are ranked fourth in the state."

"Maybe we'll win this year," I pitch in. "We're seniors. This is our last shot." Cupping my hands around my mouth to project my voice, I shout loudly, "I'm in. Our boys are in."

"Well, if Gillette says he's in, we're in," Coach Nichols blabbers, taunting me, and I know I'm going to regret it later.

"You're so belligerent," Danvers sneers. "Are you off your meds?"

"Oh, my God. Jasper and Crispin are going to kill each other," Jack whispers, sounding sarcastic as all get out. "Awesome!"

"What the–" Franny's ass wedges between my hip and Jack's.

"They're cousins," Francis starts gossiping. "Coach Nichols and Coach Danvers. A lot of the kids on the opposing teams are related. Coach was calling his own cousin a pansy ass and saying he talks like a tool. How fun!"

"Oh, fount of juicy information," Bren purrs. "Please keep flowing."

"That lanky kid who had the balls to speak up from Hillock, his name is Tyler Ross. His mom is the school board superintendent, and he's one of the ghosts in our Facebook group. Of the fifteen kids in our group, nine of us are in our gym right now."

"More. More!" Bren gets overexcited.

Head jerking up from his coach huddle, "Shut the fuck up, Kennedy!" Nichols demands.

"Yes, coach," Bren shouts back. "Sorry, Coaches."

Silent, Bren, Jack, Francis, and I start examining every player in the gym, wondering who knows our secrets. There's five kids spread out between those two teams. After Josh outed us all on Facebook, everyone in the group knows exactly who we are. It doesn't help that half of Franny's ass is on my thigh, with all four of us huddled together. We might as well put an arrow above our heads.

Bi. Questioning. Super Gay. Gay.

Most of the guys are chatting within their teams, but the five kids stick out easily. All of them are staring at me with curiosity and fear, like they can't figure me out and they're worried I'm going to out them. Without shame, I just look back and smile.

"Alright, douchebags!" Coach Nichols gains our undivided attention. "Y'all git yer asses acquainted, because yer either gonna get along, or I'ma run you into the ground."

"Jasper," Danvers cautions. "Have some fun, guys. You need to remember we're doing this for you. There is no I in team!"

"Yer such a tool, Crispin." Nichols smacks the smaller man upside the head, but he's grinning like a villain. "I don't care whatcha do or where ya go. The busses for Hillock Corners and Furrow Creek leave at nine. Git yer asses on the bus, or be stranded. I don't give a fuck. Git outta here!"

"You hillbillies got a bar around here somewhere?" Coach Smithers looks to our team. "You're teenagers. You ought to know."

"Rusty's," Duane shouts. "Right on the main drag."

"Thank ya kindly, kid." Smithers turns, leaving his team behind as he walks out of the gymnasium. Nichols and Danvers follow after him.

"Is he a drunk?" I grumble, judging the asshole.

"Nah," Francis replies, finally hopping off my lap. I rub my thigh– it was falling asleep. Francis may be rainbows and glitter but he's full-grown. "Smithers is a good dude. Men bond over beer, I guess."

"Yeah, my daddy celebrated everything with beer. He used to put it in my baby bottle." I flinch, realizing what spilled out against my will. "I guess since I'm in charge of you bastards, I better go introduce us."

I'm met halfway by Furrow Creek's and Hillock Corners' point guards. We eyeball each other for a moment, determining who's in charge.

"Wynn Gillette," I say as I hold my hand out for a shake, waiting to see who's going to go first. I remember the tall kid with the bad acne from Furrow Creek. He's a piss-poor point guard. He can't dribble, pass, or shoot the ball for shit, and should be benched. He glares down at my hand, and then walks around me to greet my team that's standing at my back.

"Colton's a homophobic prick," Tyler Ross barks out as his hand slips into mine. I glance over my shoulder to see Colton giving Franny a wide berth, but he engages with the rest of my boys. "Nice seeing ya again, Wynn. You always seem to whip my team's ass on the court. It's a good thing I don't have an ego."

"Shit, man." I huff a laugh. "I remember you, all right. You run dang good offensive plays. As for defense?" I rub the phantom pain in the center of my chest. "Elbow jab to the solar plexus, if I remember right." I laugh a bit, remembering how pissed I was when no foul was called. "Ref must have blinked."

"Yeah, and you still made the shot." Tyler sounds a bit awed, and I decide on the spot that I like the tall, lanky guy. "This strategy is going to be epic."

"Epic failure," I say with a laugh. "I'd say it was my coach's idea, but he's an imbecile. The only reason we do okay is because he runs us to death. I'm guessing it was your coach's idea. He seems like he has the brains but not the power to make you guys work for it."

"Damn straight, skippy." Tyler winks at me, like he knows all my secrets. He pulls his cellphone from his pocket, looks at the screen, and then pins me with the bluest eyes I've ever seen. "Wynn, it's only four o'clock, and I've got five hours to burn. What's fun to do around here?"

"Not much," I grunt. "It's why everyone is either drunk or high, or screwing their brains out."

"Wynn Gillette doesn't do any of those things," Tyler proves he has my number. "So, what does the elusive Rusty West do for fun? The group's been a bit chaotic without your input lately. Where have you been?"

"I see we aren't going to pretend we don't belong to the group, eh?" I lift my eyebrow in Tyler's direction, and the brat mimics me. Chuckling, I shove against his shoulder. "Dumbass."

"I get them waxed once a month." Pink tongue flicking out, Tyler licks two fingertips, makes a nasty gesture with his tongue and V-shaped fingers, and then smooths his eyebrows. "It arches higher this way. Gotta look like a badass."

"I'm all natural," spills from my lips for some reason, causing Tyler to check me out. Feeling ballsy all of the sudden, I do the same thing.

Challenge accepted.

I run my eyes from Tyler's faded blue Chucks, his jeans with the knees blown out, over his Tootsie Pop t-shirt– *How many licks does it take?* Tyler's hair swings against his jawline, and the scruffy blond stubble on his chin looks soft.

"How many licks does it take?" comes out of my mouth, and I wonder who's speaking for me.

Tyler looks a bit thrown, but he grins. "For you?" I nod like I have this flirting shit figured out. "I'd probably be creaming before the first one."

"Jesus." The visual slams into me, stalling the breath in my lungs and causing my pants to get too tight.

"Quit eye-fucking each other," Bren breaks in, arm hooking around my neck. "At least postpone it until we're out of an enclosed space filled with hillbilly homophobes."

Tyler turns his face away, but not before I notice the blush creeping up his cheeks. "Shit," he hisses, voice quivering. "You're right. These assholes wouldn't listen to Josh Truman after he came out. They beat the fuck out of him the night before he took off for Rhode Island."

"How is that scumbag doing?" Bren snarls, still sore. "Is he enjoying getting his pucker stretched by Brown's freshman class?" I put my hand on Bren's chest to shut him up, because Tyler looks miserable right now, and I don't like it.

"Josh," Tyler's voice breaks. "He's doing better. I… um… it was my fault he outed everyone. I wouldn't come out, so he was throwing a tantrum."

Bren starts to go into gossip mode, so I stop him in his tracks. "What are we doing tonight? Remember, our curfew was extended?"

"You!" Bren shouts, pointing at Tyler. "We'll be driving your ass home tonight." Tyler and I both go to ask why, but Bren cups his mouth with his palms, and then bellows. "PIZZA! If you know how to dribble a ball, free pizza! Follow me, faggots!"

"Slurs, really?" Jack shouts into my ear over the sound of forty idiots losing their shit. There's a bottleneck at the doors as they all try to charge through, having no clue where they're going. I point at Duane so he'll show them the way to Calhan's Pizza Barn.

"Hey, Duncan!" Bren shouts back, and then he's mouthing the words. "I can use it since I love dick, but they don't know that. They think I'm being a good ol' boy, and that's how you protect your ass."

"I'm moving," Jack grumbles, and it has Francis offering, "You can come with me. I'm leaving and never looking back the minute the ink is dry on my diploma."

"I'm staying," I admit for the first time. "Y'all better write."

"You know damn well I ain't going anywhere," Jack shouts, and then he jogs out the doors, leaving us behind.

"What crawled up his ass and died?" Bren's oblivious.

"The fact you like pussy, I suspect," Tyler pitches in after seeing Bren and Jack interact for all of two minutes. "I'm curious… what's the pizza place gonna think when we invade and don't pay."

"Since I'm buying, they'll probably be jumping for joy. Least this month they'll make rent on the building." Bren speaks to Tyler like they're old buddies, and I don't bother putting in my two cents. I've been inputting all of Royce's invoices into QuickBooks, so I know the score.

"Dad's way too forgiving, but it's sweet," Bren prattles off. "As long as I'm buying something from town for a good reason, he's all for it. So we'll be eating a lot of pizza after practice from here on out."

"I can't take this shit!" Jack shouts as loud as his lungs will allow. "We have to get out of here before I lose my fucking mind."

Bren, Jack, Tyler, and I are huddled around a small table in the middle of Calhan's. It's standing room only after all the tables were taken. The only reason we have a place to rest our asses is because Bren threatened not to pay if they didn't give up a table. It wouldn't be so bad, except that it's a Friday night and everyone in town is getting takeout.

"I hate crowds," Jack's still blathering. "It's like they're swallowing us alive."

"Calm your shit, Duncan," Bren orders. He reaches over to squeeze Jack's shoulder. "Just close your eyes, and breathe in and out. I already told them to make it to-go. We'll light a bonfire in the backyard. Okay?"

"Okay." Jack does as he was told, closing his eyes and taking even breaths. "I don't know why I'm like this."

"You just are," Bren says patiently, dealing with Jack in a way that reminds me of how Kade used to manage me. It makes me feel happy for them, but sad at the same time. "Deal with it, buddy. I've got your back."

Tyler and I share a look that speaks volumes. *How are they so blind?* We both shrug at each other and laugh.

"Have you been accepted anywhere?" I try to make small talk with Tyler as Bren coddles Jack.

Looking a bit sad, Tyler mutters, "Brown."

"Ah, Rhode Island." My lips quirk up in the corners. "Long distance relationship, or just parting ways until meeting back up?"

"Josh wants nothing to do with me unless I come out." Tyler looks away from me, but he keeps speaking. "I'd already been accepted when we broke up… So, where do you go off to next year?"

"West Virginia U." I point at Bren and Jack, who are completely ignoring us. "With those idiots." I mock cheer, "Go Mountaineers!"

"Basketball?" Tyler raises his manicured eyebrow at my buddies, and I know what he's asking. It's like we've been friends for ages.

"Me? Yeah. Them?" Tyler nods. "No fucking way. They suck. Take that from the man who tries to get them to listen to my plays."

"I am paying attention, jerkoff," Bren grumbles. "Some brother you are."

"I'm the best big brother you have." I flash a shit-eating grin.

"You're the only big brother Bren has, and he's not worthy." Clearly Jack's still bent out of shape over Bren screwing Trina Sherman last week– all week, and this morning in the janitor's supply closet.

"HEY!" Bren shouts all of the sudden, but he's looking behind me. "Speaking of the fact that I have more than one big brother."

Glancing over my shoulder, I mutter, "What the–"

"Awkward," Jack drawls out just as my eyes light on Kade.

Totally involuntary on my part, my entire body betrays me. A shudder rolls up my spine. My eyes become heavy-lidded, and my lips part.

Kade doesn't look anywhere else besides me as he makes his way through the crowded restaurant. It's almost been two months since I'd seen Kade last. I haven't caught sight of him anywhere. I haven't spoken to him in person or online. It was torturous. It's been so long since I've connected with those hazel eyes, I don't know if it feels good or bad to feel the snap engage between us.

I've been proving something to myself and to everyone else. I can make sacrifices and be patient. I've been upset with Royce because he doesn't trust me. I understand how Kade doesn't trust himself, but his actions scream he doesn't trust me either. Understanding or not, it makes me feel like shit.

"Hi," I breathe, no sound coming out, but Kade hears me anyway. He walks right over to me, places his hand on my shoulder, and then glides his fingertips across the nape of my neck.

"Hello, groupies," Kade says cheerfully, as if he's not wreaking havoc on my entire nervous system. My skin is quivering, trying to get closer to his touch. Such an innocent yet possessive touch is disturbingly erotic to my senses.

I thought I got hard for Tyler earlier– I thought wrong. I harden so rapidly, my dick physically aches and my nuts swell past the point of discomfort. I try not to whimper as I adjust myself in my seat by pulling at my pant leg.

"It's strange seeing you guys mixing together." Kade glances around, with a fake, strained smile plastered on his face. Every second or so, his fingertips pulse on my neck. "Seventy-five percent of the group is in this pizzeria. Bizarre."

"We're hiding amongst the straight folk," Tyler mutters sarcastically. His eyes narrow, noting how Kade's fingers are now absent-mindedly running through the back of my hair, and I'm trying my damnedest not to react. I hold my body still, as if I'm formed of ice, when all I want to do is melt into Kade's touch.

"Normal people are boring." Bren flashes us a grin, appearing innocent when he's reveling in the chaos erupting between Kaden and me.

"Breeders, always repopulating the earth." Jack sounds downright belligerent. "The thought of straight sex turns my stomach."

Bren flips around, "What the fuck, Duncan? That was a pretty intolerant thing to say."

"Sounded like a bitchy, vindictive, jealous thing to me," Tyler whispers, going unnoticed. "But what do I know?"

"I hate the words normal, tolerant, awareness, and acceptance," Kaden enters Mentor KM territory, and it makes me miss him so goddamned much that I almost latch onto him. "I get why people use them, like they're being helpful. But to tolerate us means we're wrong– or less than. You don't have to tolerate me, be aware of me, or accept me as if I'm not a normal human being. It just pisses me off."

Kade's standing next to me, his fingertips biting into the back of my neck, and he's seething. Everyone at our table is utterly silent as we absorb the gravity of his words. I reach out and wrap my hand around the back of his thigh, and squeeze a few times to center him– I turn into a living, breathing Suicidal Tendencies. Kade exacts the same amount of pressure on the back of my neck in thanks, and then I let my hand fall away.

"I apologize," Jack blurts out. "I can't say I didn't mean anything by it. I get so fed up with Bren screwing anything with a snatch."

"That's between you and Bren," Kade stresses. "But if you ever need any advice, you know where to find me."

"Okay. Thank you, Mentor–"

"Eh! What'd I tell you?"

Jack blushes, turning shy, and we all chuckle because the tension has broken. "Thank you, Kade," he corrects himself.

"Wynn?" Kade grips my chin, yanking my head to the side so I'll have to give him my undivided attention, and my cock almost misfires from the intensity of his gaze. "I didn't mean we had to avoid each other, or never see one another. You can call me, you can text me, message me. Please," the word sounds downright pleading. "I'm still your mentor."

"I want a friend," comes out of nowhere. "One who trusts me."

"I do trust you." Kaden tugs the hair at the back of my neck. "Clearly it's me I don't trust."

"You can trust me enough to know I'd say no," I bite out, not giving a shit who is witnessing our conversation. "Don't call me a child, treat me like a child, and then say you want something from me only a man can give. That's bullshit."

Kade's eyebrows dip low as frustration flashes across his features. "Older. Taller. Stronger. Smarter. Remember? I trust you not to say no to anything I ask, because that's what makes you feel safe and comforted when you're around me."

"Fine," I grit out. "I'll be a kid then. But don't get pissed if I do something childish that you won't like."

Kaden releases a growl that rolls across my flesh and takes up residence in my dick. I'm not going soft anytime soon. "Teenagers," he snarls hotly, eyes scorching mine. "Such cute little assholes that make me want to do things only I will regret."

I arch a brow at Kade in challenge. "School teacher? Mentor? Teenager hater?"

"It's not hate I'm experiencing right now." Kade's eyes snap shut, and then he takes a deep breath. "I can only be near you if Royce is with us. This is getting worse."

"Wynn turns eighteen a week before Christmas," Bren turns helpful.

"Shut up!" Kade snaps. "Stop talking to Warren, Bren. Don't twist Wynn and me up over some bullshit from six years ago." He takes a few deep breaths, trying to calm himself. "Besides, legal adult isn't the issue, so try June at the earliest."

"I guess I have eight more months to be a little asshole," I volley back. For some reason, I'm getting hotter the more frustrated Kade is getting. Payback for turning my offer of friendship into something nasty, and for making me feel like a stalker freak, when all I wanted to do was talk to him.

"Pizza for Marx!" flows from the back of the restaurant.

"That's me!" Kade shouts back, sounding relieved. Turning Jekyll and Hyde, "Well, kids, have a good evening," he says pleasantly. "Bren? Wynn? I'll see you at home for Sunday supper," and then he strides away, flowing through the mass of bodies.

"That man is about to pop a nut if he doesn't get some," Tyler mutters in awe, and then releases an uncomfortable laugh. "Holy fuck!"

"That, right there, was nothing," Bren drawls. "You should have seen how Wynn's been for the past two months, and Kade's been insufferable. Dad told Kade to get his ass to Sunday supper for a reason. He made a joke about a stud horse and a mare."

"I am not the mare in this scenario," I grit out while shifting around in my seat, trying to adjust myself. "I get the stud horse feeling, though."

"I think Dad thought if you guys saw each other, you'd stop being a miserable prick and settle down."

"I've apologized," I whine. "I can't explain it. It's like words I'm not even thinking regurgitate out my mouth. I regret it instantly, but I can't help myself."

"You've been through a lot," Jack tries to comfort me. "It's okay to give yourself a break."

"After Josh broke up with me, my mother threatened to murder me in my sleep if I didn't stop harassing my sister." Tyler scrunches up his face in remembrance. "Mom's the Kentwood school board superintendent. She can be scary."

"You're not the only one who's been acting possessed." Bren narrows his eyes, staring at Jack. "I think it's in the water. I feel like we've entered The Twilight Zone. Where the fuck did my buddies go?"

"They left the—" Kade walks by holding a pizza box, and not only do my eyes follow him, my head turns too. "Building…" I slide from my seat, and then say over my shoulder, eyes never leaving Kade's retreating back. "Listen, if I'm not back in five minutes, save me from myself."

I left my mind behind in Calhan's Pizza Barn with the boys, and I'm acting on pure, animalistic instinct. I don't know who is walking me outside the building and across the parking lot. My sneakers hit the damp pavement with purpose, and my eyes never leave my destination– Kade's broad back. I've stared so long at the gray and white flannel, I'll be dreaming of it for decades to come.

This isn't me. I don't know who it is. But I'm no longer Wynn Gillette.

Kade reaches his Durango before *Not Wynn Gillette* catches up with him.

My eyesight sharpens to the point I can see the curl escaping Kaden's bun– something deep inside of me knows I'm going to finally learn whether or not his hair is as soft as it looks.

My hearing becomes crisper. Kaden's breath hitches, almost as if he scents my madness riding the air. Delving deeper, I know I'm going to force a more potent sound from him in a moment.

My feet move without thought. My eyes register what I'm doing. My heart beats and my lungs breathe. Is it involuntary if you've fantasized about it for months?

I watch in awe as my hands shove against Kaden's back– his worn flannel shirt is so soft I groan. I hear myself say, "We have four minutes," in a deep voice that doesn't belong to me. "Move the pizza, or wear it," I threaten.

The shocked yet scared sound is more potent and sweeter than I imagined. "What the–" is all Kaden manages to utter before I forcefully shove him inside his SUV. My palms push him against the far side of the backseat, until his shoulders hit the opposing door. I kick at his long legs, making room for myself, and then I fold into the car.

"Stronger?" this man who isn't me taunts as I slam the door shut, locking us inside together. I grab the pizza box out of Kaden's hands, and then toss it into the front passenger seat. "Right now, I'll give you older and taller, but that's it."

"Wynn?" Kade's palms push on my chest, but his fingertips curl into the fabric of my t-shirt. "What has come over you?"

"I'm positive I'm gay," flows out of *my* mouth, but the words don't belong to me. "I got hard for Tyler today, and I flirted with him. I want shit I don't understand."

With hazel eyes huge in the waning light from the streetlamp, Kade just stares at me until my words register. "Getting wood over two guys isn't exactly an accurate hypothesis."

"I don't care," I hear myself say as I lean into Kaden. A quiver rolls through his body, exciting me more. He tries to press farther away from me, but the locked door is in the way. "I'm not labeling myself. I'm warning you that my body won't shut off and I *need* something." My voice breaks with hunger. "I'm going to do something stupid I will never regret."

Kaden's "Wha–" is cut off when my lips crash into his. Starve-gutted, I groan on impact. Kaden uses all of his force to push me away, but I lock my knees and elbows, refusing to budge. My sneakers shove against the door with all of my might. I push back with equal force, determined to get what I need.

Kade snarls, his fingernails snag my t-shirt, his back arches, pushing his chest into mine, and his boots connect with my shins as he flails about. I feel none of it because all thought is centered on the pounding hunger in my dick. For all the fight Kaden puts up, his mouth opens wide beneath mine and his tongue flicks out to welcome me home.

I pull away, spitting the words like verbal punishments. "You're not taking advantage of me, Mentor KM, Mr. Marx, or Kaden. This is Wynn and the Kade I used to know."

"I'm not him anymore," Kade rasps breathlessly beneath me.

"Yeah, ya are. So fuck being the nice guy. I'm a Gillette, and it's about time I remembered that. So I'm not asking. I'm taking what I want, because I'm a cute, little asshole teenager, and I'm doing what teenagers do– whatever the hell we want." My teeth sink into Kade's lip so hard I taste the coppery hint of his blood. "And I want you. So treat me like a mindless teenager, and I'll act like one to spite you."

I drop all of my weight on Kade, and the force expels the air in his lungs in a gust against my lips. He's so shocked, he no longer fights me. He lies still beneath me, his muscles pliant.

"I'm not in control of myself right now," I warn as my fingertips snare the rubber band securing his hair. "Oh, God," I groan, dick jerking from sensory overload as his silky curls caress my fingers.

"I don't know what else my body is going to do without my consent, but I wanted my first kiss to be with you."

Kade doesn't say anything, but his eyes are locked on mine. He arches his back again, but this time it's not to push me away. He wants our bodies connecting as much as I do. I press back, but I use my groin instead. Swiveling my hips, rocking back and forth, I grind my cock against the hard bulge in the front of Kaden's jeans.

Out of nowhere, I realize gay is not a label. It's innately who I am. I finally understand Kaden's diatribe on how tolerance and acceptance are an insult, as if who I am is inherently wrong and it must be tolerated and accepted. As if I need permission to be who I am. It's not right or wrong. It's just my version of normal, and I fucking own that shit.

"You didn't ask for this. You didn't say yes. So if anyone asks, I took advantage of you." I lean in to take Kaden's mouth again, and it's already open and waiting for me, with his tongue meeting mine halfway.

"I didn't say no," Kade manages to get out, even though my lips are smashing into his with my unskilled, clumsy kiss. A bit of spit slides down my chin as I slobber all over the bottom half of his face, not giving a fuck that I have no idea what I'm doing because he isn't complaining.

"I didn't ask," I remind Kade. "That's all anyone will give a shit about." I shove his flannel off his shoulders, and then return to slide my hands beneath his t-shirt. Feverish soft skin greets my fingertips, and I instantly become addicted to his touch. A hard nipple abrades my palm, and I almost pop my cork. Wiry hair tickles my inner wrists. I give it an experimental tug, causing Kade to grunt and jerk his hips into mine. I bite back a groan as my cock threatens to erupt inside my track pants.

"Well, if I keep coming back for seconds and thirds, and never protest…" Kaden chuckles into my mouth, the sound sweet to my ears and the vibrations driving me batshit crazy. "Wynn, you know no one will buy that."

"This is the only time– we won't get caught," I promise. I yank my t-shirt up, needing to feel our skin pressed together. Lowering myself, bare flesh on bare flesh, we groan into each other's mouths. Kaden is warm and hard, large enough to support my weight. Every nerve in my body is firing pleasure, soaking up a sensation that is so very new to me.

"It won't be the one time, and you know it." Kade's hands move from fisting the back of my hair, over the curve of my back, and latch onto my ass. He jerks his hips up, grinding into me deeper, while his hands press me down.

"More. Need more," I hiss, experiencing real pain. I just *want*… everything and anything. "I've got to get off with you. Tonight. In this car. Or I'm going to go postal."

"Christ, I am a pervert. I'm going to Hell, and I don't give a fuck," Kade snarls as he yanks me backward by my hair. My eyes roll back in my head from the way he controls me. "This is such a bad idea," he continues on as his hand slips in between us. "We will get caught, and I'm ashamed to say it will be worth it."

Eyes popping out of my skull, "Jesus, fuck!" I practically shout when Kade's hand slips inside my pants and boxers, and wraps around my cock. A tight ball forms in my lower back and a harsh spasm rolls up my spine. I stare down at a smug Kade with eyes gone wide with awe. The corners of his kiss-swollen lips tilt up in satisfaction, and I lose myself. "That escalated quickly," I breathlessly rasp.

"Now I'm your first everything," Kade bites out, sounding fiercely pissed off, displaying a mind-bending mercurial mood switch. "I won't do penetration, so consider yourself no longer a virgin."

I draw back at the violence in his tone. "If you don't–"

"Get. My. Pants. Open. And. My. Cock. Out." Kade snarls the words, squeezing my dick in his fist with brutal force. I wince, but a part of me enjoys the abuse. "I'm gonna die if you don't touch me. I've waited *long* enough."

Laughing for some unexpected reason, my hands are back to belonging to someone else. If I thought about it, I'd be fumbling. Instead, my fingertips are popping the button and pulling the zipper down to Kaden's jeans like I own them and wear them every day. The feel of his fist pumping my dick and the sight of his blue boxers has me on the edge of explosion.

"It's not a present to be opened," Kade protests, arching into my hand. "You don't have to savor it. We're on a time crunch in a goddamned parking lot with dozens of witnesses."

"Good, I'll lose my virginity just like most teenagers– hurried in the backseat of a car, you grumpy prick," I sputter through my laughter. I hesitate just to torture him.

"I've been this way around you and your perfect ass since I was sixteen. I've felt like a pervert ever since. So get used to it." Kade's hand slips from my dick, and I begin to protest. But then my balls are cupped, and my body goes limp. "Dick. Out. Now. Or else I squeeze," is an effective threat.

With an assist, Kade lifts his hips as I yank down his jeans and boxers. I swallow thickly, never having seen a hard cock besides my own– I never did visit YouPorn like Bren asked. Long, thick, and smooth, Kade's not quite as big as me, but he's perfectly curved and ruddy with arousal.

I don't know what it feels like to be high, but I'm guessing it's not as good as how I'm feeling in the back of Kade's Durango with our dicks out and proud.

I'm flying!

"I'm gay," falls from my lips with absolute certainty– *finally*! "I'm so fucking gay for your dick, I'ma 'bout to bust a nut just looking at you."

"You're *Gade,* is what you are. Gay for Kade." He releases a taunting laugh, like he's amusing himself and it hurts somehow. "Now stop staring at it, you little shit. You're not that innocent to think sex is a staring contest with a dick."

"No penetration? Because I'm willing," I volunteer gleefully, eyes still glued to the sight spread out before me. Kade's dick throbs, and a bead of pre-cum glistens on the tip. "I'm totally down for that. It's all I think about. Your dick. My ass. Getting off." More pre-cum oozes onto his belly, dampening the dark curls covering his abs.

"I'm old-fashioned," Kade whispers, and I watch in awe as a blush creeps over his chest, up his neck, and across his cheeks. My heart beats double-time at the gorgeous sight. "I'm saving that for a committed relationship, and I can't have that with the boy who's gonna get my ass fired. At least the hillbillies voted for sixteen as the age of consent, so I don't have to worry about going to jail. I'm embracing my inner pervert, but not *that* much."

"I'll release the teenage asshole again to protect you." I turn coy and flirty, and I didn't think I had it in me. "Just don't bitch that I don't know what I'm doing as I overpower you."

As I move forward for a kiss, Kade's fingertips twist into the back of my hair and tug me forward. We cheat a bit, because he's controlling everything from beneath me. But that's a good thing, since I don't have an idea of what I'm supposed to do.

A shudder waves through me at the taste of his tongue filling my mouth. I suck it, smooth, hot, and wet. I fall into our messy kiss, barely registering how my pants are getting tugged down over my knees, and then slipped off completely. I perk up a bit when palms slide up my thighs to cup my bare ass. Then fingertips clench, blunt nails biting into my flesh, pressing me forward.

I open my mouth to moan when our bodies connect, but no sound comes out when I try to shout his name. Hard and hot, Kade's cock slides against the length of mine, and I lose it.

"Breathe, Wynn. Just breathe," Kade rasps roughly against my mouth as he rocks beneath me. Sliding down the seat, he plants his boots on the window behind me. He grips the backs of my thighs, urging me to straddle him.

The temperature in the car heats up to the hottest of muggy summer nights, fogging all the windows. Sweat beads on our skin, aiding in our bodies writhing against one another. Using his fingernails biting into my ass with every clench and flex, Kade teaches me how to counterthrust against him. Beneath me, he slides his cock from my belly, along my length, nudging at my balls, and tickling between my cheeks.

Spasming, eyes rolling back into my skull, my dick starts spurting all over our stomachs just from the sensation of Kade's cock gliding along mine. "I'm so lame." My cry of shame turns to a grunt of intense pleasure. Muscles jerking forcefully, I feel ashamed but I can't stop my body's reactions.

Kade's moaning my name in my ear, and it's the sweetest sound I've ever heard, so I suck on his neck while I writhe around like an inept idiot. Then I don't feel as bad, because two seconds after I'm finished coming, Kade is joining me.

Arms locking around me so tightly I'm forced to grunt to get a deep breath, Kade comes undone beneath me. Shouting my name in my ear, his orgasm is more powerful than mine because he owns it, not giving a shit that he didn't last more than a minute.

Panting wildly, I savor how safe and warm and comforted I feel with Kade's arms wrapped around me, how sweet the sound of his breathing is in my ear. The only thing that would make this sweeter was if I was beneath him, with him deep inside me. I squeeze him back, never wanting to let go.

My body loses the fight to keep my muscles taut. I slump down, all my weight settling on Kade, and I feel totally relaxed for the first time in my entire life. I have nothing to worry about when I'm in his arms.

A pained groan fills my ears, then arms are squeezing me tighter and tighter. "We gotta behave," Kade warns me as if it's killing him. "This could escalate a helluva lot quicker the next time, and neither one of us are ready for that. If we don't get caught this time, it will be a miracle."

"I understand," I whisper against the side of his neck, and I mean it. "I don't know what came over me, but I don't regret it."

"Neither do I." Kade shifts beneath me, but he doesn't let up his grip. His nose runs along the side of my face, tickling at my skin. "I want grownup acting Wynn Gillette as my friend and lover. As much fun as teenager Wynn is, he scares me half to death. So only let him out when it's safe."

"I promise." I shift until I'm resting on my knees with my head bowed against the ceiling. "I won't attack you like this again. It was just something I *had* to do."

"You can attack me as much as you want." Kade waits a heartbeat. "*After* you graduate."

"I'm normally a responsible person, so I apologize for being an asshole." I go to pull my t-shirt down and notice the huge mess smeared all over my stomach and matted in my pubic hair. I arch my eyebrow, unable to wipe the smug look off my face. "I'll last longer next time. I swear."

"No complaints on my behalf." Kade's hand disappears underneath the seat and reappears with a roll of shop towels. He tears one off and hands it to me, and then takes one for himself. He cleans off his belly, and then tosses the towel on the floor.

By the time I'm cleaned up, Kade already has his pants pulled up and fastened. I'm doing the same as he's removing his flannel.

"For you," Kade says with a mischievous smirk. "Because I could tell how much you liked it by the hole you were burning into my back the entire way across the parking lot."

"You, ass!" I punch Kade in the chest, and then snatch up my prize. "You knew I was coming after you!"

He flashes me a cocky grin. "I assumed we'd get into a fight, actually."

"I–"

"Your five minutes was up twenty minutes ago!" Bren shouts from outside the Durango. "Enough cuddling. Our pizza is getting cold, and there's a fucking crowd out here wondering who the hell is screwing in the parking lot."

"Oh, shit!" I cry, real tears pricking my eyes.

"Don't." Kade puts a fingertip to my lips. "I never said no because you didn't ask, remember?" He begs me to go along with my teenage fairytale that we both knew was bullshit the moment I said it.

"Just crawl out, and he can drive away," Bren sounds reasonable. "It's just the basketball team out here. Only our boys know who you are, and they ain't saying jack. So get out here, Wynn, and look like a stud while he makes a clean getaway!"

"Go!" Kade shoves me backward, but leans forward to give me a quick peck to the lips. Scared shitless yet exhilarated, I slide from the backseat as Kade crawls into the front.

Bren leans in just as I'm getting out. "Nice Wolverines. I thought for sure you were gonna knock the window out with 'em." I try to yank Bren out of the Durango so Kade can drive away, but he leans in farther. "You're noisy when you come– whole parking lot heard Wynn's name outta your mouth. I guess it's a good thing Wynn lost his voice."

It takes both Jack and me to yank Bren from the car as he continuously razzes Kaden. "You guys are one-pump-chumps. But that's okay, 'cuz you both got off. Bet Sunday dinner will be more pleasant, eh? Except for Dad, that is."

"C'mon!" I try and fail to yank Bren from the car. A big palm appears, the same one that was wrapped around my cock and clutching my ass, and it shoves against Bren's forehead.

"Eww!" Bren squeals, darting backward. He runs in a wide circle, scrubbing at his forehead. "Get it off! Get it off me!!! Whose was it? Eww!"

Kade's evil laughter rings in my ears as the Durango pulls away, and then I turn to face the music.

Every basketball player in Kentwood Area School District is in Calhan's Pizza Barn's parking lot. A few are hooting and making rude gestures, but they are harmless and amused. A dozen kids take a step back, sneering at me like I'm going to spread a disease. Besides my boys, five others look at me with fear in their eyes– fear for me, because I was just outed on the same night I realized I was gay.

I shrug on Kade's flannel shirt like it's armor. I start walking down the street toward home, knowing those who have my back are protecting it.

"Why is Tyler carrying a stack of pizza boxes?" I reach over, taking a few off the top. It's only a three block walk home, but it's uncomfortable to have a dozen pairs of eyes burning into my back as my mind wars between shame and pride.

"New dude gets to be the grunt man." Bren takes the boxes from me, and replaces them back on Tyler's stack, until only the guy's nose and eyes are visible. "It's just the order of things. If he wants to hang in our town, on our court, and at our house, he's gotta pay his dues."

"Hazed. You're twisted," comes muffled from behind the pizza boxes. "I like you."

I chuckle when Jack's eyes narrow and his lips draw in a tight line. Bren's short and hasn't filled out into the stocky dude he will become. Jack's a bit taller but lanky. Fury giving him strength, Jack shoulders his way by Bren, nearly felling Bren to the ground.

What the hell, Duncan?" Bren hurries to catch up with our jealous buddy. "What's gotten into you lately? You're always pissed at me."

Tyler winks at me, communicating how he's just jerking Jack's chain. Feeling manic, I burst out laughing over the idiocy of the situation. I'm going to have to do something to help them along. I know how insane this makes you feel, like your words, thoughts, and actions aren't your own anymore.

We need a cure for teenage angst.

I reach over again, taking four pizza boxes so Tyler doesn't upend and ruin our dinner. Bren and Jack are silently fuming and stomping down the sidewalk ahead of us. There's ten to fifteen guys straggling behind us. Most are from Rusty Knob, a few are from Kade's LBGTQ group, and a couple don't seem to care that they just found out there's a gay dude on their team– maybe it's the free pizza?

"So… Mentor KM, huh?" Tyler drawls, but he's grinning. "Just so you know, Kade has a vanity plate that says TEACHER. You guys done fucked up."

"Yeah, I know," I breathe the words. "It's like… it's like being told not to do something when you never planned on doing it, or being told to do something when you were gonna do it in the first place. Yeah, it's like that. I just wanted to be a dick because no one trusted me. I've never acted like anything but an adult, and they kept saying I was a kid. So it's like, '*fuck you! Here's how a kid would act*!' I knew it was wrong, but I couldn't stop myself."

"I get it," Tyler tries to comfort me. "It's irrational. But I get it. Maybe it won't be so bad. Maybe they'll ignore it."

"It's gonna be the gay thing that destroys us. If Kade was straight and I was a girl… they would laugh and call him a stud. If Kade was a girl, they'd call me a stud for bagging a teacher. I feel sick right now. I'm like the most responsible person I know besides Royce, and I just mucked up Kade's life because I was throwing a tantrum."

"I've been in Mentor KM's group for a year and a half, and I just met him in person. He's almost six and a half feet tall and two hundred pounds… Kade was with you because he wanted to be, consequences be damned."

"I should have been the bigger person and told him no. But instead, I did the one thing they kept accusing me of, and I don't regret it."

"Wynn?" Tyler stops walking, and the horde behind us hesitates, unsure what to do. Thankfully, they are talking so loud and we're being so quiet, they can't overhear us. "I've made destructive mistakes and been an asshole. Josh fucked me, fucked me over, and fucked me up, and he then left. I've been there and done that, and I'd still do it again with that hindsight is 20/20 bullshit."

"Thanks." I take another pizza box to lighten Tyler's load to be nice. "I don't regret it. I regret the assholes who are going to mess with Kade because they are scared of who we are."

"Truer words, my friend." We start walking again, and I have to laugh when the crowd mimics us. "Truer words have never been spoken."

"I know I broke the rules," I mutter, feeling lost. "I get that."

"Nah-uh… NO!" Tyler shakes his head. "You didn't break the rules. Kaden Marx did. He knew the rules, and he still did it. Don't get a big head because he wanted you so much, but don't beat yourself up because of it, either."

I spot Willa in her rocking chair, blue eyes huge as she watches us flow into the yard. Royce is in the garden with Hayden, and

Hayley is chasing Bren and Jack down at the fire pit. Bren starts smashing wood with his bare hands, and Jack's even more violent. My niece parrots all of their movements, and it's so dang cute it makes me snort.

"Who's the little killer?" Amusement is thick in Tyler's voice. "She reminds me of my baby sister."

"That's my niece, Hayley. Hayden's the little feller staring at us from the garden with the pumpkin in his hands. Their momma is on the porch– my sister, Willa." I point at Royce, who's staring at me like he's worried. "That's my dad– Bren's actual dad. In true hillbilly fashion, Royce is the twins' uncle daddy."

"What?" Tyler releases an uncomfortable laugh like I'm joking.

"It's the truth." I wait a heartbeat, and when Tyler frowns, I expand on it. "The twins have three uncles: my brother and me, and then Royce. Bren's dad is the best. He adopted me and the twins. Uncle Daddy, as Hayley likes to call him."

"Only my baby brother would come home six hours before his curfew." Willa comes up to me, lifts the lid on the pizza box resting in my arms, and then takes a slice of pepperoni. "Bren texted, saying he was bringing some friends and pizza." She points at the flood of basketball players flowing to the fire pit in the backyard. "That's not a '*few*' friends."

"I'm sorry," I apologize for stressing Willa out. This is the kind of thing she shouldn't be around.

"It's okay, Wynn." My sister rubs the center of my back, something she started last month when we moved from holding a hand to actual physical contact. Willa's allowed to touch us, not the other way around. "Royce and the kids and I are gonna watch a movie in the den. Just don't let anyone in the house."

"Understood," I agree. "I promise."

"They can potty in the field." She puts her slice back in the box, and then takes the box from me. "This one is Royce's and mine. There's one with extra cheese somewhere for the kids."

Tyler and I look at each other, and then burst out laughing. "Um… I'll put my boxes on the stack again, and then take a peek for the glob of cheese." After some maneuvering, I locate Willa's pizza.

"Your fridge in the barn is stocked with water and Coke," she says as I settle the box into her arms. "Royce needs to have a private word with you before you run off with your friends… so, this feller needs to hightail it to the bonfire."

"Shit," I hiss. "How the fuck did he hear about it so quick?"

"I'd smack your hand if my arms weren't filled with pizza," Willa warns, and I eye the spatula sticking out of the pouch of her hoodie. "Kade called the second he left the parking lot. He's with Warren and Penny right now, trying to get his shit together."

I pivot, ready to run across town. "No!" Willa stops me with her momma voice. "You have your friends and he has his. You'll see him on Sunday morning. You can't be seen together in public again until things get settled."

"Oh, shit…" I mutter, voice breaking, when I spot Royce striding across the lawn to me.

"I'll just stand over here," Tyler promises, already a loyal friend, even though it's unnecessary. Royce isn't going to harm me in any way.

"Hayley! Hayden!" Royce shouts, never taking his eyes off of me, like he expects me to bolt. "Go with your momma into the house, ya hear? Go on, now."

"You okay?" Willa asks me. When I nod, she leaves us be. I watch her walk back to the house and onto the porch. By the time she gets to the front door, Hayden's opening it for her, and Hayley's walking in right behind her– Royce's little soldiers.

I close my eyes, unable to see the look of bitter disappointment on Royce's face. The shaking begins again, starting in my fingertips to radiate up my arms. My guts twist and my throat clenches like I'm going to be sick.

"I was stupid," I force out, having a hard time with speech since bile, not words, is the only thing that wants to flow.

"Are you okay?" Royce's voice is filled with a deep well of compassion. "Do you need to go to the hospital?"

My eyes pop open. "What?" I squawk, shocked.

"Are you hurt?" Royce runs his palms up and down my arms, checking for… wounds? "We should go now. C'mon."

"What?" flees my lips again. "I'm physically fine, Royce. Why aren't you mad at me? What's up with you acting like I'm dying?"

"You didn't have sex?" Pure relief is in his tone. "You're not hurt?"

A laugh huffs out of me as I try to fathom what's gotten into Royce. "Um… I'm pretty sure if I had anal sex and had to go to the hospital, either we were doing it very wrong, or very right. We're talking about Kade and me, Royce." I start sputtering. "Really?"

Royce's hands grip my shoulders, fingers biting in. "If, at any time, things get out of hand and you get hurt, go to the hospital immediately. It can cause lasting harm." His eyes are sad, with misery swimming in their depths.

"I... I..." My eyebrows knit together in the center as I try to reason him out. "What?"

"Just promise me," Royce begs.

"Okay, but... it's Kade and me. You get that, right? We might be big dudes, but we're both very passive. If it gets to that, we won't be pounding each other to death. What's up with you? Why aren't *you* tearing me a new asshole?"

"So, you're okay?" Royce's eyes make a circuit over my body. "You've both been so frustrated. I worried about how it would be when you both broke." His brown eyes dart away, refusing to hold my gaze. "I blame myself. None of this would be happening if I had allowed you to see each other again."

"I feel like we're talking two different languages here, Royce, and we both know I'm fluent in English, Appalachia, drunk, and bullshit. You're not to blame at all. It's mostly on me, with Kade not telling *me* no."

A big palm covers Royce's face, and then scrubs hard. "The first time I noticed was when Kade was visiting from college and you were waiting by my truck to begin work. He was staring at you from the window. So every time he came home, I told you not to come to work."

"What?" blows out of me in a gust.

"After he moved back home, Kade kept visiting you at the Circle K. He was being real surly, but it was in public so I let it be." Royce turns around, like he's the one ashamed. "I just didn't want you ruining your lives... what I feared, I created. If I would've allowed you two to spend time together, not pushed Kade to stay away from suppers and church, it wouldn't have looked so odd in public."

"It's not your fault that I like him." Insane laughter bubbles up, replacing the anxiety with disbelief. "I did exactly what you warned me off from doing– exactly what you said I was doing, and I argued with you about."

Royce turns back around, almost violently. His patient brown eyes are now shooting sparks of rage. "If I'd let nature take its course in this house." He points to the upper floor. "We wouldn't be in this mess. Only we'd know. It would have been private. But I didn't want to keep secrets– secrets that would destroy futures."

"Hey." I reach over to shake Royce a bit, trying to calm him down. "It's going to be okay. No matter what happens. You've got to believe it. You ought to be beating Kade and me, tearing into our ears with your lectures, not beating yourself up. Dang it, Royce!"

Looking me deep in the eye, "I was scared," he admits like a secret. "I let Bren do whatever with girls as long as he's safe, because he won't hurt them and they can't hurt him. But I was scared what would happen between you two if you got alone."

Speechless, I just stare at my dad. I know he's not a homophobe. There's something that isn't clicking into place in my head. "I know I'm dang innocent, but even I know it's not supposed to hurt enough to harm. Be uncomfortable, I suspect. Anyway, Kade says he doesn't do that."

"Okay. Good." Royce takes a deep breath, and then it shudders out. "I'm gonna go sit with Willa and the kids for a while. The boys need to be on their busses before nine, and no one can spend the night but Jack." He walks toward the porch. "Either in your room or the spare room. Keep Jack out of Bren's bedroom, please."

"Okay," I agree quickly, still confused. "Bizarre." I trail a manic laugh as Tyler hesitantly approaches me. I know he heard it all. "Am I missing something? Is sex between men like going to the slaughter?"

"No." Tyler looks a bit sad. "It's uncomfortable sometimes. But you can get really hurt if someone wants to hurt you."

"I…" I reach for the top half of the pizza boxes, feeling bad that Tyler didn't just go to the bonfire instead of sticking around for me. "I feel like shit right now. If Royce would have yelled at me, been disappointed in me, grounded me, I would have felt better. It's a billion times worse because he's upset with himself."

"Wynn?" Tyler calls out when I start heading toward the team. "Your dad… he… he's been hurt real bad. Someone wanted to harm him. He doesn't realize that it's just as normal for us as it is between him and a woman. That's what your mind won't let you light on, because you're petrified of the truth."

I walk to the bonfire in a daze with tears swimming in my eyes. I'm thankful for the waning light so no one will call me out on crying. My body is warring with itself. I want to run halfway across town to give and seek comfort from Kade, but I also want to go in the house and give Royce comfort as well. But I know better. Royce is a prideful man who wouldn't want his sons to see him break. I think that's Willa's job now.

"'Bout time!" A few guys shout when we approach. "I'm starving," Bren continues on, but he's looking at me like it's killing him not to ask what his dad and I talked about.

Our fire pit is a large hole dug into the ground, with flat rocks surrounding it so the fire won't spread. There are a few logs set out as seats, and an outdoor storage box filled with matches, lighter fluid, and roasting sticks for hotdogs and marshmallows. Royce loves to sit out here and stare off into the field and the hills beyond.

Some of the guys are sitting on the logs, but that's not what they're for. Bren and Jack have it right, sitting on the ground with the log as their backrest. I settle down on the ground next to Jack, not wanting to be interrogated by Bren just yet.

Placing the pizza boxes on a sawed-off stump, "Okay, asshats!" Tyler shouts. "We've got a meat lovers with a shit-ton of jalapenos."

"Me!" Tyler's Power Forward takes the box, and he and two buddies go after it, taking slices.

"Another meat lovers. I'm sensing a trend, here." Bren lunges forward, steals the box from Tyler, sits down next to Jack, and then props the box on their thighs. "Vegetarian? That is just a travesty."

"Mine!" Francis grabs the box out of Tyler's hands, giving the kid a once-over. He sits next to Bren. After grabbing three slices of vegetarian, he passes the box to Jack. I laugh while watching the idiots make pizza sandwiches out of one slice meat lovers and one slice vegetarian, all because their Franny doesn't eat meat but can't eat a whole pizza himself.

"A fag that don't eat meat? You guys are seriously fucked in the head." Rob from Furrow Creek taunts, but his voice is light and there is a sympathetic smile on his face. "You better bring it on the court. We don't need any more jesters."

"Three pepperoni– y'all can fight over those." Tyler plops the boxes on the ground, and a couple of guys grab them up. "Chicken Wing. WIN! That's mine." He's looks around for a safe place to stash it.

"I'll hold it." I try to take the box but Tyler won't let go. A game of tug-of-war commences as we laugh. "Don't worry, I won't touch your pizza. I can't eat it without it making me sick." The box is tossed on my lap in a heartbeat.

"Another meat lovers, seriously?" Tyler just hands the box to the chubby kid, knowing it's his. "Barbeque chicken? Mmm... I want a slice."

Duane grabs the box, reaches in, and tosses two slices on top of Tyler's Chicken Wing pizza, and then retrieves two as compensation. He then settles down next to Francis. I snort, noting how we're all together yet still segregated. Rusty Knob is sitting together at one log. Furrow Creek at another, and Hillock Corners at the last log across the fire.

"Last but not least... Plain cheese? Who eats that?" Tyler taunts, walking over to sit next to me, breaking the segregation cycle. "Even Franny has an imagination. Wynn, plain?"

"Wynn has tummy aches," Bren teases me around a mouthful of half-chewed pizza. "If he's upset, he eats boring food. When he's not, he goes balls to the wall and empties out the cupboards."

"Cheese won't hurt as much as meat lovers on the way back out," I mutter underneath my breath. "So, let's just pretend I didn't screw around in the parking lot of Calhan's, and that you all know it was with a guy. It doesn't affect my performance on the court. So if you want to work hard, learn some new tricks, and get better before we graduate and go off to college, then now's the time to swallow whatever bullshit you want to say to me and get to work."

After a few nasty remarks, we spend the next hour and a half eating pizza, sharing stupid stories, bragging about our stats, and getting to know one another, because there is no *I* in team.

LET US GROW UP

I'm standing outside of Royce's office with my ear pressed against the wooden door, trying with all my might to eavesdrop. About five minutes ago, Kaden arrived for Sunday supper. I saw from the upstairs window, and my heart flipped out at the sight. By the time I got down here, they were locked together in Royce's office.

Friday night I tried to call Kade and he shut me down. I logged into the group, and he wasn't on. Like a stalker, on Saturday, I went to Warren and Penny's, dragging the twins and Bren in tow. It was an excuse to spy on Kade, but everyone saw through it. Warren said Kade took a drive to get his head on straight, that he was with his grandfather, and I was to leave him be.

It's been the longest seventy-two hours of my life.

"Uh-oh, I'm rubbing off on ya," Bren whispers in my ear, and then snickers. "Anything good happening in Dad's office?"

"I don't know." I press my ear closer to the door. "I can't hear anything."

"Amateur," Bren drawls as his fingers twist the doorknob. My heart beats out of my chest when the door cracks open soundlessly. Bren raises an eyebrow at me, silently saying, "*I'm the master*."

"How could you be so stupid, son?" Royce's voice is stiff with disappointment. "I've warned you about this for over a year, and you didn't listen."

"Which is it? Am I a kid, or an adult? You have to pick." Kade sounds furious, and I turn to look at Bren in utter shock. "I'm twenty-three, and you treat me like a child. When you were my age, you were married and a father. Give me some credit."

Bren just raises his eyebrow higher, lips twisting into a smirk. "*Dad treats Kade the same as he treats you*," he mouths back at me. "*Good Luck*."

"Jesus Christ. Don't start that shit again. I hear that enough from Wynn." I arch my head to the side, trying to peek through the crack in the door. Bren's palm landing on my shoulder makes me meep. I'm pressed down to my knees.

"We need to get out of eye level. No one looks down," Bren whispers in my ear. "They will see the crack at most, not your eyes glowing back."

"I know you love Wynn, but you don't understand him." Kade is walking around in a tight circle while Royce sits behind the desk. "By default, adult Wynn is responsible. When you piss him off by not trusting him, he turns into teenager Wynn, and that kid is terrifying." Kade points right in Royce's face. "Your fault."

"He *is* a teenager." Sighing, Royce rests his forehead in his palms.

"Which am I, Royce? Adult or child? You need to pick, and you need to do the same with Wynn." Kade slumps into a chair, looking like he's been lectured in this office too many times to count. "Kids don't pay bills. They worry about their grades, sports, their friends and family, where they are going to college, and who they want to screw. I don't see how Wynn is acting out of character, and neither am I."

Glaring, Royce grits out in a grave tone. "In this, you're an adult and Wynn is a child, and you're both fucking up your lives."

"I'm an adult, and as such, it is my responsibility to make my own decisions. Do you have any idea how hypocritical I feel right now?"

"What?" Royce is thrown by how despondent Kaden sounds. Only Bren's hand on my shoulder keeps me from barging into the office to comfort Kade.

"This isn't even about my six year obsession with Wynn, even if you've all made me feel like a pervert."

"You're not a pervert," Royce clips out. "I've never said that. It was always in your head."

"Whatever," Kade grumbles like he doesn't believe it.

"Speaking of acting like a child… So, why are you a pervert and a hypocrite now?"

"I'm not a pervert," Kade grumbles. "The school board knows I'm gay. The superintendent raved over my idea about the Facebook group. But I was told by them and by you to keep it private. Do you have any idea what it felt like to have my foster dad tell me to hide my true self?"

"You have to tell me this shit, Kaden. I'm not a goddamned mind reader." Royce's voice is tight with frustration. "Everything I do is well intentioned."

"Every day I mentor kids about being true to themselves, owning who they are, and I'm living a lie."

Sounding confused, Royce leans across the desk. "Is it worth losing your job over it, son?"

"Yes," Kade answers unequivocally. "If it makes a statement, so be it. If Rusty Knob won't accept me for who I am, I don't give two shits about Rusty Knob. They won't run me out of town. If I lose my job, trust in the values you instilled in me that I will not stop doing what is best for these kids. Maybe seeing me stand up for myself will feel as if I'm standing up for them, too."

"So, fucking a senior in your car, in the middle of a parking lot for the whole town to see, that was your version of independence? You're shitting me, right?"

"No, Royce," Kade says gruffly. "That was me doing something I never got to do when I was a teenager. Between your celibacy bullshit, the horrors of penetrative sex, and your warnings of lynching the faggot kid, I'm stunted."

"That was for your benefit." Royce reaches across the desk to pat Kade's shoulder, affection coloring his words. "God... the thought of you being in pain kills me. You're very fragile in a way."

"Thanks for metaphorically cutting my balls off," Kade snarls. "And thanks for threatening to literally de-nut me if I touched Wynn again, my version of actually gaining a pair in the first place."

"I... I don't get it," Royce stammers.

"Of course you don't. You're straight, and it's simpler. You met the girl of your dreams, asked her to marry you, and didn't think twice about being inside her. It was thought of as normal." The side of Kade's fist connects with the edge of the desk, causing all four of us to jump.

"That's what life's about, son. I don't know why that's upsetting you."

"This *is* my normal." Kade thumps the desk again. "And I won't apologize for it any longer, nor will I hide from it. It sends the wrong message to my kids, and your bullshit is confusing yours."

"That's not true," Royce mutters in denial. "I'm not confusing the boys at all."

"I'm one of your boys, remember?" Kade challenges. "How old were you when you lost your virginity."

"That's private."

Not backing down, Kade bulldozes forward. "We're both adults sitting here, answer the question."

Royce says without hesitation, "No."

"I'm trying to make a point," Kade stresses. "Answer the question. How old were you?"

Snarling, "I was attacked at age nine," Royce tears our hearts out. "Is that what you wanted to hear?"

I reach up to squeeze the hands gripping my shoulders. Bren releases me, and then sits against the wall, facing me. I can't look at his face for more than a split-second, before the pain causes bile to rise in my throat.

"Shit," Kade hisses. "That's not what I meant, and you know it. We've been through all of that before, and you know I hate it when you yank out the '*funny uncle*' story to put me in my place."

"Fine," Royce concedes. "I was fourteen… with Annie. I haven't been with anyone since she died."

"Knock your shit off, Royce. Don't use emotional extortion to stop me from proving a point." My eyes flick to Bren's in astonishment over how Kade manages Royce. We have a lot to learn from their interactions.

"I was fourteen," Royce states plainly, not adding anything that wasn't asked.

"How old am I?"

"Don't do this," Royce warns. "Don't make me do this."

Kade doesn't back down. "How old am I?"

"It's not safe. You could get hurt, or harm someone else if you're not careful." Royce begins stammering again. "There are diseases to think about."

"Yeah, but not pregnancy," Kade all but growls. "But that's okay if Bren knocks up some chick on accident, as long as he's not doing a dude. Then he'd have to marry her, right? I know you're not a homophobe, but your actions and words make you out to be one."

"I'm looking out for your best interests, and you know it." Royce leans over his desk, getting into Kade's space. "Don't take my actions out of context and then throw them back into my face."

"The intentions are good, but they make me feel bad about myself," Kade murmurs quietly, as if it's impossible to speak the words any louder. "I'm almost the same age you were when you were widowed, and you expect me to live a life of celibacy– a lie – all because I want to be with men."

"I… I… I don't mind you being with men. I just don't want you being harmed. I never said you had to be a virgin at your age–"

"Yes, you did," Kade cuts Royce off. "You're okay if I wanted to go out and screw a girl, or pick a guy up in a bar for a blowjob. But you raised me to want more, to want a commitment and a relationship, and your bullshit cuts off the possibility of one. No sex without a commitment, but don't actually have sex. Say what?" Kade squawks. "And that is what has you so pissed off at me and Wynn, because we decided the feeling was mutual."

"So you fuck my son in your car to screw me over– to prove a point? I want more for you than that, and I want more for Wynn than being used because you have daddy issues."

Instead of being angry, Kade tilts his head backward and releases a spine-tingling laugh. Voice arrogant and smug, "Trust me when I say neither one of us thought of you when we were in the moment, and both of us took responsibility for our actions."

"So when you lose your job tomorrow morning, and Wynn is so ashamed of himself and bereft with guilt, I'm to send him to you for suicide watch? Jesus Christ, Kaden. I've got two boys on my hands who tried to kill themselves and they gravitated to each other. What do you think I should have done differently?"

"Nothing," Kade whispers. "I get it. You love using the word fragile for Wynn and me, and I understand why you're terrified. But we're not going to bond over a suicide pact. If anything, we'll help each other cope."

"What about the fallout, though? If you're adult enough to fuck, you're adult enough to clean up your own messes. You're both my children, and it's my responsibility to keep you from destroying yourselves and each other."

Kade leans over the desk, blocking out all sight of Royce. "You need to trust yourself enough to have faith in the way you've raised us. You need to trust Wynn and me. You need to understand that we love, trust, and respect you, and the only reason we ever get mad at you is when you don't trust us in return." Kade returns to his seat, and says, "Let us grow up."

"Wynn's still a kid," Royce repeats for the billionth time, and I don't fail to flinch.

"Wynn's my equal." Kade's response causes my heart to stutter. When my heart restarts, it beats a rapid tattoo in my chest. I quickly glance at Bren, and find his mouth hanging open in utter shock.

Royce's snort is as loud as a gunshot in dead silence. "Equal? Pfft… Which are you in this scenario? Are you saying you act seventeen, or that Wynn acts twenty-three?"

"Wynn's as mature at his age as I am at mine. When I was seventeen, I was a gangly child with no direction in life. I was dumb, ugly, skinny, and broken. I was freaking out over being a pervert. I might look like a grown man now, and have the degree to prove it, but I don't feel it yet because I have no experiences. Wynn's a grown man with his shit together, so you need to quit stunting him."

"So, what?" Royce sounds disgusted. "I'm just supposed to let you screw each other?"

"Don't denigrate what Wynn and I could build," Kade snarls. "Not only do you not stop Bren from scratching all the girls in Rusty Knob, you encourage it. So instead of accepting that I want to be Wynn's friend, that I want to be near him, you have to make it dirty and nasty."

"Are you honestly going to deny that you don't want to fuck him? Screw him in the way I warned you against?"

"What would you have done if you were my age and Annie asked you to be with her? Would you have relegated her to a life of grinding against each other and call it sex? And don't utter that bullshit about how you had to make kids. You couldn't afford kids, and it's not a prerequisite for marriage."

"It's not the same goddamn thing!" Royce slaps his desk, turning furious. Face boiling red, the vein in his forehead is visibly throbbing with his heartbeat.

Calm in the face of the storm, "Yeah, it is. You loved Annie, and you wanted to connect with her, so you did. Wanting to be inside a man, or have one inside me, is no more abnormal than you wanting to be inside a woman. So don't push your issues off on me and expect me to believe what I crave and need is wrong."

Royce lunges from the desk, and begins pacing around his office. Bren and I share a confused glance, communicating how we hate Royce being upset, but knowing he needs to hear the truth.

I reach over to grip Bren's hand, give a sharp tug until we're both standing upright, and then I walk into the office.

Startled, Royce whips around, hand still raised to rake through his hair. "What the–?"

"Seriously? When will you ever learn?" Bren swaggers across the room to take a seat in his father's chair. "It's me– I snoop like it's my day job." He points at me, rolling his eyes. "Kade's in here, and you honestly believe Wynn wouldn't be stalking him?"

"Apparently, y'all think I'm a shitty father." Royce yanks Bren out of his chair, and retakes his seat. "You were a curious child, and I could never break you of your obsessive snooping."

"You would have had better luck if you'd told Wynn to screw Kade." Bren slumps to the floor, lying on his back like he's super comfortable. "Just some advice before Hayden and Hayley are teenagers. Telling a guy no will make him want to do it even more… telling two of them…"

"Did I? Have I? Am I somehow confusing you?" Royce stammers, eyes flicking between Bren, Kade, and me. "Do I make you feel bad about yourselves?"

Bren turns away so none of us can see his face. "I'm not answering that."

"You're the best dad I've ever had," I try to comfort Royce. "You don't hit me, scream at me, or bleed me dry. You genuinely care about me, so I give you a pass when you fuck up."

"Being compared to Corbin Gillette is not a ringing endorsement, Wynn." Royce leans back in his chair, groaning. "What am I supposed to do?"

"Let us grow up," Bren repeats Kade's words. "Let us fuck up so we can learn this shit on our own. We'll come to you if we need your help. I promise."

Doubt crosses Royce's features, but he remains silent.

Hazel eyes bore into the side of my face, causing a blush to spike my blood. "You need to put all of your attention into the little ones," Kade says to Royce while staring at me. "I will clean up my own mess, and I will suffer any consequences that may come my way."

Royce leans forward in his seat, resting his arms on his desktop. "You shouldn't have to."

"It's my fault," guilt spews from my mouth. "I… I'll try to talk to your boss, or something."

"I already took care of it." Kade's words are reassuring, but the way he's clenching his fists speak more truth. "I called the superintendent on Friday night. What's done is done."

"So you lost your job, then?" Bren crawls to his feet, looking concerned.

Needing a distraction, or possibly trying to distract me, Kade tugs the band out of his hair, allowing his curls to swing around his chin. He leans forward, raking his fingertips through the ringlets. "I don't know," comes muffled. "Possibly. Probably. It's too soon to tell. I've been honest with Mrs. Ross since day one, even going as far as to tell her about Wynn."

Utter shock pours off of me. "You told your boss about me?"

"I had to, Wynn." Kade wraps the band back around his hair, and then stands up straight. "Royce is right about me watching you for far too long. I knew when I came home I'd be tempted to do something stupid. It didn't help that you were so eager to join me."

"I'm sor–"

"Don't apologize," Kaden demands. "Don't feel guilty or ashamed. Don't regret it. If I lose my job, so what? I'll find another one."

Bren and I stare at Royce– Bren with big, brown puppy dog eyes, pleading with his dad to fix it, and me hoping to seek some guidance.

A loud snort fills the silence. "Don't look at me like that." Royce stands from his seat. "I've got more of you assholes I've got to keep in line. So I'ma do what you asked me to do. I'ma let you grow up. If you fuck up, enjoy the consequences."

"That suspiciously sounded like an '*I told you so!*' Didn't it?" I shout at Royce as he leaves his office. Deep laughter flows, and us gluttons for punishment follow after it.

GOOD BOY!

"Winnie the Pooh!" Penny's squeal stings my ears a split-second before I'm engulfed in a bear-hug. Tiny arms clutching at my waist, with her big belly pressing into my hip, Penny knocks me backward into Kade.

Large hands steady me, but the deep laugh spikes heat through my blood. "Princess Penny," flows smoothly. "How are you feeling today? How's the babe?"

"Good! Good. Just missed my Winnie the Pooh, is all." Penny steps away, and then punches me in the arm. "You don't visit enough."

I rub my arm, wondering if Penny's been taking boxing lessons. I glance down and take note that it was the ring on her finger inflicting the damage. "Jesus, girl." Laughter spills from everyone as I shake my head back and forth. "I see you every freaking day at school, and at least once a day I'm at your house. Do you remember church this morning? The playground after? How much more time do you need? I've got to sleep at some point."

"You left me." Penny sniffles and pouts, causing her copper ponytail to bob up and down. She flashes me sad, brown eyes that probably render Warren speechless, but have absolutely no effect on me whatsoever.

"I left you with him." I point at my grinning brother. "You picked him, so you get to keep him."

"I hear you thinking '*good riddance*' in your head, bro!" Warren punches me in the same spot Penny did, and he doesn't pull his hit. "But I don't know which one of us you're happier to be rid of. Penny is not easy to live with. Sure you don't wanna move back in and be our buffer?"

"Fuck!" I hiss, gripping my arm when Warren punches me again, only to hiss again when I'm flayed by the cussing spatula. "What did I do to deserve such violence?"

"Be a good boy." Willa taps my chin with the rubber-pain-inflictor. "Stop making Penny weepy. Stop worrying Royce so. Stop screwing in parking lots. Lastly, stop swearing. It's unseemly."

I turn to my sister with a nasty remark on the tip of my tongue. But no one can be angry with Willa when she's made such strides to return to the human race. It was only last week when she finally pulled her sandy blonde curls away from her face, no longer using it as a shield.

I grin down at my older yet tinier sister. "You get the irony of yelling at us for swearing, right?"

Willa's eyebrows knit in the center of her forehead as she thinks. It's not often she speaks without thinking about it for a bit first, and usually it's so her words come out properly. "I'm making sure we don't turn into them. We need to have a better vocabulary."

I do what I do countless times a day when Penny surprises me, or humors me, or makes me laugh or feel proud. I lean down and press a soft kiss to Willa's forehead before my mind catches up with me, before I realize it's my sister and not Penny I'm kissing.

I freeze after flinching, waiting to hear the shriek of fright, worried I ruined the mood, and feeling guilty for expressing affection Willa wasn't ready to experience. But after we all take a collective breath, Willa smiles up at me brilliantly, like I just made her day for not treating her like fragile glass.

"I'ma go finish making supper," Willa stammers, blushing a pretty shade of pink.

"Do you need any help?" flows from my lips immediately.

"Penny's helping." Willa's words are not a suggestion. "But thanks for asking. You're such a good boy."

Penny glares at me as she trails after my sister, like I'm cheating on her or some shit.

Willa's a natural-born cook, whereas Penny's creations are still… rough. Penny's great with kids and horrid at keeping a house. Willa tries so hard to do it all, but it's a struggle. Only cooking comes naturally to her. The two women do and don't get along for the most part.

"I'm not helping," Hayley grumbles while tugging at her skirt. "I'm never going to cook anything."

"Then you'll starve." Hayden's a good boy, too. He drags his twin into the kitchen to help.

"I guess I'll set the table, then," I mutter to no one in particular, catching sight of Royce's face. He's simultaneously pale and flushed, like he's shocked speechless. I grin at him, and he goes even whiter.

"I… I'll go take the turkey off the rotisserie spit," Royce stammers, backing out of the room. "Ya know, on the grill."

"What's up with him?" I direct to Kade and Warren.

"Willa, I suspect," Kade answers.

Feeling enlightened, I hum, "Ah!"

Bren comes out of the kitchen carrying an armful of plates. He plunks them down, knowing I'll put them where they're supposed to go. After only eating when we could find food, Willa has embraced eating every meal in the dining room. Royce and Bren love it because it was just the two of them most of the time, eating takeout in the kitchen or den.

I drag the stack of plates across the table, and begin setting them on the placemats. A warm palm settles on my hip as Kade leans forward to help. "You're such a good boy," is breathed into my ear. "But I really enjoyed the bad boy in the backseat of my Durango."

I melt into Kade, not caring that I must look like a fool. I'm just happy we're near each other, even if we mucked up Kade's life. We can face more things together than separate.

"I thought teenager Wynn was terrifying," I taunt Kade in a flirty tone. "Hmm?"

"Among other things," he replies, voice rough and husky. Placing a few plates, he uses that as an excuse to align the front of his body with the back of mine. I give up all pretenses of setting the table, and steal a quick kiss to the side of his neck.

"Jesus Christ!" Warren snarls as he charges from the dining room into the kitchen. "Don't go in there. It's gross!"

"I've walked in on you–" I stumble over the word *fucking*, not wanting to be bruised by the spatula again. "With Penny, and I can't bleach my brain. So just deal!"

"It was probably when they were making that evil spawn." Bren returns with the silverware, wearing a shit-eating grin. "Everyone knows gingers have no souls."

Kaden busts out laughing. "If the kid pops out with dark hair, all hell will break loose."

"Motherfucker!" is shouted from the kitchen, warping into a sharp shriek of pain. "C'mon, sis! I get punished for defending my wife's honor?"

"She ain't yer wife yet," Willa replies, slipping into the diction she's been trying to overcome.

"Ah, so this is what a real family dinner feels like?" Kade says to Bren as he sits in my usual seat. "It wasn't like this before."

"Pure freakin' chaos." Bren sits next to him, and I'm left standing, wondering where I'm going to sit. "Remember how quiet it was eating in front of the TV."

"Yeah, that was nice." Kade sighs heavily.

They both ignore me as they go on and on about how it used to be. I move to sit on the other side of the table, but a hand hooks around my waist.

"Sitting in my seat at the table… using my old bedroom… sleeping in my bed… it makes a guy think he's being replaced." Kade pulls me onto his lap, but we're too big to sit like that. Try as I might, I don't fit on his lap. I end up in the chair with Kade standing next to me.

"You moved away." Bren grins at us. "Dad had to find a better replacement."

"Instead, Royce went ahead and found me a *friend*." Kade's laughter is infectious as he pulls a chair over, situating it next to mine at the end of the table, cattycorner to Royce's seat at the head of the table.

"No shit? I'm in your room?" I flush at the thought, and my jeans get a bit tight in the crotch. "I'm in your bed?"

"Hmm… Definitely used to be my bed," purrs throatily. "Navy flannel comforter and fuzzy blue sheets?"

I breathe, "Yeah," feeling hot and giddy all of the sudden.

Kade leans into me, making sure the eavesdropper can't overhear. "You were my personal Goldilocks." He pinches one of the curls on my head. "Someone was sleeping in my bed. When I'd come home from State College on weekends, you weren't allowed to work, remember?"

"Yeah." Bren leans forward so he can talk to both of us, shameless in his eavesdropping. "Dad put the kibosh on coming home except for major holidays after he caught you eye-fucking Wynn." He laughs heartily. "Those sheets were washed before and after every visit by the both of you."

"Pity," Kade whispers, still fingering my hair. It would be creepy if it wasn't so hot. He blinks out of it, dropping his hand to his lap. "Royce thought I was a pervert in the making. He could have put you in any other room and accommodated us both, but he was rightfully terrified of us being in the same place at the same time."

"Still am," Royce says as he enters the room carrying a platter laden with smoked turkey. "There's a No Touch Policy in this house from now on," he orders gruffly. "No macking on each other."

"NTP, seriously?" Bren rolls his eyes. "Warren's tongue was shoved in Penny's mouth earlier today at the park, and you didn't even blink. Mixed signals, much?"

"They're not my kids," Royce says bluntly as he sits at the head of the table. "They're getting married and having a baby. I don't give a shit what they do."

"I've never noticed how intolerant you sound," Bren grumbles, voice thick with emotion.

"First of all, I see Kade and Wynn as my sons, so it freaks my ass out to think of them touching each other in a way that would make them puke if they touched you."

Bren makes a gagging sound while Kade and I cringe.

"Yeah, chew that over, why dontcha?" Royce looks over his shoulder toward the kitchen, making sure we're not being overheard by the little ones. "You've never had the balls to kiss someone in front of me, and you better not until there is a ring on your finger. Same for the twins. It has nothing to do with orientation, and everything to do with being disrespectful."

I ignore everyone except for Kade, because guilt is suffocating me. "I'm sorry I took your room. That wasn't right or fair. You must have hated me every time you wanted to come home and couldn't."

"It wasn't you I was pissed at." Kade's eyes cut toward Royce, who is still debating Bren. "Besides, Penn State wasn't exactly boring."

"Yeah... but... I never want you to feel like you weren't wanted, especially because of me. I would have stayed in Gillette Holler so you could have come home more on weekends."

Kade's lips twist into a sad smile. "You really are too good to have been born into the Gillette family tree." His fingers twine with mine beneath the table. "I understood. Don't for a second think Royce didn't spell it out, or that he didn't drive up to see me during the week."

"Wynn was the sweetest kid ever." Willa carries a big bowl of mashed potatoes into the dining room, and I nearly salivate. "He was such a peach. Always following everyone around, asking if he could help them."

I blush fiercely as that warm sensation of home slams into my heart. I'm practically glowing by the time everyone files into the room, carrying various dishes to the table.

"Remember when you and Wynn made me a new doll out of the recycling in the yard?" Willa asks Warren as she starts scooping food onto plates. We hand our plates around the table, everyone plopping a couple spoonfuls of each dish.

"Yeah, after Daddy burnt your Barbies in the fire because you were an ungrateful ingrate who didn't appreciate 'em."

I snort when most people would cry at how sick that sounded. "Daddy has never figured out that he's repeating himself. Ingrate means unappreciative."

"Daddy's a fucking idiot," Warren deadpans. Quicker than the eye can see, he's catching the spatula in his palm before it can whack his wrist. "I'm exempt. I don't live here."

Smiling naughtily, like Warren will suffer later, Willa breaks my heart. "I still have the doll. It was the only thing that mattered to me. I took it when I married Donny, and I had Royce rescue it twice: when I was in the hospital and when I was in rehab. It's sitting on my dresser as we speak."

Everyone chats together while I hide the tears stinging my eyes. Royce is just as silent, as we eat around the food Penny prepared, and try to enjoy the yummy food Willa made. I notice we all have pushed the oddly textured scalloped corn to the side, except for Warren. He's inhaling it to make Penny feel good.

"I think Willa ought to take up tennis," Kade teases the spatula-wielder. "I'm impressed."

Pointing at Kade, "Oh, my God!" Willa turns animated for the first time since I was ten. "Remember when you couldn't hit the broadside of a barn with the rifle? You got so pissed, you took a tennis racket to the beer can targets sitting on the fence."

"I was a late bloomer," Kade grumbles beneath his breath. His tan skin pinks and a high blush stains his cheeks.

"No, you were a skinny beanpole who tripped over his own feet," Warren taunts his buddy. "You were covered in zits and bruises, and your hair looked like you'd been electrocuted." We all turn to stare at Kade, seeing the big, strong, gorgeous man he is today. "Who would have ever thought you'd look like this? You're still not as perfect as Golden Boy."

"I don't remember you looking like that?" I stare transfixed at Kaden, wishing we were alone in the backseat of his car on Friday night, knowing I would make that mistake over and over again. "Who's Golden Boy?"

"You are!" Everyone at the table shouts, with Warren adding, "Instead of being jealous, I decided to take ownership over how awesome you are. That's my brother!"

"What?" I grumble, confused.

"Dude." Bren bumps his shoulder into me. "You being blind to the fact is part of your charm. If you try anything, you excel at it. It sucks, so I had to do what Warren did, or else I'd hate your guts. But I'd feel guilty for not thinking you're the shit."

My face turns beet red. "You're exaggerating." I take a forkful of mashed potatoes, not tasting it as I chew.

"You were the only twelve-year-old I've ever met who was tall and corded with muscle. You intimidated the hell out of me." Kade whispers in my ear. "Among other things that made me feel like a pervert."

"Pfft... please! I wanted to hang out with you and Warren when I was little, and you guys ignored me. I followed after you all the time, and you were *not* a late bloomer."

Jumping up from his chair, "I've got proof!" Royce rushes from the dining room, returning a second later with a small picture frame in his hand. It's thrust at me. "Here, check this out."

"No, don't," Kade protests, trying to pry the frame from my grip. "Don't look! It will ruin it– all of those hours at the gym and stuffing my face to gain weight. All you'll see is what I used to look like, not as I am now."

I turn toward Bren, using my back to shield me from Kade. I hide the frame on my lap so no one can take it from me. On a camping trip, Royce is standing proudly with a hand on both of his boys' shoulders. Bren was a chubby kid with huge apple cheeks and an even bigger grin.

"How old were you?" I ask of the emaciated looking boy. All of his glorious hair is shaved to the scalp, with no way to hide the bad acne marking his face. Kade looks so sad yet happy, it hurts my heart.

"Sixteen. I looked like a lollipop with that huge head and skinny body." Kade laughs at himself, wrenching the frame out of my hands to pass back to Royce. "I'm seriously going to go home and lift weights." He tucks into his food like he's ravenous. "Can't ever get skinny again."

"Never thought I'd hear those words." Penny snorts. "Us girls always gotta make sure we're svelte."

Raising an eyebrow, "Svelte?" Warren looks at Penny like she's been replaced by an alien lifeform.

Flashing a wicked smirk, "Cosmo. Those church ladies are naughty. I have an unlimited supply of every magazine on the market. It's an education, I'll tell ya."

"Are they really throwing you a bachelorette party?" Willa turns to Penny. "I got an invite last week, and I thought it was a joke."

"They really are," wonder is heavily lacing Penny's voice. "I thought they'd judge me, but they never have. When all those women get together, they get a lot done, and nothing goes without attention. I'm amazed."

"My cousin had a bridal shower and a baby shower at the same time, with the men invited," Kade offers in. "It was the creepiest thing I've ever seen. They were passing around onesies and lacy underwear, and I'm pretty sure it turned me gay. No offense."

"None taken." Penny stares at Kade for a heartbeat, giving him the stink-eye. But not because of the offhand comment. She's always been a bit jealous of me giving attention to anyone else– Bren is still on her shit list. But Kade is a big issue for taking both Warren's and my time from Penny. "I said no to the showers, and I hope they listen. I didn't want to look like a money grubber out to take whatever I could get from complete strangers. So if anyone wants to get the baby anything, that's fine as long as they are actually my friends or family."

"Bit creepy to be resting our boy's head on sheets somebody we don't associate with bought." Warren shudders. "Creepy."

"Terry had five showers for her first kid. Church, work, friends, family, another set of friends," Penny rattles off. "Then she did that again for the next kid, and the next. I argued with this woman for a good hour, how I thought that was gross."

"Has to be a townie thing," Willa muses. "How gluttonous… and who needs so much attention brought to them. Obviously I didn't have any showers, or even a wedding. I was forced to sign the license, and then dragged off." My sister looks around at our horrified expressions. "I want better for you, Penny. So if those ladies want to host parties for you, let them."

"Maybe someday you'll get remarried and have some more kids," Penny hesitantly suggests.

"Even if I do, I don't want a fuss made." Willa points her fork at all of us. "You hear me? No surprise anythings."

"Yes, ma'am." Royce tries to suppress his laugh by smiling into his glass as he takes a drink. "I'm not into surprises myself."

"So how the hell did you afford that rock on your finger?" Willa leans forward to examine her soon-to-be sister-in-law's shiny new bauble, and Penny blushes the same shade as her hair.

"Hey!" Bren shouts. "That ain't fake. What the fu– nk?"

"I came into a windfall, you could say." Warren smirks at Kade. "I thought my woman deserved the very best."

"Compensation for marrying you, eh?" Bren taunts, never giving up the opportunity to press Warren's buttons. "If I were a betting man, I'd guess that ring cost close to a grand, with tax."

Warren leans forward, pointing his fork at Bren with a huge grin twisting his lips. "And you'd be a winning man."

"I could be losing my job," Kade announces, making me feel guiltier. "I can't afford to be a betting man."

Warren and Bren crack up, leaving the rest of us to watch them with confusion. Except for Kade; he's murdering his buddy with his stare.

"Once, a long, long time ago, old man…" Warren's voice flows smooth, like a seasoned storyteller. "I was living in the holler, in a shack falling down around my ears. I hardly had a pot to piss in, yet I was the proud purchaser of a fourteen hundred dollar AKC Registered Pug named The Pervert Virgin." He points his fork at Kade. "I'd say we're almost even, brother humper."

"Perty's named The Pervert Virgin?" Penny's the first to bust out laughing, with all of us but Kade turning into hysterics.

"It was worth it," Kade whispers, and then he's joining us in laughing at himself. "I'd pay it again if I could be left alone for an entire evening."

"NO!" Royce's fist pounds the edge of the table. "I don't need to know the specifics to figure out what Warren and you are talking around. No more of that horseshit. Got it?"

"Yes, sir," Warren and Kade say in unison, with Bren coughing into his hand, "Says the Kennedy who is known for buying Gillettes." He clears his throat, and then coughs for real.

"I'm not an idiot, ya know?" I glare at Warren, knowing he's at fault. "I'll never get over Daddy and Momma having no issue selling my ass. I expected better out of you, brother."

Warren rolls his eyes. "I think you've been hanging 'round Royce too long, learning the art of guilt and manipulation."

Penny leans across the table to pat my hand. In a sweet, concerned voice, she murmurs, "Winnie, you sure you ain't a girl?"

"Oh, my God." I release a few snarls and choice cuss words, and Willa doesn't dare swat me for it. "I'ma kill you if you keep that shit up!"

"Just riling ya up, dummy!" Penny and Warren laugh together at my expense, obviously conspiring against me.

"You guys have been replaced." I flash a glacial glare at them. "Bren's my new brother. Willa's my favorite sister. And Jack will always be my best friend. So you guys can take a big suck of my ass."

"That's what he wants." Willa points at Kade, voice and expression serious. It takes a heartbeat, where we're all shocked that came from Willa, and Kade's the first to crack. The table erupts into hysteria, with everyone lobbing euphemisms for gay sex acts at Kade and me. I join in, realizing they're desensitizing themselves to something that makes them uncomfortable.

"Momma." Hayley tugs on Willa's sleeve, never abiding by her mom's NTP rules. "Can we play games later?"

"Hmm…" Willa surprises us all by wrapping her arm around Hayley's shoulders. "After supper is cleaned up. But not for long, 'cuz you've got school in the morning."

With big, blue eyes filled with innocence, "Can we play for money?" Hayley negotiates.

"*What the hell kind of kids are these?*" Kade mouths to me. "That vulture is not my sweet student from last school year."

"Babe, we'll play Bullshit with a winner's pot." Warren makes Hayley's day. "Go on now and get to cleaning up. Your brother will help you." As soon as the kids scamper to the kitchen with plates in their hands, Warren says to Kade. "We're Gillettes, and games are only fun if you have something to win or lose."

"Gillettes cheat." Kade narrows his eyes. "I remember well."

"Just part of the game," Warren sings as he stands from his seat.

"Kennedys are no better." Kade glares at Bren. "Those kids are the evil incarnation of two very bad bloodlines."

Bren stacks a bunch of plates, and then says over his shoulder as he walks toward the kitchen. "If I ever have kids, I want 'em to be just like Hayden and Hayley. As for cheating, I call that creative playing. So don't be a pussy, bro, and ante up."

I decide to help clean up, but first I make sure everyone knows I'm honest. "I don't cheat."

"Of course you don't," Royce grumbles, and then he rolls his eyes. "But maybe you ought to start."

"Don't release Teenage Wynn, Royce," Kade says in an ominous voice. "You've been warned." An evil twist to Kade's lips captures my attention, and everything else is blocked out when they touch mine.

I'm hit upside the head before I can even react. "No," Royce snarls. "Kade, I know you're trying to piss me off since you waited for everyone else to leave the dining room. Don't test me, boy."

"Just proving a point, is all." Kade's laughter lingers even after he leaves the room.

Royce's, "You be a good boy," rings in my ears all night, and it riles me up. Seventeen or not, I'm my own man. I respect Royce, but I've been taking care of myself for this long, I can't go backward and pretend I'm the kid I never was.

"Okay, kids. It's time to go to bed." Royce stands up, stretching his back out, effectively ending our fun. "C'mon. Let's wash up."

We all groan for different reasons: the kids because they don't want to go to bed, and the adults because the kids are card sharks. Hayley's sitting on the floor, wearing the satisfied smirk of a budding gambler, counting her winnings out loud in a smug, girlish tone.

Warren and Penny left about an hour ago when the stakes were getting too high. My brother simply said, *Too rich for my blood*," and walked out of the house. My wallet is ten bucks lighter, and I was winning some. Poor Bren– his wallet's empty now.

Kade points at my niece, gaze filled with pride. "I taught Hayley that. She was one of my brightest students, especially in math."

"First grade, dude. First grade. You're not teaching Rocket Science." Bren rolls his eyes dramatically. "Pretty sure Penny taught the kid how to count change at the laundry mat… just saying."

Hayley's eyes flick up to us as we stand around her. "Mr. Marx taught me how to read. But it was Uncle Wynn who taught me how to count."

Kade's eyebrow raises in question, and I simply mutter, "Don't ask." Hayley learned her mathematics just like the rest of the Gillettes did. How many beers has Papaw had? One to four? Hide. Five to ten? Stand your ground. Eleven to fifteen? Call an ambulance for when he beats one of us. More than a case? Let him rot in his own piss and vomit.

"I want a bedtime story, Uncle Winnie," Hayden nearly whines. He drops his winnings onto his sister's pile to be put toward their future iPad– one more round of Bullshit, and they might not have to share. "The real ones, where they're scary."

"Hayden has a thing for the Grimm Brothers," I offer as an explanation. I reach down to ruffle his hair, and then muss up Hayley's curly fauxhawk. The girl keeps cutting it every time it grows out. "I'll be up in a bit. I've got to say goodnight to Kade."

"Night, Kade!" Royce waves like he's a little kid, then grabs the twins' hands and makes them wave too. "I'll call you later. You go on out through the front door." Turning a smug smirk my way, he goes from friendly to pissed in a heartbeat. "Now you can read the kids a story."

Kade's laughter is loud and infectious, and I'm pretty sure he keeps repeating *ass* when he takes a breath. "Night, *Dad*," comes in a warped tone. "I'd like my brother to walk me out, if you don't mind."

"Oh, I mind," Royce drawls. "Hey, Bren? Walk your brother out. Wynn's busy reading to the kids."

Bren raises his hands out in front of himself, refusing to get in the middle of this. "I ain't got no horse in this race. Leave me out of it."

"C'mon, kids, Wynn, let's get upstairs," Royce urges, trying to herd us out of the den.

I look to my sister for some help, only to find her laughing into her hands. "I can't... I just can't..." She's out of breath from trying to keep her amusement quiet. "I've never seen anything like this in my life. My God, this is hilarious."

"Uncle Daddy?" Hayley's voice is sweet with calculation, not confusion. "But I gotta get washed up first. Uncle Wynn's got time to see Mr. Marx off."

Royce snarls, looking like a cat readying to hiss. "Hayley? Remember how I said that doesn't sound good? Either Daddy or Uncle Royce, not a combination. Okay?"

"Daddy?" Hayley turns on the charm, batting her long lashes. "Will you change my Band-Aid after I brush my teeth?" She holds up her fingertip covered by Disney characters.

"Yeah, darlin'." Royce takes her hand, swallowing it up in his. But he turns to issue a warning. "No leaving the porch. No going to Kade's car. Willa stays in the front room at all times, and Bren is going with you. Got it?"

"I want Hansel and Gretel," Hayden chirps as they leave the room.

"No, Rapunzel," Hayley argues. "You got to pick last night."

"Okay, but we're reading in my room. I don't like having to get up to go to my bed when the story makes me sleepy."

"Deal."

Filled with a mother's love, "They are such good kids." Willa gazes after the twins and Royce. Then she turns to me. "Those aren't the original stories, are they?"

"Ah…" My eyes go wide, not knowing how to respond, causing Willa to hightail it upstairs to find our huge tome of Grimms' Fairy Tales. "Good thing the cover fell off, so she won't know which book it is."

"Learn to lie, bub. Learn to lie." Bren pats my shoulder. "Shall we retire to the porch so Mr. Marx can get a good, refreshing night's rest in preparation of expanding the minds of tiny sociopaths?"

"I pity that girl's future husband." Kade's eyes are transfixed on the staircase, like he can still see the twins. "At seven, Hayley manipulates better than anyone I've ever seen."

Bren points at his puffed up, scrawny chest with pride. "I taught her that!"

"Stay!" I treat Bren like he's a dog. "If your dad comes downstairs before I'm back inside, just tell him we threatened to beat you."

"Pfft… yeah, right. Like he'd buy that with you two pacifists." Bren shoulders his way past me, yanks the front door open, and lets the screen door slam when he makes his way onto the front porch.

"You really need to get a handle on Royce, or he'll walk right over you," Kade warns me. Before I can respond, he palms the back of my neck to draw my lips to his.

Leaning forward and rising up a bit to reach Kade better, I'm completely shameless in our kiss. Inexperienced, I try hard not to slobber all over him, but fail miserably when my tongue has a mind of its own. I end up awkwardly licking his chin on accident.

"We need to practice," Kade chuckles against my lips. "Lots of practice."

"I can do better," comes in a raspy voice. I shut off the part of me that is thinking, and go on pure instinct. I curl my fingertips into Kade's shirt, tugging him closer. At the same time, I nip his bottom lip.

Whimpering, Kade opens his mouth, and I know I'm doing something right. Our moment is cut short when a door slams upstairs and voices float down. We hop apart, both of us glancing at the staircase.

"Seriously." Kade drops a quick kiss to my lips. "Ask Bren for the same advice he gave me." He steps away when all I want to do is get closer. "No one understands how you feel about Royce more than I do. How appreciative you feel. How you worry about disappointing him, like you're an investment he's making, and if you fuck up he'll take it all away."

I stare at Kade, speechless, feeling like he's somehow entered my private thoughts. Chuckling with satisfaction, he rubs the center of my chest to calm me.

"Royce gave you something you didn't ask for but desperately needed. That doesn't give him the license to boss you around for life. Nor does it take away your voice. Compromise on everything but being you. Everything else is a negotiation." His hand drops from my chest, and I shiver from its loss. "Take Bren's advice. It works."

"Yeah, listen to me," Bren croons in a spooky voice inches behind me, causing me to jump and nearly piss my pants.

"What the fuck?" I shake it off. "Did you get trained by a Ninja?"

"The siren call of moans summoned me from the porch." Bren's teeth flash when he grins. "I'm a nosy bastard. I had to watch."

"Gross." Kade shudders, but he's smiling. "See ya around sometime, my annoying baby brother," he says in parting to Bren, but he gives me a wink.

"You both need to get laid," is Bren's advice. "If you don't use it, you lose it."

"I figure your dad isn't going to get much sleep for a while, so that ain't happening any time soon," I grumble as I ascend the staircase.

Bren follows me right into my room, shuts the door behind him, and then leans on it. I ignore him as I strip down to my boxers and tug on a pair of pajama pants and a t-shirt.

"Here's the thing, Golden Boy. You're too good."

Folding my jeans, Bren's words stop me in my tracks. I look at him over my shoulder, trying to figure out where the hell he's going with this. "And that's a bad thing?"

"Hell, yeah!" Bren walks around my bedroom, snooping while chatting. "Look at me. I suck at everything. I'm mediocre, but I think I'm awesome."

"Are you serious?" I snort, and Bren looks offended.

"I am," Bren drawls. "I'm amazing because I truly believe I am. I'm short, dorky, and clumsy, but people still love me. It doesn't matter that I'm not perfect. If you have a mix of achievements and fuck ups, no one will give a flip if you make a mistake. But if all you ever do is excel, the second you fail, everyone will be on your ass."

"I don't like failing," grumbles unbidden from my lips, making me feel like I'm whining.

"That's your problem!" Bren points at me, bugging his eyes out. "You put so much stress on yourself, to the point you tried to shoot your own head off." I glare at Bren for bringing my biggest mistake back up again. "You did! You need to relax. Fucking up is not the end of the world, and it can be liberating."

"And I'm to what?" I toss my jeans on the floor, feeling a bit guilty for not taking good care of something that was given to me. "Misuse my shit, treat everyone nastily, and don't give a fuck about anything?"

"Nah, dude." Bren reaches into my dresser drawer, hand sweeping beneath the clothing, looking for my darkest secrets. He scowls when he comes up empty-handed. "You're boring," he pouts. "You can't let Dad stop you from fooling around. He'll be telling you what to eat, what time to go to bed, and what to wear when you're seventy. Cut the cord."

"I respect your dad." I slump to my bed. "I can't do that."

"Bro!" Bren mock-punches me in the arm. "There is nothing you could ever do to piss that man off enough to where he won't love you. Trust me."

"I don't want to disappoint him."

"Do you love Willa and Warren any less, or do you love them more for overcoming their mistakes?"

"I…" I reach down to pick up my jeans, fold them, and then place them in my dresser. "They are Willa and Warren. I expect them to act like Willa and Warren, and that has nothing to do with me."

"Exactly." Bren reaches into the drawer of my nightstand, and his hand returns palming my lube. He grins hugely, happy to see I'm not a saint. "You just be you, and don't worry about what Dad thinks about that. That's on Dad."

I snatch the *Anal Eze* out of Bren's hand, and toss it back into my drawer. "I got it online," I mutter bashfully. "I was curious."

"You're human." Bren quickly steps into my closet, and returns scowling. He stomps to the door, pissed he didn't find anything interesting in my room. "Act like it," is said as the door shuts behind him.

I de-stress using my nightly ritual: lying in bed with my laptop and my headphones on. I laugh shamelessly at the Buzzfeed video of The Try Guys. I've got a serious crush on Eugene. There's been too many late nights rewatching videos to count. On a few mornings I've walked around like a zombie, and I fear tomorrow will be one of them.

"God, take it off, Eugene." I groan, my hand venturing south. "Mmm… You look damn fine wearing ladies' lingerie, but I bet you'd look even hotter with it off. Mmm… hmm…"

I fight the urge for my eyes to shut as my fingers dip below my waistband, skimming along my hardening dick. Giving up, my eyes slip shut and my ass cheeks flex. My laptop slides from my thighs to rest on my bedspread. On auto-pilot, my hand reaches into the drawer in my nightstand, coming out with my lube.

Back arching, hips gyrating, I marvel over how great my life is versus how it used to be. Privacy is a luxury, but nothing is as good as getting hard at will because I finally know what turns me on. With a groan, my hand strokes my length while Eugene and Keith laugh together.

Not bothering to take off my pajama pants, both of my hands are working furiously beneath the fabric. The thick lube paves the way as I get way into it. I roll my balls between my fingertips, getting off on how it shoots darts of electricity up my spine. It hurts so good.

Last week I found this new technique of drawing out my orgasm, stoking me until I can't take it anymore by grinding my knuckles into my taint. Jackknifing off the bed, eyes squeezing shut, I wrap my hand around the base of my dick and my nutsack to stop me from spurting, at the same time, the knuckles of my other hand rub and roll along my taint.

"Oh, fuck!" I flop back to the bed, spine still bowed, when a knuckle makes contact with my asshole. "Jesus Christ." My cry ends on a whimper. But I still don't allow myself to come.

Eyes still shut, to the backdrop of Eugene's voice, I squirt more lube into my hand. I wiggle a bit, legs spreading as far as my pajamas will allow, I slip a fingertip inside me for the very first time.

An odd gurgling noise rumbles up my throat, a mix of pain and ecstasy. Dick and balls and taint long forgotten, I find my new favorite plaything. I keep my hand stationary while I roll my hips up and down on instinct. I fuck about an inch of my fingertip, marveling over how it burns a bit, but I can feel myself loosening.

"UH!" I grunt when my asshole sucks my finger in deeper, like something gave and I can finally move freely. Hips jerking, finger counterthrusting, my throat is spilling moan after moan as I ride the most intense wave of my life.

Every muscle in my body contracts at once, my mouth opens up to release a building scream, and my balls tighten so hard I fear I'm going to shoot them out the tip of my dick.

"Argh–" a heavy palm covers my mouth, pressing hard. I begin to struggle as my dick erupts and my finger impales me deeply. Terrified, my orgasm is so intense I can't stop to protect myself.

My headphones are wrenched off my head, and then a pair of lips whisper insanity. "Don't stop, you little shit. Don't you dare fucking stop." Kade's hand presses harder to my open mouth, my gasps and groans reverberating against his slick skin. "Fuck yourself– pretend it's me."

Kade's hand covers mine with my pajama pants acting as a barrier. His fingers tighten against my wrist, controlling my movements, not allowing me to slow. Faster and faster, my finger slides in and out of my ass, and my hips join the movement.

A heavy moan pierces the air– mine –for the split-second Kade's hand leaves my mouth to be covered by his lips. Tongues and moans mingle as I ride out the most intense pleasure of my entire life. I'm not sure I will survive to reach the end.

"A gift from Heaven– a natural bottom," Kade rumbles as he flops on the bed next to me. "Maybe there is a God after all."

"What? Huh? Seriously? What the fuck?" I lay boneless on my bed, random words rambling out my swollen lips. "How? Huh?" Then it dawns on me. Kade is in my room. Kade just saw me jerking off to The Try Guys. Not only jerking off, finger-fucking my asshole. "Fuck," spills from my mouth in a rush.

"Hmm… now this is awkward." Kaden's intoxicating laugh fills my bedroom, and it's too much, too soon after getting off. I writhe on my mattress, riding it out. "You just lay there and get your bearings."

Nearly comatose, wishing I could die of humiliation, I lie in bed while Kade cleans me up. He uses my t-shirt to wipe the spunk off my belly. Then he pulls my hands from beneath my pants, and wipes them off too. Now I really want to die, because I can guess what's on my fingertip that he is meticulously cleaning.

"You are an odd little shit, I'll give you that." Kade chats with me as if he isn't cleaning poo off my finger. "When I was your age, I had at least ten different gay porn sites bookmarked. But you." He abandons the cleanup to tug the plug to my headphones from the jack on the laptop. Eugene's sexy voice fills my bedroom. "Buzzfeed? Really, Wynn? You're jerking it to Buzzfeed? Wow. Just wow."

"The Try Guys are hot. Each one in their own way." My voice is slurred, sluggish. "Eugene– there's something about Eugene."

"Hmm… I pegged you as a verse who had a thing for manly men. Did I get that wrong? Do I need to stop working out?" Kade shuts my laptop, shutting Eugene up while he's at it. "This Asian guy seems a bit effeminate. He's straight, though… and I caught you finger-fucking yourself, so I guess I was wrong on you being versatile."

"First time," I gasp out. "First time for that. Instinct or something. Usually when I'm jerking it, in my head we take turns."

"My childhood faith has returned," Kade says sarcastically. "Nice lube. Good shit. I tried out a dozen brands before I found the right one and settled on this one. It's great when using a plug."

"Too advanced for me." I roll across the bed, grabbing my laptop on my way. I set my baby on the floor out of harm's way, and then rest my back against the headboard.

"Well, I do have a few years of self-exploration on you." Kade just sits on my bed, staring at me.

"Why are you here? How did you get in? Why didn't you stop me?" I press my face to my thighs, hiding my humiliation. "Why did you make me think I was going to get murdered while coming? Why did you try to suffocate me?"

"Why am I here? I never left. I walked to my car, and then realized I was a grown man and this is still the house I lived in for nearly six years. Royce is not going to push me out, and I need to teach him some boundaries. How did I get in? My key. I walked right in and sat in the kitchen. Bren caught me licking all of his cookies in retaliation like he used to do to me. So we sat downstairs shooting the shit, and Bren ate the cookies anyway."

"Eww…"

"Hey, you suck my tongue, so don't even try to say my saliva is gross." Kade maintains a straight face.

Shuddering, I look at Kade, wondering if he's for real. "Yeah, but it's Bren."

Kade just shrugs. "The ass used to stare at me when I was eating. If I paused, he'd spit on my food so he could have it. I was trying to gain weight, so I spent a lot of time beating the shit out of him."

"Are you serious? I can't fucking tell right now? You're acting weird. Why?"

"True story. The little asshole had good aim, too. Projectile spitting– always on my sweets. He'd take the pounding, and then eat my dessert in front of me." Kade is not even cracking a smile. I just stare at him, waiting for the punchline. "While Bren was consuming my saliva, Royce came down in a panic, screaming about how I was upstairs fucking you. Then he started shouting about calling an ambulance."

"What?" I gasp out, eyes bugging from my skull.

"What?" Kade mimics me. "I was eating a cookie, so we were all confused how I was upstairs fucking you. Bren just wondered what the ambulance was for." Still, he maintains a straight face. "I volunteered to either murder whomever was in your room violating you, or assist, if the case may be– not that I told Royce that part."

"Stop it," I snarl, getting more and more mortified by the second. "I'm missing something."

"Why didn't I stop you? Because it took all of my self-control not to join you, that's why. Why did I try to suffocate you? Because you were lying there with your headphones on, sounding like the main cast member of a solo porn video. You were building up to screaming. That's why."

"Oh. My. Fucking. God. NO!" I hide my head in my hands, and then Kade lets loose, laughing so hard the bed shakes beneath us.

"If I live to be a hundred, nothing will ever be hotter than you finger-fucking yourself to The Try Guys." Kade yanks my hands from my face. "I swear to God, Wynn, I creamed my pants the second I laid eyes on you." My hand is tugged lower, until it's cupping the front of Kade's damp pants. "See?"

No matter how mortified I am, my fingers still clench and give a few pulses to his soft bulge. I pull away, roll to my side away from him, and then lie in the fetal position. "I'm going to go die now."

"I miss this room." Kade moves around on the mattress as he gets comfortable. "I love that it felt like home from the second I moved in. As fatherly as Royce is– and trust me, that gets annoying fast –I needed it. Bren was the perfect annoying, little brother. I always looked forward to coming home on holidays. After Dad died, I thought I'd be lonely all the time. But it's impossible with Royce and Bren."

I tug my pillow over my head, hiding. "You saw me shoving a finger up my ass. You saw my poo. I wanna die."

"We both want my dick in your ass… and it wasn't as bad as you think," Kade tries to comfort me. "I'd probably want to die if you walked in on one of my more adventurous masturbation escapades. Maybe someday I'll have the balls to show you."

"That good, huh?" I peek out from beneath the pillow, looking at Kade from over my shoulder. He's just sitting on my bed, looking around the room, memories playing out over his features.

Kade turns to me. "Oh, God, yes!" His hazel eyes slip shut, mouth parting on a pant. "So good. You, little shit, I'm a virgin. So I've had to be creative in my solo missions."

"Give me your worst so I don't feel so embarrassed." I roll over to my back, and then sit cross-legged. "C'mon. Tell me."

"Okay." Kade sighs like I'm torturing him, then he flashes a naughty grin at me. "I'll give you my most embarrassing sexual moment, followed by my most adventurous sex. Trust me, that won't be embarrassing. It's so fucking good I could come just thinking about it."

"Bullshitter," I mutter, trying to dampen my excitement.

Kade gets up from the bed, and starts checking out the changes I've made around the room. "I like what you've done with the place." His fingertips glide over the antique trunk I refinished. "And I get off on knowing you're sleeping in my bed."

"Unlike you, I still don't feel at home here… or anywhere."

"You will. Trust me." Kade examines the crown molding I encased the windowsill in. "You trust Royce, but after your dad, you won't find home until you make one. My house is *my* home. This room was a layover."

"I want that."

"You'll get it. Be patient." Kade laughs when he spots the copy of Out magazine I found underneath the mattress. I'd thought it was Bren's. "I was awkward and horny. I was eighteen before I tried to not be so gross."

"You were never gross," I growl.

"Yeah, I was," Kade says without any emotion. "I begged Royce to fix me. I got antibiotics for the acne, a dietician to fatten me up, workout equipment in the basement, and salon visits until I tamed my hair. I know when you look at me, you see similarities between us, but that's bullshit."

"How? What do you mean?"

I expect Kade to look away, instead he hits me head-on with his gaze. "You are naturally selfless, and I'm selfish. I lie; you don't. I cheat; you don't. I fuck up; you don't. You are smart, athletic, a hard worker, giving and compassionate– a good person. I graduated with a C average, and college didn't come naturally to me. I struggled to get through every class that bored me. Everything was a struggle, and I had to overcome being lazy to get anywhere."

"So what?" I scoot down the bed to sit at the foot of it. "I like you, Kade. I meant what I said before. You're still Kade– the Kade I remember, and that's a good thing."

"I'm glad, because I'm still embarrassed of the old Kade. I got to Penn State thinking I could… ya know…" Kade stumbles over his words. "Experiment. Learn some shit." His shoulders curl into themselves, making him look so much smaller. "That didn't happen. Not once, even after I grew into my looks. I was awkward.

"My most humiliating sexual experience was every day over four years of my college education." Kade sits next to me at the edge of the bed. "My roommate was a slut– a hot slut. Every night was another girl, even when he had a girlfriend. I'm ashamed to admit I'd whack off while he fucked them in front of me. I was transfixed by my roommate. I didn't want to date him. I didn't even want to fuck him. I just got off on watching him."

"Damn," I drawl, utterly shocked.

"We were friends. Not like best buddies or anything, but good friends. He knew about how I thought I was a pervert and why I wanted to wait to have sex. So I didn't realize Danny caught on until junior year, when he'd actually done so during our freshman year. He'd been posing for me, making sure I enjoyed myself. At the end of our last semester, he brought this twink to our room. Uriah."

"I don't like where this is headed." My voice deepens with jealousy. "Not one bit."

"It's not what you think." Kade rests his hand on my knee. "Imagine Francis five years from now– that kid is going to own Berkeley. That was Uriah. He was more sexy and feminine than all the girls Dan had brought home for four years, but manly too. I can't explain it. I lasted ten seconds into my lap dance."

A growl echoes around the room, and I don't even realize it came from me until Kade is chuckling.

"Uriah was a bit disappointed because I looked like I do now by then. He thought he was getting a playmate for the night, and Danny thought he was going to get even by watching me for once. But I popped immediately. Nothing like a pity fuck courtesy of your roommate."

"Um… I do get that. I've had Bren ask Jessica to ask me if I wanted a blowjob a few times to take my edge off. But I couldn't do it. We're more alike than you realize, I guess."

"Bren and Jessica do not have a healthy relationship." I'm surprised by the sad tone in Kade's voice. "I ended up getting the education of a lifetime. Danny was keyed up and Uriah was willing, and I was the one who was given a show."

"Your *straight* roommate?"

"I didn't actually believe gay-for-you existed, but I was proven wrong," Kade mutters wryly. "I'd never seen Danny like that– he even surprised himself, I think. So for the rest of the semester, not a single girl stepped foot into our dorm room, and Dan almost flunked out of college. He fucked Uriah continuously, making sure I watched. Both of them telling me anything I'd ever want to know. And they always made sure to masturbate with me so I didn't feel like a freak."

"Did they touch you?"

"No," he says matter-of-factly. "I wouldn't let them."

"Oh." I'm surprised that I sound mildly disappointed. Part of me wanted to live vicariously through Kade. "That sounded like it might have been… fun. What happened next?" eagerly spills from my lips.

Kade falls back against the mattress, and stares at the ceiling. He huffs a laugh, and I almost beg for him to continue. He flashes me a sly smile. "We've kept in touch since we graduated, meeting halfway every month or so. They live just south of Pittsburgh, so it's not that far of a drive. This past summer, I was their best man at their wedding."

"Again, I gotta say this: your *straight* roommate."

"I'll have Uriah visit soon, and you'll see why he'd appeal to my straight roommate. Danny doesn't care that Uriah has a cock because he loves him, and I think he loves the cock almost as much now, too." Kade releases a laugh I've never heard before. An intimate manly one exclusive to sex. It runs along my spine and curls in my belly.

"The bachelor party was at a male strip club, but it was Uriah who gave me a lap dance. This time I didn't pop because it was like overstimulation– chaos everywhere. But we did get drunk and end up getting spunk all over the inside of the limo. Me from watching them fuck... the stripper."

"Jesus Christ," I breathe out in a gush. I reach down to squeeze myself before I pull a *Kade*. "That's too advanced for me."

"Me too. Well, not the watching and whacking... the actual fucking. Uriah wanted me to do him while Dan watched for old times' sake, neither having been with anyone since they met. But I told them I was taken, so they settled on making me watch them with the stripper."

"Was the stripper hot?"

"Eh... not really. They were hotter." Kade starts laughing, a belly-deep sound of amazement. "I didn't think it'd be like this with you. So easy. It's like talking to a best friend, but better. Best friend, brother, boyfriend, and lover rolled into one. I've never been able to share this with anyone but Dan and Uriah. I always feared getting a boyfriend and having him judge me. Like how you see girlfriends act, all jealous and spiteful. They're automatically right, no matter what, and the guy is always wrong, even when he's right. *Me. Me. Me.* But I forgot you're you. Mr. Selfless. Thank fuck for that, because I'm not."

I reach over and rest my palm against Kade's chest. His heartrate is through the roof, probably worried about what I am thinking and feeling. The odd thing is that I feel more connected to Kade than ever because he's telling me the truth, even if it might hurt me or piss me off.

"I am jealous, but more curious than anything." My fingertips clench against Kade's t-shirt. "Did you want to fuck them?" My tone is serious, but without judgment. "Do you now?"

"Yes," flows gravelly deep. Kade turns to pin me with his stare. "And yes." He waits a few heartbeats for that to sink in, how he is attracted to other people.

"I've had so many people tell me what to do, what to think, how to feel. Where to work and how my money is spent. Where to go to school and study what. What, where, and when to eat, sleep, shit. I'd never do that to you, because I need you to be the first person in my life to give me the freedom to be who I am. So I'm not gonna get pissed because your dick gets thick over some hot piece of ass. You didn't get mad at Tyler when it happened to me because you knew I wouldn't do anything about it."

Kade stares at me for a very long time– intense and deep –and I stare right back, open and exposed. His hand cups the nape of my neck, fingertips curling possessively. Neither of us blink, silently communicating. Then his lips are on mine, rough and hard. Demanding.

In a flurry of questing, impatient hands, we tear each other's clothing off while grinding against one another, mouths never parting. My pajama pants are gone in an instant, but Kade's boots and t-shirt are more difficult. Getting angry with it, with a harsh yank, I rip the fabric from his back.

Tearing his mouth from mine with a growl, Kade shoves me off of him and steps away. In a few heartbeats, his boots are tossed to the wayside, and his jeans follow after. He pauses, looks at me, looks down at his boxers, and then looks at me again. The boxers fall to the floor in an instant, displaying six and a half feet of naked male.

My brain takes a vacation when I get a good look at him, but he's too impatient to stand still while I devour him with my eyes. I nearly pop the top off my dick when Kade's hands cup my armpits, lift, and then toss me up to the head of the bed. He's on me in an instant, laying his heavy body on top of mine.

"I won't fuck you," Kade rasps out in my ear, sounding like the words bring him physical pain. "Neither of us are ready for that yet, and I won't in this house."

Before I can reply, my arms are wrenched above my head. Lips descend, landing on my throat. "Oh, God!" A deep groan is pulled from my chest at the first bite of Kade's crooked front tooth sinking into my flesh. I arch up, wanting more. "I like that. Harder."

A heavy palm smothers my moans. "I'm not the Sandman, and you're not sleeping," Kade reminds me, not removing his hand from my mouth. "Last thing we need is Royce barging in here to take you to the emergency room."

My laugh vibrates against Kade's hand, but it turns into a grunt when he attacks my chest with his lips. My back jackknifes off the mattress, wanting more of everything he's giving me.

"I feel so alive," murmurs against his palm. "So goddamned happy to be alive."

"Me too. We're alive because we were supposed to be here in this moment," comes in a voice I don't recognize. So deep, almost a groan. I will always associate that sound with sex. My cock jerks between our bodies because of the way Kade is turned on by me.

Kade leans back, all of his weight resting on the hand covering my mouth. The first trickle of panic slithers in, but I shove it away with the trust I have in Kade. At his touch, I cry out so loud the sound escapes around the edges of the suffocating palm.

Echoing around the room, I writhe and jerk and quiver as Kade runs his tongue from my hip, up my side, over my ribs, and lands in my armpit. Mouth opening, Kade devours me, and I'm shocked at his reaction. A continual moaning vibrates my armpit as he feasts, with his cock pressed tight against my thigh, pumping pre-cum to dampen my skin.

"Christ," Kade groans. "I've waited six years to do that. You smell so goddamned intoxicating. I'ma lick your scent off every single inch of your skin." He slides down my body, hand still pinned against my mouth. "Hush, now. Don't scream," and then he presses his face between my thighs.

I scream but no sound comes out as Kade eats me. Swallows my dick, sucks my balls, bites my taint, and tongues my ass. My thighs are rubbed raw from his stubble, but the pain feels exquisite. I come down Kade's throat in a torrent. Driving me to the brink of insanity, three fingers are crammed in my ass, thrusting like a piston. Sound escapes my lips, causing fingertips to bite with bruising force against my cheek, ensuring my climax is a quiet one.

"I feel so alive," Kade repeats my earlier words as he slides up next to me. His dick leaves a trail of cum from my calf to my hip. "I'm so goddamned happy to be alive."

Voice thready and weak, I say Kade's part. "Me too. We're alive because we were supposed to be here in this moment."

MISS ME?

After waking a few times in the night to find Kade curled around my back, I was disappointed when my alarm went off and he wasn't beside me. Stretching, I laugh to the ceiling. "Holy fuck!" I crawl out of bed and quickly do my morning ritual, prepared to face the consequences of my actions. My face blazes bright red when I remember what brought Kade to my room in the first place.

Backpack slipping off my shoulder, I hunch to set it into place as I open my bedroom door. Not paying attention, I walk straight into Royce. Backing up, I mutter. "Whoa… whoa… whoa… no need for a trip to the hospital." I can't help but bust out laughing at his glacial glare.

"You're not funny," Royce bites out through gritted teeth. Guilt momentarily hits me when I take in the strained wrinkling around his eyes and the bruise-like bags from a sleepless night, but I'm in too good of a mood to feel bad. "Are you okay?"

"I… I'm sorry." I apologize to be proactive. "Not for Kade staying over, or for what I was doing beforehand. But for upsetting and disappointing you."

"Are you okay?" Royce doesn't relent.

"I am–" I really think about it. A brilliant smile stretches my lips and I can't stop it. "Perfect."

Royce rolls his eyes at me while shaking his head no, like I'm a doofus. "Your Sandman is sitting down to breakfast, and he assured me you're okay. So no need for hospitalization jokes."

"Kade is still here?" My voice pitches high with excitement. I move to pass Royce, but his fingertips grip my bicep to halt me.

Gruff, Royce turns into *Dad*. "We've got some shit we have to get straight first."

I slump against the hallway wall in defeat. "Punish me. I deserve it."

"You're a goddamned fool," Royce snarls. "Don't pull that shit. Worse, I can see you really mean it. I'm not gonna punish you for anything. You weren't in the wrong."

"What?" I squawk. "Who are you, and what did you do with Royce Kennedy? Of course I did wrong."

"No punishments." Royce grips my shoulder, fingers pulsing in a soothing rhythm. "Boundaries. Here's my compromise. One, no dating Kade until you're eighteen because he's an adult. Two, you can see him all you want during daylight hours or when you're with the family. Three, once you're eighteen, you can stay with him one weekend night a month, but you and Kade have to spend time here at home. No more sleepovers in this house. No sex of any kind in this house. If you plan on playing with yourself, take your headphones off so you can hear what we're hearing."

"Oh, my fucking Lord." I raise my hands to cover my face. "I'm so humiliated."

Royce's lips quirk up at the corners and his eyes dance, but he doesn't comment further on my embarrassing moment. "Once you graduate, you're your own man, but if you aren't in this house four days a week to at least visit, I'm locking you in your room."

I huff a laugh, finally getting with the program. "You're worried you'll miss me, aren't you? Is that what's been going on?"

A blush stains Royce's cheeks, and he quickly looks away so I can't see him. Muttering softly, "Kade was hard to tie down. He moved to State College, and when he came home he'd already bought a house. I had to go to him. I'm not letting him steal you away too, because then I'd never see either one of you again."

"Thank you for the optimism on the longevity of Kade's and my friendship." My chuckle is cut short as warmth blooms in my chest and explodes. I finally feel like I'm home. "I'm not going anywhere when I have so many reasons to be in this house."

"Willa and the kids," Royce murmurs, sounding a bit sad yet happy.

My smile is huge. "Now who's the doofus? I have a feeling Kade avoided this house because I was in it, making him feel like a pervert. You'll probably have to kick him out if you get sick of him now."

"Probably." Royce looks away bashfully. "I'm glad my son has finally come home, but it's a conflict of interests."

"Well, I can't speak for Kade, but I'm not going anywhere because of you." I reach for Royce, finally– FINALLY –feeling like I belong somewhere. I tug him into a manly, back-slapping hug. I lean in and whisper near his ear. "Thank you." I squeeze him tighter, my words breaking with emotion. *"Thank you.* I love you, Dad."

I walk away, leaving an emotional Royce in the hallway. I brush a few tears of my own from my cheeks as I descend the stairs. Voices filter in from the dining room, making me realize the tears are happy ones.

"Mr. Marx," Hayden's voice targets my heart. "Is my homework good?"

"Kade," Kade's amused tone makes my lips split wider.

"Mr. Marx?" Hayden asks again, tiny voice sounding confused.

I turn the corner, entering the dining room, just as Kade repeats. "I'm Kade, kid. Your Uncle Warren is my buddy. Your Uncle Wynn is my boyfriend. Your Uncle Royce is my foster dad. No more Mr. Marx. *Kade.* But I'll gladly check your homework."

"Mine too!" Hayley can't be left out of anything. "Tell me mine was better than Hayden's. Pretty please."

"Can I call you Uncle Kade?" Hayden trumps anything anyone else could have said, judging by the way Kade looks like his heart just exploded.

"Sure kid," Kade says gruffly, hiding his emotions behind a cough. "Uncle Kade. I like the sounds of that."

I stifle a laugh at the sight that unfolds before me. Kade is trying to eat a waffle, but Hayden is hanging over the back of his chair, homework in hand. Hayley's trying to worm her way into Kade's lap while shoving his plate out of the way. Kade's hand follows his plate, fork still trying to spear a piece of waffle, and Hayley's homework is where his plate used to be.

"I'm a nobody now." Bren frowns at me, genuinely hurt. He eats his bacon with the enthusiasm of turkey bacon. "They didn't even notice me walk into the room."

I sit next to Bren, knowing my niece and nephew forgot I existed too. "They probably still think he can give them an A." I reach forward with my fork, stabbing an English muffin. My hand automatically bypasses the waffle and nasty, *not*-maple syrup. "After a few days, someone new will grab their attention."

"Whoever checked your homework last night did a perfect job." Kade gives me a wink. "Skedaddle, and eat your breakfast."

"I stayed up all night watching Buzzfeed," Bren starts in, and I groan in mortification. "Eight hours later, I'm still not seeing what the BFD is. Wynn," I get elbowed so I'll take my hands from my face. "You're a freak… and I don't think you looked in the mirror before heading down here, 'cuz you have fingertip bruises on your cheeks."

"Christ!" I bolt up from the chair, laughter following me. I run into my sister, and have to quickly grasp a container of orange juice before it smashes on the floor.

"Ya better pull the collar down on your shirt to show off your hickey," Willa deadpans, taking the orange juice back from me. "That way if social services is called, they'll figure it was a rough fuck, not domestic violence."

"Uh!" Bren's sharp intake of breath is startling. Followed by his insanity. "Halle-fucking-lujah! FUCK is back in my vocabulary. F. U. C. K. FUCK! Fuckity fuck fuck… fuck… fuuuuuuuck…"

"You sure you don't wanna run away to my house?" Kade arches his eyebrow in my direction.

Grinning back, I mutter with conviction, "There's no place I'd rather be than right here right now," with everyone razzing a giggling Willa in the background.

OWN IT!

During the last play of practice, everything goes to shit– yet again. "Ross, did you see what I did there with the play?" I stride up to Tyler as he wipes his sweat-covered face with the back of his hand. "It doesn't matter who you are outside of this court when you're standing on it. If you're naturally passive or aggressive, you have to be assertive to lead. You are the one who has to set the pace and tone. You can't let them lead you."

"I'm trying to act like you, but they're not listening to me." Frustration warps Tyler's voice, and I know how he's feeling. "I know how it needs to play out. I see it working perfectly in my mind, but they just won't fucking *do it!*"

After a month's worth of practices, I've noticed a trend. *Don't listen to the fag, even if he's your Point Guard!*

I never thought I'd get bullied– not Wynn Gillette. Every incident has slowly changed me. Countless insults have been launched at me from my teammates and classmates because they can't take me in a fight. A month-long nightmare of sitting with Kade in Royce's office because of ignorant parents thinking a gay elementary school teacher will molest their child or turn him gay. Last week when I was walking down the sidewalk, some asshole I've never seen before slowed up his truck and unrolled his window to shout at me.

"We let you ass-bandits marry. Next thing ya know, they'll let molesters marry kids, or daddies marry daughters! Ya wanna marry a sheep? Legal!"

I don't regret coming out, and neither does Kaden, but it hasn't been a pleasant journey. I'm still selfless and compassionate as Kade and Royce like to call me, but I'm more Gillette than ever. Warren wouldn't back down for anything, and neither do I now. The second this shit flares up, I jump on it and shut it down.

Even Colton, Furrow Creek's resident homophobe Point Guard, is being ignored. "Next asshole who doesn't listen to us–" arm raised, middle finger pointing, I turn in a complete circle in Center Court "–is getting cut."

"You can't do that!" Daryl from Hillock Corners bellows in my direction. He lobs the basketball at my head in a fit of rage. I palm it, turn, aim, and then shoot.

Swish.

"I can't do what?" I cup my ear, sick of their bigot bullshit. "I can. If you won't listen to me, you don't get to play with me."

"Gillette's on his period," some asshole calls out, but I can't be sure who. "I thought after he got fucked he'd be less of a pussy."

I don't even turn around to look at who's bashing me. "Leave!" I point at the door. "Leave. Don't come back. I don't care if you play with your team, but not on my court. Leave." I turn in a circle again, glaring at everyone. "It doesn't matter if I crave dick or pussy, I'm still a better ballplayer than you'll ever be. You want a scout to notice ya? Follow my lead."

I stalk off the court, catching a glimpse of our three coaches. They're silent, confused at how much I've changed. Even Coach Nichols is stumped. With upraised palms, I charge through the locker room doors.

The team is spilling in behind me by the time I strip down and step into the shower. My nerves are coiled, and I need something– anything –to take the edge off. I'm this close to punching something.

I lean forward, allowing the cold water to cascade over my neck and down my back. "What's up with Gillette?" Duane asks anyone who will answer, voice being drowned out by the slamming of lockers.

"Tonight's Kaden Marx's school board hearing," Tyler answers for me.

"Shit," flows from several sources, but Bren's, "What? Why didn't I know?" is a punch to the nuts.

"I found out from my mom and told Wynn." I wrench the knob to the shower, furious over the pity in Tyler's voice. "I thought he knew."

"Is Mentor KM gonna get fired?" Franny's asking, but he freezes when he sees me stalking toward my locker.

"Yes," I mutter gruffly while attacking my padlock. "They were humoring him until the marking period ended, so we couldn't call foul on discrimination. Kade is a great teacher, but it won't matter." I yank on my lock, but it doesn't pop open. Frustrated, my palm meets the front of my locker with a sharp rattle. "FUCK!"

"Here." Jack nudges me to the side, no one giving a shit that I'm buck-ass naked. "I'll get it for you, bud. I'll get your clothes out for ya, too. You need to towel off."

"When's the meeting?" Bren hands me a towel while averting his eyes. "Does Dad know?"

"The meeting starts at six in the auditorium. It's open to the public." I bunch the towel in my hands and slump to the bench, not even caring that my bare ass meets plastic. "Dad knows. I know damned well Kade told him. They're trying to protect me from the guilt."

"It's not your fault." Jack hands me my boxers first.

"Chicken. Egg." I yank on my boxers, and then reach for my socks. "I get the hypocrisy of it. I can bitch about all the times they let this go between other teachers and students, but we did break the rules, and they have the right to enforce 'em."

"But it's not right," Francis cries. "If Kade was screwing a girl a few weeks shy of eighteen, they wouldn't care."

Arguing, explaining, and talking it to death with my friends will change nothing. Standing up, I quickly dress, and then start for the door. It takes me a few seconds to realize my friends are following me– supporting me, and Kade by default. My dirty, stinky friends.

"You guys need to shower," I remind them. "You won't be missing much." I walk out the side door to the cafeteria, and then cut through to the hallway. "I don't think Kade wants this large of an audience when he gets fired."

With a shrug, I cross the front lobby, with my friends still following me. "Suit yourself," I mutter as I walk into the noisy auditorium. I've never been to a school board meeting, but I doubt they draw a full house. Tonight, it's packed tight as I fight my way to the front by the stage.

"Fags molest kids," a chubby momma is bitching at her husband. "I don't want our Kara being touched by that monster."

I stop in my tracks, halfway up the aisle. Bren grunts when he collides with my back. "Do you hear yourself, lady? Do you ever listen to what you're saying?" I get into her face. "If all fags are molesters, then what the fuck do they want with your *daughter*?"

The lady gasps and recoils like I slapped her. "You!" she points at me. "You're that kid infecting all the basketball players with your perversions."

"Jesus Christ, woman," Bren groans, and then he's using all of his might to propel me away from her. "Ignore that cunt."

"Didn't ya hear?" I can still hear the woman running off at the mouth. "All these gay basketball players are cropping up. It's spreading like a disease."

"It was that goddamned teacher," a man's voice raises in pitch, overpowering the voices around him. "He targeted them on Facebook."

An old lady's, "Facebook is no different than the funny uncle driving around in a van passing out candy to kids," just about has me losing my shit. My team literally grabs me and carries me up to the front to stop me from committing murder.

"I don't think it's possible to pack more ignorance into an enclosed space." Jack plunks me on my feet with Bren and Duane assisting.

"Irony: we're in an educational institution," Francis points out to our disgust.

My body meets a wall of solid flesh. "What are you doing here?" Kade accuses in a voice tight with silent rage. I glance over his shoulder, spying Warren, Penny, Willa, and Royce. "There was a reason I didn't invite you."

"I very much doubt you invited all of these assholes." I gesture to an auditorium filled with Kentwood Area School District's finest.

"I didn't want you to have to hear this shit," Kade snarls in my ear. He grips my biceps and forces me backward. "Go!"

"I don't live in a vacuum," I remind him. "I'm saying what I came here to say." I reach back, and Tyler plunks a packet of evidence in my palm. "Then I'll go."

The squelch of the microphone has us all grimacing. "Testing… testing one, two, three…" I glance up to the stage where the school board is sitting. Superintendent Ross taps the mic one more time, and then she seems satisfied. "I'd like to call the meeting to order."

I fall into the seat between Kade and Bren, just now noticing the podium standing in the aisle of the first row between two sections of seating. "You shouldn't be here," Kade whispers out the side of his mouth, but the sting of rejection is lessened by his hand twining with mine.

I ignore all the preliminaries. Instead, I focus on the posture of the board members to gauge their decision. It reminds me of what I had to do to survive Daddy. A table full of men are out for blood, with Tyler's mom sitting front and center looking frustrated and furious.

"We're here this evening because Kaden Marx is accused of an inappropriate relationship with a Kentwood Area School District student."

"Inappropriate?" Bren shrieks, causing Tyler's mom to cringe. "The fuck?"

"I don't want my kids being taught by a faggot!" An asshole is standing at the podium without being addressed first. "I ain't raising my son to suck cock."

"Suck this–" Bren lunges from his seat, shocking us all. Kade catches Bren before his fist makes contact with the man's face.

"Duane! Jack! Get our boy out of here!" Kade breathlessly demands as he struggles with a flailing Bren. "This is why I didn't want you here. This!"

Snarling like a rabid animal, it takes Warren to contain Bren. "Knock it off. Yer making this worse."

Three more assholes shout slurs through the microphone while we watch Bren get towed out the back doors to the auditorium. "A man who'd diddle his own foster brother ain't worth having 'round here. That ain't the Lord's path. That's incest."

"Seriously?" Francis turns around in his seat, resting on his knees, and talks right to the old man at the podium. "For a God-fearing man, you sure did miss the sermon about what incest meant. Look at your six fingers, and then say that again." A low rumble of laughter rolls through the auditorium, and Francis turns around looking proud of himself.

"May I say something, Superintendent Ross?" I rise to my feet, not wishing to prolong this more than necessary. "Facts, not hillbilly old wives tales, bigotry, or the bastardization of religion?"

"You practiced that, didn't ya?" Penny whispers loudly, embarrassing the hell out of me.

I don't wait for Tyler's mother to give me the go-ahead since it's been a free-for-all so far. I don't bother with the podium, either. I hop up on stage instead, carrying my packet of facts.

"Wynn." Superintendent Ross sighs my name. "I hate this. I do. You've put me in a hard place. Rules are rules. Kade took advantage of his position as a teacher when he began an inappropriate relationship with you."

"I own that, I admit. But I don't regret it." I turn to face the crowded auditorium, clutching the packet to my chest. "Truths first. I'm Wynn Gillette. I grew up in the hollers but was adopted by Royce Kennedy a few months back. I'm a survivor of child abuse, and I tried to take my own life because of it. I've overcome a lot of things to be who I am today. I'm Rusty Knob's Point Guard and will be their salutatorian come June. I have a basketball scholarship to West Virginia University. I'm three weeks shy of my eighteenth birthday, and I'm of the legal age of sexual consent in this state. I'm 6'3" and weigh 176 pounds. There is nothing about me that can be preyed upon."

I turn around and flop the packet on the table resting before the members of the school board. "I know Kaden Marx broke your rules. But I'm going to point out some facts. I've known Kade since my birth. He is not Mr. Marx to me. He was my brother's buddy, not my authority figure. I'm a senior, not a first grade student. Kade is twenty-three, and I'm going to be eighteen. That is the very definition of normal across the country. I ask, how was that inappropriate?"

Superintendent Ross reads from a book before her. "The rule states that a teacher cannot consort with a student of Kentwood Area School District. The non-tenured teacher will be terminated. I'm sorry, Wynn. It's black and white."

I reach for my packet, and then raise it. "There are forty-seven counts of black and white rule breaking in our school district going back to 1973, with not a single termination. Four were between a teacher of one school and a student from another. Twenty-one were with students in their class. Nineteen were with students below the age of sexual consent. Thirty-nine were male teachers with female students, with eight female teachers with male students. More than half were non-tenured, and no charges of molestation were brought against those who were abusing students who couldn't legally consent."

I flop the packet on the table– the sharp slap reverberating around the auditorium. "One single case of a male teacher with an adult male student. One case of termination." I look out to the crowd but talk over my shoulder to the school board. "We all know you're going to fire Kade and why. I just thought I'd educate everyone for the first time in this ignorant, goddamned high school."

I jump down from the stage, rage boiling in my blood. Penny's, "You did practice that, didn't you?" grates on my nerves.

"Yeah," I grunt absentmindedly. "Tyler's mom is the one who gave me the packet." I head straight for Kade. He's stock-still, awaiting the decision. Both of us know what I said didn't make a difference, but Tyler's mom wanted me to do it anyway.

I lean down and press a kiss to Kade's lips, but he doesn't respond. "We're going to be okay. I'm proud of you. I'm not sorry, and I don't feel regret or guilt." I kiss him one more time, just a press of a touch, and he presses back. "I love you," I say for the first time.

I rise from our kiss to the backdrop of pure chaos erupting in the auditorium. I close my ears to what they say as I walk up the aisle with my head held high. I can't listen to the moment they fire Kade.

I can't.

We broke a rule everyone else has always broken, but we're the only ones to suffer the consequences. If we didn't want them to use their rules against us to push an agenda, than we shouldn't have broken their rules.

To own our choices is to earn our consequences.

GOODBYE

Warren said I wasn't to drive up this road again until it didn't make me feel the urge to off myself. I'm angry at the world at large, but more so myself. There is nothing that would force me to harm myself, because then I wouldn't be able to target those who deserve my wrath.

It took me over six months to get the balls to get in my truck and head to Gillette Holler. The truck drives the path on autopilot, but to me it feels foreign yet familiar. Even in the dark, these trees, hills, fences, rocks, and soil look the same. Even the ruts in the dirt road haven't changed.

I'm who's different.

I huff a laugh when my headlights cast a beam on the sign Warren, Willa, and I made when I was a little shit. The project was my first, and it bred my love of working with my hands. I'd taken a hardwood board and chiseled the words into the sign, Willa had painted over the marks with white paint, and Warren nailed it to an old fence post at the end of our drive.

GILLETTE HOLLER
RUSTY KNOB WV

Lying half in a ditch and half on the road, even our welcome sign is done with life. Its creators have moved on, and it's time to put it out of its misery. My hands clench on the steering wheel, and at the last second, I swerve to run the sign over.

In my rearview mirror, with a red glow cast from my taillights, I watch as the wood flips up, spirals in the air, and lands in the ditch.

Turning sharply to enter our old driveway, I say goodbye.

Shifting in park, I sit in the yard, looking out over Gillette Holler, just as I did on my last night. The night I should have died. The night the old Wynn Gillette did die.

My heart aches at the beauty of desolation and isolation the hollers offer. On this December night, the grass is white and shiny in my headlights- crystalized with ice. The clear sky shines countless stars overhead… and before me sits the shack of my childhood, agonizingly beautiful.

Between me and the shack stretches a few acres of the yard dumpster with its prehistoric remains of bygone useful items and empty soldiers in the war of alcoholism. A warm, yellow glow lights up the night, only this time it's not from in between the slats of broken boards acting as siding. The shack now has a waterproof metal roof, painted siding, and brand-new windows.

Rage strikes me deep, but it quickly fades. At first I think my parents sold me for a roof and siding, then I realize they'd never be practical.

Royce Kennedy.

Dad.

Dad knew I'd come back here someday when the guilt got the best of me. How I'd worry about my daddy and momma, even after they sold me. The roof, siding, and windows were Royce's way of giving me comfort, removing the guilt I feel over abandoning my blood when they threw me away.

Movement catches my eye in the large picture window. When I sat here last, I had a shotgun barrel shoved beneath my chin with my finger pulling the trigger three times. No longer is the window broken, but the view never changes. Wasting away, Daddy's in his chair, only it's a new chair, arm bending to bring a beer to his lips. With Momma at his side, cigarette dangling from her withered fingertips.

No words need to be said, because none of them would be the healing kind. They would only drag me back down to who I used to be, and I won't jeopardize my future by hearing them. I reach to twist the ignition key, starting my truck, and then I back up and drive away.

I never want to go back to who I used to be. I don't look in my rearview mirror as I drive to who I'm going to become.

Wynn's head is bent over his work, thoroughly engrossed to the point he doesn't hear me step foot into his barn. His arm is furiously chiseling at a piece of beveled wood. It doesn't matter how many times I look at the kid, I can't believe he wants a thing to do with me.

Wynn says I'm the same Kade he used to know. I tend to agree with him. When I look in the mirror, I don't see an adult. I don't see the face and body of my dad staring back at me. The sad eyes of a boy marked for death gaze back at me from an emaciated, pockmarked face. When I shake someone's hand, I don't recognize mine unless I'd forgotten to use makeup on my scars that day.

I feel like a fraud– a skinwalker wearing my dad's flesh.

"Hi!" Wynn finally notices me leaning against the wall. Probably because I was burning a hole into the side of his face with my gaze. I push away from the wall with a huge grin stretching my lips. The little shit always lights up like the goddamned Sun when I enter a room, so who am I to argue with what he sees in me?

"You're smiling– does that mean?"

I hate bursting Wynn's bubble, *but*… "I taught the first grade for exactly a year and a half. I have a degree in Elementary Education from Penn State, which took me four years of a heavy course load, followed by a year of working my ass off to get licensed, only to have that mean nothing because I'm gay and stole Rusty Knob's golden boy."

Wynn's Adam's Apple bobs when he swallows down his guilt. A small part of me wants to rub it in ever since that day six years ago when he broke me. But the larger part of me is in love with the little shit.

"I–" Wynn sets the chisel down on his worktable. I step forward to cut off his apology because I don't need to hear it and he isn't at fault.

"It's *our* fault, but it's not." I lean my hip against the table, looking down at what Wynn's working on with a raised brow. The kid is too fucking sweet for his own good. "I'm glad it's Royce who's out of four years' worth of tuition. If I had to pay back student loans until I'm old and gray for a degree I can't use, I'd probably kill myself or murder Kentwood Area School District's entire school board– minus Miriam Ross that is. Then I'd chop off my dick for getting me in trouble and tear out my heart because I followed it."

The choking sound Wynn makes in the back of his throat has me feeling satisfied, and that's how much of a bastard I am. "Shh… It's gonna be okay," I murmur to soothe him because I made him hurt just so I could. My fingertips feather through the back of his curls. "This is for the best. I was too dumb to be a teacher anyway. I'm really not very smart."

Bright blue eyes glare at me, and it makes me flash a devilish grin. "I'm not like you, Wynn," I warn for the billionth time. "I'm not good. I'm selfish. I lie. I cheat. I break the rules because it feels good in the moment, and then it gives me an excuse to hate the world."

"That's not true!" The kid needs his head examined if he truly believes that. "I know the real you."

"Hey, I'm not complaining." I laugh without humor. "I like this guy you've made up in your head. But I wasn't saving myself for you, no matter how romantic that sounds. The reason I didn't fuck my roommate and his husband was because, even though I look hot now, it's all a lie. I'm awkward and gross, inside and out."

"I think you need more therapy." Wynn gets up from his stool, but his next words rock me to my core. "I'll go with you."

My head cocks to the side, really, *really* looking at Wynn. "You'd do that for me?" He nods his head, forever compassionate and selfless. "Well, I've got nothing but time now." I laugh for real this time, no longer sounding bitter and twisted.

He reaches out to snare my hand, twisting our fingers together. "What are you gonna do now? You can go to WVU with me. I always thought you'd be good at social work."

"I don't know." I tug Wynn to me, and then wrap my arms around him. I feel better instantly, my dark mood evaporating. "I'm bitter about losing my job, but I have no regrets. We stood up for who we are. We didn't hide. The kids growing up here won't feel so alone now."

"Tyler's mom told me to do what I did." Wynn's voice is bashful and embarrassed. I can't see his blush, but I can feel his body temperature rise. "I don't understand why when she knew it wouldn't help."

Pressing my face into the crook of Wynn's neck, I chuckle at how confused he sounds. "Miriam is angrier than I am. After Josh outed her son and took off, Tyler's had a hard time of it. He had his heart broken and his school turn on him. Then the teacher she handpicked– the teacher she brought on to help her son –is fired because he's gay… that's why. Miriam was throwing herself, and using you to do it. I appreciated the sentiment, though."

I pull away from Wynn, needing to have some distance between us. He makes me lose my head, forget all of my problems, and feel good about myself. Which is a real bitch when I have to solve a problem, because all I want to do is fall into him.

I pace around Wynn's barn, never happier for having him in my life. "Silver lining… I won't be wasting my time dealing with kids who don't have an identity yet. I always wanted to work with twelve and over, but I went with an elementary education degree because that's what Rusty Knob needed. Now I'm free to explore this using unconventional ways. Miriam isn't going to let me walk away. No way, no how. The woman fought her ass off in a misogynist wasteland, only to have a gay son who wasn't going to be treated as a human being. The woman is gonna use me to make our area tolerant."

"Are you gonna be okay with that?" Wynn sits back on his stool, picking up his chisel.

"Yeah, because it's what the kids need." I walk back over to him and curl around his back. I watch his hands work with precision, and I marvel over his talent. "God, you always smell so intoxicating, like wood and man. I feel sick for admitting it, but the scent of sawdust always sparks memories of my dad, and you always smell like sawdust."

"You can talk about him with me, ya know?" Wynn looks at me over his shoulder, smiling. "It makes me feel better to know there are good dads out there, so I don't feel as guilty for saying goodbye to mine because he was a bad one."

Palm running from Wynn's waist, up his spine, and over his nape, my fingertips twist in his sandy curls. I give a sharp yank, twisting his head to the side so I can catch a taste of his lips. I put all of my anger and bitterness into the love and passion I feel for Wynn.

"Hey! Hey! Hey, now…" Bren interrupts us before we get lost in one another. "NTP! NTP!" Bren's carrying several pizza boxes, and I wonder if the little bastard licked all the slices with olives and sausage.

"NTP?" Jack looks around for an answer. The cute kid sets a takeout tray of Buffalo wings on the worktable, perfectly content if no one actually answers him.

"I'm in my barn, not the house." Wynn grins, all proud of himself for finding a loophole. "No Touch Policy rules do not apply here."

"Nice try, son," Royce's gruff voice spills from the barn door. I glance over to watch the stocky man hold the door open for his minions and their skittish momma to walk through. "Whatcha working on there, Wynn?"

Clasping his work of art to his chest, Wynn blushes while stammering, "Okay. Okay. Okay. I'll show you, but don't laugh." He thrusts the sign forward to be seen by all.

WE ARE RUSTY KNOB
GILLETTE·KENNEDY·MARX·DUNCAN

NATIONAL SUICIDE PREVENTION LIFELINE

1 (800) 273-8255

http://www.suicidepreventionlifeline.org/

-ACKNOWLEDGEMENTS-

A lot of work goes into writing a novel, and it isn't just by the writer herself. **My parents:** for their unconditional support. **My readers**: thank you for reading my twisted words and spreading my books to the masses. For without you, no one would have ever heard of my stories. My readers are my lifeblood. A shout out to the members of the **M&M of Restraint Group on Facebook**: thanks for the endless entertainment and inspiration. Thank you to my street team: **Erica Chilson's Deviants!** You guys ROCK! **Wicked Reads**: (in all its incarnations) **Angela G.**, thank you for taking over and making Wicked Reads better than I could have done by myself. & thank you for helping promote my work and the work of other authors. Angela? Have I told you lately how much I appreciate you? A huge thank you to the **Wicked Writer's Betas** for keeping me grounded and encouraging me to keep trudging along when I get frustrated. Your thoughts and observations are invaluable. ((Hugs)) Beta readers who worked on Rusty Knob: **Kris D, Suz A, Sandy D, Darcy V, Di C, Angela G, Diane P, Jacki G, Linsey T, Alexis W, Alicia P, Billie Jo H, Shelby H, Tassie M, & Liz S.** Someday, I'd love to meet you all in real life- it would be the experience of a lifetime.

ABOUT THE AUTHOR

Erica Chilson does not write in the 3rd person, wanting her readers to *be* her characters. Therefore, writing a bio about herself is uncomfortable in the extreme.

Born, raised, and here to stay, the Wicked Writer is a stump-jumper, a ridge-runner. Hailing from North Central Pennsylvania, directly on the New York State border; she loves the changes in seasons, the humid air, all the mountainous forest, and the gloomy atmosphere.

Introverted, but not socially awkward, Erica prides herself on thinking first and filtering her speech. There are days she doesn't speak at all. If it wasn't for the fact that she lives with her parents, giving her a sense of reality, she would be a hermit, where the delivery man finds her months after expiration.

Reading was an escape, a way to leave a not-so pleasant reality behind. Reading lent Erica the courage she gathered from the characters between the pages to long for a different life. Writing was an instrument of change, evolving Erica into the woman she is today– a better, more mature, more at peace thinker.

Erica has a wicked mind, one she pours out into her creations. Her filter doesn't allow all of it to erupt, much to her relief. Sarcastic, with a very dark, perverse sense of humor, Erica puts a bit of herself into every character she writes.

Erica Chilson loves hearing from readers. If you would like more information on release dates, works in progress, teaser chapters, and random bits of madness...

FB Fan Page: https://www.facebook.com/thewickedwriter
Website: ericachilson.com
Via email: wickedwriter.ericachilson@gmail.com
DEVIANTS ONLY, if you'd like to join Erica Chilson's SECRET Facebook group, M&M of Restraint: SIGN-UP Form available on website. 18+ due to mature conversations and content.